THE DARK ELF'S PET

The Fey Adventures of Devon Mosteller

THE DARK ELF'S PET

The Fey Adventures of Devon Mosteller

MICHAEL DON ANDERSON

CRIMSON WEREWOLF LIMITED • USA

Dedication

My education has always been best served by my friends, rather than any higher institutions of learning. Their interests, as Humans tend, are nicely varied. <u>Richard</u> gave me an interest and information in British Architecture and history (not to mention the best tours of the British countryside); <u>Rain</u> renewed my interest in biology and reminded me that the diversity I coveted must by definition include some less desirable manifestations which are just as valid; <u>Miyuki</u> offered me the chance to experience Japan as a guest and not a tourist, showing me loyalty and dedication hard to find even in a boyfriend; <u>Joe</u> lent me his courage, his confidence and his sense of daring; <u>Coreen</u> shared so many of my initial life experiences with me that I sometimes forgot that we didn't also share one mind; <u>Josh</u> reminded me of the loneliness of being gay in a place where eldest sons are more than expected to produce children and that even in that loneliness can offer unembittered love; <u>Stacey</u> taught me to curse much more frequently because it sounded so cute when she did it, but in all other regards she was quite the proper lesbian; and <u>Roxanne</u> gave me the Philippines and Xavier.

*Most of all, these people gave me love that was not based on judgment; and they accepted that I would not judge them in return. This series of the **Fey Adventures of Devon Mosteller**, is dedicated to them.*

THE DARK ELF'S PET

The Fey Adventures of Devon Mosteller

By

MICHAEL DON ANDERSON

CHAPTER ONE

The California sun was directly in my eyes and that irritated me. But not as much as the car tail-gaiting my Chevy S-10 pickup. The white Chrysler LeBaron was close enough that if I slowed down even a little, it would kiss my rear bumper and not in a good way.

I glanced back at the driver through my rearview mirror, wondering what sort of idiot was driving. When I saw a decal on her windshield bearing the emblem of California's growing *Human's First* hate-group, I felt a surge of deep-seated disgust. It made me want to tap my brakes. I knew that if she hit my beat-up truck, the impact would hurt her expensive car a whole lot more than mine. And I could afford the damages, even if the police ruled me at fault. Not that they would.

"No, Devon." I shifted my foot back onto the accelerator, keeping the S-10 an inch or two away from the LeBaron's bumper.

I had to remind myself that despite pockets of reason and intelligence, that Fresno, California, was mostly mid-century conservative. Whether anti-gay sentiment, or illegal immigrant fears, or even the desire to destroy anything not quite human, too many people here were strongly against anything that they couldn't understand. I also had to remind myself that the LeBaron driver was entitled to her opinions, even if they were small-minded, bigoted or just plain hateful. *Human's First* member or not, if she got seriously hurt because I wanted to punish her for reckless driving, I'd never forgive myself.

I focused on the intersection coming up fast, but even my radio seemed to be against me. It began playing one of my least favorite songs and I took one hand off the wheel to turn it down as I rounded the corner onto Van Ness Street. I was going too fast and the tires on my S-10 squealed. The left pair try to leave the asphalt but I clutched at the wheel and slammed on the brakes with a bark of profanity. The tires bounced back onto the wide street, but my heart kept thudding. Even without slowing down, the LeBaron barely missed clipping my tail as she zoomed past.

"Stupid!" I cursed at her a few more times under my breath before slowing down to the speed limit.

I was grateful that there was no other traffic, because it allowed me to focus on the large yards. I knew that the tall, dense trees which lined the historic street could sooth me. It was hard to believe that the wealthy had ever chosen Fresno as a place to build million-dollar homes back in the sixties. Maybe it was for the fact that there weren't many Fey here.

Fresno County had the occasional Troll up in the foothills and birds that weren't really birds, but very little else, preternaturally speaking. The wealthy really didn't like magical creatures. They couldn't control them. Well, except for the prestige that exotic High Elves brought as the occasional house-guests.

The Fey hated deserts. At least, most of them did. Which was why Fresno was pretty much free of Pixies, Sprites and other woodland preternatural creatures. It was the hottest city in inland California and the whole San Joaquin Valley would have been a desert if we hadn't irrigated it to life. On the other hand, the heat made the area perfect for agriculture, which was how it had earned its nickname, '*The World's Fruit Basket.*'

Fresno County shipped more fruit to other parts of the world than any other growers in the United States. I agreed with the Fey, I preferred more temperate surroundings. But here I was.

My name was Devon Mosteller, a thirty-year-old West Coast native. I was six feet tall, with wavy brown hair and blue eyes that stood out against my tanned skin. Like many Californians, I worked out to keep my body tightly muscled, but I did tai-kwon-do three nights a week to stay supple. I wasn't attracted to muscle-bound guys and honestly, I didn't want to be one, either.

Still, as I'd been told when I'd first started going out to clubs at twenty-one, if you wanted a better body, you needed to have a better body. That wasn't entirely true, even in the gay community, but it was mostly true. It was also true for my work. I needed a better body when working on law enforcement preternatural cases. If I got hit on more often as a side-effect, I could live with that.

A silver-haired couple on the sidewalk waved at me, drawing me out of my memories, and I smiled back at them. Mr. Fuller and his wife Tilda had lived in the same house for decades and had never broken themselves of their Germanic, Pennsylvanian habit of waving at their neighbors. They had been delighted when I waved back because apparently no one else would.

I glanced at the yards I passed, wishing just once I'd see evidence that they Fey had finally settled into the neighborhood. Instead, there was only the usual evidence of wealth and extravagance. Cadillacs, Trans Ams, Porsches and other expensive cars were parked along curved driveways, set far off the street on oversized lots. Many of the properties were close to half an acre each, and the homes had a grandeur that newer buildings lacked. That's why I'd bought a house there. The trees were older, the yards were lush with seas of green grass and shrubs, which helped against the heat. And the gardens had a sense of age about them that you could feel, even without using magic.

Despite the beautiful sylvan landscape, only about one out of five-hundred homes in Fresno sported a personal Fey. It was quite different from places like L.A., where one out of every fifty homes had personal garden Faeries. Until recently, most of the people living in the San Joaquin Valley had gone about their daily lives and never saw anything preternatural from birth to death. But the last few years, more and more of the Fey were being driven into residential areas as Humans encroached on their woods, pastures and fields. And many of them should have been naturally drawn to these larger estates, for the same reason that I had been. So if they weren't here, where were they?

I approached my driveway and slowed down to a crawl. Unlike the pleasant Fullers to the south, my neighbor on the north side of the property was the sort to complain about anything. If I gave her the chance. Even though I had more money than she did, she acted like I was out of place. My pickup clearly was.

I pulled the S-10 through the open wrought-iron gates and onto the wide cement drive. Turning the steering-wheel sent a spike of pain through my left shoulder and I braked to a crawl. My shoulder had started hurting a couple of days ago, the kind of pain you get when you tear a rotator-cuff. But it wasn't a torn ligament. It wasn't anything at all as far as the doctor could determine. The shooting pain seemed entirely random.

When the pain finally ebbed, I noticed a small piece of paper tacked to the front door. It fluttered against a soft breeze, white against the dark cherrywood. I frowned. None of my friends would have poked a hole in the expensive wood just to leave a note.

As I pulled to a stop in front of the flagstone walkway, I saw the tiny fabric-doll holding the paper in place. I suddenly had an inkling of an idea about the source of my pain, but I couldn't quite believe it was that simple.

I got out of the truck and cautiously approached the doll, half expecting it to leap off the wood to attack me. If this were a trap of some kind, the person setting the trap probably hadn't left a note, but my life had gotten pretty strange these days. Not just because of the new millions in my bank accounts, either.

I paused at the steps and looked around the yard. Whoever had left the note didn't seem to be hiding in the bushes. I wasn't really worried about being mugged. That wasn't what I was looking for in the shadows. No, there were other things that I worried about more than muggers.

I glanced casually around the large porch, behind the waist-high boxwood shrubs, peering into the early afternoon shadows of the cypress trees and willows, but saw nothing suspicious. The Fey could blend in if they wanted, so that didn't necessarily mean anything. My blue eyes were as innocent as I could make them, which was probably the only lie they could tell. Sometimes I wanted the bad guys to attack. I just wasn't cut-out for delayed gratification. Ask any of my ex-boyfriends.

I walked up the steps of the porch toward the door and turned my focus to the note and strange doll. A silver pin was stuck in the faceless doll's left shoulder; the same side causing me pain. Considering that the doctor had found nothing wrong with me, I was sort of glad to see the crudely stitched doll. It meant that there really was nothing wrong with me.

I sensed a subtle pulse of magic from the cloth figure and the world faded to shades of blue-grey, except for the glow of magic woven into the doll. Being gay wasn't the only different thing about me. I also had the Sight.

The ability to See and Manipulate magic was the rarest of genetic characteristics known to modern science and I was among those very few blessed with it. Some perverse geneticist had named it the S&M gene, which naturally had stuck. It manifested in puberty and when my father couldn't figure out how to make money off of my gift—well, let's just say that it hadn't made my family proud. It was just another reason for them to remind me that I didn't fit in. I was gay *and* I could See magic.

I was not officially with any law enforcement organization. But I was often called in by the police to examine the intentionally low-profile cases involving various forms of witchcraft, devil worship, voodoo and any other form of magic which seeped into mundane life, such as this doll on my door. Occasionally, even the Feds brought me in to consult. Alright, not occasionally—once.

But I knew this spell was personal. It was spun around the doll's rough-stitched body like a shining string of gossamer, and then connected to strands of Human hair on the faceless head. My hair, I presumed. Sad to say, my ability to See magic was the least complicated part of my life. The doll on my door was proof of that.

I reached out with my right hand to untie the bit of magic, although I really didn't touch it physically. It was more like my fingers directed my power and manipulated the weaving. The magical thread came free and the spell faded away, dispersed into the air as ambient magic.

I clutched at my shoulder as it spasmed that last time, then yanked the pin from the doll. Once the spell had been unwoven, the pin could no longer harm me. But I removed it out of sheer frustration.

I read the note. '*Call me.*'

"That's what I get for dating a voodoo princess."

Jiao Bauptiste was not really a princess. But he was a first rate Brazilian *Olorisha* in the Santeria religion. He also dabbled in voodoo. An '*Olorisha*' was a type of priest, but Jiao more often than not referred to himself as a '*hechecero*' or 'sorcerer.' He was prone, however, to pettiness, like any typical princess.

In my book, just because a guy was majorly effeminate didn't automatically make him a 'queen.' Titles of royalty had originally been assigned by gay men to other gay men because of implied pettiness. I'd had an effeminate boyfriend or two and I'd never thought of them as queens unless they showed that meanness of spirit. I would admit to anyone that I didn't like pettiness and that meant I didn't like 'queens.' If you took that pettiness to an extreme, you got a 'princess.' And that was Jiao.

I was not in the mood to deal with the emotionally turbulent *hechecero,* although I realized I could not put him off too much longer. But I was troubled. The last I knew, he was still in Brazil. So how did the doll get here? I knew the shoulder pain was only to get my attention. If I waited too long, I was pretty sure the pain would stem much lower down.

I had the house key in the second lock when the phone started ringing. "Shit!" I twisted the key and shoved open the door using the bad shoulder. I flinched but only because I'd forgotten that the pain was permanently gone.

I grabbed for the phone annoyed and glared at the voodoo doll as if it were Jiao. "Hello?"

"Devon, I know we're supposed to have lunch, but I got an emergency call." The caller was Yuriko Morimoto, one of my best friends.

She worked for the Fresno County Animal Control section of the local police department. It wasn't hard to guess what the emergency was. "An animal in distress?"

"Yeah. Can I pick you up? We can grab food after I take care of it?"

She knew me well enough to know my answer before she asked the question. It was a long story, but she had lived with me almost two years before moving into her own place. No, not that way. Purely platonic on my part. Even wanting kids, I'd never been able to get it up for a girl.

"Sure, ready in ten."

"I'm almost there," she said and hung up.

I crossed the enormous living room-kitchen and walked down the hallway to the last door. It was a six-bedroom house with a classic, curved banister staircase leading to the second floor. I rarely went upstairs. That floor was for guests and I hadn't really had any yet.

The door I entered was my one of two downstairs bedrooms. It was the smallest in the house, but my California King bed and two dressers fit perfectly. There wasn't room for anything else, but the high ceiling made it feel huge. It had a private bathroom and was close to the kitchen, even if it wasn't the master bedroom. I lived alone after all.

I took the time to switch from a t-shirt and gym shorts to a dark-blue plaid, long-sleeved, cotton button-up shirt and my favorite black Bench jeans from the Philippines. I had just zipped up the fly when there was a light rap at the door. My hearing was excellent—for a Human—and my closest friends never banged out of politeness. I knew it was Yuriko.

I walked to the entry and pulled open the door without peering through the peep-hole. Yuriko stood in the doorway, hand on one hip, her black hair cut in a Japanese bob style. It reminded me of *Neon Flux*, the American anime character. Yuriko was thin and wore expensive jeans that made her skinny legs look long and willowy. Her blouse was cut low to reveal the tops of her large breasts. She had recently lost weight and they were finally the right size for her modesty. They had been much larger when she first came from Asia, too large for Japanese standards she had complained, but perfect for California bikinis. Now she could have gone back to visit her parents in Osaka and would have blended in. Women, unfortunately, could not always control where they lost the weight when they tried.

I hugged her warmly, expecting the usual stiff-but-sincere embrace in return. She had acclimated to a lot of American culture but she still found hugs with anyone except her boyfriend Antonio slightly uncomfortable. Even from her gay best-friend. "I like the new haircut!"

"Thanks. Can you tell it was done by an Asian guy?" She pulled at the tufts that curled about her cheeks uncertainly. "You always complain I'm too conservative with it."

We stepped outside and I closed the door. "This definitely isn't conservative."

I grinned at her as we walked to her vehicle, a vintage 57 Chevy Apache pick-up truck that she had restored herself. It dwarfed my S-10, but the color alone overshadowed it. She had painted her truck 'sunflower yellow.'

The Apache's large wooden bed and wide cab were useful when dealing with animal control issues. There were caged compartments in the truck bed for all manner of critters. The back window had been fitted with official police lights and behind the bench seat was a very potent siren. Something rattled around in one of the cages, clanging and struggling to get free. I couldn't see it, so I ignored it. Usually my curiosity got me in trouble. Maybe that's because usually I didn't ignore it. I was trying to break old habits.

"Is it easier to maintain?"

"No. My hair curls weird because I have cowlicks and it takes longer."

She pulled at another tuft of hair sticking out just behind the ear, but opened the driver's side door with the other hand and climbed in. I followed on the passenger side. The door was stiff and I had to yank hard to get it to close with a heavy clang. I locked the modernized seatbelt into place as she sped out of the drive and raced down the road.

Yuriko was an aggressive and heavy footed driver—one of my best pupils. I knew with her at the wheel I was as safe as with anyone. I had trained her to drive L.A. style, which was starting to come in handy with the ever increasing Fresno traffic. Not to mention that the Apache was a real truck with a very heavy, protective metal frame. If we hit some poor, modern fiberglass-bodied vehicle, they would be the ones feeling the pain, not us.

"Where to?" I asked.

"That new development just outside of Clovis. *Ravenclaw.*" Yuriko didn't look at me, constantly checking the mirror as she made her way through the two-lane traffic. She drove like the devil and pissed off a lot of really slow drivers as she headed across town.

For twenty minutes, Yuriko said nothing, concentrating on her driving. It was rare for her not to talk to me while driving. I studied her face for a clue as to her thoughts until she finally glanced over at me. "What?"

I raised my brows at her as a silent question but said nothing. She reached over and swatted me on the shoulder. "Stop staring."

"You haven't said two words to me on this drive. Either the animal we are rescuing is in horrible shape and you're getting pissed off about it—"

"Or?"

"Or you have something on your mind about your personal life that you really want to talk about but can't express. Even to me."

She started out slowly, trying to find the right words to say, then it burst free. "You need to do something about your fucking boyfriend!"

Okay, that was pretty much opening up! Shit! What had Jiao done now? Not just the voodoo doll and note, then. Yuriko Morimoto was not one to use the f-word lightly.

"He's not my boyfriend," I stammered, apprehensively trying to figure out how Jiao had involved her. He knew Yuriko because she had been with me in Brazil when I had met him. It had been a group holiday with Yuriko and another good friend of mine, Sonny Perez.

"You're fucking him. For you that makes him your boyfriend." Yuriko shot me an unhappy look, but there wasn't anything hurtful in it. She was just annoyed with me, which was rare. "We're here."

We reached a newly installed, gated archway and she slowed down before turning the big truck into a new complex. It was being constructed in the middle of former pastureland which meant that it was pretty isolated. I could see fruit trees in the distance on either side, but no houses outside of the complex itself.

"Okay, I can't argue with that." I was a little bit afraid of what the voodoo princess had done.

All of my friends knew I didn't have sex casually. As part of dating in the gay community, to know if people really meshed, you had to have sex. Hell, it was true of the straight community, but they had a slightly simpler selection of slot-As and tab-Bs. For me, if there was another date after we got around to sex, it meant the guy was boyfriend potential. There were exceptions of course. And my relationship with the voodoo princess was *hella* more complex than that.

I'd been forced to have sex with him as part of an *Olorisha* bastardized ritual to save some kidnapped schoolkids. That had led to other things, including a large sum of money being deposited into my name and even the tax liability paid on the gift. Yeah, that's how I got rich, but I'm not some kind of high-end whore. It wasn't Jiao's money. Like I said earlier, my life had gotten really strange of late.

"I didn't expect things to get out of hand." I stared at the housing complex as we talked. The lots were in various phases of construction. Some had completed houses with dirt yards, while some had expensive, instant greenery from welcome mat to sidewalk. But all of them lacked the feeling of permanence I'd found on Van Ness. I sighed. "Okay, give. What'd he do?"

"Later. I need to find the address." She gave me a side glance. "It's okay. I don't blame you. He is hot. But why do you always wind up with psycho boys?"

"It saved the life of fifteen kindergarten kids. For that, I'll take complicating my life up some. But I won't let some little *Santeria* queen fuck with my friends."

Then I had a sudden twinge of guilt at the eight digits sitting in my various bank accounts. If the money had come directly from Jiao, I'd never have accepted it. No, it wasn't payment from the family of the kids I'd saved, either. I hadn't done that for any money. My new millions had another source and the situation was equally complicated. It was related to Jiao, but if he had known why, I'd be in even more serious trouble with him. "Everything changed because of the promises I had to make to save them."

"I know that!" Yuriko made it sound as if I was stupid for thinking otherwise. "4501 Talon."

I looked at the street signs as we passed. The streets were far apart, with the lots about an acre each, but this was the edge of the country so that wasn't a surprise. The names, however, were disturbing. *Pard. Feather. Stealth.*

"Er, what kind of development is this place, Morimoto-*san*?" I grew suddenly alert.

I looked about for magic, but Saw nothing in that blue-grey rendition of the world. After a few seconds, I switched my vision back so that the world consisted of natural colors again.

"I know. I thought you might find it interesting. Is it meant to make people think of a connection with animals—?" She craned her neck to see the signs.

"Or is a Lycanthrope community being set up in our very own Fresno," I finished.

"Clovis, actually. Even Lycanthropes are class snobs. There." She nodded at the next street, *Talon*.

"Why do the numbers start so high? These streets have to be specific for this complex. Must have cost the developers a pretty penny to push Clovis to let them use new names."

Yuriko pulled into a wide driveway and stopped the truck abruptly. I couldn't complain that she parked badly. I charged stop-signs and parked crookedly. I only ever said I was a good driver and that I had trained her to be a good driver. The stopping part always seemed to be more difficult. Friends said it was because I'm compulsive. Not obsessive, I *can* stop. Just that it's abrupt when I do. Like Yuriko just then. And like my driving, so was my love life. I was never sure if I was parked between the lines.

"Well, I suspect we are going to find out if there are preternaturals moving in." Yuriko used to hate words with approximants in them— r's and l's. But now, a word like 'preternatural' rolled off her tongue. She had spent a lot of hours perfecting 'Marilyn Monroe' as practice. "The animal in question has been howling the last four nights disturbing the neighbors. If this were a Lycanthrope community, they wouldn't have called for outside help."

"So some of them at least are Human." I nodded and pushed open the truck door. I was so grateful that the shoulder pain had stopped that I actually smiled. Maybe I should call Jiao. It was flattering that he wanted me so badly.

The 'something' in the back of the truck rattled and I glanced at Yuriko. She was already walking away from the Apache up to the front door of the single-story Victorian home with a wrap-around deck. I rushed to catch up with her.

"Hold on, there, Morimoto-*san*!" I spoke softly, as if there was something I feared disturbing in the sparsely developed tract.

There wasn't even a construction crew working on any of the unfinished projects. It looked as if something had swept through the place killing anything alive. My over-active imagination was hard at work.

Yuriko paused at the door, waiting until I caught up before knocking. Unlike her tap on my front door, this was a healthy knock. I looked around the development for some evidence of Human existence. Nothing.

"Whoever made the call said the owners didn't answer the door when they knocked. Probably they went out of town and left their dog with some irresponsible jerk." Yuriko moved toward the side gate. I trotted after her.

She let me reach over the fence to open the interior latch since I was almost a foot taller. Then we slowly walked inside the backyard. She had her gun out, filled with standard issue tranquilizer darts. I didn't have a gun on me.

"There's no evidence of digging in the backyard. No dog toys or shelter." Yuriko gave the yard a quick inspection. "Must be an inside dog."

"Which means we have to get inside?" I knew that ordinarily cops needed search-warrants to enter a dwelling but 'probable cause' was an exception. Did a howling dog constitute 'probable cause?'

Yuriko pulled a piece of paper out of her back pocket, "Already taken care of."

I smiled and glanced at the double-paned French doors at the back of the house. One of the glass doors was open more than a crack, although the wall-length curtains kept the inside of the house obscured. I noticed then that all the windows were covered from an outside view by fabric.

"The door's open," I said.

Yuriko nodded, giving me a wary look. I nodded back. A missing owner could be simple irresponsibility. A door ajar could mean a whole lot more serious stuff. Especially since a dog could have pushed the door further aside and come out if it had been hungry or thirsty. There was a fountain with fish which would provide both food and water. The door was open but the dog had been howling from inside. Not good.

We approached the opening and although I was bigger and clearly stronger, she was the authority. I let her go first. My chivalry frowned at this, but my sense of self-preservation was stronger. Not because I was afraid of anything inside. I feared that she would have killed me herself. Not literally, but she would have been rightly pissed off.

Yuriko held the tranquilizer gun out in front of her as she slipped inside. I hadn't taught her to shoot and had no confidence in her aim. In fact, I'd never seen her shoot. I sort of hoped it would stay that way today.

The inside of the house was dark. The thick curtains allowed in so little light that it was perpetual night in the sprawling living room which opened into a huge kitchen. But with a switch in Sight, I noticed immediately the mystical signs that would have been missed by anyone else. It was why I got paid the big bucks—when I was actually getting paid.

"Yuriko, hold on." I moved to the kitchen. She held her position, her back to me in the kitchen and the gun pointing toward the dark corners of the other room.

I approached the counter-top, looking at the shadowy blue-grey objects sitting against the wall, almost invisible in the dim light. One of them, however, was surrounded by a sheet of magic that literally glowed in my other Sight. I studied it for a few seconds, puzzled by the exotic weaving of the spells. I say spells, because there were more than one layered upon what must have been, what? A cookie jar?

Invisibility, deflection, avoidance—all the magic was intended to make the jar unnoticeable, even to a thorough search. I realized that I couldn't see the container itself, only the sense of it underneath the layers of magic. If I had not been what I was, I would never have found it.

I must have reached out a hand to the spells upon the object because Yuriko hissed at me and I stopped myself from touching the jar. I pulled my hand back to my side and once more in normal sight, she gave me a look that said '*didn't I tell you not to touch anything?*'

"There's a spelled item here. The cops aren't going to be able to sense it. Even if you tell them it's there." I looked at the stylistic weaving of the magic but couldn't place it. It was clearly not from any cultural magic I had previously studied. But I only had a B.A. in the

Anthropology of Magic, so I was sure that there were many types I'd never seen.

"It's not our problem. Finding the poor dog and dealing with him is." Yuriko started to move across the living room toward the hallway which connected it to the bedrooms. Reluctantly, I followed. It wasn't like me to leave new magic unexamined. Curiosity may have killed the cat but it was part of my compulsive behavior. The fact that I left it behind showed I wasn't obsessive, right?

Yuriko had reached the first room by the time I rejoined her. I couldn't tell if she had opened the door or found it open. Either way, she was frozen at the threshold. I didn't say anything but stepped close behind. When I put a hand to her shoulder to peer past her, she flinched.

She turned away from the room and put her hand to her mouth. I stood at the doorway and looked inside. It took a moment to identify what I was looking at on the floor of the otherwise empty bedroom.

A body was face down with a pool of blackened blood gathered around her torso. How did I know it was a 'her?' Easy. I immediately recognized the female shape of the buttocks. Let's just say I had spent a lot of time studying the shape of men's backsides to quickly note the non-male breadth and slight pear shaping of this woman's cheeks.

The upper back was boyish and well-muscled, neither masculine nor feminine, but the shoulders were narrow and somehow delicate. Her legs were smooth and taut, swimmer's legs or something like them.

Suddenly, all my detached, analytical thinking faltered for a moment. Instead of a stranger laying there dead, it was my mother. I flashed back to a moment at the funeral home, Olivia Mosteller laying on a metal slab, lifeless. Only, it hadn't been her, not really. It had been an empty shell.

That moment had raised a very unexpected question in me, and one which had dominated quite a few years of my preternatural studies.

Was a person's humanity in the blood, or did it merely cling to the body for a short while into death? I didn't want to believe that by allowing her to be embalmed I had destroyed what spirit remained. I had to trust that it was the fact that one more day had passed.

"Can I take a closer look?" I asked.

Yuriko had regained her composure. She nodded and followed me into the room. I jumped when the lights came on. She had used the fabric of her work gloves to flick the switch, then proceeded to actually put the gloves on. I had no such gloves, so I needed to be extremely careful not to leave prints. Yuriko knew I would be careful because of my earlier lapse. We understood each other very well.

"Ritual killing," I commented. She nodded.

There was a blood circle painted around the body and each of the woman's hands and feet just touched the circle. The mystic purpose for which it had been drawn was either spent or had yet to be played, because I saw no telltale threads of power as I shifted into the Sight— except, there! It was so tightly woven into a small stone resting on the small of the woman's back, that I almost didn't see it in the blue-grey shadows. Once I saw it, I recognized it immediately. My B.A. came in handy with this spell, even if it hadn't with the jar on the kitchen counter.

"Shit!" I blinked as my normal vision returned.

Yuriko had pulled her police walkie-talkie from her belt case and I put a hand to her arm as she stood over me. She moved the device away from her mouth and raised a brow to look at me.

"Can you wait a minute before you call? There's something really nasty here and I need to fix it. If the police come, they'll keep me from it."

"What?" She glanced at the body.

"See that stone at the small of her back? There's a spell tied to it. I don't know who or what this woman did to deserve dying, but her soul has theoretically been sent to a specific Hell into the hands of a particular demon. Not that I believe in necromancy, but this spell was meant to take a living soul. If there's even the slightest chance that it works, no one deserves that kind of torture. At least, I don't believe they do." I stared defiantly at Yuriko, as if she would refuse me.

"If the police find out you messed with the evidence, you could get into serious trouble." She paused, translating what I said into concepts and words she could understand. "You're saying even though she's dead, her soul is in the hands of a demon? Being tortured?" Yuriko looked at the woman with renewed horror.

"If the spell really works. The experts say that there's no such thing as necromancy but some argue this kind of thing isn't necromancy. So it might really work."

Yuriko didn't fear magic, but she hated torture. She'd watched her mother get raped and beaten in Japan when she was just eight. It had left an impression. "Do it. Now."

"Gladly." I reached out to the stone, but only symbolically, using my fingers to direct my ability to manipulate the threads as everything else faded again to blue-greys. I pulled at the knots of the glistening spell which was bound to the dead body and the soul.

I had seen this particular spell in the collection of Jackie Gillespie, my former professor of the Anthropology of Magic. I had been getting my first B.A. at California State University at Fresno and she was an actual witch who had Anthropology and Biology PhDs from Stanford and Oxford, respectively. Her field research had been on tribes in South America and Africa. I didn't know if her being a witch came before or after she had studied their magics. It didn't matter; she was a brilliant adept with an amazing collection, even though she only used her magic for theoretical purposes and research. And for training students like me.

I had been the only student she'd ever had who could actually See the magic she talked about. Not that I had let her know at first. She found out when I got involved with my first police investigation. She was one of their only local magic experts. Or rather, she had been. Now she was back doing field-work in Kenya—some long-term project and I had a standing invitation to come join her.

Before Dr. Gillespie had found out about my talent, she had wondered how I'd managed to get 'A's in all of her classes. There were so few of us that she remembered all of us by name even years later. When she found out about my Sight, she had offered me a full scholarship if I would work with her on my PhD in the 'construction of magic.' I had told her that someday I might.

Although I still suffered from a slight case of hero worship of the woman, these days my life was already too full. And I wasn't ready to spend a year in Kenya, no matter how pretty some of the men were.

It was simple enough to untie the spell. It was nearly identical to the spell in Dr. Gillespie's collection. I had taken a serious interest in any magic which supported the claim that there was an afterlife as a result of my conflicted religious upbringing and my mother's death.

As the spell pulled free, I made sure the magic disintegrated to prevent it settling back into the stone or some other inanimate object. In an early fit of grief over my mother's death, I'd once even contemplated having that very spell cast upon me to find out once and for all if there was life after death. But I realized that my mother wouldn't be in Hell. And that's where this magic supposedly sent you just before your body died. Sadly, as far as I knew, there were no similar short-cuts to check for the existence of Heaven.

I glanced at the dead woman's head, the way her auburn hair splayed about her back and face. Her right ear showed through the reddish locks and I saw the slightly pointed end. I glanced closely at her well-tanned, olive complexion. There were no freckles. Her skin was flawless. Whatever wound had spilled her blood was on the front half of her body, facing the floor.

"Freeze!" exclaimed a voice from the doorway.

Yuriko screamed while I jumped backwards. Obviously neither of us froze, but we stood and turned with arms raised up. A beat cop stood there, gun pointed at us. His partner lurked in the hallway watching the other's back.

"I'm police," said Yuriko with a trace of anger. Her police walkie-talkie was in one hand while the tranq-gun was in the other. "Animal control."

"Not real police," said the older of the two cops, which earned him a frown from Yuriko and me, both. "What about him?" He motioned toward me, stepping into the room and his partner followed.

I read the name on the badge of the first cop, 'M. Sorenson.' He looked like his name, six-foot-one, late-thirties blonde with broad shoulders, blue eyes and a square jaw. Definitely not my type. He was built like a line-backer, not the usual sort of cop one saw these days in Fresno. The name told me he was probably Mennonite. Many of them had settled into the area about thirty miles southeast.

His partner, on the other hand, caught my eye. Not just because he was a lean-but-muscled five-eleven inches—my favorite height. He was also a dark brunette with green eyes and smooth olive skin.

No, he caught my gaze literally, held it just a trifle too long and I knew he was 'family.' I used to get embarrassed about the term 'family' for identification of other homosexuals. The gay community was anything but one big happy family. I'd gotten over it.

And don't get into an argument about nature versus nurture with me. If it was nurture everyone would have the fluidity to screw either sex. Not me. I was one homosexual with a strong sense of my own biological imperatives. It was chemical, down to sense of taste or smell.

However, none of this had anything to do with the present situation, two guns drawn, one pointed at my chest, and me getting the eye from the junior member of the partnership, 'T. Ramirez.' I looked up at the green eyes again and saw the faintest trace of Mexican bone structure.

That accounted for the sensual shape of the jaw, boyish but masculine. Yeah, I was definitely interested. Just what I didn't need, another guy to complicate my life. At least this one might be normal.

"He's police liaison on occasion. We were here on a dog disturbance." Yuriko didn't lower her hands for her ID. Her badge was half hidden under her vest. "The county budget doesn't allow back-up for animal control."

That won a softened look from the blonde cop and T. Ramirez let his eyes wander down my body with a coy but interested gaze. I shifted so that my thighs flexed in my Bench jeans, drawing his eyes back to me when they started to drift to the body beside me. It wasn't intentional, but I was aware of the effect when I saw it. And it wasn't just the jeans. Horseback riding was great for killer thighs. Yeah, it didn't hurt my butt any either.

"Go ahead and pull out your badge. You too, 'liaison.'" Sorensen relaxed the grip on his weapon and T. Ramirez holstered his. Sloppy work. Even though we had explained that we were the good guys, we hadn't proved it yet. Ramirez put his sexy lips to the police walkie-talkie and called in the body.

"You touch anything?" asked Sorensen. Yuriko had her badge out and the tall blonde looked it carefully over. She shook her head.

I didn't have official ID, as I was not officially with the police. I pulled out my California Driver's license and he scowled at me. "What the fuck is that?"

"I'm a consultant, not an actual police affiliate." I hated contradicting Yuriko, but I figured I was cornered. If I pretended to be something I wasn't, it could hurt my credibility when I needed it. "My driver's license is all I have."

"What kind of consultant?" asked Ramirez, waiting for a reply from the station. His voice was rich and masculine and made my fingers anticipate touching smooth skin. I curbed the flash of attraction, although I made serious eye contact which he boldly returned. I was distracted by the smile on his lips as he noted my flirtation.

"He asked what kind of consultant!" demanded Sorensen when I'd paused too long. Ramirez blushed and I smiled a small victory smile. He wanted me.

"Magic Crimes Unit. I'm called in as a consultant when the presence of magic is suspected." I watched Sorensen's blue eyes turn hard and flinty.

"A fuckin' witch," he spat out the words and I saw Ramirez stiffen.

Something in my heart fell into my stomach at seeing that. Why did all the respectable, good-looking guys react that way to finding out about my ability? I didn't bother to correct him that I wasn't a witch. But he didn't leave it at that. "Only thing worse than a fuckin' witch is a fuckin' faggot."

T. Ramirez stiffened even more and my stomach unclenched. It wasn't me that Ramirez was uncomfortable with. He didn't like that his partner was a bigot. That was going to make the younger cop's job really hard if he didn't get a change in assignment. But it renewed my faith in him.

"Officer—Sorensen is it?" Yuriko's voice had a familiar bite to it and I stiffened the same way that Ramirez had. She didn't care as much about her career as she did protecting her friends. And Sorensen had really pissed her off. It was one of the things that I adored about her.

"You get double the pleasure, Sorensen!" I exclaimed interrupting. Yuriko glared at me but I gave the blonde asshole my most flirtatious smile. "I'm a fag and a witch." I really wasn't a witch, but I wasn't going to bother explaining to him. He wouldn't hear it. "Don't worry, you're not my type. Too much prick and not enough balls."

Sorensen sputtered and Yuriko took back over. "I'd hate for my friend here to file a report about sexual discrimination. I hear they've really stepped up the sensitivity training for cops in Fresno and Clovis who cross the line. Too many repeat violators."

Sorensen looked at Yuriko like he'd stepped in dog shit, but didn't fight her. Instead, he put his gun away and regained his composure. I still didn't like him, but it showed me that he was a better cop than I would have thought. First impressions weren't always the most reliable.

"Get away from my crime scene. If you've touched anything," he directed that at me, "I will see your ass in jail long enough for you to enjoy yourself as any man's bitch."

I sighed. Because of my boy-next-door good looks, people just didn't think I looked intimidating. Apparently I didn't look like a top either. Maybe I should cultivate some scars.

"Why officer, I'm afraid that while your interest in my ass is flattering, I'm strictly a top." Ramirez glanced involuntarily at my crotch then looked away at the dead body on the ground. "And no, I didn't touch anything." Which was technically true. Sorensen clenched his fists and seethed.

"I don't know why you're raising such a stink, Sorensen. They always call Devon in for these types of crimes anyway, you might as well try and get along," said Yuriko.

"It won't be my investigation if MCU steps in, so I don't care who they call. But until someone else is here, I don't want you part of my crime scene. If you're here for the dog, go take care of the dog!" snarled the cop.

Ramirez replied to a voice on his walkie-talkie and Yuriko nodded for me to follow her. I glanced at Ramirez's backside, which he'd automatically presented to us when he turned away to hear the voice on the radio. Sorenson saw me and that took most of the pleasure away. I didn't want Ramirez to get shit for my interest him. I sighed. Better to protect his career than out him for a date's sake.

"Too bad your partner's straight. Now he's my type." I laughed. It was the most I could do to let him know I was interested while protecting him. If I said I thought he was straight, then he must be. All us fags thought everyone cute was gay.

Sorenson put his hand to his holstered gun, more threat than intent. But from the protective look, he hadn't noticed Ramirez's half of the flirting. Good.

Who said that the hero always gets the guy? Okay, I always wound up with the guy, but half the time they were the bad guys. Just once I'd like it to be a good guy. A great guy would be even better.

I followed Yuriko down the hall, away from the living room and kitchen we'd entered, past the other doors till we reached one that could only lead to the garage. There was enough light through the curtains to let us navigate without flashlights, so Yuriko didn't bother.

"If someone locked up an animal here, it probably wouldn't be in the house itself. I'm so used to dealing with runaway pampered pooches and outdoor abuse cases, I wasn't thinking," she sounded sad and I knew it wasn't just about any animal we might find. She was worried about me. I was the eternal optimist and when I met bigots, it did something bad to my inner child. She had commented on it more than once.

Yuriko put a hand to my arm and paused before the door. "You okay?"

Perhaps I had been affected. After all this time, you'd think I'd develop a thicker skin. What serious alpha male was as big a pussy as me? One with a heavily balanced yin and yang, I have been frequently assured, although not by Yuriko. She wasn't into the whole Asian thing.

I motioned toward the door and she took a breath before opening it. I'd seen photos of some of the horrors she'd uncovered. Emaciated bones of animals trapped without water; puppies suckling on the teats of their long dead mother; a cat tied to a radiator with crochet needles through an eye and jaw, someone's idea of appropriate behavior management. I didn't think it weak of her. No, that she did this job day after day was bravery in itself. I couldn't have done it. Yeah, a big pussy.

The garage was darker than the rest of the house and it took Yuriko a second to find the light switch. She glanced back at me as her fingers stopped moving and I knew she was giving me a warning. I squinted and the lights flared. About the same time, the smell rolled over us and I turned away. It wasn't the smell of death which would have cost me the bile in my empty stomach. Dog urine and feces, not to mention something musty and unhealthy, filled the garage. If starvation had a smell, it would have been mixed in that barrage of scents.

"Wolf-hybrid?" said Yuriko and I turned back toward the scene.

Chained by the neck, a skinny wolf was curled on its belly, its dull eyes opened and watching us. It tried to lift its head, but whimpered weakly instead. It was reddish brown with a black mask around the eyes and black paws. The eyes were as green as freshly unfurled leaves, the most beautiful eyes I'd ever seen on an animal except for the dull spark of starvation. I could tell that it had tried to keep away from its own feces and urine, but there was evidence toward the end it had not had the strength. It lay in a puddle of dried fluids and smeared shit. My heart lurched. I had a soft spot for dogs the way some people did for new babies.

"No. Wolf-wolf." I instinctively moved toward the helpless creature. Its ribs were showing through the thick fur. I risked a hand to stroke the head but it was too weak to snap at me. Something sparked to life in those eyes, the most it could do in that moment when I touched it. "Definitely a full-blood or at least enough it might as well be."

I didn't know everything, but I did know some things. I knew bees, bats and wolves in the animal kingdom. This was not a dog, although it had been raised as a pet. It looked at me hopefully, the way something taken care of looked at Humans. I recognized the submissiveness in its nature and it recognized me as dominant. There was something almost electric in the connection and I wondered how animals sensed the alpha in me immediately while Humans went into denial.

"He seems to like you." Yuriko chuckled and I felt the beast's muzzle rub against my crotch. I blushed and pushed the animal gently away. Why did dogs and men always go for the gold at first meeting? I mean, after a couple of dates, by all means! But let's form an emotional connection before we get that intimate.

Yuriko continued to talk while I stroked the spot between the ear and cheek, making up for my gentle rebuke. "Which is good, because he's gonna have to go with you."

"What?"

"I don't have any room at the shelter and we don't have the facilities to nurse a full-fledged wolf," she complained. "No, don't argue. We're full. Even if it had been a sweet golden retriever I'd have to ask you to take him."

"You're lying to me." She never lied to me but I could read it as plain as anything. I was highly empathic and it cut both ways.

"Okay, okay." She laughed again and looked at me as if I was to blame that she couldn't lie to me. "I didn't want to say anything, but my boss hates exotics. She's almost phobic about them. Says our job isn't to take care of the ever increasing number of wild animals made pets. If I take this wolf back to the shelter, she'll have it put down"

"That's all you had to say. What made you lie to me?"

"I didn't want to tell you why because I was afraid you'd go and do something about it." Yuriko bent down and stroked the wolf but it ignored her, rubbing against my leg and trying again for the crotch which I had shifted out of its reach. "Barbara had a very rare gryphon fledgling killed while I was out of the office. Too dangerous she said. If I was tempted to hurt her, I knew you would do more."

"Why shouldn't I? Someone with that kind of attitude shouldn't be allowed—" My tirade was interrupted when the door opened. Ramirez walked into the garage, a look of contrition on his face.

"What do you want?" demanded Yuriko.

"You were right." Ramirez was apologetic, but his eyes never left my face. "We called it in and described it. The chief told Sorensen to call Devon Mosteller as a specialist on the scene. Sorensen said you were here and interfering with the scene and the chief chewed him a new one. Apparently you left out the part about the chief being a buddy of yours."

Although Ramirez's tone was slightly chastising, the grin on his face and the gleam of his eye said he approved thoroughly. He noticed the wolf then and his gaze softened. He liked dogs. I approved even more of the Hispanic cop.

"He never asked," I smiled but then grew serious. "Besides, I don't play on that friendship. Glad that Richard felt compelled to defend me though. I've saved his ass a few times." I had to push the wolf's muzzle away from my crotch again, although the poor beast was so weak I felt bad doing it.

"Saved it or—?" asked Ramirez, a little tinge of jealousy playing in his expression. I was going to like this boy, if I could figure out how to get his number.

"Saved it," I answered firmly. "So Sorensen sent you in here to ask me back inside?" Ramirez was so innocent he didn't get the unintended innuendo.

"Yeah, said he'd be outside waiting for another squad car to provide you with police supervision. For now you get me."

"Well, things are looking up," I gave Ramirez my best innocent gaze. He blushed and glanced at Yuriko as if caught in some indecent act. I was so trying to pretend she wasn't there.

"Don't worry, Officer Ramirez. I have no problem with Devon's sexuality. Or yours." Yuriko stood up. She gave me a knowing look and motioned at the wolf. "I'll get him loaded into the truck. You go do your—job. When you're done, we'll finish our conversation."

"Yes, Ma'am," I muttered sarcastically and followed the very nice view of Ramirez's backside back to the crime scene. "By the way, Ramirez, what does the 'T' stand for?"

I might not have another chance, so with Sorensen out of the house, I decided to ask. The hall was filled with the smell of wolf-shit and death, but hey, it was better than meeting someone at the bar.

CHAPTER TWO

It took an hour to do my part of the crime scene survey and by then, the house was crawling with police, none of them from the Magical Crimes Unit. Most of that hour I had spent carefully walking the house looking for spells that might have been related to the murder while Ramirez followed me around. His sexy presence was more than a little distracting, but I put on my best professional demeanor. I had found other spells, but nothing related to the murder. A glance outside revealed that Yuriko was sitting in her truck, talking on her cellphone, which kept her from getting impatient as I did my job.

"Where's MCU?" I glanced at Ramirez.

"Something going on with the feds. They called the team in this morning. How come they didn't call you?" He studied me as if trying to figure out how important I was. Or maybe he was looking for romantic queues.

I shrugged. "I'm not really a witch."

Ramirez grinned, tentatively touching my arm. "I know, I asked."

"When did you have time?"

It was his turn to shrug, his cop eyes softening with mischief. "Too busy walking around with a glazed expression to notice me. You really can see magic?"

"Yeah."

Sorensen suddenly loomed in a hallway that gave him a view of us and other portions of the house but his gaze was sternly locked on me. I got the message—*back to work*. Except I was done.

"There's nothing else here of importance."

"Then I guess you don't need to be here, do you?" growled Sorensen. "The Chief said to let you do your job. We did. So leave the crime scene!"

The blonde stormed off but Ramirez handed me a card. "In case you need to contact me."

"About the case?"

"That too." He smiled but Sorensen roared for him and he gave me a curt nod before trotting off.

I left without making detailed notes on what I saw. The feds would have demanded it. If they got involved, which they would, Sorensen would get another ass-chewing. And not the good kind. But he wasn't my problem anymore. Not unless Ramirez and I became an item.

Despite my interest in Ramirez, my mind was busy with more important things as I walked outside. There was no doubt that the woman lying dead on her floor had been part Drow. Subtle spells were woven at every window and door to conceal the inhabitants from detection. Those wards wouldn't have helped her much, however, as the walls and the foundation of the house should have been spelled, too. They weren't.

Most things that go bump in the night wouldn't hesitate to tear through the wall instead of using the door. But she apparently had thought they would enter through a man-made opening. That *was* significant. I told the detective in charge that much before they threw me out.

Such an oversight by the dead woman suggested that she had been raised in Human culture, not by the Drow. Elves didn't think in conventional terms of doors and windows. But if she hadn't been raised among Elves, how had she learned enough about Drow magic to ward her windows and doors?

I walked outside, past the uniforms at the front door to Yuriko's truck. I looked in the cages on the truck bed for our newest addition, which wasn't easy. The panels weren't just mesh-wire, they were solid bits of steel as well.

I finally found the wolf curled tightly in the center cage against the tailgate, silent and looking very near death. I reached fingertips in and touched the top of its head, then jerked my fingers back and yelped as the cage behind it rattled and shook. Ashamed of my skittishness, I withdrew my hand entirely and peered past the closest squares of metal but I couldn't see into the other occupied cage. I reminded myself that Yuriko was waiting for me and headed for the cab instead of investigating. I nodded to myself. *See, not obsessive.*

Yuriko glanced at me as I slid into the passenger seat and finished up her conversation. "He's done. Okay. Bye." She hung up the phone.

"The boyfriend?"

"Yeah," she sighed. "Wish you guys got along. Then I wouldn't have to cancel lunch plans with you for my early dinner with him." She started the engine and backed out of the drive. Two uniformed officers waved and she smiled at them. White middle-aged guys tended to like skinny Asian chicks, even cops.

"It's not my fault you date homophobic jerks."

"He was at a gay bar when we met," she answered, exasperated. "I only talked to him because I thought he was gay."

"I know. You always meet straight guys at gay clubs, even though you only talk to them because they seem gay. Just once, it would be nice if they weren't so—never mind."

More rattling came from the back. I turned around in the seat to look through the back window of the cab. I couldn't see into the cage that was making all the fuss. I started to ask her what it was when she had the bad taste to remember our earlier conversation.

"Devon, you cannot cause problems down at my work."

"Why not?"

At first she just looked at me. When she spoke, her voice was full of complaint. "You know the budget is tight. The department is under review. If exotic animals become an issue for how it's being run, they will call out the federal department of game and wildlife. Cut our staff again and reduce the holding time from three weeks to one week."

"You mean euthanize unclaimed animals after one week?" I asked, appalled.

"Legislation is on the floor about exotics. Werewolves, exotic familiars of witches, anything not normal are funded at the federal level. The money has to come from somewhere. And if a domestic animal is believed to be a magical familiar, it gets shifted, too. They're thinking it may just become too problematic and the whole Animal Control department should be made federal."

"So no more job." I glanced at her. She stared straight ahead as she drove, fuming.

"Fuck my job! All the homeless cats and dogs, farm animals—they get killed quickly just to save money." She took a moment to gather herself. "Sorry. I'm not mad at you. But you can't cause trouble. Even if you think it's the right thing to do."

"It may happen anyway from what you say," I warned her. I believed that denial is something for weak people. Yuriko wasn't weak. Not in that way.

"I can live with it if it happens." The look on her face was tragic. "I can't live with it if you help make it happen."

I sat in silence. She rarely asked me for anything. Not that I'd say 'no' to her. Of all my closest friends, she went out of her way to try and pay me back for all of my kindnesses even long after I felt like we were even. Another Japanese trait—every gift obligated another.

But all she had to do was ask. "Okay."

"Okay, what?" she asked suspiciously.

"Okay, the wolf can stay with me." To Yuriko Morimoto, who had been my friend for seven years, it was a promise to help her out and not cause trouble at work.

Yuriko shifted gears and continued to study the traffic, but I could see the faint smile of relief playing at the corner of her mouth. Sometimes, she was such a guy. Not that she couldn't say 'thank you.' She had many times before. But it was more often than not simply understood. Except when her boyfriend was involved. Then she thanked me from the bottom of her heart. Why was *I* the one who always had to tolerate *them*?

CHAPTER THREE

From the mirror in my bathroom, I glanced at my king-size bed and the freshly bathed wolf resting there. He had curled on my comforter like he belonged there, but he was wide awake. His eyes never left me as I walked back, but it was probably the bits of raw steak in my hand. In the morning, I'd find more suitable food. For now, sleep was important.

He watched me as I took off my shirt, which I threw into the open clothes hamper in a corner. Looking down at my chest, I noticed I was starting to develop a few hairs. I hadn't really looked at myself in a long time and it startled me that I was no longer completely glabrous.

"Guess I can't stay young forever in the one way I liked."

The wolf which perked its ears at the sound of my voice, but it raised its head to watch me as I undressed. I slid my Bench jeans down and stepped out of them, tossing them over an armchair. They were starting to look frayed at the bottoms and the knees had been worn thin. I'd need to visit the Philippines again soon to replace them. I hated wearing the same shirt or briefs and socks for more than a day, but I tended to wear out my favorite pants and tennis shoes.

Of course, I could ask Evangelina Vera Cruz, another of my close friends, to ship me a replacement pair or two. Evangelina was doing her PhD in linguistics in the Philippines, which meant all I had to do was send her enough cash. She'd laugh at me, of course, for requesting ten pair of identical black Bench denim jeans, but she'd do it.

I started to remove my briefs, tighty-whities, which were my idea of sexy. But I hesitated, staring into the green eyes of the wolf. I slept naked, but I was reluctant to be naked with a wolf in my bed. Animals tended to sniff out and lick very inappropriate regions with clothes on. This wolf had already proven that point. Naked could only be worse. I left my briefs on, yawned and crawled onto the bed.

Given its ordeal, the wolf needed companionship as much as food right now. Instead of slipping under the covers, I curled up against the beast on top of the covers. It was too weak and submissive to hurt me and I was used to cuddling with dogs, not just boyfriends.

As my arms went around its ribs, it let loose a sigh of canine pleasure. I could feel its heartbeat strong and steady, but it didn't try to move away from me. I had been right that it had been raised as someone's pet. Wild animals didn't react this way, especially not to strangers.

Yuriko would come by later with paperwork for the long-term care of the wolf and I realized I didn't mind the obligation after all. I was so comfortable laying with the wolf, like spooning a long-time lover, that I was the one who fell immediately asleep, exhausted.

CHAPTER FOUR

I woke to the fuzzy pleasure of being relaxed but not ready to stir, and a warm body beside me. I pulled the body against me tighter, snuggling my morning erection against a firm, naked backside through my briefs. I nuzzled the hair at the back of the head, sniffing the clean maleness. My hand slid down a smooth, narrow waist to confirm the nakedness of the hips where I pressed up against him. My eyes flew open and I froze.

The pale white body against me wriggled up against my crotch, shifting me into a more penetrating position despite my underwear. I stared at the short blonde hair with horror. Where was the wolf and which of my ex-boyfriends had crawled into bed with me this time? It was a short list given that he was a blonde. There had only been three in my life.

"Underwear." He tried to reach a smooth hand back to pull at my briefs, but it was as if he hadn't the strength.

I didn't recognize the voice. "Who are you?"

Waking up next to people I didn't remember was not a familiar experience for me. Even with the occasional blackouts from too many Long Island ice teas, I had always remembered the bits before I got wasted. Only this time I hadn't been drinking.

"It's okay, you can do it," he murmured.

I sat up to get a better view, not quite extricating myself from our embrace. The blonde looked young because he had a petite frame, firm skin around his neck, ears and butt. In fact, I couldn't be sure he was even legal without looking at his face. I pulled my body away from his.

The noise that came out of his mouth was like a painful whine. My hand went back to its familiar place on the meat of his naked hip, but my erection faded completely. It wasn't the right kind of pain noise. "Are you okay?"

"Do me." His tone was desperate and I pulled my hand away.

I slipped out of bed and glanced around for the wolf. I walked around the bed but saw no evidence of the animal in the room. Had it crawled into some corner of my house to die?

I glanced at the face of the stranger in bed and grew anxious. I had never seen him before. I was sure of that because he was too good-looking to forget. But he was also way too young. He could have been eighteen. Or he could have been sixteen. I was thinking the younger of those two possibilities.

How had he gotten into my bed? Was this a ploy to blackmail me for money? Whatever the answers were, I was angry. "I don't even know who you are!?"

The blonde seemed disoriented. I was betting on drugs if he had broken into a stranger's house hoping to have sex. If it was an effort to blackmail me, I expected to learn later that someone had taken pictures of us while I slept. They might still be in the closet, although the door was wide open and there was no one visible.

"Why does that matter?" he sulked.

"How old are you?"

He closed his eyes for a moment, his mouth a grimace. He looked ill and then I realized something when he re-opened his eyes. They were the color of newly unfurled leaves.

"Holy fuck," I said.

"More like illicit fuck," said a male voice from the doorway.

How many people had broken into my house? I jerked my head up and saw that Antonio Ramos, Yuriko's boyfriend and a member of the California State Bar, stood looking at me with disgust. This really was the *Twilight Zone*, and I was doing an episode in Hell. At least Antonio was fully clothed. That was not a dream I wanted to have.

It was when I saw his judgmental gaze go to my crotch that I remembered I wasn't dressed. Yeah, I had on briefs and he was a guy, but I tended to be shy like that. I always had been. Thank God my woody had gone away.

I started to tell Antonio to get out when Yuriko walked in with paperwork in her hands. She froze when she saw me half-naked and then her eyes went to the boy in my bed. I grabbed my oversized t-shirt and pulled it on. It hung down just enough to hide my crotch.

"What's going on?" she exclaimed. "Where's the wolf? And when did you have time to pick up a boy?" She almost sounded impressed.

"Oh, come on, Yuriko!" sneered Antonio. "You've never heard of the internet? Sexual predators love using it for teenage boys."

He really didn't like me any more than I liked him. Of course, it was because he didn't like me that I didn't like him. Well, part of it anyway.

"I'm more likely to pick up an underage boy than Devon." Yuriko was angry at him, but it was also the truth. "He turns down more jailbait than most guys meet in a lifetime."

"Stop covering for him. I know he likes younger guys. He always refers to them as 'boys.' Looks like one finally said 'yes.' I'm calling the police." Antonio smiled with vengeful satisfaction.

"'Younger guys' means like twenty-three or something! And most of us use 'boy' to refer to maleness, not 'children.'" I hated letting him get under my skin, but he was so smug. For Yuriko I tried to be tolerant. "Yuriko calls you her 'boy' and you're only a couple of years younger than me." I was being defensive, but then I was still shocked by the morning's revelations. "Besides, he's not a guy." I nodded in the direction of the blonde curled up on my bed too weak to move.

Antonio was already opening his cellphone flip top, but that made him pause. He glanced at the naked blonde and if you asked me, his gaze lingered a bit too long on the boy's naked crotch. I couldn't help but be suspicious. Yuriko *had* met him at a gay bar.

I pulled on my jeans, fastened and zipped them then knelt on the bed next to the man-boy. I touched his hair and his large green eyes tracked my every move. His lips moved softly and I leaned in closer to hear, "Sorry."

I looked into those lost and empty eyes and saw some emotion flicker in the background before fading away. "Did you bring that electrolyte drink for the wolf?

Yuriko rummaged through her oversized purse and brought out a plastic bottle of clear liquid. "Here."

"That's for the wolf!" shouted Antonio outraged.

Yuriko gave her boyfriend a warning look as she handed me the bottle. Antonio was more confused than offended. That ultimately was the source of his outrage. Anyone who said you had to be smart to be an attorney hadn't known very many attorneys.

"And what did you mean he's not a guy. He's clearly not a girl. You going to try and tell me he's related to you? Sex with a minor is still an offense, even if it's your cousin! Hell, especially if it's your cousin!"

I ignored Antonio and dripped bits of the liquid onto the boy's lips. He licked the moisture and swallowed weakly. I continued to give him more until he tried to gulp down half the bottle. I looked up at Yuriko. She was staring at the naked boy unabashedly. Amazing the things that didn't make her blush but made me go pink in the cheeks. On the other hand, she hadn't been kidding when she said she'd have been more likely to wind up in bed with a sixteen-year-old than me. In Japan, the legal age for boys to have sex was thirteen. Not that she liked them *that* young.

The expression on my face must have made her realize something strange was happening, because she approached the bed with eyes slightly wide. "Where's the wolf?"

I turned back to the youth in my bed, studying the angles of his face, the shape of his nose. He looked fully Human. Only the color of his eyes and the texture of his blonde hair gave him away. As he drank more of the fluid, his features seemed to fill out. His coloring went from a pale, greenish hue to simply pale.

"What's your name?" I asked.

He blinked, licked his lips, and then gripped my wrist with both hands. I wanted to jerk away but he sighed deeply and his eyelids fluttered rapidly before they shut. He began snoring and all my questions would have to wait.

CHAPTER FIVE

"What do you mean he's a Werewolf?" shouted Antonio Ramos as we stood around the kitchen counter, a Diet Pepsi in my hand.

This time, he assured me, he was yelling not as Yuriko's boyfriend, but as a court-appointed representative of the Fresno County District Attorney's office. I didn't like him much better in his official capacity. Let's just say he wasn't much better at listening.

"I went to bed curled around the injured wolf and woke up with that—'boy' in my arms." Even Yuriko looked at me doubtfully. "C'mon, Morimoto-*san*! That wolf was so far gone it needed the comfort of a dominant male to make it feel safe. Like it had a reason for pulling through. I'm not into animals any more than I'm into little boys."

"I didn't say anything," she complained, but a flash of guilt raced across her expression. It was quickly replaced by resolve. "If Devon says it's a Werewolf, it's a Werewolf."

"Yuriko, Hon, I know this pervert is your best friend, but—!"

Antonio the D.A. had pushed the one button which Yuriko had asked me to ignore for the sake of her department and the animals it protected. Whether I was a pervert simply for being gay or a pervert because he believed I wanted a teenage boy in my bed, I'd had enough.

Yuriko saw the look in my eyes and she grabbed Antonio's arm. It wasn't like I could do magic of my own. My talent wasn't like that. I could See the threads of magic, but I couldn't create spells. She wasn't afraid I was going to make his balls drop off, although if I could have in that moment, I probably would have been tempted!

"You shallow, cock-sucking sack of shit!" The words that rolled out of my mouth parroted my father's vile curses from my childhood. When your father called you those things as a kid every time he was mad at you, they became automatic. "You have been pissy with me since Yuriko said you weren't my type. What the fuck does a straight guy want to know if his girlfriend's gay friend thinks he's cute? And how straight are you if you get pissy because I don't think you are attractive? Trust me, Yuriko *can* and *has* done better!"

Mr. D.A. couldn't find any words as he looked from me to Yuriko, ready to explode. I wasn't anywhere near done. "In case you happened to forget, Antonio, you ramapithecine-bred shit! I work for the police as a criminal consultant. I present evidence which helps you prosecute the real bad guys! And while I would never withhold evidence or tamper with a case, I sure as hell can get you black-listed from any case with preternatural aspects. I can press sexual discrimination charges for the whole gay-pervert thing. And I can also get my friends at the police department to start refusing to cooperate with you."

"The police won't refuse to cooperate with the D.A.'s office," sputtered the dark-haired man.

"Who said anything about the D.A.? I said *you*. What kind of status in the department will you have if the police and their civilian consultants refuse to work with you and only you?" I looked at Yuriko who had the good sense not to ask me to calm down.

"Apologize to Devon, Antonio. If I told you he wouldn't lie, why don't you believe me?" She confused him by making it about her. And some people wondered why I loved women more than men.

"Why aren't you taking my side?" He obviously didn't know Yuriko well enough, yet. Not even after six months. She didn't take sides unless someone was being unfair.

"You called me a liar!" she replied.

"I didn't!" Antonio turned to her, panicking.

Personally, I'd hoped Yuriko would wise up and dump the smug, son-of-a-bitch. I'd never once heard him compliment her, other than to say she was a great lay. What kind of asshole tells a girl's friend that? Or that they have sex four times a day and she likes to get out of control while fucking? What happened to saying that she makes him feel special or that he can talk to her about things he couldn't say to other women? Not 'she's an animal in bed.'

I wasn't the violent sort or I would have punched him when we first met. Six months later, I didn't like him any better. I pretended in my imagination sometimes that I was violent and that the only reason I didn't off him was that it's hard to hide a six-foot-three corpse. She liked tall guys, but it did make for more to dispose of.

"You did. She said he was telling the truth and you called him a liar," said a voice tentatively from the hallway. We all turned and the naked blonde was standing there gripping the wall. "Freshman college logic textbook."

"College?"

Whether Antonio was smart enough to change the subject or was just dead set on hauling me in for contributing to the delinquency of a minor I didn't know. I didn't blame him, seeing the blonde's naked body upright. Unlike most college boys, the blonde's patch of crotch hair didn't continue up past the hips to form that tiny trail along the stomach. He had the smooth flat stomach of a high school swimmer or polo player.

Of course, Antonio didn't know from firsthand experience that my belly didn't have hair either and I was thirty. We didn't know if it was the Choctaw or British blood that accounted for it, but I was still mostly glabrous. It didn't make me sixteen.

"She let me read her books," said the blonde uncomfortably.

I studied him and realized that maybe he wouldn't have been mistaken for sixteen. But he couldn't have been much older than eighteen. All I knew for sure was that he was a natural blonde.

"I was gonna say, since when did they let sixteen-year-olds into college," snorted Antonio bitterly.

"I'm nineteen." The blonde stood taller, throwing back his shoulders which had the hint of width to them. "I only so look young because I'm malnourished."

"You were the wolf we found?" Yuriko stared at the naked boy and finally had the decency to blush when he scratched at himself. He seemed unaware of his movement or the embarrassment it caused her.

"You gonna take me to prison?" He took a terrified step toward me, but then stopped. He seemed uncertain who to face, because he tracked Antonio's movements the way a wild animal watches a predator. Finally, his gaze returned to me, full of confusion.

Unexpectedly, he pressed himself back against the wall and clutched at his stomach. His body trembled and although it revealed a defined six-pack, he looked terrified instead of sexy. He also looked ready to collapse.

"Antonio isn't here as the D.A.. He's here as Yuriko's boyfriend. Since you are not a minor and he has no status over Lycanthropes, he was just getting ready to leave."

"You can't make me leave. I want proof—!" Antonio reached for his court-badge as if it made a difference to me.

"Antonio, please! Just go outside, let me handle it." Yuriko grabbed him by the arm and pulled him toward the door. "Wait outside. We're trespassing and you don't want Devon pressing charges against us, do you?" Yuriko had learned that some Americans dealt better with threats of criminal charges than simple reason.

"Probable cause." Antonio threw his hands in the air. But he stepped toward the entrance.

"Probable cause to shove my foot up your ass," I muttered back as he walked out the front door and slammed it. I looked at Yuriko. "Why do cops and asshole D.A.'s lie to civilians about the law as if we don't know anything? He had no probable cause to enter my place. Just because he finds something after illegally entering doesn't mean it's retroactive. He was here because you have an open invitation to visit and brought him. Probable cause—idiot!"

"I know, I know. But it got him outside, didn't it?" We'd never fought until this man was in her life. I resented him more for it.

"Don't get pissed off at me, I didn't do anything!" I snarled. Hearing the growl in my voice, I looked over at the young man who was starting to slide down the wall. "Shit, grab him!"

I rushed to the blonde. Yuriko came over to help me carry him to a recliner near the kitchen counter. He looked frightened as we grabbed him. In his weakened state he couldn't even hold onto us, but his eyes tracked me desperately. "Help me."

I stroked his thick, coarse hair, as I had when I thought he was just a wolf. I realized in that moment that there was no difference in the way I played with a boyfriend's hair and a dog's. The things you learn about yourself sometimes.

"I won't let them take you. Not now." I wanted to tell him that I'd never let Antonio or someone like the D.A. take him, but that would have been a lie. If he turned out to be involved in the murder of the Drow woman, I couldn't help him.

Yuriko pulled out her cellphone and hit one of her speed-dial numbers. I went to the refrigerator and grabbed the rest of the sliced, raw filet-mignon. I'd find something else for my lunch.

"Hello, Agent Jacobsen? We've got a situation. Yeah, the wolf turned out to be a guy. Lycan. The murder house from yesterday."

Yuriko talked brusquely, looking at me reassuringly because she wanted to apologize. Another guy moment between us. No words.

The federal agent she spoke to was the department head of the Fresno branch of the federal Office of Preternatural Affairs. I'd worked with him twice, once on my single federal case and once when the feds assisted the local MCU—Magical Crimes Unit. He played fair which is more than I can say for some G-men.

She nodded and looked at me again. "Yeah, I've placed him with Devon. Yeah, he *is* a good guy. No, the Lycan won't be a problem. Not hostile. Let me ask." She put the phone to her chin. "Can you handle him if he goes bad on you?"

I didn't know if my talent at magic manipulation could work on Lycanthropes. But I did have a 10mm with a round of silver shot somewhere. Federal rules had required it after they pulled me onto that first case and made me a consultant.

"Yeah," I lied.

My instincts said he wasn't trouble. Not the sort that would threaten my life with claws and fangs. But if he went around naked presenting his silky smooth bubble-butt to me and saying 'do me' over and over, I might weaken. Sometimes I was a guy.

"He's fine with it." Yuriko listened to the phone for a while, gave him my address and phone number and then hung up. She took the time to put her phone away before talking to me. "He can stay here till they have a chance to question him about the murder. You are not to question him prior to an agent arriving. Guess you won't need my paperwork after all."

"Thank you," said the blonde. I realized that I kept calling him the blonde in my head and that was annoying.

"What's your name? And this time, wait till after you tell me to pass out."

He flashed me a cautious grin. "Jake. Jacob Winters."

"Hi, Jake," I said reassuringly. "I'm Devon. This is Yuriko."

"Thank you for saving me." I saw a peek of adoration before his bright green eyes grew cautious and guarded.

"Don't mind me. I don't exist," said Yuriko.

I shrugged at her, but Jake continued to focus on me. I did tend to collect stray boys, but even Yuriko had to agree that this one wasn't my fault. I'd have argued that a *lot* of them weren't my fault, but the truth was more important than my culpability.

"Let's get you some clothes," I said.

It wasn't a naked guy in the room with me that bothered me. It was a naked guy I was attracted to and a friend all in the same room. Some things just weren't natural, I told myself as I rushed toward my bedroom. You'd think that the fact that he had been a wolf just a few hours earlier would have been more unsettling. It wasn't.

CHAPTER SIX

A short while later, Jake was back in bed in the spare room adjacent to mine. We had tried to get him to take a bedroom nearer the kitchen, but he panicked at the idea of being so far from me. He was wearing another of my oversized t-shirts and a pair of white briefs, which we had struggled to get him to wear. If he hadn't been so weak still, I doubt that we would have won. He didn't seem comfortable in clothes at all. Thankfully I liked my briefs tight on me and he had enough butt to keep them from sliding off his skinny waist.

I returned to the kitchen and stood at the coffee-maker, filling it with water. Yuriko would have preferred coffee, but she wasn't going to be staying long. Instead, I put two cinnamon flavored tea bags, two vanilla-hazelnut flavored tea bags and two regular black tea bags into the glass pot and turned it on.

Outside the front door I could still hear Yuriko and Antonio arguing.

"You did ask me if he thought you were cute!" Yuriko wasn't quite yelling, but it was close.

"I didn't ask you to tell him I asked!" retorted Antonio for the fifth time.

"How the fuck was I supposed to find out if I didn't ask?" You could tell how mad she was when she began cussing.

I leaned against the counter listening to them fight and waited. Part of me was involved in their discussion while part of me thought about the wolf-boy—Jake—in my spare bedroom. I had no actual experience with Werewolves, just what I got from books or classes. But there was one woman who I knew had hands-on experience.

Melanie O'Keefe was an old college buddy who had gone on to become a veterinarian, getting her degree from U.C. Davis and spending a few years in Europe interning. She had returned a little less than a year ago, setting up a practice in Clovis. I'd visited her occasionally the last few months, but she had seemed so very different from the girl that I'd known so well. During her time in Europe, she had decided to specialize in non-mundanes or animal Fey, which fit her personality. However, she had also brought a mysterious German husband home, about whom she was very private. That was very unlike her.

Still, of all the people I knew, she could help. Werewolves apparently were much more the mainstream on the Continent. Not in the UK, but the Continent.

I picked up the phone. The feds were supposed to show up, but my sense of right and wrong sometimes made me push the boundaries of authority. If Jake turned out not to be an innocent, well, I'd deal with that when it came up.

"Hello," said a familiar voice on the receiver.

"Melanie! What's the doc answering her own phone for?"

"Devon?" I hadn't called often enough, otherwise she wouldn't have sounded slightly unsure. "I'm like you—student loans and starting up a new business, can't really afford to hire a receptionist yet." She didn't sound upset.

"We need to get together and talk," I said. She didn't know I was wealthy now. Didn't matter the excuses, I'd been avoiding her. Too much history and too much love still there. Too much love without sex and that was the problem.

"Anytime. Business isn't that booming," she answered.

"You still sticking strictly to non-mundanes?"

"I love preternaturals, you know that. But if things don't change, I may not be able to. Why? You have something for me?" Her voice took on a familiar eagerness.

"How are you on Lycanthropes?"

The phone went still for several seconds. 'Lycanthrope' was the technical term for Werecreatures but most people called them 'Lycans' for short.

"What kind?"

"Wolf," I answered. She released her breath.

"Not a problem. Wait—is there a problem? You know someone can't be cured unless the first full moon hasn't passed. And even then—"

"You are talking to the Werewolf king or did you forget?"

"Sorry. You know more lore about Werewolves than anyone not medically trained or a Werewolf themself," she joked. "But some of my patients in Europe!" I could feel her shaking her head on the other end of the phone.

"No, my fault," I apologized. "We haven't spent much time together the last few years." I listened at the doorway and the argument was still in full swing. "I have a young Lycan that was locked in a garage without food and water for a time. Days at least. We've given him liquids with electrolytes and small amounts of raw meat. But he's still weak and sleeping a lot. I thought maybe you should come look at him?"

"Any chance you can bring him to me?" She sounded conflicted. "I know I said I wasn't busy, but I have a couple of patients I'm watching and, like you noticed, I'm even answering my own phones."

"Okay, I haven't seen the new place, yet. At Shaw and Clovis, right?"

"Oops, gotta run!" she exclaimed into the phone. "See you then."

The connection was broken and I slowly put the receiver in the cradle. I picked it back up and dialed the FBI. Their switchboard answered and I left a message for whichever agents that they were sending to call me when they got to the house.

Yuriko came back inside as I hung up the second time. I heard a car start up in the driveway. "We're leaving now."

"So are we." I motioned toward the spare room. Yuriko stood there looking at me blankly. "I'm going to take him to see Melanie. My friend who's the vet. You guys still haven't met, have you? I think we should have Jake examined in case it's more than simple dehydration."

"You're right. I know better than that!" Yuriko was as rough on herself as I was over little mistakes. "The department doesn't pay out extra for outside vet care, so it wasn't my first thought. I know you can afford it, but do you mind sticking the bill?"

"Not a problem. And it's 'picking up the bill.'" She rolled her eyes and I grinned as I slipped on my tennis shoes before heading to the bedroom. "Help me get him to the car first?"

"He's not that heavy. You can carry him yourself."

"Let's just say I'd feel better having a chaperone until we prove for sure that he's over eighteen," I answered. Yuriko didn't respond but followed me into the bedroom. Jake was laying on top of the sheets and had removed the t-shirt but not the briefs.

"He's like you, doesn't like to wear clothes to bed," she said. "If he's over eighteen and isn't a murderer, he is really cute."

"He's a Werewolf! And I don't need you to set me up with another boy, thank you," I retorted. I studied his sexy form and shook my head. "I'd have ditched the briefs before the tee."

"You gotta ditch that Jiao. I never did tell you what he did!"

"And it will have to wait. I need to get Jake looked at and back again before the feds think I'm hiding a witness."

"Okay. Antonio is impatient about going to dinner now anyway. He has a case to work on tonight." I shot her a glance but she waved me off, "No, another murder. This one near the university. One of the football players again. Killed his girlfriend or something."

I bent down to pick up Jake, but he was heavier than he looked. I shifted the extra weight in my arms and then nodded at the door. "I'll carry the body, you get the door."

Jake wrapped his arms around my neck without waking and nuzzled his face against my chest. Yuriko chuckled and gave me that look. "He likes you."

"He's a Werewolf!" I snarled exasperated. She laughed some more but got the door for me. "I want to date a normal guy. Like Tony."

"Who?"

"T. Ramirez." I turned through the doorway so Jake didn't hit his head. I imagined we looked like the cover of a gay romance novel.

"The cop?" asked Yuriko. "Yeah, he was cute, too. But I hate his partner!"

"Join the club. But I'd be dating him, not his partner."

"You've never dated a cop before." She opened the front door for me. "Love me, love my partner."

"Home wrecker," I chastised her as we stepped outside.

"Homo wrecker." She grinned at me until Antonio honked impatiently.

"Whatever." I waited while she opened the passenger side of my S-10 and then deposited Jake in the passenger seat. She stood there with one arm raised and I gave her a brief hug. Over her shoulder I saw Antonio scowl and hugged her even harder. She made a soft noise of complaint and I let her go.

"You gonna come by tonight and check on the wolf-boy?"

"Don't want to interrupt anything." Her laugh was a low, in-her-throat sound that hadn't always been so confident. Or sexy.

"There's no full moon tonight, so if you don't hear any howling coming from the house, I guess it's safe to come in." The words that had come out of my mouth surprised me.

"I knew you liked him," she teased me. "But yeah, the cop is better, even if he is older."

"I like older! Just not stodgy or jaded! *You* like them really young." I slid into the driver's seat.

With a glance at the beautiful blonde in the seat next to me, I felt my breath catch. While I didn't consider him a child, I felt that same urge to protect him that men had written about women for centuries. The few times I'd felt this way about a guy, something bad had happened. I tried to memorize his peaceful features while trying to convince myself that Officer Tony Ramirez was the better choice. He was more my normal type. I preferred brunettes.

Yuriko got into Antonio's silver Chevy Camaro, watching me for one worried moment. Jake had done something to me and I knew it. Yuriko knew it, too. She finally shook her head and motioned Antonio to drive off. I followed the Camaro out of the driveway in my S-10 then turned onto Shaw while they continued straight for a romantic dinner out. What chance did I have for romantic nights out with a Werewolf? I guess I was going to find out.

CHAPTER SEVEN

Melanie O'Keefe's veterinary office was downright cozy. It smelled good, like vanilla and spice. The waiting room was lined with shelves filled with older, worn books. The prints on the walls were European and somewhat dark. There were moonlight landscapes with wolves, Gargoyles on medieval embattlements, and a pastoral scene inside a white-washed barn where a pale-yellow Fairy looked as if it would shred the skin off of the children hiding in the hay. None of them were the Unicorn-kind-of-brightness she had once favored. And not a single Dragon print in the place.

Melanie took Jake's temperature through his ear and smiled at me. The blonde was laying flat on his back on one of her two examination tables. "He's going to be fine."

I watched how carefully she had to move about the examination table because unlike Yuriko, her breasts were Playboy sized, the Holiday Edition. When she leaned against the sterile counter her chest molded around the edge like firm Jell-O. Contrary to popular belief, a large number of gay men were fascinated with women's breasts. I was one of them. But it had nothing to do with sex appeal. It was a perverse curiosity about the physics of lugging those things around.

Melanie stood at five-foot-eight, with curly strawberry blonde hair and built like a modern Mae West. Her alabaster skin burned easily, so she avoided the sun. She wouldn't have died like some story-book Vampire, but the effects would have been just as bad. Unlike Yuriko and me, Melanie liked men older than herself. Her husband Ulrich, the mysterious European, was a good ten years older.

"I'll look at the bloodwork to double-check my diagnosis, but he is clearly dehydrated and malnourished." She continued to work as she spoke. "Lycanthropes suffer from those illnesses sooner than Humans or their natural wolf counterparts."

"So just keep feeding him raw meats and electrolytes?" I asked.

"Ordinarily that would be fine. But a Werewolf is never meant to go without food for a whole week. I mean, it sounds silly, but his body will use up everything you give him the next time he changes and probably kill him."

I put my hand on Jake's head and brushed his cheek with the back of my hand. If I had one enemy in the world, it was Death. Melanie knew how I felt about things dying on me. Men, women, animals— didn't matter. Although my mother had been the worst.

"There are some metaphysical things his pack could do for him." She looked at me questioningly. I shook my head and she frowned. "Without that, he needs an IV now and some special protein supplements for later. Might as well make them liquid form since he could use the extra fluids. But," Melanie looked at me painfully and then at the ground. I remembered her expressions too well even after all these years.

"Go ahead, tell me."

"I can't eat the cost, Devon. And it's not cheap." The look on her face hid a lot of emotions, including something that asked me not to bring up her new husband. I loved her too much to say anything that would intentionally make her feel bad. She had once been my only best friend. Now there were five of them, eleven years later.

"The IV isn't too pricey," she said, "but Lycanthropes need special amino compounds. The protein supplements are expensive. If he had only been without for a day or two, maybe three, I'd say risk it."

"My circumstances have changed, Melanie." I realized I was caressing Jake's hair without thinking about it and I stopped.

"No, you should keep doing that. That's what a pack member would do. Lots of physical contact is important psychologically. You know that."

"Yeah, I just—,"

"He's totally your type isn't he? Except for the blonde thing." She smiled at me sympathetically. "Touching him when you are attracted to him doesn't make you bad. You are just a very affectionate man." She sighed sadly. "You've always held yourself to an impossibly high standard."

"But he's ill and unconscious. If he were a kid or I weren't attracted to him, I'd be fine. Totally guilt free."

"Which boyfriend had to tell you it was okay to make love to him when he was drunk because you refused to take advantage?" she asked playfully. "He was only getting drunk so that it was easier for you to have your way with him, silly man." When I scowled instead of replying, she grew serious. "What's the change in your circumstances? You aren't sick?" She studied my face as if she might never see me again.

"What? No, Oh god, not that. No," I chuckled realizing what she was asking. "No, I've just come into some money. Lots of money. I can afford it."

"Your dad's okay?" she asked with a tinge of concern. Not that she liked how my dad had treated me. But he adored her and had treated her accordingly. Melanie was conflicted, so I didn't make her choose, even if the man had killed my mother.

"He's great. That bastard will probably outlive us all. The meaner they are, the longer they last."

"Then where?" she didn't finish the question. There was a rattling from the cages at the back of the examination room and she rushed off.

I followed and froze a good ten feet away from the two occupied cages. Not frozen from surprise. Frozen because of that blood chilling, terror so strong it paralyzed your legs. Creatures the size of chimpanzees, with overly large heads and skin the color of dried grass peered at us through heavily lidded eyes. Fangs protruded up from their lower jaws, visible on the outside of their sagging lips.

"What the fuck are those?" I asked, horrified.

"Don't tell me the brave and fearless Devon Mosteller is afraid of a couple of Foothill Trolls?"

"You know me. Only afraid of three things—Humans, Werewolves and gorillas. And now, apparently, Trolls."

"You're only afraid of Werewolves because of your fascination for them. Like when we were hiking in Yosemite, attacked by that pack of wild dogs. Instead of running like any rational Human being, you, Devon Mosteller, charged the lead alpha and roared at him. I don't know if you scared them or me more."

"It was just an instinct or something," I muttered.

Melanie approached the caged Trolls and started cooing at them and speaking softly. "There, there, my little luvs, it's alright." She reached for bits of bananas on a nearby table and gently fed each of the two brutes. They took the fruit from her fingertips carefully, as if afraid they'd hurt her.

Still using her gentle voice, she continued to lecture me. "And you are afraid of these little darlings because they share facial features and overall body morphology with great apes. Your parents should never have let you watch all those gorilla horror films when you were a little boy."

"I can see the similarities," I conceded and hugged myself, "from right here." Some things a person was just phobic about. I had no reason to interact with the Trolls, so I refused to try.

"Some farmer took pot shots at them," she explained angrily. "Then his wife made him rush them here. He's not planning on paying for their care either, but the State is going to step in. I think. Hell, they better."

"I didn't know we had Trolls this close. I thought only the foothills?"

"We didn't. Not in the numbers we have now or as close to Humans as before. Something is driving them up from their burrows and down from the higher elevations. You used to maybe see a Troll or a small clave of Trolls every couple of years in the mountains if you were lucky. Now they are starting to be spotted near the Tollhouse community and even on some of the farms at the base of the foothills a few times a month."

"Environmental?"

Melanie shook her head. "No, there's been no change in habitat. Something's driving them out. Possibly a new predator. Since the laws have changed about non-mundanes, more things are coming to light than in the old days."

"Funny that I've not heard about sightings of these guys before." I'd known that there were occasional Trolls in the upper foothills but in my mind, I'd thought that they were unseen and as elusive as Bigfoot. Of course, Bigfoot wasn't real.

"Actually, they're sort of on the hush and hush. Before the new laws, they were one of the first protected species. Not just Foothill Trolls, but all the lesser Trolls. They were hunted and sold because of their natural gentleness and how easy it is to make them into slaves. You know the Drow used to keep the larger Mountain Trolls as slaves didn't you? It wasn't just Werewolves they kept."

"No, I didn't." The first thing I thought of was the murdered Drow woman. But there had been no Trolls there, only the chained up Werewolf, Jake.

"The only reason the Drow didn't fight to keep them when they first came to the U.S. was the fact that no one really wanted the Drow to get protected rights in the first place. By agreeing to let the Trolls and any other slaves they kept free, they garnered sympathy."

"Which isn't much, even to this day."

"Yeah, well, that's why the Drow maintain such private communities and keep to themselves." She peered into the cage at something on a Troll's body but shook her head. "I think there's a glade of them just north of Modesto. One of my UCSD cohorts works up that way. He wasn't positive, but he works big animals out in the country there. Occasionally he's seen stuff. Anyway, regular people can't tell the difference between them and Christian demons just because of the darker skin and pointy ears. Absolutely stupid people, as if they know what demons looked like." Melanie ushered me back toward Jake. Away from the Trolls, she paused and put a hand on my arm. "You really can afford the treatment?"

I laughed at her sheepishness and hugged her. The contact startled her and made her step away. It would never have surprised her in the past. Although I continued to smile as she set up the IV, I wondered if our friendship would ever be the way it had been before she'd left for Europe.

"Fill 'er up Doc. And don't worry about making a profit. If anyone should make money off of me, it should be a friend."

"Thank God." She was suddenly her old self. "Would rather take advantage of a friend than a stranger."

An old joke that brought back old memories, some painful. I stared at the beautiful blonde lying on the white sheets of the metal examination table. He reminded me of another blonde young man from years earlier who had been nothing but trouble. Melanie had been by my side then, helping me through that mess. But blondes had never boded well for me.

"What happened to the Unicorns and Dragons?" I finally asked. Melanie's expression flickered to discomfort. "On the walls."

"Ulrich doesn't care much for Dragons. They terrorized his village in Germany and were responsible for the loss of his parents."

"What about the Unicorns?"

"A girl has to grow up some time." She stared at the wall, fiddling with the IV line. Her cryptic response was an accusation from the past about our friendship. "Some things just aren't real, Devon. It was time to move on."

I didn't say another word. I watched her work in silence and mourned the loss of her innocence. For some reason, I'd expected her to be living in total bliss. It was hard to believe that someone achieving their dreams could still end up living in sadness. Who the hell was I kidding? I was the poster-boy for dreams leading to sorrow.

We were in Melanie's office for two hours. There had been no phone calls or appointments. How could she and Ulrich survive like this? From what she told me, Ulrich hadn't had much luck finding a job yet. He was limited by his visa and unfamiliarity with the area. I used the time to figure out how I could funnel business their way without pissing either of them off.

Jake woke up after the second bag of fluids had dripped into his arm. He smiled at me as if I were his savior. It was hard not to want to flirt but I did my best.

"Sit up," instructed Melanie.

Jake looked at me. I put my hand to his shoulder which was warmer than I'd expected. He moved as if I'd ordered him.

"At least he's well trained." Melanie fed him from a bottle of some protein mix labeled 'chocolate,' but offered me a smile. "You like them that way."

"Chocolate flavored?" I ignored her comment.

"It's specific for Humanoids."

"Just wondered if a real wolf or cat would have preferred chocolate."

"I love chocolate," said Jake between mouthfuls. "It tastes like chocolate meat!"

Melanie's eyes blazed with joy at the amazement in his voice. "I've been experimenting with supplemental proteins specific to a Werewolf's metabolism. It's nice to know you actually can taste what's good for you in it."

"God, he looks older already." Jake looked closer to mid-twenties than nineteen. His features had matured just from the nutrients.

Melanie didn't seemed pleased with my observation. "You been spending a lot of time in wolf form?"

"The mistress preferred me furry."

"What difference does that make?" I asked.

"What? The Werewolf King doesn't know the problems associated with extended animal shape?"

"I'd read somewhere that animal characteristics might get fixed," I replied but Jake laughed at me. "What's so funny?"

"Superstition." His teeth were straight and white and the green in his eyes glowed with alert intelligence.

"Devon has never been called superstitious. I like this boy." She leaned for a moment against a counter. I watched her breasts flatten underneath and the tops squeeze against the containment of her bra. "Yeah, Devon, it is an urban legend."

"So what can happen?" I felt the color rush to my cheeks.

"Accelerated aging." Melanie angled Jake's face up to the fluorescent lighting, studying his features. "How old did you say you were, Jake?"

"Nineteen." He kept his head still as he replied. Apparently once I'd encouraged him to obey her, he continued to do so.

"Going on twenty-six," she muttered angrily. "Who the hell is your mistress? Werewolves don't refer to their leaders as mistress and master. Not even a female Fenra."

A 'Fenris' was the most dominant male member of a pack and their recognized leader. If it happened to be a female, she was a 'Fenra'—terms borrowed from popular fiction, even by the Werewolves themselves.

Jake got quiet and wrapped his arms around his knees. The look in eyes turned empty again, like when I first found him. Melanie looked at me and I shrugged.

"Do you have a pack, Jake?" I asked.

He looked at me hopelessly then shook his head. "No."

We all jumped when my cellphone rang loudly in the silence. I flipped it open and Melanie slugged me on the shoulder. I hadn't meant to leave it on maximum volume.

"Hello?"

"Devon, this is Federal Agent Shelby. I'm standing outside your house."

"Sorry, Agent Shelby. I had to take our Lycan friend to get medical help."

"Was he injured?"

"Only from long term isolation. We are almost done here."

"How far away are you?" he asked.

"With traffic, maybe forty minutes."

He didn't answer for a second then laughed. "Okay, I suppose we could grab a bite to eat before we get down to interrogation. I'll be generous, you have an hour. Please be here. My boss isn't as relaxed about these things as I am."

"Thanks Shelby. It will be nice working with a reasonable government type for a change."

His voice grew cold. "Don't forget I am a federal agent, Mr. Mosteller. I'm in this profession because it has my utmost respect."

"No disrespect intended, Agent Shelby." The phone went dead. Shit. We had been off to such a good start. I had meant it as a compliment.

"We've got to leave within ten minutes," I said to Melanie. She nodded and Jake started to stand up.

"Hold on, there, buckaroo. Let's get you disconnected first." She began to remove the IV needle from his arm. "Devon, I'll send enough supplements for two days. It's all I stock. Make sure he drinks it as I prescribe."

"No problem."

Melanie filled out some paperwork. I glanced at the top sheet, curious about the prescription. It was the bill. I looked at Melanie who pretended to be distracted by collecting the protein mix.

"Am I good till tomorrow?" I asked wryly, although I reached for my wallet.

"I'm sorry." She gave me a look of desperation. "I'll need to order more and they'll make me pay up front."

"Fine, here's a credit card. Or do you need cash?" She plucked the credit card from my finger without further comment.

CHAPTER EIGHT

A federal sedan was parked in my driveway as we pulled up. Jake was buckled in on the passenger side of the S-10, but even with the lap belt, he tried to lean over to snuggle me. I pushed him upright with one hand and slowly parked beside the FBI vehicle. He was still dressed only in my borrowed briefs as we got out of the truck. "The feds are here, Jake. Try to behave?"

"Federal Agents Shelby and Gunnerson." The shorter of the two agents held up ID. He was about my height, maybe a quarter inch taller, African American and built like he worked out every day. From his voice on the telephone earlier, I guessed he was Shelby.

"Agent Shelby," I acknowledged.

"Don't have to ask if this is our boy." He motioned at Jake.

"Jacob Winters." I confirmed.

"Nice house." The other agent, Gunnerson, was very Nordic looking. He had platinum blonde hair and icy blue eyes, but well over six feet tall. Unlike Shelby, Gunnerson was thin and lanky, like an overgrown kid.

I unlocked the front door and helped Jake reach the recliner once more. Then I grabbed his protein supplement and headed for the kitchen. "It's the medication for Jake. Do you mind?"

"If it will make him a better witness, go ahead," said Shelby magnanimously. Unless you've worked with law enforcement agencies, you can't really appreciate a cooperative agent for the rare and special creature he is.

"You're a prince." I went to the fridge to mix the supplement with milk and noticed the coffee-maker full of cold tea. I cursed under my breath. Wasted the whole pot. Shaking my head, I mixed the supplement and returned to Jake.

"Drink it slowly. Then a glass of that electrolyte sports drink. Then," I said turning to Agent Shelby, "You can begin your questioning."

"I can wait," said Shelby. "Mind if I have a seat?"

He was examining the house, but his expression looked cynical. I motioned to any of the chairs in the room. He took a stool at the kitchen counter.

"Didn't know preternatural consultants made such good money. Or were you born into it?"

"I'm new money. You might say I sort of hit the lotto," I answered as Jake began to drink the liquid. Every time he started chugging I tapped the end of the glass and he slowed down.

"You the one that saved those elementary school kids? That was Brazil if I remember right." Shelby's voice was neutral, so I wasn't sure whether he thought I was one of those guys that interfered when he shouldn't or if I was one of the good guys.

"Yeah, that was me."

"Good work. I have a soft spot for children and animals." I glanced at his large black hands and saw the gold wedding band. He saw my reaction and replied as if I had asked a question. "Three children of my own. Two girls and a boy."

"Someday I hope to have kids."

He gave me a double-take, which was almost funny. It was common knowledge that I was gay because of the Brazilian affair. But when I saw that Jake had also turned to gape at me, I laughed. Gunnerson was the only one who nodded as if that had made sense.

"Just because I'm gay doesn't mean I don't want biological kids, Agent Shelby."

I went to the kitchen and refilled the glass with a sports drink from the side-by-side fridge.

"Here, Jake. This is the last for now. Then you need to answer Agent Shelby's questions," I held Jake's gaze and gave him a stern look. He nodded and took the glass to drink.

"Man, that is one sweet refrigerator." Gunnerson whistled as he plopped onto the couch. He propped his black dress shoes up on the coffee table and I raised my brows. He ignored me, but he made a point of making it obvious that he was ignoring me. His idea of being funny.

I opened my mouth to comment but then shook my head. Instead, I took Jake's empty glass and walked it to the kitchen. "What about legal counsel?"

Shelby looked at me. "For you?"

I shook my head.

Shelby put his hands on his hips, staring at the carpet like it had pissed him off. He looked up at Jake. "You been read your rights?"

Jake looked at me. "Do you want me to answer his questions?"

"I do, Jake. But I don't want you to incriminate yourself without being advised by an attorney. I'm sorry, Agent Shelby. I didn't think about it when you called. I guess I assumed the FBI would send someone to advise him."

"No, Mr. Mosteller, you're right. You saved my ass a whole lot of trouble by pointing that out before we asked anything." Shelby was incredibly reasonable and I knew then that I'd go out of my way to help him if we ever worked a case together. "Someone must have let the ball drop at our office. I confess, Mr. Mosteller—."

"Devon," I interrupted.

"Devon. Our department is still new here in Fresno. Most of the preternatural laws haven't been in effect that long, and new ones keep getting proposed. Would it trouble you too much to let us wait here until a duly appointed legal advisor can be sent for? Because of the hour, the condition of Mr. Winters, and the fact that our offices are pretty stark, I'd rather we did this here."

"No problem, Agent Shelby. Can I offer either of you coffee? Soda?" I re-opened the fridge door waiting for a reply. Shelby waved away the offer as he spoke into his cellphone. Gunnerson walked over and peered past me into the fridge for himself.

"Wouldn't mind a regular soda of some kind. Sugar helps keep the brain going." He helped himself as he answered. When he turned away, I shut the door for him and watched him twist open the plastic lid and take a swig. He gave me his best smile after I'd stared at him long enough. "Sorry."

"While you're here, please help yourself." Sarcasm wasn't my thing, but Gunnerson seemed the type to enjoy it. I grabbed my Diet Pepsi and went to the couch, kicking off my shoes on the way.

I sat down and made myself comfortable near Jake. He looked helpless in the chair. "Okay, okay. If you want, you can sit over here."

I patted the spot on the couch next to me and the Werewolf moved with preternatural grace to curl up next to me. His naked thigh and arm were pressed up against me in a very distracting manner and I was very aware of his clean, masculine scent.

Even with all eyes on him, Jake clutched my bicep with one hand and nestled his face on my chest, like a child. A twenty-six year old man-child. Not only had his facial features matured, but his body had grown more mature as well. He still had no chest hair, but his shoulders were broader, his muscles more thickly layered on his frame. It was as if he immediately turned the protein supplement into muscle mass.

"This explains the ID we found at the crime scene." Gunnerson held a small laminated piece of paper. Shelby was still talking softly on the phone so I took the proffered paper. "Not a driver's license. One of those state-issued ID cards."

"Wyoming." I studied it, but the name and age agreed with what Jake had told us. "Looks like you really are nineteen, Jacob Winters."

"I wouldn't lie," he whispered. "My mistress would make me stay in wolf form longer if she thought I lied." Jake gripped my arm tighter and pressed more of his body against mine.

"Let's keep the questions and answers to a minimum, folks." Shelby clicked his cellphone shut. "An attorney is on his way here. Anything Jake says before then can be problematic for us."

"Thanks," I said.

"So, what do we do till the attorney gets here?" asked Gunnerson playfully.

Shelby glared at his fellow agent. "You have something specific in mind, Gunnerson?"

"Oh, just wondering about that Brazilian rescue story." He sat up and put his elbows on his knees. "I read the file last year. How the heck does someone get talked into having sex to rescue a busload of kids? I'm a bit of a voyeur. Even of gay sex. Purely out of intellectual curiosity, though. I'm one hundred percent hetero." Gunnerson winked at me but leaned back in his seat in anticipation. "We don't count experimenting in eighth grade, right?"

Shelby offered me that apologetic expression, again, but I smiled and put an arm around Jake. It was good for his health, I reminded myself. But for some reason, I didn't want him to hear the story. Damn, Yuriko. If she hadn't put the idea in my head that I should be interested in Jake, I wouldn't be thinking about it. Yeah, right, and on the next full moon, I'd turn furry myself.

I sighed and motioned for them to get comfortable. "It's a little bit of a story."

Shelby joined us on the couch and Jake looked up into my eyes as I began. "Once upon a time—!"

"Come on, Devon, seriously," complained Gunnerson.

"Fine, fine. Let's see, where to start?" I relived the incident in Brazil for them, although I made it the short version.

Sonny Perez, Yuriko and I had gone to Sao Paolo for a holiday. Sonny was another of my best friends, who'd lived his whole life as a workaholic and I'd made it my mission to talk him into a serious vacation. We'd only chosen Brazil because Yuriko's then-boyfriend had actually lived there and offered to put us up which made the trip possible.

We had been at a mixed-crowd, gay nightclub when the news broke. A busload of elementary school kids had been kidnapped by terrorists who wanted money for their war against democracy. That's at least how the newscast touted the incident. The children were in fact from some of the wealthiest families in Brazil.

My involvement began when Jiao Bauptiste had come up and bought me a drink at the tail end of first report of the kidnapping. He had black-hair and was an athletic five-foot-two in platform shoes. He also happened to own the nightclub. His opening line was the most innovative come on I'd ever heard and the least savory. "I could save those children without any ransom, *Guapo*."

"How?"

I didn't have to wonder how he knew who I was or what I could do. A national newspaper had carried a story about my ability to manipulate magic. It had been fed to all the affiliates along with my photo. Suddenly I was a celebrity of sorts, and Jiao had recognized me.

He hadn't continued to speak, waiting for my drink to arrive. He had smiled, savoring my confusion as he sized me up like a present he hoped to unwrap. In the meanwhile, the news had continued to paint a hopeless picture for the children. The parents of some of the children had been contacted earlier, but either they hadn't believed the threat was real or they had been unable to liquidate assets quickly enough. A young girl in pig-tails had been shot in the forehead at point blank range. Brazilian news didn't censor such images like American news did. She was an example of what they would all suffer if the money were not forthcoming.

The choice Jiao had given me was simple. It would require the fresh blood of an human body to destroy the terrorists, or, Jiao had suggested seductively, I could have sex with him to build the spell to fruition.

He had warned me that if I chose blood, it would have to come from Sonny. Yuriko's blood was wrong for this magic, although I was pretty sure that was because he thought Sonny and I were a couple. Obviously I chose sex.

For the magic to work, the prolonged act need only finish with a climax. But the sex option wasn't as simple as I had hoped. In the middle of our intimacy, Jiao had claimed love at first sight. I found him attractive, but love required more than a hot body or great sex.

"Go on, this is getting interesting!" urged Gunnerson.

I glanced at Jake. He was looking forlorn as I built up the details of my sexual experience with Jiao. I wasn't planning on going into graphic details, but then he didn't know that.

CHAPTER NINE

After my story, Gunnerson had shared some of his most interesting experiences, but finally grew disgusted when none of us turned out to have his voyeuristic interest in such stories. He rose and went to the fridge for his third soda when someone knocked on the door. I was two ahead of him.

"I'll get it." Agent Shelby actually walked over and opened the door, completely at home. I appreciated the gesture, because it was hard for me to get up from the couch with Jake snuggling tightly against me.

"Li Leung, attorney for the public defender's office," said the neatly dressed, slender Chinese woman in crisp American tones. She was around five-foot-six, probably in her mid-fifties, with a grey skirt-suit that looked like it belonged in the court room and not in the office. She wore a striped, black, blue and grey power-tie and looked at the sports drink in Agent Shelby's hand as if he were being derelict on duty.

"Welcome, Ms. Leung." Agent Shelby motioned her inside. "Your client is the underwear model on the couch."

"Why is my client being subjected to public embarrassment? Where are his clothes?" demanded the woman without any sense of humor.

Shelby looked at me for help. I grimaced and replied, "He arrived without any clothes, Ms. Leung."

"Animal form?" she asked without blinking an eye. Jake clung to me as she walked around the couch and approached him like a predator. I didn't blame him, she scared me, too. "Could you provide him with a t-shirt—Mr. Mosteller—I believe?"

"Yes, but please, call me Devon. And for the record, I already gave him a t-shirt. You'll have to be the one to make sure he keeps it on this time." I stood and Jake started to follow me. "Stay. Just to be clear, the briefs are loaners too. Unfortunately, I haven't been a size twenty-six waist since high school, so no pants to fit him."

"Surely a man in your trim physical condition has elastic waist gym shorts? If you wouldn't mind," said the attorney. It didn't sound anything like a request.

When I came out of the bedroom with my gym shorts and the extra-large t-shirt for Jake, Ms. Leung was already sitting with him on the couch. He seemed to have gone from afraid to extremely comfortable with the woman, because he had one hand on her forearm. It surprised me that she hadn't shaken it loose. She didn't seem like the type who would tolerate physical contact. Maybe I was being harsh, but she was way more professional than I thought was Human.

"Here," I said and Jake actually looked at his attorney instead of me for approval. She nodded and he slipped on the t-shirt first. He looked at the gym shorts and sniffed them. They weren't exactly clean and I blushed, but a smile crossed his face before he put them on. He slapped the waist band across his stomach. I got the impression he was as pleased as a high-school girl wearing her boyfriend's letterman jacket.

"Thank you Mr. Mosteller," said Ms. Leung very formally. "I was just explaining to Jake his rights, but he seems to feel if you are present, that he doesn't mind answering any questions." Ms. Leung stood. "May I have a word with you, privately?"

I nodded and followed her outside. But she didn't stop there. I saw her Lincoln four-door parked at the end of the circular driveway and followed her all the way to the car. She opened the door with a press of a button and motioned for me to get inside.

Once we were seated with the doors shut, she spoke freely. "As you may be aware, Werewolf hearing is especially acute, even in Human form. I wished this to be a private conversation."

I nodded but said nothing. Instead, I momentarily flickered into the Sight. The entire interior of the car was alive with spells of protection. They pulsed like copper filaments ablaze in familiar patterns. She might be a high-end, modern attorney, but her car was protected by ancient Chinese magics. I glanced at her and saw that her delicate silk tie was laced with other spells, not merely for protection. Ms. Leung was packing serious mojo.

"What you may not be aware of," she continued, "is that Lycanthropes, more than Humans, are likely to be imprinted upon by any alpha who rescues them from a traumatic experience. Usually, Lycanthropes aren't subject to the sort of torture I understand Mr. Winters suffered. Since you are responsible for rescuing him and he has been deprived of his pack for support, in all likelihood, you have imprinted on him as his savior."

"What does that mean, exactly? I mean, I didn't do anything on purpose," I said, slightly defensive.

"Oh, I understand that. You did everything correctly, of course. Except, had there been other pack members to turn him over to, then what you did would have been less appropriate. In this case, you did the next best thing. Regardless, the result seems to be that he has bonded to you. I'm afraid that you must take this seriously. The fact that he responds to me suggests that he is submissive by nature and will respond well to alphas in general. However, his fear level and the fact that he trusts things to go right if you are present is proof that you have imprinted on him."

"Okay." I put a question into that one word.

"I am a Lycanthrope specialist among other things," she explained. "I just happen to be in Fresno so that I can be with my family. Not that Fresno needs a specialist of my sort."

She glanced at the house as if making sure we weren't being spied upon. "Now, what I need from you is, of course, to look to me for cues as to the appropriateness of questions and things along that line. It will be in Mr. Winter's best interest if you keep him with you as long as possible during his recovery, so that his sense of safety is maintained. However, he will rely on you for what is in his best interests, which means he will not wait until I am present to answer questions. I need you to assure me that you will not encourage him to answer when I am not present. I will request that the court appoint you *guardian ad litem* in this particular instance. Any problems or objections?"

"I have no problem with it. But I feel I should point out a couple of things. One, I'm gay," I waited for her reaction but she looked at me as if I should get to the point. "Two, he's expressed sexual interest in me already. And three, honestly, I am afraid I'll get myself in trouble if he stays."

"None of that is relevant to you protecting his legal interests or being *guardian ad litem.*" She looked into my eyes and I saw the first smile the stern Asian features had assumed since she walked in the door. "I respect your honesty and concern for my client. As traumatized as he is, the sex would actually be good for him and it would help him bond to you better. Honestly, Mr. Mosteller, I don't see a problem. He's of legal age. He's traumatized but mentally sound. And if he finds you attractive, sexual attraction isn't a sign of imprinting. It's his interest in you as his protector and a man."

She reached for the door handle and then turned to me. For the first time, I saw a flash of bitterness in those stern Asian eyes. "My son Daniel is gay and I hate his lover. He's older than Daniel by almost twenty years, but acts like he's fourteen. Daniel has become shallow and vain and I don't think either of them knows what responsibilities come with a relationship. If he weren't in that relationship, I'd introduce you. That's the Chinese mother looking out for one of her kids. It's also my way of saying, I don't care that you or Mr. Winters are homosexual."

I wanted to offer her the magic words that would make her feel better about her son. Unfortunately, some guys got drawn into their partner's superficial values and I couldn't find anything substantial to reply. I said the only thing I could think of. "I'm sure with you as his mother, he's got quite a lot more character than you think."

"Perhaps I'll introduce you to him anyway," she said as a compliment. "I'm not sure he has any friends that have the kind of character you expressed in five minutes' time. They would have just used the boy and not worried about it." She opened the car door and I followed her back inside.

She disappeared inside the house and I followed with my head spinning. When I walked inside, that window of openness into her personal life was closed and she was all legal professionalism.

"Thank you, Mr. Mosteller," began Ms. Leung. "For the record, Jake, Mr. Mosteller and I agreed that we will let you answer these men's questions. But!" her voice grew very firm and she made sure she held Jake's eyes. "If either Devon or I tell you not to answer a question, you stop immediately. Understood?"

"Yes, Mistress—I mean, Ms. Leung," Jake seemed confused how to address his attorney. Ms. Leung raised her eyes to me and the expression was exquisite.

"He has referred to the woman found at the murder scene as his mistress. At least," I looked at Shelby and Gunnerson. "I've been assuming that's who he's been referring to. Did you bring photos so we can verify that?"

Gunnerson nodded and reached inside his jacket pocket. "They aren't the sort of 8x10s we use in the office, but I brought the Polaroids just in case. Told you, I'm a voyeur."

"Let me see them first," demanded Jake's attorney. Gunnerson handed them over with a frown. She took the packet of pictures in her slim hands and shuffled through them quickly. Her expression said nothing of her reaction. Surprisingly, she offered them to me next, as if I were entitled to view them before asking Jake to comment.

I looked through them, blanching a little bit at the close-ups of the wounds. "This is the woman we found at the murder scene." I started to hand them back to Gunnerson, but Ms. Leung waved her hand for them.

"I'll present to Jake any material you have questions on." She shuffled through the photos again and pulled out a single one. It reminded me of a magician's trick. "Do you recognize this woman, Jake?"

Jake looked at the picture then looked away. His demeanor changed. He brought his knees up against his chest and hugged them with both arms. He looked at me sadly. I nodded encouragement. "Go ahead, Jake. Please answer."

"It's my mistress," he started to tremble. After a pause, he continued, "I could smell her from the garage for days. Her death filled the house. I howled and howled but no one came to set me free. Until you."

"Why did you stay a wolf? As a Human, you could have freed yourself?" asked Agent Shelby. Jake's attorney nodded.

"I can only change around the time of the full moon or with special magic." He shot me a secretive glance. I was sure the rest of those watching saw it as well, though I had no idea what it meant. Thinking about it for a moment, I remembered he had changed with me last night. Was that his secret? Did he have a magical means of changing? I would wait to ask him. I knew Ms. Leung would object otherwise.

He continued, "My mistress could force the change. When I smelled her death, there was nothing I could do till the next moon."

"But there was nothing to stop you from offing her, coming back to the garage, chaining yourself up and changing back during the last full moon," added Gunnerson.

"When was the woman killed Agent Shelby?" asked Ms. Leung before Jake could answer.

"She'd been dead five days," replied Shelby. "So he couldn't have changed without some help."

"Given the level of dehydration," Jake's attorney turned to me, "how long had he been chained up without food or drink?"

"Dr. O'Keefe said it was at least seven days. Could have been as long as ten." Jake stared at the ground. I started to ask a question but Ms. Leung caught my eye. She shook her head carefully.

"So all we know for certain is that he was cut off from food and drink before she died," commented Agent Shelby.

"What was the name of your mistress?" asked Gunnerson from across the room.

"She was called 'Lenora,'" Jake stammered her name.

Shelby leaned forward. "Who called her that?"

Jake looked at me and I looked at his attorney. She nodded and I passed it along to him. "Go ahead."

"When we first moved into the new house, some people came to see her. I was locked in the garage, but the door was open and I could hear them. I heard a man call her by name."

"How long have you been with Lenora?" I asked without thinking about it. Ms. Leung sighed and I mouthed an apology.

"Since I was eight."

"Eight?" exclaimed Ms. Leung. She seemed thoroughly disconcerted. "Is she a blood relative?"

"No."

"Then how the hell did she wind up with you?" Shelby's tone revealed a similar sense of outrage.

"My alpha sent me with her," he said, his voice even softer.

"It's okay, Jake. No one's mad at you. We just want to understand what happened," I used my very best animal-calming voice. I looked at his attorney and she nodded almost imperceptibly. "Why did he send you with her?"

"He—," Jake sucked air in through his teeth and pinched the bridge of his nose.

"Why, Jake?" I repeated. Even Ms. Leung leaned forward waiting.

"She—," he stammered again and wouldn't look any of us in the eye. I put a hand on his leg and he stopped rocking. "She used me."

"Holy shit," said Gunnerson unhappily. I guess there were some things he wasn't a voyeur about any more than I was.

Ms. Leung leaned back and looked pale against her black hair. "He was eight."

"She had sex with you?" Shelby asked the question that we all needed to have answered aloud.

Jake looked up surprised and he laughed. But it was a morose kind of sound. "No, not her. She used me for my *blood*."

CHAPTER TEN

"We have motive." Agent Shelby leaned against the black sedan. Gunnerson stood on the other side of the car, with his elbows on the cab. Ms. Leung and I stood next to Shelby. We had come outside to let the cool air clear our heads. Jake's story had ended with him crying and us disturbed. To be honest, Shelby's eyes were the only dry ones in the house.

"What do you mean, 'motive?'" complained the attorney. "It's obvious he couldn't have done it."

"Not alone, Ms. Leung. But he could have participated. Eleven years of torture. I wouldn't even blame him. A jury wouldn't either. That Bobbitt woman got off when she had other options."

"Yes, but Jacob Winters is a Lycanthrope. Juries aren't kindly disposed toward preternaturals." Ms. Leung's anger startled us all. "He didn't do it. She'd kept him locked in the garage almost a week before she was killed."

Shelby looked at me, "The veterinarian will testify to that?"

"Definitely," I said without hesitation.

"Look, I understand taking the kid's blood for her spell casting, but why the other torture?" Gunnerson shook his blonde head, troubled.

"What kind of person would be willing to buy a child, even a Lycanthrope child, to cut on a daily basis for blood in the first place?" I let Gunnerson see just how pissed I was. "It's only one step from that kind of cruelty to serious torture."

"If you can get a written declaration from the vet about Jake's medical condition," Shelby turned from me to Jake's attorney, "We'll put Jake to the back of the list of possible suspects. But I'll want him to come to the murder scene tomorrow to provide further information. Ten in the morning?"

"We'll be there," replied the petite Asian. "You can bring Jake, can't you, Mr. Mosteller?" Ms. Leung looked at me and I nodded. She shook her head and snapped her fingers at Shelby. "No further questions tonight. The boy has been through a lot. What he needs now is some strong physical affection and sleep."

"Well, then good night, Ms. Leung. Mr. Mosteller," said Shelby.

He gave me a knowing look as he slid into the sedan. Gunnerson saluted casually and got in on the other side. Ms. Leung and I stepped back so they could drive off.

"Thank you, Devon." There was genuine warmth in her eyes. "You helped with Jake very nicely." She had called him Jake for the first time when not to his face and she had called me Devon. "I am concerned about something though."

"What?" I studied her hazel eyes and carefully plucked brows. She had probably been a very pretty woman once, except that her ears stuck out and flawed otherwise delicate features. I wondered then what her gay son looked like. Call it another case of my inappropriate curiosity.

"If she got him at eight, then he missed a lot of his formative years in the pack. He may not know nearly as much about pack law and social etiquette as he should. I had assumed we'd return him to his pack when this was over, but now I'm not so sure." She walked to her car and I followed her again.

"What should I do?"

"Meet us at the murder scene tomorrow like Agent Shelby said. And give Jake lots of tender care. In some ways, he's still a child. But his sexual needs, they're still valid. He's nineteen and god knows how she tortured him in that capacity. Celibacy alone is cruel and unusual, but he hinted at exposure to pedophiles in the beginning." None of us had pursued that line of questioning. We were already heart-sick enough.

Ms. Leung got behind the wheel of her Lincoln and backed out of the driveway. I waved for a moment then walked back inside, more than a little nervous. I was finally alone with a sexy, half-naked guy that I was attracted to and I'd practically been ordered to have sex with him. Who had that kind of will-power?

CHAPTER ELEVEN

The pounding on the door had me not only awake but standing naked on my feet before I even knew where the sound was coming from. My physical responses and light sleeping habits were the amusement of all of my friends. My brain narrowed down the sound— it was the front door.

I looked around my bed, expecting to find Jake there again, but he was still in the spare room next door. At least I assumed he was. I had tucked him into bed an hour or so after the feds and his attorney left. He hadn't gone to sleep alone willingly. I had let him cling to my arm until he calmed down, sitting beside him making soothing noises as if he were a child. But I hadn't been able to go any further with him under the circumstances. It wouldn't have seemed like acceptable sex. He had finally dozed off and I'd crawled into my own bed.

The knocking repeated and I grabbed my t-shirt and threw it on along with my other pair of gym shorts lying on the floor near the closet. After I was dressed, I looked in on Jake as I passed his room and found him sleeping soundly, curled into a ball.

"Coming, coming," I muttered, worried now that the noise would wake him. It wasn't the kind of knocking friends or ex-boyfriends did in the middle of the night, so I stopped in the kitchen to grab my 10mm handgun from the cookie jar on top of the fridge. There were no pockets to hide it in so I held the weapon under one arm-pit as if I were cold. But I left the safety on, just in case. "When it rains it pours, apparently."

"Open the god-damned door!" I immediately recognized the accent, even though I'd only met him twice before. I unlocked the single dead-bolt and pulled the door open. Ulrich Gotterdam, Melanie's husband, pushed into the house, knocking me aside.

"How dare you interfere in my domestic life!" he spit the words out through tightly clenched teeth, making his German accent hard for me to understand.

I looked outside but there was no sign of Melanie. Ulrich had made this pilgrimage solo. He turned his angular face toward me and from the heat in his eyes, I was glad I had the gun.

"What are you talking about, Ulrich?" I didn't hide my confusion.

"You bring business to my wife so that you can show her how much better the man you are? To make her humiliated by the fact that her own husband cannot find a job?" His fists were clenched and I took a step back. He was a wiry, dark-haired man who stood at five-eleven. I knew I was stronger just by looking at him, but I didn't want his anger to get to the point of us hitting each other. Melanie would never forgive me, regardless of who started it.

"I don't know what you are going on about, Ulrich. I came to Melanie with an official government problem." I kept the gun tightly clenched under my arm. He didn't seem to hear me. "You do know that your wife is the only preternatural veterinarian in all of Fresno County, right?"

He stormed back and forth as if fighting an urge to strike me. His eyes were glazed over and bloodshot to the point of appearing red. I wondered then if he'd been drinking. Maybe having the gun in my hand wasn't so smart after all.

"She loved you so much. It was so hard for her to fall in love with another man." He had begun to shout so I shut the door. I didn't think Melanie would be happy if my neighbors called the police on her husband, either. "You cannot let another man have happiness? Even with a woman you do not desire? She moved back here to be near you! What kind of Human are you?"

"Ulrich!" I shouted his name this time, putting heat in my voice. Some of the glaze left his eyes. He blinked at me, as if not quite seeing me. "It was official government business. Melanie was the only one available to help the federal government."

"The government?" he echoed as if unsure he'd heard right.

"Yes. The government hired Melanie to help an animal." I chose words to distance my personal involvement from the situation. I wondered then if Ulrich might not be on drugs. It would account for Melanie being so secretive about him. "They authorized payment."

"You didn't come to show me up?" The intelligence slowly returned to his eyes and the redness faded.

"No. I want you and Melanie to be happy." I used my soft voice, the kind for scared or angry dogs. "I would never hurt you like that. It would only hurt her."

"Your word as a gentleman?" His German accent faded as he regained control of himself.

"My word as a gentleman that I did not attempt to embarrass you or make myself look good. My word that I only brought business to Melanie because she was the only person I knew who does this sort of work. She saved her patient's life." I chewed my lower lip, realizing that Jake might need Melanie's help in the future. "I will have to bring her the government's business for a while longer. But if you'd rather, I can send someone else in my place."

"Melanie said you were good for your word." He obviously had wanted to believe otherwise, but I saw the defeat in his sober, rational eyes. "She has only lied to me once and even then she knew I knew.

So I cannot entirely call that a lie. If you say it is true, then I must believe you." His expression grew sullen and shamed. "Forgive me. I sometimes do not have very good control."

"There's no problem, Ulrich. Please assure Melanie that her patient is coming along really well, thanks to the supplements she provided."

"Oh, no. No, please." He clutched at his jacket and looked older than his forty years. "Please do not tell her I came here, like this. It will shame me in her eyes."

I looked at him sadly, but not with pity. I knew what it was like to want someone's love and to be denied it. In my case, I'd chased my mother's love, but she had eyes only for my father. It wasn't a love triangle. I don't know that he loved anyone at all. I knew he loved money, but we never had any.

"She will never learn from me that you came here tonight. Not if we understand each other. Though, I think you underestimate her feelings for you, Ulrich. And overestimate them for me."

"You are an honorable man, Devon Mosteller. I can see why my wife holds you in such high esteem. Though I wish she did not."

He walked to the door, but my free hand was still on the knob. I decided that I had nothing to add and opened the door for him, keeping the gun pressed tightly under my armpit, hoping that he wouldn't notice it. He nodded at me in a very European manner and shuffled outside.

I stood there until he'd driven off and pulled the door closed. "God. Didn't see that one coming."

I locked both locks and leaned back against the door. The flashing red light of the answering machine disturbed the tranquility of the darkened kitchen and my stomach knotted. It could have been Jiao again, but leaving voice messages wasn't his style. I set the gun on the counter, dangerous end away from me, and reluctantly, I pressed the play button.

"Hello, Devon. This is Tony. You know, the police officer from yesterday?" I smiled. His voice sounded so eager yet uncertain. Cocky was fun, but coyness brought out the romantic in me. "This isn't about official business. I—look, I'd like to go out with you. If you aren't seeing someone. If you weren't flirting with me, then I apologize. Otherwise, please call me. My private number is—," I wrote the number down on the pad next to the machine and saved the message anyway.

My heart raced and I smiled. "Score." I could barely contain my excitement as I stood and walked around the counter to put the gun back in its drawer.

I walked down the hall and peeked in the bedroom again. Jake was still curled in a ball, but he was trembling. I sat on the bed at his back, putting my hands on his body.

"Jake?" He trembled so hard that the bed shook. Was he having a secondary reaction to the trauma? Then I realized that he was crying. "What's wrong?"

I caressed the smooth skin on his forearm, reassuringly. Emotion was very erotic to me. His sorrow was no exception. I gazed at the line of his narrow waist, the firm roundness of his butt, and the smooth muscling of his thighs and became aroused. Eventually, he turned onto his back, staring at me with anguish in those beautiful green eyes.

"Am I really only an animal to you?" he asked mournfully.

I tried to make sense of what he asked. When had I—? When I was calming Ulrich down. I had used that word to distance my involvement from Melanie.

"Oh, Babe, no!" I stroked his arm and then rested my hand on the upper part of his belly. His flesh was almost hot enough to burn. There was nothing predatory in my touch, despite my erection. I'd called him 'babe.' How else did you comfort someone? "I was trying to calm Ulrich down. I was trying to make Melanie's role more like a veterinarian and less like a friend. Honest."

He sniffed a bit then wiped his nose with the back of his hand. Very male and not very attractive. "You smell like you're telling the truth."

"Why would I lie?"

"Alphas always lie." He curled into a ball again. This time he didn't put his back to me. I tugged at his long blonde bangs.

"Not this alpha," I answered. "I don't lie."

"Are you my alpha?" His voice was barely above a whisper.

I didn't reply. What were the specifics of Werewolf law? A pack alpha was a Fenris. But what was he specifically asking? What would I be if I said I was his alpha? How much harm if I said 'no?'

"For now, all that matters is that I am an alpha and I don't lie." I avoided his question.

"You told that man you'd lie," said Jake, a little louder. He wanted to believe me, but he was afraid to.

"No, I told that man I wouldn't tell his wife about his visit. I never said I'd lie to her if she learned about it." Didn't people realize that I couched my words carefully? I was a damned good communicator if anyone bothered to listen!

"I don't understand. Isn't that a lie?"

"I used to think so, Jake. I used to think so." I nuzzled his shoulder with my cheek, as if he were a child. "Get some sleep. We'll talk in the morning."

I stood and watched him for a few moments. With the filling out of his body, I couldn't help to see him as a man. A sexy man in white briefs. His smell was masculine but not feral. I actually forgot about Tony's message as I stared down at Jake's beauty.

Then I swallowed hard. He was a sexy young man at the moment. But he was a man who would turn into a beast at the next full moon, furred and clawed, with a hunger for killing. A man who had been sliced open for eleven years, who had probably never been touched for his own sake—except possibly by pedophiles. But that would not have been for his sake.

How could I touch him knowing all of that?

CHAPTER TWELVE

I was laying on my back on the mattress but I was wide awake. The pain in my shoulder had kept me awake several nights in a row, but tonight it was my mind that wouldn't let me sleep. I was far too aware of Jake curled up one room away. It didn't help that I knew he wanted me.

Every time I closed my eyes, I kept picturing my mouth on Jake's, my hands running along his smooth sides, pulling him close to me as a potential love, not just lover. And my thoughts would wander to Officer Ramirez, just as passionate, just as sexy underneath his uniform. In my fantasies, they were light and dark versions of each other and I romanced them both. Sometimes separately, sometimes together.

I froze at a soft, stealthy sound. The door knob to my bedroom turned quietly. I had double-locked the front door when Ulrich had left, so I knew who the visitor should be. There was enough ambient light from the kitchen appliances that I could make out Jake's naked shape standing in the doorway. He'd stripped down again.

"Jake?" Instead of my earlier fantasies, I suddenly pictured the snarling fangs of a wolf. I put a hand to my throat reflexively.

"I can't sleep." His boyish but masculine tone soothed away the imagined snarling. He took one step into the room. "Can I sleep with you?"

As he stood there, I pulled the sheet and blanket up to my armpits, suddenly shy. "I'm naked."

"You were expecting me?" he asked hopefully.

"No!" I actually laughed in surprise. "I always sleep naked. I was just warning you."

"You didn't sleep naked with me last night." His voice was a soft, deep hum in the dark. When he said 'naked' it stirred my libido. I didn't think Werewolves had voice magics. No, it was just him and that word. Sexy. And I was tired of being alone.

"You were a wolf and sleeping naked with non-boyfriends is just wrong." I focused on my words, but I wanted him to slide into my bed no matter what I'd said. He had been a victim most of his life. If he really wanted this, he had to make the move on me.

"Why?" He took another small step into the room.

"Because," I started to give him a glib answer, but it was too much like a lie. He didn't deserve to be lied to anymore. No one ever did. "Because my family is uncomfortable with being naked. Naked means sex. I don't have sex with animals or friends. I only have sex with guys I'm dating or boyfriends." There, I'd given him the full answer.

He stood there coyly, watching me with such earnest that I was the first to give in. I should have known that I would be. "Give me a minute to put on at least underwear and you can sleep in the bed."

"No," he said and I stopped sliding toward the edge of the bed. "I want you naked."

"I told you—"

"I know. I want you to sleep naked with me. You're alpha. It's your right to fuck me." I tried to see his face in the dark.

"It's my right? Jake, sex should be what each of us wants. Either to please the other or ourselves. But not just because it's a right."

He only stared at me. I really did want him to want me that way, but my responsible adult-self swam to the surface. "You're injured and under my protection. It wouldn't be right."

"If I'm under your protection, then take me." This time, his voice had more demand to it. And to think I'd just gone soft for a moment.

"I'm not going to take advantage of someone under my protection!"

"Then you won't protect me. I have no one to protect me."

"I said I'd protect you. Why do I have to have sex with you to prove I'll protect you?" Was this part of the Werewolf mentality or something that had been done to him? I suspected the latter.

"A submissive has to give themselves to their protector. If I don't, then you have no obligation to protect me. They won't smell you on me and I'll be open for attack." His voice wavered.

"The government doesn't work like a Werewolf pack. If I say I'll protect you, they don't have to smell me on you for you to be safe." His idea of pack rules was twisted. Sex was not the most common symbol of protection.

"Not the government. The other packs. My mistress warned me. I won't be safe without your protection." He began to tremble again. "Please, Devon. Protect me."

Why did 'protect me' sound exactly like 'fuck me' all of a sudden? Melanie's voice entered my head almost as if she were there. 'You always hold yourself to a higher standard, Devon.' I tried to keep Ulrich's criticism from joining her in my thoughts.

"Fine," I said through gritted teeth. "Come get in bed. We'll talk about the sex stuff once you are warm under the covers."

He raced across the carpet and slipped into bed with preternatural grace. Then he pressed his body tightly up against mine, wrapping his muscular legs over mine, his head pressed into my arm-pit. His hand on my chest was uncomfortably warm but I didn't complain.

I turned to face him, lying on my side. I put my hand on his hip, but I fought to keep from sliding it back to caress the meat of his bottom. I couldn't hide my physical reaction, pressed against his smooth thigh. One of his hands slid down to grasp me and I grabbed his wrist, stopping him before he touched me there. I had phenomenal self-control at times when it came to sex. This was not one of them.

"Jake," I said but his mouth brushed my chest with soft full lips and my mind went blank. Then his mouth slid down, along the side of my chest below the arm-pit. He lifted his body so that his lips were not even an inch away from mine. I could see in his large green eyes the expression any man wants from his lover. Adoration. Trust. Need.

I think I actually kissed him first. But he kissed me back. It wasn't the kiss of lust or of a one-night stand. It was a kiss of need—of wanting me. I could taste his uncertainty about my desire for him. He made sure that I knew he wanted me.

His body trembled when I ran my fingers over his side. My other hand grasped him firmly at the back of the neck. I entwined my fingers in his hair and forced his mouth harder onto mine. His submissive awoke my alpha, but his fear stirred my gentleness so that I was dominant and tender. My mouth moved to his neck, then the meat of his shoulder. I sank my teeth into his shoulder, sucking at the bulge of his bicep, forcing his arm over his head and licking the line from his arm-pit to his waist.

I stopped chewing at his flesh and nibbled at his ear before whispering breathily. "Let me get a condom."

"We don't need one," he said, equally out of breath as he pushed back against me.

"I'm not sure that's smart."

"I'm a Werewolf. I can't get diseases, including AIDS. Or give them," he reassured me. "I'm not even contagious for Lycanthropy unless I'm in animal form. So put it in, please."

Did I say I had will-power? I didn't stand a chance then. My free hand gripped his nearest wrist and I held his arm away from our bodies as part of my dominating him. It turned him on and I lost myself to his writhing and moaning and heavy breathing. Somewhere along the way I had slipped inside him and he made a noise so erotic I almost came at the sound of it.

He turned his head to the side to try to kiss me, so I left his neck and put my mouth on his. He writhed and whimpered passionately with each thrust. I knew I wasn't going to last long this first time. He was too perfect in his every movement and sound. We finished at the same time, his voice crying out inside my mouth and our sounds blended like our bodies.

"I'm sorry," Jake said breathlessly as I released his lips from mine. I looked at him still with the glazed euphoria of that incredible if brief love-making and he blushed embarrassed. "I made a mess on your side of the bed." I burst out laughing and everything seemed hopeful for the first time that day.

CHAPTER THIRTEEN

Jake and I pulled into the Ravenclaw complex in my Chevy S-10. This time I was more interested in the surrounding houses and inhabitants than I had been on my first visit. It was late enough in the morning that someone should have been up walking their dog, but I didn't see a single person.

"You ever meet any of your neighbors?" I asked.

He held my hand contentedly and gazed at me. I might have been the only person to ever touch Jake without trying to hurt him and he adored it. "Only one."

"And—?"

"Oh, um, Chuck or something like that. I wasn't allowed out of the house except occasionally at night in the back yard."

"So you met Chuck?"

"One time. I was walking through the living room to the garage and he was there." Jake sulked. "Mistress gave me her angry eyes and I ran into the garage and shut the door."

Two police cars and the federal sedan were parked in the drive way of the house on Talon. "Your attorney isn't here yet." We were fifteen minutes early. Bad habit.

"She's scary," said Jake laughing.

"I thought you liked Ms. Leung."

"I do. She's very alpha and disciplined. Mistress was never so disciplined."

We pulled up behind the nearest cop car and I turned off the engine. "Remember, you can't answer any questions until Ms. Leung arrives. It's for your own protection. Understand?"

"Yes, master, I understand."

"Whoa, wait a minute. What's this 'master' crap?" I startled Jake by shouting.

"You are my new master, right? You're my protector. You did me." He put his hand on my arm. His eyes got a twinkle in them. "Twice this morning alone."

He would not call me 'master!' "Call me 'Devon.' I mean it, Jake."

"Okay. Devon." He stammered over my name as he had Lenora's.

"Look, Jake. I know you've had eleven years of being told one thing. But we agreed that I'm dominant to you and I expect you to obey this thing for me. You call me Devon. Never 'master.'"

"Yes, Devon." He stammered less. "I'll try not to forget."

We got out of the car then. Jake hurried around the front of the truck to grab my hand. He held my forearm with his other hand as if he were afraid I'd get away. This wasn't Santa Monica Boulevard in West Hollywood where it was okay to hold hands. Glancing around the neighborhood, I still didn't see anyone, so I reluctantly didn't shake him loose.

Li Leung's black Lincoln pulled in behind my S-10. We waited as the petite Chinese woman stepped out of her car. She actually smiled at us.

"Good morning, boys." She seemed in particularly good spirits.

"Good morning, Ms. Leung," I said.

"Actually, Devon, it's Mrs. Leung. And off the clock, please call me Li."

"Someone is in a good mood. But you don't smell like sex," said Jake. My mouth dropped open and I waited for Li to explode.

"My husband hasn't been well enough for sex for quite some time, Jake. No, my son and his boyfriend are fighting." She looked at me with guilty eyes. "I know, I know, it sounds petty. I have six kids, Devon. All of them happily coupled, except Daniel."

"That's why you are smiling this morning?" It seemed out of character for the stern but charming woman.

"Well, that's only part of it. Seeing you two together just made this old heart smile, too. You look good together. Even if it's probably only a short-term thing." She stuck out her hand to shake mine first, then Jake's.

"Why would you say it's short-term?" Jake panicked. "Devon?"

"Let's just wait and see, Jake. I'm not expecting to get rid of you." I frowned at Li who looked apologetic.

The door of 4501 Talon opened and T. Ramirez stepped outside with his partner. A look flashed across his face when he saw Jake attached to my arm. I hadn't had a chance to call him back. So much for winding up with a normal guy.

"Couldn't you just let it be?" I pleaded under my breath to an imaginary god. In all fairness, after what Jake and I had already done, I couldn't see Ramirez forgiving me.

"Well, well, well. If it isn't the witch and his bitch," said Sorensen. Ramirez frowned but said nothing. Obviously I'd hurt him.

"Who are you?" asked Mrs. Leung coldly.

"Officer Mark Sorensen. My partner and I were the first real cops at the scene of the murder. Who are you?"

"I just want to get your name right when I file charges. I'm Mrs. Li Leung, attorney from the public defender's office. I represent the witness Jacob Winters." She motioned to Jake.

"I wasn't calling you the bitch," said Sorensen, taken aback.

"I didn't imagine you were. If you had, I couldn't argue," said Mrs. Leung. "But since you were referring to my client and new anti-racism laws prohibit law enforcement officers from making slanderous remarks to non-Humans, that's a different matter."

"Non-Human?" Ramirez looked at me and the expression turned sour. Apparently he thought I preferred my men a little on the preternatural side.

"Lycanthrope," said Mrs. Leung.

"The dog?" repeated Ramirez still trying to sort out his rejection.

"Who knew?" I said, trying to make light.

Ramirez looked at Jake holding my arm one more time and went back into the house. He didn't look happy. It bummed me out, too. I'd done too much fantasizing about the cop as a boyfriend already after one night.

"Do we have to go inside?" Jake pulled back on my arm as I tried to follow Ramirez inside.

"Yes, Jake. We promised Agent Shelby you'd come answer more questions."

I hadn't told the local police about the hidden container in the kitchen. I don't know why, but for some reason I'd withheld the information. The federal agents I'd worked with on a previous case had encouraged me to delay releasing unusual magical details to the cops. Something about the local police not being properly trained. But this time, something else had stopped me; maybe just how much I didn't like Sorensen.

"You're the alpha," Jake sighed and stopped pulling back on my arm. "But I don't think the cop wants to share you."

I balked and looked at the blonde. He didn't look me in the eye but his expression was smug.

"I'm right behind you, boys," said Mrs. Leung. Sorensen remained outside.

Just inside, we were stopped by a uniformed officer I didn't recognize. Agent Shelby happened to notice us from where he stood in the kitchen and motioned us inside. The officer nodded and let us pass. He gave us an unfriendly stare. Not a lot of cops were gay friendly. Even if this were a simple Lycan species behavior, it wasn't going over big.

"Good morning, Mr. Mosteller. Mr. Winters." Shelby's eyes glittered with humor at Jake's hold on my arm.

"You remember Mrs. Leung?" I asked.

"Yes, Mrs. Leung. Good to see you this morning. I guess since we're all here, we can begin?"

"Let's start with the garage," Shelby stepped aside to let Jake lead us. He looked at me hesitantly.

"Go ahead, Jake." I gently pushed him forward.

"I want to see her body." Jake's defiance was out of character.

"Jake, she isn't still here." I turned to Agent Shelby to help me out but he looked embarrassed.

"Actually, she is."

"What? That's outrageous! You guys don't leave bodies lying around. Once all the experts have examined the scene—," I paused and looked at Shelby. "You're waiting for another expert. What, a preternatural expert? You didn't trust my analysis?"

"I knew I smelled her still." Jake missed the important part of my objection.

"Devon, it's not like that. If this were an ordinary case, the head guys would be happy with what you've provided. But once the word Drow came up on the reports, they insisted a federal specialist be called in."

"Who?" I asked.

"Shiandra Mistry, sort of a floater between districts at the moment. She's a regular in these cases. It's not personal." Agent Shelby waited for me to sulk. I disappointed him.

"No, that's fine. The truth is I don't know that much about the Drow," I conceded. "I can recognize their magic as distinct from any other magic. But as to the details and stuff, I'm not the first person you should call. I understand."

"Her flight arrives late this afternoon. I've had the pleasure of working with her before, she's a good agent and personable."

"Ma—Devon, can I see the mistress?" Jake tugged on my arm.

Mrs. Leung stepped forward and put her slim hand on my shoulder. "Devon, I think you should let him. He will be distracted otherwise and unlikely to answer the Agents' questions completely."

The black federal agent nodded and Jake pulled me toward the bedroom. We passed Ramirez leaning against the kitchen sink. He must have been there simply as back up to the feds. He wouldn't look at us as we passed him.

The door to the murder scene was open but Jake paused at the threshold. He turned to me and I nodded encouragement. He sniffed the room.

"She had sex," was the first thing out of his mouth. He sounded puzzled. Jake stepped into the room.

"He cannot touch anything," called Agent Shelby from behind us. "Walk on the paper path."

Jake stepped close to the circle of power and the face-down body. She had started to reek a bit.

"I can smell sex and death. No Elf magic though."

"Are you sure?" Shelby followed Mrs. Leung into the room. The Chinese woman put her fist to her mouth and looked away from the naked body.

"When your blood has been used for eleven years to practice Drow spells, you'd never forget the smell."

"So not a Drow on Drow killing? Agent Mistry will be glad to hear that," Shelby commented. "Complicates matters in a way she didn't like."

"I also smell something strange." Jake sniffed deeply and looked at me with wonder in his eyes. "A new thing. Devon, I never smelled this creature before. Underneath it, Human."

"Human Human, or Drow Human?" I asked. Shelby looked at me puzzled. "The woman wasn't a full blood Drow. I didn't know how specific Jake was being."

"Mistress would have killed you for calling her hybrid. She struggled for years to be taken as a full Drow. The other smell is purely Human."

Jake knelt at the edge of the circle and Shelby started reach out to pull him back. I put a hand up and Shelby hesitated. Jake stayed outside the circle, careful not to touch it. He looked at the naked body with a mixture of sorrow and uncertain relief.

"She's really gone," he said to himself.

"You're no longer her property," said Mrs. Leung. "You're free."

Jake stood and looked at each of us, face by face. He stopped at Mrs. Leung and asked with such terrible emptiness, "Free to do what? I have nowhere to be." He stepped toward me. "I can smell your reluctance to keep me."

"I will keep you, if you had nothing to do with her murder." Shit, I'd stepped in it again.

Jake looked at me and relaxed. He took my arm again. He was used to being bullied. It would comfort him for now. But in the long run, he would have to learn to not be comfortable with it, or we'd never get along.

"Can you tell us anything else about the murder site with your sense of smell?" asked Agent Shelby.

Jake sniffed the air. He let go of me and moved about the room, looking at me puzzled. "Devon, how did you know there was magic here?"

Shelby echoed his expression. "That's a good question. I hadn't had time to read your FBI dossier."

Mrs. Leung interrupted. "While I do not represent you, Mr. Mosteller, if there is any reason you shouldn't answer the question—."

"No, thank you, Mrs. Leung. It is general knowledge within the department about my ability to manipulate magic. I have the S&M gene. It's why I get called in on hush hush magic related cases, to disarm dangerous spells." Then I had a thought. "Why aren't news crews camped outside this house? How did you manage to keep this locked down?"

"To the Fresno PD, this is just another homicide," answered Shelby without hesitation. "Only my division knows that the vic was part Drow and that it was a special circumstances murder."

"At least till the press gets a wind of it."

"Good point, Mr. Mosteller. Good point. Gunnerson!" Agent Shelby strode out of the room like a freight train.

"Now that we have a minute, is there anything we want to share in private?" asked Mrs. Leung.

"Not that I can think of," I answered. Jake continued sniffing about the room and the Chinese woman folded her arms and studied us both. "Honestly."

"If you say so."

A moment later, Shelby walked back into the room. "Devon, I was wondering. Can you demonstrate this gift of yours?"

I shifted into the Sight. To my surprise, a new spell was in place. "Has this body been under constant surveillance since we found it?"

"Around the clock. By the local PD," hedged the black FBI agent. "Why?"

"Because I see a spell that wasn't here before."

"Then why can't wolf-boy here smell the magic?" asked Shelby.

"I don't know." Jake sounded uncertain of his abilities for the first time since entering the room.

I knelt down at the circle, expecting to see another post-death torture spell in place, but this spell was unknown to me. It was—I could only described it as 'slippery,' like every strand vibrated, avoiding my power.

"Weird." It was hard for me to make sense of the pattern. A hand went to my shoulder and I turned to see Jake in my normal sight. He gazed at me apologetically.

"I only smell death."

"Death," I looked again at the spell, flicking between the mundane world and the Sight. With effort, I found a single one of the knots that tied the threads in a spell and it became a pattern with a purpose, recognizable by my mind. "Necromancy?"

"There's no such thing as necromancy," said Mrs. Leung shocked.

"If there were, it's on the list of things absolutely illegal under federal law," added Agent Shelby.

"Someone doesn't want Lenora called back into her body to give testimony," I said with conviction. "My guess would be the murderer."

CHAPTER FOURTEEN

Before Shelby could react fully to the news that someone had tampered with the crime scene, Agent Gunnerson appeared at the doorway, his cellphone on speakerphone. "Go ahead, Agent Mistry."

A sultry, female voice answered. "Just leaving the Fresno Air Terminal."

"I knew you couldn't stay away from me for long," joked Gunnerson and the woman on speakerphone laughed.

"You're the one who called me, remember?"

Shelby glared at the blonde agent and Gunnerson cleared his voice. "I'm getting the evil eye. You better just get here pronto fast."

"You know that's redundant don't you?" she asked.

"Uh, yeah," he lied and hung up on her. "I'll go back to the garage."

"You do that," agreed Shelby.

"I take it they know each other?"

Shelby nodded. "Speaking of knowing things, where's that pompous, incompetent cop?" He marched out of the room and we could hear him harangue Sorensen as the ranking PD officer for letting evidence be tampered with.

There was heavy footsteps and the blonde cop came in and refused to look at me. He physically put himself between the body and the three of us. "Out."

"Jake, can you come to the garage?" Shelby's question came down the hallway like a command and I instinctively headed out the doorway.

"You don't have to come," said Jake.

I thought about it and realize that Jake was probably reluctant that I be reminded of the condition in which we'd found him. Yuriko had already told the agents how we'd discovered him in his own excrement. He'd been embarrassed by that disclosure so I nodded at him.

With Sorensen in the bedroom keeping a personal eye on the body, and Mrs. Leung following Jake to the garage, that left the kitchen for me to wait in. As I came around the refrigerator, I froze. Ramirez was by the sink filling out paper-work.

"The FBI wants to know my whereabouts during my shift." He gave me a sad smile and my heart ached with regret. Not regret that I'd been with Jake, but regret that it had cost me the sexy Mexican cop.

"About the call last night."

Ramirez cut me off. "Don't worry about it."

"I was going to call but things got a little crazy." I took a step closer but his eyes grew cop cold.

"Look, it's not an issue any more." My expression had to reflect my disappointment, because Ramirez softened for a moment. "I'm sorry I called."

"I wasn't." I started to walk out of the kitchen, aware that he didn't want me there. But I remembered the hidden container and paused at the edge of the counter.

I must have looked like I was waiting for something because Ramirez spoke to me again. "You latched onto him awful quick."

There was an chilly edge to his voice that was both wounded and unforgiving. It was judgement and I didn't do well with people judging me unfairly. I started to reply with a nasty comment but I remembered Jake in my bed. Ramirez hadn't said anything that wasn't true.

"He latched onto me pretty quick," I said with surprising bitterness. Why was I bitter? It wasn't like I'd cheated on a boyfriend. Hell, we hadn't even actually arranged our first date. So why did I feel so ugly? I studied him and recognized the truth in my reaction. I didn't like to be perceived as a person who was that easy to hook up with and that's just what I had done.

"Sometimes you click that fast." I don't know why I said that. Even though it was true, it felt final somehow. Like I was shutting the door on Ramirez once and for all.

"Yeah, sometimes you do. Even at first sight." His voice wasn't cop cold anymore and I turned around, startled. He was staring at my back. Not my butt, but my shoulders and hair. At Devon Mosteller, the person.

If he could admit that much attraction for me, even after I'd slept with Jake, I could offer him the same. "I'm still interested. Very."

"Let me know if you're ever single again." He bent back over his paper-work. I waited a moment, but he refused to look up again.

I sighed and turned back to the counter. I switched to the Sight, but there was no spelled container. Had the feds found it? Or had someone else known it was there and taken it. Whoever had placed the new spell on the corpse could have just as easily taken the container.

"Shit." Ramirez ignored me, perhaps thinking I was saying it about him. I'd screwed up and now I really needed to talk to Shelby.

When I walked into the garage, I was prepared to tell Agent Shelby about the missing container. What I saw, however, stopped me. Jake stood holding a collar in both hands—the one which had kept him attached to the chain on the wall, away from food and drink. His expression was somber as he stared at the leather strap. Shelby,

Gunnerson and Mrs. Leung watched in silence and I couldn't bring myself to interrupt the moment.

Gunnerson, however, found his voice first. "If you're a Werewolf, how did a simple leather collar hold you?"

Jake lifted his eyes, as if coming out of some faraway place. I answered for him. "It's spelled."

"You guessing or you can see it?" asked Shelby.

"I can See it." The cords of magic on the leather were thick and layered, from years of use. "She used the same collar for such a long time."

I approached Jake and the collar in his hands. He kept his eyes on me, standing still, almost as if he was afraid I'd ask him to wear it again.

I reached out for the leather without touching the collar, and waved my fingers along the configuration of spells. I found the knots which held them together far easier than I found the new spell on the body. I found not only spells to strengthen the leather against a Werewolf's preternatural might; but spells to make the wearer unwilling to remove the collar, to not fight against the bindings. It was meant to sap will as well as strength.

Bit by bit I unraveled the years of compounded spell-casting. As I grew familiar with each of the types of magic, I was able to pull the threads faster. They were simple spells, despite that there were so many of them.

The most complicated spell I'd found in the house so far had been on the missing container. Even the demon-bound stone, although it was a powerful spell if it actually did anything, was not especially complex. The necromancy spell—that was less complex than oddly difficult to See or touch with my mind.

When the last bit of magic fell away from the collar, I flicked the raw energy into the air. It was habit. I smiled with a sense of accomplishment. It would never be used to keep Jake helpless ever again.

"I hope you didn't do what I think you just did," said Mrs. Leung. I looked at her, confused. "That magic was evidence in Jake's defense."

"Oh."

"Do it Jake." Gunnerson's eyes met mine with an understanding that surprised me. Jake looked at Gunnerson and then me.

"That collar will never bind you again," I said. Jake looked at me, tears of anger in his eyes. "Do it, like Gunnerson said."

The young blonde's fists tightened around the collar. No magic remained, only the mental conditioning of many years. Jake didn't believe he could break it.

"I am telling you to do it!"

He pulled against it with frustrated strength. When the leather snapped in his hands, psychological chains snapped inside him. He yelled with rage and starting shredding the leather into little bits. Ramirez and the uniform at the door came running into the garage guns drawn.

"Ease down, boys." Shelby waved them back with an open palm. His expression was sympathetic. I expected Mrs. Leung to chastise me again but she was wiping tears from underneath her glasses. The softy!

Jake fell to his knees, sobbing. Mrs. Leung touched my arm and nodded toward Jake. I dropped to my knees beside him and put my arms around him. He threw himself against me, gripping with more strength than I expected. Over his shoulder, I saw Ramirez frown and leave the garage. Strike two.

"Jake," I whispered. "Jake, please, you're going to crush me."

He loosened his grip on me slightly. His sobbing wracked him. I would be bruised tomorrow, but I gripped him tightly in return. Then I felt him shudder, like something breaking free inside him. His crying changed its tempo and his shoulders relaxed. His grip on me went from rigid to something more like need. Not the sexual need that he'd expressed the previous twelve hours. This was something different.

"Are we done here?" Mrs. Leung looked pointedly at Shelby and Gunnerson and the two men left the garage. Mrs. Leung squeezed my shoulder briefly before she followed the agents.

Jake continued weeping, oblivious that we were alone. I rocked him, uncertain what to say, especially when Jake started whispering over and over one word. 'Mistress.' I noticed then the college of ratty textbooks neatly organized on the bottom shelf of a bookcase, within range of the chain which had held Jake. They looked well-worn but well-loved. It reminded me that I hadn't just been attracted his body or his need. There was a keen mind in this sexy body as well.

After what felt like a long time, but which couldn't have been more than five or ten minutes, he stopped shaking. Jake gently loosened his hold on me and he leaned back, wiping his glistening green eyes. He sniffled a few times and I looked around for tissue. I turned to help him search, which triggered a flash of my Sight. I'd hidden my ability so much of my younger years that I sometimes lost control. This was one of those moments.

I stared at the cluttered garage countertop and held my breath. A kitchen-style *ginzu* knife glowed more brilliantly than the collar—but red, with layers of blood magic. I stood up and approached the counter, but I didn't touch the blade. I froze, horrified by what I saw.

"It's one of the knives she used to take my blood." Jake stood close behind me. He wrapped his arms around my waist and put his chin on my shoulder. It was a comfortable feeling, the way he attached himself to my body. There was nothing sexual in it, just a desire to be close.

"Let's go tell Agent Shelby. There are a couple of things he needs to know." I gently pried Jake's arms from around my waist and he took one of my hands instead. We walked back inside and found everyone sitting at the kitchen table.

"You okay?" Agent Shelby was wearing his sunglasses inside, so I couldn't tell which of us he was asking. When Jake didn't respond, I answered for him.

"He's fine. I found something." Shelby stood up as Ramirez poured him a cup of coffee. I felt the way he kept himself from looking at either of us. "A knife in the garage. The one used for cutting Jake."

Mrs. Leung accepted her coffee next in turn, focused on her cup, but listening.

"It's bespelled."

She didn't look up but smiled briefly to herself before taking a sip. Something had upset her. We hadn't been in the garage that long. Perhaps it had just been seeing Jake traumatized. I'd ask when it was just the two of us.

"Officer Ramirez, please stand watch in the garage." Agent Shelby motioned toward the face of the house, before he looked me in the eyes. "I got a call from Agent Mistry that she just entered the development. She's only a few minutes ahead of the press."

"They didn't waste any time figuring out something was going on," I muttered.

I squeezed Jake's hand and he smiled sadly. He was stronger than he'd been going into the garage. Allowing him to tear up the collar had been the right thing, even if it had cost the defense evidence.

"Agent Gunnerson," said Mrs. Leung softly. We all turned to look at her. "How did you get involved in the preternatural division of the FBI?"

Gunnerson stared at Mrs. Leung without any of his usual humor. What the hell had happened while Jake and I had been alone in the garage?

Agent Shelby didn't wait for Gunnerson to answer. He walked to one of the front windows to look for Agent Mistry's arrival. Ramirez took that as his que and he left for the garage. It was just the four of us at the table and Mrs. Leung kept her gaze on the blonde agent.

"My parents, Mrs. Leung, were killed while skiing in Colorado." Gunnerson spoke calmly, without emotion. "They had unscrupulously swindled an old widow out of her home so that they could obtain this prime cabin area. Had her found mentally unfit. Unfortunately for them, the widow was also a witch."

"She attacked them with magic?" asked Jake, like he was hearing a scary fairy tale.

Gunnerson stared at the Werewolf and gave him a wry smile. "No, Jake. The widow asked for one more day to remove spells from the woods around the cabin. She'd had to protect herself from a troop of Goblins over the years—it was part of their natural migratory territory you see. But my parents forced her out so quickly she didn't have time to get them all." He grinned bitterly. "All she needed was one more day to make the place safe. Like I said, my parents were unscrupulous. They just laughed at her and threw her out, then skied into one of the spells."

"So you became interested in magic out of revenge?" Mrs. Leung clearly disapproved of the notion.

Gunnerson laughed, a mangled sound of anger and regret, but it was Shelby who answered without turning away from the window. "The widow was his grandmother."

"Granny raised me in my dead folks' mansion. Suited us. She taught me an awful lot about magic before she passed. I was getting in trouble with it until I was set straight by a pretty impressive FBI field agent. They recruited me right out of high school."

"You don't miss your parents?" Jake's eyes were full of disbelief. Having been given up by his family, he couldn't understand someone who hadn't not caring.

"Jake. Some people, even someone's family, can be total bastards." Gunnerson stopped smiling and got up from the table. He hadn't touched his coffee. He left the kitchen and disappeared down the hall.

"I upset him?" Jake leaned into me sadly.

THE DARK ELF'S PET | 113

I smiled and brushed the back of my hand along his cheek to reassure him. "The truth upset him, not you."

"She's here," interjected Shelby at the sound of several cars pulling onto the street.

Oh boy, I thought. Things were going to get interesting now.

CHAPTER FIFTEEN

Agent Shiandra Mistry was the first non-American FBI agent I'd ever seen. Clearly, as her name indicated, she was East Indian. Probably Guajarati. My first linguistics professor had been Guajarati and I'd learned a little bit about the culture from him. Agent Mistry was quite beautiful. She reminded me of a dark Angelina Jolie, with as much sex appeal. She was lean at the waist but full figured enough up top and in the rear to rate as a model instead of a special agent.

"Agent Shelby, good to see you, again." She shook his hand and then turned to me. She offered me the same well-manicured, strong fingers. "You must be Devon Mosteller. It's a pleasure."

"Same here," I replied. "This is Jacob Winters, Lycanthrope."

Mistry smiled at Jake but she didn't offer to shake his hand. I bristled a bit at that, wondering if she had a problem with Werewolves or maybe it was just gay men.

"Well, I know they are holding the body for me, shall we?" She seemed impatient.

"I understand you are an expert on Drow?" I asked politely.

"My doctorate was on the Dark Elves, although I'm working on a certificate in Lycanthropy for the agency. Hard to gain access to some of the inner workings of either culture, but the Drow are the worst. Where to, Agent Shelby?"

"Wow, Mistry, you're looking phenomenal as ever." Gunnerson came back into the kitchen from the bedroom where the murder victim remained. He was smiling again, all evidence that he'd been sad gone.

"You're looking well too, Ivan." I heard just the faintest bit of East Indian accent slip out.

Mrs. Leung stepped up to the female agent and extended a hand. "I'm federal attorney, Li Leung. I represent our young Mr. Winters here. He is both a witness and *apparently* a possible suspect in the murder you're here to inspect."

Mrs. Leung had told Sorenson that she was with the Public Defender's office but now she claimed to be with the federal government. Who was our Chinese attorney, really?

"This way, Shiandra." Gunnerson swept his arm toward the bedroom with a flourish before he patted Jake on the back in a genuine camaraderie. Jake flinched at the contact and that sobered up Gunnerson. The blonde agent shot me a look of contrition before he took lead and escorted Agent Mistry to the body.

"Not often I'm brought to a bedroom by a hunky stud," said Mistry to Gunnerson. The blonde agent glanced at Shelby and blushed. Mistry only chuckled. "Don't worry, Ivan. Shelby knows we're old friends."

"Agent Shelby, since this doesn't involve Jake, may I take my client back to the kitchen?" Mrs. Leung held Jake back which stopped me as well since Jake hadn't let go of my hand since leaving the garage.

"Sure, knock yourself out."

Mrs. Leung nodded reassurance at me and tugged at Jake until he released his grip on me and followed her without asking my permission. We were making progress. Perhaps he wasn't as badly damaged as I'd thought.

At the entrance to the bedroom, Gunnerson stood aside and Mistry stepped past him inside. Gunnerson dropped in behind her and Shelby followed. I brought up the rear, curious what she would do or say about the dead woman.

Someone had opened up the curtains and the whole room was brighter. Looking on the corpse in daylight made it look less mysterious. Maybe even less Human and I wasn't referring to her lineage.

Mistry paused halfway into the room. Her hand went to her mouth and she seemed ill. I didn't blame her. The smell had not been masked and the body had been sitting there hours, though it didn't look much different from when Yuriko and I had first discovered it.

"Just a moment, gentlemen." Agent Mistry breathed deeply. Smart woman. My first reaction had been to take shallow breaths which had left me light-headed.

"Take your time, Shiandra," said Agent Shelby. "Never get used to the smell."

Mistry gave a terse, grateful smile before nodding to herself. She pushed her shoulders back and walked along the outside of the dried circle of blood on the floor. She leaned forward here and there to get a closer look, pausing at one point, as if the angle of the body were important. She looked up and motioned me over. The smell hit me badly, but if she could tough it out, so could I.

"You de-activated a spell here?" she asked. I nodded. "Good. Nasty piece of work that from what Gunnerson told me. Not Drow, mind you. They don't do necromancy. But nasty."

"I recognized it." I felt Agent Shelby's gaze heavy on me.

Ramirez stepped into the room. "Paparazzi in the front yard." Shelby acknowledged the statement and the cop left, his eyes still avoiding me.

"Nothing about this ritualistic death smacks of the Drow." Mistry was clearly relieved. "But, you were right. She's a mixed breed. I'd guess a quarter? Too Human for a half. Drow genes are fairly dominant. She looks nearly Human."

"That's what I thought," I agreed.

"So there's nothing to indicate that this was done by the Drow?" asked Shelby.

"Oh, it was intended to emulate Drow ritual killings." Mistry sounded confident. "But it's definitely not. Someone Human tried to make it look like Drow were involved."

"That's good, right?" asked Gunnerson.

"Definitely. If it had been Drow on Drow, I'm not sure we have the resources to investigate that." That thought definitely troubled the beautiful agent.

"There are a couple of other things you should look at," I added.

"You mean the knife?" asked Shelby.

I couldn't keep the embarrassment off my face. I had left one thing out of the report. "And a missing container. Shielded by Drow spells. I kept it from the police when they didn't want to know anything else about magic at the scene. I intended to turn it over to you. When I looked for it today it was gone."

"So whoever added the spell to the body also took the container? Maybe one of the local PD?" suggested Gunnerson.

"No. When I say it was shielded, I meant from sight or touch. You had to know it was there."

"The woman was around a quarter Drow." Mistry rubbed her chin in thought. "Surely she could have cast the spells?"

I thought about the knife, collar and the hidden container. "No, I don't think so. I mean, yeah, the knife and collar are hers. Jake told us as much. But the missing container, that was clearly not the same hand."

"How do you know?" Agent Mistry could mask her surprise.

"Spells are woven after the fashion of their nature," I explained. "But the caster also leaves stylistic fingerprints on the spell. Subtle, like differences between Monet and Manet, regardless of the period in which they painted. Though I'm not expert enough to catch all the distinctions, painters or spell-casters, the container was not bespelled by the same person as the collar and knife. There was a certainty to the weaving; a strength not found in the collar and knife. And not just because those spells were so much less complicated."

"That would be the nature of Drow magic in general. Some of the most complicated rituals I've ever seen," agreed Mistry. "Amazing, I'd no idea individual spell-casters could be identified."

"Given enough comparison and enough time to examine a spell, yes," I confirmed.

"Does the department know that?" asked Shelby.

"I can't remember if I told Agent Jacobsen. I answered all of his questions as fully as possible when I first assisted the FBI. To be honest, though, I've only worked one case with the feds. Mostly it's been the cops. You can't say I'm very heavily valued."

"Nothing personal, Devon," said Gunnerson reassuringly. "The department doesn't much trust outside help. Now, if you were one of us!"

"No, thanks. I mean, working with you two has been entertaining. But in general, I don't like to follow the rules as strictly as you have to."

Gunnerson nodded sympathetically but Shelby didn't seem impressed. "Agent Gunnerson, could you open the window. I'm afraid the smell is getting too much for me," interrupted Shiandra. "And the jet-lag. I need a minute."

Shelby nodded and the blonde agent reached for the window latch to open it part way. We all flinched at the sound of shattering glass. I thought that he'd pulled too hard.

"That didn't come from in here," yelled Shelby as Mrs. Leung began to scream from the kitchen.

I was first out the door with both federal agents close behind me. Ramirez wasn't around but Sorensen and the uniform cop at the door rushed in from outside. Mrs. Leung and Jake were both on the kitchen floor and there was blood everywhere.

"Everybody down!" shouted Shelby.

He and Gunnerson threw themselves against the wooden base of the cabinets, guns drawn and gripped in both hands. Sorensen and his fellow officer pressed themselves flat against walls out of sniper vision.

I saw the broken glass on the floor and looked up to see the kitchen window, curtains opened wide, shattered from the outside. A hand grabbed my shirt and yanked me to the ground. I fell next to Gunnerson.

"Everybody includes you, Mr. Mosteller," hissed the platinum-blonde agent. He called across the room, "Mrs. Leung, Jake, which one of you is bleeding?"

"Jake," exclaimed the Chinese attorney, trying to maintain her normal dignity. "The glass shattered and he cried out in pain. Blood splattered from his shoulder and that's when I screamed. No warning sound, just the shattering glass!" Mrs. Leung sounded close to panic. "There's so much blood!"

I slid across the floor toward Jake. Gunnerson grabbed at my ankle but I shook him off and crawled through a pool of Jake's blood to reach the Werewolf. The coppery stench of it filled my throat with bile.

"He can't afford to lose so much blood so soon after his trauma," I said to no one in particular. Mrs. Leung pressed her small hands over the wound, but the blood oozed out. "Let me try."

We swapped hands and I pressed tightly. Although I could feel the blood seep under my hands, I could not account for the amount that pooled onto the floor.

"The bullet! It must have gone through him." shouted Agent Shelby. "Check for an exit point!"

Without a word, Mrs. Leung put her hands back over mine, to cover the entry wound. I reached my hands, slick with blood, and found the thick liquid dripping from the exit point. I saw a dishtowel dangling from a rod and yanked it down. It helped staunch the flow.

"Got it!" I shouted. In the silence of the kitchen, we yelled to hear each other over our racing heart beats.

Agent Mistry was on her hand-held radio. "We need back up. Sniper fire at 4501 Talon Avenue. The Ravenclaw development. No, no agents down. But send an ambulance! We've got one civilian casualty."

"The local hospital isn't equipped to deal with Lycanthropes," I shouted to Agent Mistry. "There's a local vet who has training and probably the medicines he'll need."

"I don't think he'll make it." Mistry dropped to her knees in the blood next to Mrs. Leung and me. "Not unless he changes. The change will heal the wound and he'll recover faster in Werewolf form."

I remembered then what I had forgotten from the night before. How had Jake transformed from wolf to Human in my bed so many days away from a full moon? I wanted to trust him, but that question created a certain degree of doubt.

"The full moon is a few days away. We have no means of forcing the change," said Mrs. Leung.

"Yes, we do," said Mistry. "I've never tried it but I know a spell which can force the change. It's illegal blood magic, but we've plenty of blood on the floor."

"Well then do it for god's sake!" I yelled. Jake looked paler than when I'd first seen him in my bed. Lycanthropes were tough but they weren't invulnerable. He was weakest in Human form.

"As his attorney, I have no objections." Mrs. Leung's eyes met mine sympathetically.

"He won't be able to turn back to Human until the full moon," warned Mistry.

"Wait, can he talk in his other form?" Agent Shelby stretched up to peer through the shattered glass. Sirens could be heard in the distance.

"He should be able to," confirmed Mistry.

"If it's the only way to save his life, we have to try!" I repeated.

"Fine, do it! It's going to be my ass on the line for this though," muttered the handsome black agent.

Mistry didn't wait a moment more. She slapped one hand into the pool of blood and began speaking in a language I didn't recognize. It didn't sound Human. Maybe High Elf or something nearly as old.

Jake's body grew warm to the touch and Mrs. Leung looked uncertain. No, she looked afraid. Not of the sniper, but that she would fail Jake. I recognized that look from the mirror and offered her a reassuring smile. "Press onto the wound as long as you can."

She nodded, disheveled, blood splattered and slightly green. I didn't look much better. But Jake looked worse than either of us and I felt helpless—helpless the way I'd been when my mother had died.

There was a keening sound that scratched at my temples. I could hear it despite Mistry's alien chanting. The blood pooling around her hand started to vibrate, reacting to the power she raised in the room. The East Indian woman grabbed Jake's wrist with her other hand and his entire body arced as if lightning coursed through him.

He screamed in agony and Mrs. Leung let go of his shoulder with a start of fright. She stared at her hands as if they had betrayed her, but they were red—scalded from the heat of his body. I had to release him, too. Was he burning up because of the magic or because he was changing?

I slid back, horrified and amazed. I'd never seen a Werewolf transform in person before. The surface of his skin rippled with the start of the change, his muscles tense as he continued to scream. I'd never read that it was so painful, and I had to fight myself to keep from reaching out to hold him.

It was only then that I remembered I had another way to view what was happening. My genetic gift of the Sight didn't just allow me to *See* magic. Mundane surroundings were pushed into the background. Everything ordinary sat in blue-grey shadows, so that anything with mystical composition rose to the fore. That's why I didn't just walk around using my gift all the time. But I used it now.

Threads of red power swirled around the woman's palm in the blood, as if she'd trapped some tentacled thing under her open hand that struggled to pull itself free. One by one those tendrils of blood-magic found Jake's body and coiled about him. There were hints of color in the blue-grey shadows of the Werewolf, but the unpleasant red glare of blood-magic drowned out any lesser magics.

The writhing tendrils wrapped tightly around Jake's chest and waist, throat, arms and legs until he was firmly entangled by the spell. I was unsure what to expect next. I had never witnessed this sort of magic before. Blood magic was not only illegal, it was very dangerous to both the source of the blood and the person casting the spell.

How different was it from the spell that Lenora had used to force the change on Jake? And had it always been this painful, each and every time? Perhaps this was a form of Drow magic. I wouldn't know until it was done.

A thick coat of red energy flowed up Mistry's palm from the blood on the floor. Like the tendrils of the spell, this energy moved up her arm, across her chest and back to the hand touching Jake. It surged when it reached him, pushing its way into his body. He spasmed as his muscles contract involuntarily.

Mistry's voice rose to a shout in that other language. The blood around her hand evaporated into the spell, carried away by magic. The last bits of blood-red energy flowed into Jake. The power shimmered just below his skin, separating into double-helix threads which my magic recognized. When the strands reached the surface of his skin, they sprung taut like a tightly stretched web along his skin into a two-color pattern which every Werebeast on the planet wore. The dark redness of fresh blood faded from the magic as if blood-magic had never been used, but he was different. Jacob Winters had transformed into a Werewolf.

I mentally shifted and my sight returned to normal. Jake collapsed onto the floor with a shudder, then he lay there unmoving. The wound was closed and there was no blood anywhere in the kitchen.

"I'd never done that before," said Agent Mistry, out of breath. Her long silky hair was mussed as if this had been a physical trial, not just casting a spell and I remembered once again how dangerous using blood magics could be. Her eye-lids fluttered and I barely managed to grab her waist and shoulders, leaning her against my chest as she passed out. Unlike Jake, Mistry felt cool, almost clammy.

A swarm of federal agents and local police burst into the house and all hell broke loose. When the first person shouted 'hands in the air,' I didn't know if I should let Mistry hit the ground or risk being shot. Ultimately, I took my chances.

CHAPTER SIXTEEN

"It's alright!" Agent Shelby shouted at the top of his lungs for at least the third time. None of the other agents seemed to recognize him or hear his voice. All of them had aimed their weapons nervously at the unconscious Werewolf on the kitchen floor.

"Sniper! Outside!" Gunnerson stood up from the kitchen floor disgusted. "But then, so are about twenty reporters. Chief Jacobsen, we have men hitting the perimeter?"

Preternatural Department Chief Alex Jacobsen stepped into the kitchen as I held Agent Shiandra Mistry slack in my arms. Like Shelby, he was a big, tall man who worked out, although he was a little softer around the paunch than the black agent. Jacobsen surveyed the scene with angry grey eyes. His finger-length brown hair was parted on the side. I'd wondered if his nose had been broken a few times because it had that shape and size to it. His square jaw offset high cheek-bones and his lips bore a perpetual frown.

He glanced at me, nodded briefly then crossed the kitchen low to the ground and took a position under the window next to Shelby. "We just didn't expect to see a full blown Lycanthrope on the floor. I thought they could only take one of the two end forms during the day-time, wolf or Human?"

"Agent Mistry performed a spell to transform the Human to the beast to protect the witness," replied Gunnerson.

The blonde agent had lost all of the playful banter and irreverence he had displayed earlier. I should have known that Gunnerson had to have some of that FBI no-nonsense attitude somewhere in him, but it was a scarier transformation than Jake's to Lycanthrope form.

"The shot came through this window, hit the witness." Shelby motioned above the sink. "Single-story rooftop angle or higher."

Jacobsen got on his radio, "Look for a rooftop shooter, facing the West side of—what is this called again? Oh yeah, Talon Street. Watch out for the reporters. No, I take that back, collect everyone in the area and haul them in for questioning, *including* the reporters."

He and Shelby exchanged a knowing glance. Mrs. Leung tried to stand up but Agent Shelby took her arms in his large black hands and carefully lowered her back to the ground. He shielded her body in the process. Another agent might not have been so chivalrous.

"I'm alright." Mistry startled me because I hadn't felt her stir in my arms. She sat up, patting my shoulder by way of thanks.

"Agent Mistry, I'm Chief Jacobsen—."

"We spoke on the phone," replied Mistry with a polite nod.

An ambulance crew came inside the house, carrying a gurney. The EMT looked at the unconscious sprawled Werewolf on the floor. "Uh uh, no way."

"What's wrong, Thom?" asked the second EMT. He was busy looking at all the federal agents with guns drawn moving through the house. Thom, the first EMT stepped aside.

"No way we're hauling a Werewolf in our ambulance," asserted Thom a second time.

"Shit, is that a real Werewolf? I thought they were Human in the daytime?" asked the other EMT.

Great. Not only weren't they willing to transport Jake, they didn't know anything about Werewolves. "I thought they'd be up to date on the laws passed that give Lycanthropes legal rights?"

Thom rushed his partner back outside. Agent Jacobsen glared at them retreat from where he crouched, disgusted, before he turned to meet my gaze. "You're his guardian for now. Mind hauling him to the hospital?"

"Not the hospital," I said. "But I'll take him to a qualified preternatural veterinarian. If I can get someone to come with me."

"They'll get there faster in a marked car," said the black agent softly.

"Good idea." Jacobsen searched the gathered assortment of federal agents and local police pressed against the walls to avoid the sniper. "You! What's your name?"

Sorensen was the focus of Agent Jacobsen's question. His expression was no more pleased than mine. He held his gun at the ready, his gaze flickering out the window at every little movement.

"Sorensen," replied the cop tersely.

"Well Sorensen, I need you to help Mr. Mosteller, here, transport this witness to get medical assistance."

"I don't feel comfortable," started Sorensen.

Chief Jacobsen stood from the shelter of the cabinets to face the blonde cop angrily. Shelby tugged on his pant leg. "Down, Chief!"

Jacobsen squatted back down but he still managed to be intimidating. "It wasn't a request, Sorensen. I don't care if your grandmother was eaten by the big bad wolf! Help him carry the body to your squad car and take them where Mr. Mosteller tells you!" He snarled like the big bad wolf himself.

"Fine." Sorensen seethed through closed teeth and came over to Jake, keeping low to the ground. He refused to make eye contact with me and I was glad for the silent treatment. I doubted that it would last.

I got off the ground and reached under Jake's arms leaving Sorensen the feet. The federal agents covered us through the broken window, although they could not have stopped the sniper from putting a bullet in my back. Sorensen pulled on plastic gloves before he picked up the Werewolf. In his furry Wolfman shape, Jake looked bizarre in my t-shirt and gym shorts. His Werewolf coloring was the same as his wolf form—a ruddy-brown with black mask around his eyes. Weird, as a Human he was so blonde and glabrous.

His body was heavier than he'd been as a Human, but I'd expected that. Studies had shown that Lycanthropic muscle tissue was denser than Human muscles. It explained their added strength, although not their metaphysical properties. Had I not worked out as much as I had, I wouldn't have been able to carry him even with Sorensen's help. The blonde cop grunted at the unexpected effort of lifting Jake's extra mass.

"Damned heavy, huhn?" Gunnerson looked over at Jacobsen who was busy on the radio. "You taking him to the babe with the huge tits?"

"How the hell did you know?" I whispered. Sorensen scowled and tried to force me to move.

"We're the new preternatural division here in Fresno! You think we wouldn't have already checked out resources?" Gunnerson winked at me and moved somberly towards Jacobsen who beckoned him.

Sorensen forced me to walk backwards as we carried Jake out the door. I let him, since I didn't want the cop to drop Jake out of spite. When we were outside, three officers appeared as a perimeter around us. I was annoyed that they didn't offer to help carry Jake until I saw the reporters with television cameras that they held at bay.

"Which car?"

Sorensen didn't answer, but growled and shifted so that he was walking parallel to me and nodded toward one of the closest police cars. The wall of officers trailed us, keeping back the reporters. He opened the back door which was unlocked; although I knew it would be locked from the inside. Rather than putting Jake's feet in, he pivoted me around so that I had to sit and slide across the seat with Jake to get him in. Sorensen shut the door and walked to the driver's seat while I was trapped in the back.

The reporters shouted questions at him but his silence wasn't only directed at me. He didn't even look at them as he slipped behind the wheel and slammed the door of his squad car. "Where the fuck are we going?"

"Shaw and Clovis. The northeast corner," I replied.

If he thought I objected to being locked in the cage with Jake, he was wrong. It helped that I'd made love to the Human version of the beast. I wasn't panicked by his Werewolf form. On the other hand, if Jake woke up and attacked me, I might die in excruciating pain. Sorensen wouldn't unlock the rear door under those circumstances. I was sure of that.

The blonde cop drove and I tried not to concentrate on the sharp teeth visible from Jake's slightly opened jaws. Inside that wolf body was a timid Human being. But would he have a Human mind if he woke?

CHAPTER SIXTEEN

Closer to her clinic, I called Melanie on my cell-phone and told her to expect us in five minutes. She held the door open as Sorensen and I hauled Jake's limp body into the lobby. Ulrich was there looking suspiciously at me as we carried Jake into the back and laid him on the examination table.

"You didn't tell me he was in lupinoid form." Melanie sounded gruffly puzzled as she set up an IV. "For that matter, how the hell did he get into a lupinoid form since yesterday? He wasn't strong enough."

Ulrich continued to hover outside the examination room, while Sorensen leaned up against the doorway with his arms folded. He was mildly distracted by Melanie's breasts, and content to stay out of our way. Fine with me.

"A spell forced the change because he took a bullet to the shoulder," I said.

"A bullet wound wouldn't kill him. Why force the change?" She inspected each shoulder, carefully digging through the thick fur.

"He'd lost so much blood and hadn't recovered enough from the starvation. We panicked."

She ran her fingers through the hair of his belly, leaning close to check along his flesh as she shifted higher up his body. Once she reached his head, she rolled back an eye-lid, shining a light into it. "Pupils responsive, if a bit slow."

"Ulrich, you remember Devon?" Melanie offered her husband a hesitant smile.

"Yes. Hello, Devon," He greeted me as if he hadn't seen me last night. His German accent was almost negligible.

"Ulrich, good to see you," I said pleasantly. "Thank goodness Melanie was so close to the murder scene. A sniper shot Jake through a window. The EMTs refused to transport him and so the FBI ordered Sorensen, here, to help me deliver him personally." I held Ulrich's eyes to make sure he understood.

"You're welcome any time Devon. Police business or no," he said. I thought I saw suspicion die in his eyes. "We can use the business."

"You know each other?" Sorensen's eyes were aimed in Melanie's direction, but he wasn't making eye-contact. If I had been Ulrich, I might have stepped inbetween them to make a point. The thin dark German didn't seem to notice. I was the only threat in the room as far as he was concerned.

"Melanie and I go back ages, Sorensen," I answered. "Best friends at one point." Melanie looked at me, troubled by my choice of words. I tried to put her mind at ease. "We haven't seen each other much recently. She's been starting her practice and I was travelling. Now she's got a different sort of best friend. Her husband Ulrich."

Sorensen had the decency to look embarrassed for having checked out another man's wife right in front of him. He studied the furry body on the table instead. "Should we restrain it?"

"*He*," corrected Melanie without any trace of gentleness, "is not a criminal and doesn't need to be restrained. Werewolves— Lycanthropes in general, do not lose their intelligence when they change. He is, however, contagious in this form." She looked at me as if to say, 'just a reminder.'

"That sounds like reason to restrain him." Sorensen clearly wasn't the tolerant sort.

"You didn't restrain him when I was in the back of the cage with him." I made it an accusation. He just stared.

"If you prefer, you can wait in the lobby, officer." Ulrich put a firm but supportive hand on Melanie's shoulder as she prepared an injection.

"Naw, I'm not getting in trouble because I left you guys alone with this thing," said Sorensen. "What's the needle for?"

I stood at Jake's chest, away from his face and fangs. I ran my fingers through the fur on his forearm, testing the texture but aware of the sexy muscles underneath. With a shift in my gaze I Saw the lined pattern laying just under his skin that tied his beast to his body. Not a spell, but the blood curse which infected him with Lycanthropy. Twisted double-helix strands shaped like DNA, attached to his very being. A power stronger than my mind was required to unravel those twisted helices. That's why they were called curses.

"Adrenaline. In his lupinoid form, it will jump-start his healing process. The IV will feed nutrients and if we can get some protein in him, he'll actually heal faster than if he'd stayed Human or been a wolf."

"He *had* been a wolf," muttered Sorensen, looking at me suspiciously. He was a bigot, but perhaps not stupid. Those were the worst ones—smart people with prejudice.

"What do you mean, 'he had been a wolf'?" Melanie glanced up from under those thick lids with her icy blue eyes.

"When Mosteller found him. Day-before-yesterday." The cop nodded in my direction.

Melanie looked at me intently. "Here goes nothing." The needle went into his furry arm and she leaned back on the countertop. "Give it a few minutes. If he wakes, we can give him protein more naturally."

As Jake lay there, I reached out to try and unweave some of the magic on his body, just as a lark. He spasmed and screamed in response. One powerful arm lashed out and knocked me against the wall. I saw stars and could hear Melanie screaming at Sorensen.

"Put the gun away!"

I stood, wincing at future bruises, and shook my head. Jake was sitting upright, panic on his face. Melanie was attempting to reattach the IV which had torn loose while Ulrich was holding Jake's arm still. Despite his Wolfman form, I could see the anxiety in Jake's eyes and he panted, like a stressed dog.

"I don't know why that happened. Nothing we are doing should hurt him like that" Melanie looked at me with the guilt of someone who had failed—the way Li Leung had looked guilty for not being able to hold Jake down. But I was the one who had caused Jake's pain, not Melanie. I wanted to say something, but Sorensen had not reholstered his gun.

"It seems to have passed," observed Ulrich, although his eyes were angry and focused on me. He didn't know I'd caused Jake's reaction. But I was the reason Jake was here and if she got hurt, I would be the one he blamed for that.

Melanie brought a cup of the protein supplement she'd prepared and gently held it to Jake's lupine lips. "Here, drink this." Her breasts brushed up against Jake's arm and he leaned away. She moved closer, but didn't brush against him this time. "Come on. If you want to stay conscious, drink this."

Jake's bright-green wolf eyes looked at me. His Lycan mouth couldn't form the full range of Human expressions, but I could read this emotion. Jake was afraid, even to touch me.

"It's okay Jake. It was an accident. Drink. Please," I said in my best coaxing animal voice. I was patronizing him, but what else could I do? It was instinctive.

He took the cup with one clawed hand, his nails clacking against the plastic as he carefully drank the liquid. He lapped up the last of it with his very long tongue. Nothing sexy about that mouth or tongue. I couldn't imagine kissing him now the way that I had that morning.

Could I date a guy who was fuzzy half the time? Would he expect me to want to touch him like that? Would he want to touch me? I shivered at my own fear. Was this how Sorensen felt when he thought about homosexuals? About witches? It was harder to resent him for it even if it was wrong.

"You okay?" It took a moment before I realized Melanie she was talking to me. She came around the examination table and put her hand on my shoulder. The worried expression on her face was gratifying, but for Ulrich's sake, I shook her off brusquely.

"Yeah, just a little dazed," I muttered and approached the table and Jake. He trembled. "Hey, I'm not mad." He glanced at my hands and then away. Then I understood. He could smell my fear. I'd forgotten.

I started stroking the fur on his bicep and along his shoulder-blade. He turned his head to me startled. After caressing him for a time, his trembling stopped and he closed his eyes. I learned something new then. A Werewolf could shed tears.

"We should get more fluid down him while he's awake." Melanie spoke gently, but she didn't try to touch me. "And if you forced him to change, he probably needs some sleep."

"I want to find out who shot him," I muttered angrily. "Our murderer thinks that Jake knows something."

Melanie grew grim. "Well if he does, he won't tell us till the next full moon. Whatever you did to him, it didn't work right."

"What do you mean?"

"Jake can't talk."

CHAPTER SEVENTEEN

Jake consumed as much protein as Melanie felt he could handle, and then escorted us outside. "Be careful. Both of you."

We got in the cop car and Sorensen drove us back to my house. The phone rang and I put it to my ear. "What's up, Shelby."

"I hope that was caller ID and not some psychic bullshit, Mosteller."

"No psychic bullshit here. There a problem?"

"The crime scene is off-limits for now. Can't say more at the moment, but you'll have to pick up my truck later."

"Alright, I'll have Sorensen drive us to my place."

There was no reply, just the sound of Agent Shelby hanging up on me. Sorensen glared at me in the rear view mirror. "What now?"

"I need you to take us to the Van Ness Extension. Off of Shields."

"The sooner I get rid of you the better," was his response, but it was the justification he needed to play chauffeur to two people he clearly despised.

When he reached my neighborhood, he stiffened in his seat but when I had him pull into the drive, he couldn't help himself. "Rich spoiled f—brat." He shot me a surly glare in the mirror, the first time he'd looked at me since Shelby's call. "Who's that?"

Yuriko Morimoto leaned against the door of her Apache truck, arms folded and holding a large coffee container. Sorensen knew who she was. But not the tall, broad-shouldered man with reddish hair who stood talking to her a few feet away. His shoulders were hunched in an angry manner and his huge hands were half in his leather jacket's pockets. The red-head looked like a major thug.

"Never saw him before in my life."

Sorensen might not like me, but I suspected he had no problem with skinny Asian chicks. Might even bring out the protector in him, considering the aggressive stance of the red-head. I didn't think I'd fare too well against someone who carried twice my muscle mass, so I was hoping the blonde cop would hang around.

Jake was in no state to fight either. But what worried me wasn't his weakened condition. It was the fact that in this form, he could transmit his Lycanthropy with a bite or shared blood. Like a mystical version of AIDS. The AIDS-Lycanthropy issue was currently raging before the legislature—it had been all year. Should it be legal to allow people to intentionally contract Lycanthropy to cure HIV? While they might eventually find a cure for HIV, there was no cure for turning furry at the full moon. I guess I would want the choice. Of course, I also believed that suicide should be legal, so clearly I valued the quality of life over life itself.

Grudgingly, Sorensen commented aloud but his eyes never left Yuriko "We're supposed to keep an eye on the witness, so I guess I better check it out." Yep, his hero-complex, the one that had made him want to be a cop, stepped up. Gotta save the maiden fair. Yuriko's body language didn't seem intimidated, only agitated, but I didn't point this out to the cop.

Sorensen got out of the car and started toward them. The red-head studied the cop car with suspicion and Sorensen put his hand to his holster. That's about when I pounded on the back-seat window. The blonde officer hesitated, pissed, but he came back and let us out with a scowl.

"Thanks."

Sorensen walked away from the open door while I got out and watched Jake crawl out in Werewolf form. The only thing that kept my terror in check was the worried expression in his beautiful green eyes. Yeah, I was a sucker for big sweet eyes.

His gait was a cross between walk and trot, and he couldn't seem to make up his mind whether he should walk on two legs or four. When the man talking to Yuriko saw Jake, his eyes widened. Surprise, not fear. In fact, he walked away from Yuriko in mid-sentence and headed toward Jake. He was going to walk right past Sorensen without acknowledging him except that the cop grabbed him with one hand. Or rather, he tried to grab him, because the red-head kept coming and Sorensen was jerked along until he let go.

"Hold it right there!" the blonde cop demanded. His voice held a touch of panic.

"Stand behind me, Jake," I said to the Werewolf. He slunk around me and pressed himself against the back of my thighs and butt. It was a reassuring animal behavior that I'd experienced with dogs I had owned. But this is a person, Devon! Remember that!

"What the fuck did you do to him?" The powerfully built red-head reeked with preternatural energy. *Werewolf.*

"Who the hell are you?" I snarled back. Just like Melanie had said, I leapt toward danger.

"Connor Winters. He belongs to our clan," roared the man furiously. "I'm his uncle and legal guardian. Now what the fuck did you do to him?"

I was a little fuzzy on the biology of Werewolves and some of the fine details of inter-pack relations, but I did know basic etiquette and rules. In particular, I knew the ones that might keep me safe right now. "What claim do you have on Jacob Winters?"

"I told you, I'm his uncle!" The brute closed the distance between us.

"You have no claim, here, Connor Winters. You come for Jacob Winters and do not provide your pack or your ranking. You offer no proof of pack or kinship."

"What the fuck do you think you know?" he demanded, but I could see hesitancy flicker in his eyes. "Get out of my way."

"You have no legal claim here, Connor Winters. You have no claim under pack law. I challenge your authority by *rite of information.*" It was a non-combative rule of the pack. If he made a claim, I could challenge him to provide certain information or the claim had to be withdrawn. Otherwise, all pack disputes would have resulted in bloodshed. Werewolf society was built on strength of the fittest. That included intelligence, not just physical prowess.

"And what is gonna stop me from ripping your head off?" he asked, evasively.

We both turned as Sorensen's shadow drew close. He had his weapon out and pointed at Connor's chest. Behind him, Yuriko had drawn a tazer. She looked uncomfortable, but determined to use it if she had to.

"It won't be necessary, Sorensen." I wanted to forestall a physical fight that would end up with one of us badly hurt—in all probability, me! "If he refuses to answer my question and lays a hand on either Jake or myself, his own pack will be obligated to tear him to shreds. It's a pretty serious rule to protect pack cohesiveness." I hoped I was right.

"Jake didn't tell you that," said Connor with certainty. "Fine. I am Kimric Clan." Information could be used against him, which is another reason I'd made the challenge. Packs liked to keep a low profile even if there were laws to protect them.

"And?"

"You are not Clan. I do not have to reveal further information to you. I have a copy of Jake's birth certificate. You have to give him over to me. Your own laws say so."

"No, I don't. He's nineteen. What makes you think you can claim him by Human law?"

"I told you, I'm his legal guardian. My claim is under Human law. He's not nineteen. He's still a minor. Here's his birth certificate." Connor seemed hyper aware of the gun pointed at his back.

The Werewolf could move fast enough, even in Human form, to dodge the bullet and take out Sorensen and Yuriko both. Instead, he slowly reached inside his jacket. Sorensen's finger tightened on the trigger.

"I'm getting a piece of paper, not a gun. We don't consider guns weapons." Disgust dripped from Connor's lips as he slowly pulled out a very wrinkled piece of paper. I reached for it, watching his hands to make sure he didn't grab me. I doubted he'd attack a police officer or steal a federal witness, but he barely contained his rage.

The birth certificate was probably the original. Definitely not a State-issued duplicate. The creases made it hard to read, but finally I located the date.

"Now give me, Jake."

"You're right, he's not nineteen," I said slowly and watched Connor gloat before I smiled. "He's twenty. Must be real close to your nephew."

The red-head tore the fragile paper out of my hands and took as long to find the age as I had. He hadn't looked at this paper in years, if ever.

"You have no legal claim to him," I repeated.

Connor stood there trembling, crumpling the paper in his hands as if he wished it were my head instead.   "Under Kimric law—"

"Under pack law, you failed to respond to challenge for information. Pack name is not enough. And you instead made a claim based on Human law," I countered. Connor started to sputter additional arguments but I forestalled him. "You may not be aware, Mr. Winters, that Jake is a federal witness under my protection, as a federal agent," stretching the truth. I didn't care if my credibility was weakened with the bad guys. If I mixed truth with lie, he might not smell the lie.

"So?" He was confused.

"So, even if you were Kimric's Fenris, your claims to him would be subjugated under federal law. In other words, you need a court order to have him released." I could feel my heart pounding despite my bravado. I wasn't used to dealing with flesh and blood Werewolves, despite my not-so limited Lycan knowledge or brave front.

"I can smell your fear." He took a long, deliberate sniff along my upper-body and sneered. He leaned so close I thought he was going to kiss my throat. I had to stop myself from elbowing him in the face out of panic. He whispered so that only I could hear. "I can smell him on your skin. Dirty little secrets that can come back to haunt you."

"Because you failed to respond to challenge and you attempted to rely on non-clan law, you have forfeited any rights to challenge me by your own pack rules. You must now rely on the alternate law you attempted to exercise." In a moment of bravado, I goaded him. "Guess what, Wolfy, you lose!"

I flinched and jumped back when Connor Winters roared at the top of his Human lungs. There was something slightly non-Human to the noise, but it was the frustrated rage of it that scared me. I expected to see Sorensen smirking at me, but he was sweating the fact that he almost discharged his weapon.

I watched Yuriko walk up to the furious Werewolf and stick the live tazer against the small of his back. He stiffened, startled as the voltage ran through him. A tazer wouldn't stop a Werewolf, not even in Human form. To my surprise, he crumpled to the ground instantly.

She revealed her other hand and I saw the tranq pistol. I looked down and saw the dart sticking out from his back. Double zapped.

"It's a crime to assault someone." She folded her hands and looked at Sorensen who gaped at her. "Officer, do your job. Cuff him." She looked at me, pleased with herself. I opened my mouth to speak, but for a change, I couldn't think of one thing to add to the moment.

CHAPTER EIGHTEEN

Sorensen called Agent Shelby instead of his own precinct, still parked in my cobblestone driveway. The blonde cop wanted to dump the trouble Connor Winters represented onto the feds' shoulders. Yuriko had acted within the law, but knocking a Werewolf unconscious and detaining him was outside of the Fresno Police Department's experience. Hell, it was outside of my experience, too.

Without money to retrofit prison cells to handle preternaturals, the feds had been given the authority to intervene in such cases. I could only hear Sorenson's half of the conversation, but the cop looked pleased.

"Shelby said to restrain Connor. Agents are on their way. They want to question him about the murder of that woman and why she had him locked up."

I approached the cop, who stood with his weapon out, standing over the prone figure of Connor. "Look, Sorensen, I just wanted to say thanks for backing me up. Another cop might have just let me take my lumps and then bothered to stepped in."

Sorensen didn't take his eyes from Connor but he finally jerked his head in acknowledgment. "I may not like or respect certain perversions, Mr. Mosteller, but I respect the law."

"Either way, thanks," I repeated dully and led Jake inside the house. As I walked past, I gave Yuriko a questioning glance.

"I'm going to stay with Sorensen. I've got three more tranq darts designed for Lycanthropes. They're expensive, but I think protecting a fellow officer is worth it."

"If it'll cut you any slack with your boss, I'll pay for replacements."

I put a hand on her thin shoulder and she smiled at me. "Anything to keep the department open." She loved animals more than people. They never gave her heart grief. I understand the feeling.

Jake tugged at my shirt, uncomfortable around his uncle, even when the man was unconscious, so I followed him inside. He started toward the bedroom, *my* bedroom, then paused to see if I was following. I stopped in the kitchen to check the answering machine. Jake came back and went to all four at my feet. He put his nose in my crotch and I laughed despite my apprehension. Those jaws were powerful enough to bite right through my Bench jeans. Not a mental image I liked and I put my open palm between his nose and my groin.

"I'm not going to bed again, Jake." For a moment I had thought of him as an animal and not as a person who could understand me. "The police are going to ask questions. Hell, I have questions I want answered."

He looked at me with those large green eyes and then licked my belly under my shirt. I reacted as if a dog had licked me, not a lover, giggling. He had to understand that it couldn't be any other way. I pushed his head out from under my shirt.

When he showed signs of physical excitement, revulsion rose in me. As a Werebeast, he didn't have one of those nasty red, dog-like erections. It was Human shaped, covered completely in silky hair, but that didn't make it better. They weren't my favorite thing in general, despite being a gay man. I moved away from him and he sniffed the air. My scent betrayed me again.

"Go get some sleep, Jake. Your body is weak and food alone won't restore it." I made excuses, trying to distract him from my discomfort. He lowered his head to the ground but as I tried to caress it he pulled away. I said by way of apology, "I've got work to do."

Jake moved sadly toward the bedroom with a wolf-like slink which alternated into a bipedal scurry. Not the graceful movement I expected from a Werewolf. I was apprehensive that he would want to sleep in my bed, so I was relieved when he slipped into the spare bedroom.

If I was relieved, then why did I feel like shit? Because I'd had sex with him just that morning and now he could tell I didn't want him naked in my bed as a Lycanthrope. Maybe I was being an ass but I couldn't help it.

The door opened and Yuriko entered. It had taken her a long time to feel comfortable enough to come and go in my house as if she lived there. I was afraid that the incident with Antonio would change that so I was relieved that she just strode in. But behind her were two men in dark suits that I didn't recognize. Shelby had wasted no time sending agents to the house. Maybe they had been on their way before we called.

I motioned to them to come in absently as I went to the fridge to grab a soda. "You want anything, Yuriko?"

She didn't answer. I grabbed a bottle of soda and shut the door. I walked out of the tiled cooking area and one of the two men was holding Yuriko in the air by the back of the neck, her legs dangling underneath her. The other man leaned against the closed door, arms folded. I shifted my vision and Saw the pulse of magic just beneath their skins. They were like Jake and his uncle—Lycanthropes.

"Who are you?" I kept my hostility low, considering one of my closest friends was hanging in the air in the grip of a man stronger than both of us combined. "Is Sorensen okay?"

"That cop? He's alive, if that's what you mean," replied the man holding Yuriko. "But I can't say the same for the little lady if you don't hand over Jake Winters."

"I take it you outrank Connor Winters in the pack?" I asked, stalling as I tried to remember more details from the classes I'd taken years earlier and from books that I had read. Anything that would get me through this without costing any blood. Mine, Yuriko's or Jake's.

"No." I could tell he wasn't happy about the answer. "Why do you ask?"

"Because under pack law, Kimric has no claim on Jake Winters without a federal court order. Connor refused to comply with the challenge for information." This one looked tougher, but listened better as I spoke. "He elected for a Human legal-system redress."

The two Werewolves looked at each other. "Jorge, get Connor. And have Lionel call Lukas. Now!"

The man by the door slipped outside. Yuriko made a muffled noise of complaint and the Werewolf shook her a bit. "We'll all just wait and see about this."

A moment later, the door opened and a new person entered. He was only six feet tall, the shortest of the Kimric pack I'd seen to date, if you didn't include Jake. Lionel, I presumed. He looked out of breath. "What is it?"

"Where's Jorge and Connor?" asked Yuriko's captor, annoyed.

"Jorge is having Connor talk to Lukas." The shorter man glanced at me furtively. "He decided he wasn't happy with the cop."

"Did he hurt him?" Because Sorensen had backed me up, I felt protective. Fair was fair.

"Where's the kid, Carl?" Lionel looked around. He didn't look at me again, nor Yuriko, as he stood there.

"Down that way. I can smell him," said Carl. "He smells sick."

"The woman your pack gave him to liked to tie him up in the garage like an animal," said Yuriko defiantly. Carl and Lionel didn't look happy.

"You didn't answer my question. Did he hurt Sorensen?" I took a step toward my kitchen phone and Lionel was there in a heart-beat, lifting me up by my shirt and looking around for someplace to throw me.

"Put him down!" yelled Yuriko.

"You are in my home on Connor's claim, which he has forfeited. You hurt either of us and not only will we have legal recourse, we can call for blood price." I yelped as Lionel threw me across the room like I was a doll. I heard Yuriko scream as I hit the wall shoulder-first.

"Get the boy. Where the hell are Jorge and Connor?" snarled Carl. Lionel ran toward the bedroom.

I stood, bruised but otherwise uninjured. I debated rushing Carl to help free Yuriko, especially since I had felt the strength of a healthy Lycanthrope in Human form. He could snap her neck without effort.

I had expected the sounds of scuffling or at least wolfish snarling from the bedroom. Instead, Lionel walked back into the living room with Jake meekly following him on all fours. When Jake saw me, he started to move toward me. Then something changed in his eyes. I saw doubt and he continued toward Carl.

"What did they do to him?" asked Lionel in disgust.

"Let's just go." Carl tossed Yuriko toward me and she landed on the couch unhurt. "My apologies for the rough stuff."

The door flew open and Connor and Jorge rushed in. "We can't take him," said Jorge angrily.

"Lukas said bring him." Connor tried to stand taller than Jorge.

"Connor violated challenge. If we bring him back, we violate clan laws," replied Jorge bitterly. "And he's a federal witness. Do you want the feds on our back, too? We're just now getting out of the red."

Carl glared at Connor as if he'd kill him and Connor actually backed down. That was a challenge which they would settle at another time. Carl turned to look at me, next. His scrutiny lingered on me but not as meat for a Werewolf meal. "You weren't lying. My apologies. We will not violate clan law. No matter what Lukas says. Leave him, Lionel. Jorge, Connor, we go, now!"

"We can't disobey Lukas," demanded Connor.

"He'll make us pay." Lionel would clearly rather break pack law than defy his Fenris. "The feds are pussycats by comparison."

"If we violate clan law and any one learns of it, we won't have a clan," argued Carl. "I am not willing to do that."

"You aren't Fenris." Connor gained confidence from Lionel's support. "Lionel, take Jake."

"Jorge?" Carl wanted to know how the lines were drawn.

"Shit, Carl. I'm sorry. I don't want to violate clan law any more than you do, but without *Shab*—." The other Werewolves gave Jorge dangerous stares and he stopped. "I'm with them, only because if we violate clan law by following Lukas's orders, the punishment falls on him before us."

Lionel took Jake outside, but the twenty-year-old Wolfman turned to me one final time with a sorrowful gaze. I raised a hand toward him but he turned away and disappeared outside. Connor raced out after them. Jorge shook his head at Carl angrily and he too disappeared out the door. Carl stood there but took no notice of Yuriko or me, lost in thought. He heard a car start and raised his head.

"I am outranked and outmuscled. If you want to save your Jake, his fate is safe till the next moon," Carl looked at me intently and he finished that one word which Jorge had not. "*Shabatka*."

Then Carl raced out the door. And before Yuriko and I could follow, their vehicle sped off. We rushed outside and saw Sorensen lying on the ground, clutching his arm.

I knelt beside him and saw that he was conscious. "How bad?"

"Broken arm. Those bastards are strong."

"Where the fuck are the feds?" asked Yuriko. I'd never heard her cuss so much. She was rubbing the back of her neck where Carl had held her.

"Oh, they're here." Sorensen looked pointedly toward the street. I followed Yuriko down my cobblestone driveway to Van Ness. A black sedan was on its side, fifteen feet overhead in the neighbor's favorite tulip tree. Two federal agents were trapped inside, pounding on the glass.

CHAPTER NINETEEN

After only a little more than a day with him around, the house felt empty without Jake. I didn't know if I missed him as the wolf or the man, in all likelihood, both. The Werewolf thing, that I didn't miss.

"You couldn't have stopped them," said Agent Shelby as his men finished their forensic investigation of the house and grounds.

I was embarrassed that he mistook my sorrow as something altruistic when I was being plain selfish. "You posting agents outside the house in case they come back?"

"They have what they came for, but," Shelby replied. "Sorensen said you stared down one of the big bad wolves trying to take Jake. You were willing to get your head smashed like an egg-shell protecting the boy." He watched me expectantly.

"What?" I was too tired to do the faux mind-reading bit. And I needed to sort out my own emotions before I could figure out someone else's.

"Why?" the black agent asked bluntly.

At first I thought he was being sarcastic. But the expression on his face was as tightly masked as I'd ever seen it. Did he want to hear that I was falling for our young man-wolf? Or did he want to know why any Human being would risk his life for a virtual stranger—especially a non-Human?

"I took responsibility for Jake. On more than one level by the time Connor came for him." Hearing the truth helped assuage some of my guilt. "He expected me to protect him and I said I would. If I'd let him go without a fight, I would have done worse than failed him. I would have broken my promise to him. The only reason I didn't fight when the other Werewolves came was that they could have snapped Yuriko's neck like a twig." I punched the back of the couch. "What really pisses me off is, I don't know if Jake knows that. I hate more than anything that he left without knowing whether or not I tried to keep him. No, whether or not I *wanted* to keep him."

"Just trying to figure you out, Mosteller." Agent Shelby's square face was somber. "Okay, let's wrap it up and get out of here." He turned to leave but stopped and faced me again. "You okay with Mistry coming by in about an hour or so to talk to you about the case? We're looking into the Kimric group even as we speak. They have to register with our department because of Lycanthropes being so territorial and all. We try to keep wars from breaking out over location. But some packs move around a lot. From what we know so far, this Kimric group has been pretty nomadic. They've apparently moved twice since they last reported in. They are in more than a little bit of trouble with the federal government for that. They won't like having the FBI riding their asses. Well, some of them won't." He broke into a smile and even I couldn't help myself.

"Smart ass," I muttered fighting the grin.

"Mighty fine ass my wife tells me," he chuckled and followed the last of his men out of the house.

I turned in place, searching the corners of my house like I'd never been there before. Yuriko had gone to seek medical attention, but she had promised to stop by on the way home from the hospital. The place was a ghost house, empty of life but my own.

A while later, someone pounded on my front door again. I jumped off the couch, putting down one of my old textbooks on preternatural studies and went to the door. I was itching for a fight, so I didn't even bother with the peep-hole. I just turned the knob and yanked the door open. Agent Shiandra Mistry stood there beaming at me. Behind her were two more federal agents looking around cautiously.

"Trouble?" I asked.

One of the agents, a woman I didn't know, grimaced at me. She was tall, about my height, with a square build, not especially attractive. Her face was too long, her nose hooked. The only thing handsome about her was her dark burgundy hair and it wasn't natural. I'd have guessed she was Italian, but it could have been something else European.

"Worse. Reporters," she said with dry humor. "Agent Tina Clark."

I shook the offered hand. With the two women was an African American agent I recognized. Mistry introduced us anyway. "Devon Mosteller, meet Agent Palmer." I remembered Agent Palmer from my first federal case. He was cute but serious. Oh and straight. We nodded at each other.

I stepped aside and Agents Mistry and Clark came inside. Palmer remained outside, shaking his head as Clark shut the door behind her. The burgundy haired agent studied me with open curiosity.

"I imagine you have a lot of questions." Mistry performed a casual security clearance of my kitchen-living room as she moved through the house.

"Can I offer you something to drink? Tea, soda, coffee?"

"Oh, no, nothing, thank you," she said politely for them both.

"Fine, then have a seat and let's get down to the questions."

"Is this alright?" Mistry sat at the center of the couch. It forced me to sit on the loveseat, to avoid being pressed against her, but Clark remained standing.

"Sure, as long as you're comfortable."

"Very nice. Go ahead, ask your questions."

"How did you learn so much about the Drow to become an expert?" It was meant to be conversational, but I was curious. "I've tried finding text books on them but there's just nothing out there—non-fiction that is. I just did a Google search and the articles were less than overflowing with details."

"My people helped exterminate them in Asia over the decades, so I took a personal interest. I've made a few social contacts through the years, but it wasn't easy." She shook her head. "They like to think that they are misunderstood. 'Wouldn't you hide if you were persecuted all the time?'"

"Not me. It's like being gay. I refuse to be locked in a closet and keep my life secret." She didn't react badly to that statement, so I continued. "Too many people have given their lives so that I can have the freedom to be known for all my facets, not just the ones mainstream America once thought were normal."

"Which is supposedly why the Drow lobbied as they did for privacy as well as protection under the law," responded Mistry. "The only books you can find are legends and myths. Some think the Drow are secretive because they have a stash of ancient gold and gems. Others want to tap into their supposedly dark and demonic magic. I have to take what my sources tell me at face value but like all Elves, they consider misdirection an art."

"The murder victim is part Drow, right?" I asked. Shiandra nodded. "So where would a part Drow be raised? The Drow do not tolerate their own hybrids. Who would have raised her?"

"Probably her mother's family."

"You didn't say her mother. You said her mother's family," I leaned forward. "Why?"

"That's an easy question." The dark agent smiled. "Because female Drow ova aren't compatible with Human sperm. The best of our kind's swimmers would never be able to breach the wall."

"So a male Drow would have to impregnate a Human."

"Exactly. However, if a Human mother carries a part-Drow baby to term, without mystical protection for her womb, the child's innate magics will usually destroy the mother during the birthing process. And, no, the Drow do not accept mix-breeds. They consider them something of an abomination. If such a hybrid were to survive to puberty, however, he, or in this case, *she*, could petition the enclave for acceptance by right of survival. Survival is rare, so the child is normally sent to live with her mother's family. They do not kill children. None of the High Elves do."

"But a mix-breed living with Humans would never learn how to do Drow magic," I stated for clarification. "And you think her a second-generation? Completely raised among Humans?"

"Learning magic, no, absolutely not. She would grow up only learning Human things. Why?"

"Our murder victim had some Drow-spelled items. In fact, she had spells of warding throughout the entire house, but only on doors and windows."

"Why that's silly, anything that wanted to get to her could just go through the walls. Why would she—? Oh, I see." Mistry stopped, her eyes wide.

"She was thinking like a Human."

"Yes. So, where did she learn Drow magic if she was raised by Humans? If she'd been raised by the Drow, she'd never have made such a basic mistake." The East Indian agent stood and paced.

Clark focused on the other woman immediately. "Any idea why that might be?"

"I would have thought that the Drow would keep an eye on her. While some of the other Elves have prospered in this age of forced integration with Humans, the Drow have not. Two to three Light Elves are born a year. Perhaps twenty to thirty Lesser Elves. But the Drow have not seen a new birth in twenty years. Nothing full-blooded anyway according to my sources."

"How many Drow have died in those twenty years?" My voice went soft. The loss of any species was appalling to me.

"That's just it. Ordinarily, none would die in that time. For them, twenty years isn't so long. But through accident, Human interference and political infighting, twelve Drow have died in the last twenty years. That is unheard of."

"How many survive in total?"

"The Drow enclaves are small and spread out, although they all must report to the Drow High Queen or her advisors a few times each century. The numbers aren't exact, but there are less than two thousand remaining Drow in the entire world."

"Does the government realize they are endangered?" I asked.

"The Drow are afraid that if the government knew how few of them remained, that they might simply eradicate them out of fear. It happened forty years ago in Eastern Europe and Asia. Thousands were killed, entire enclaves wiped out in a mass genocide. The remaining Drow, already secretive, took to guarding themselves dearly. It's why I got interested."

"I had no idea."

Mistry shook her head. "No one does except the Drow and the responsible parties. People may fear the Drow, but China and India and Russia would face public retribution if Humans knew that they were capable of killing an entire race of people, especially children and so preciously rare pregnant women. They already have poor Human rights records."

"So, do the Drow know anything about this case?" I asked. "Can you find out?"

"I don't know," her expression grew thoughtful. "I've been away from most of my contacts for a few years."

"Then I need to talk to the Drow directly."

"They won't!" she exclaimed startled.

"The Drow may be involved in this. We don't know that they aren't. Someone taught this woman Drow magics. Someone who wasn't this woman cast very complex Drow magics and those magics are now gone. Someone knows the identity of this woman, but we don't."

"I'm positive that the ritual magic used to kill her was only meant to look like Drow. It wasn't Drow," countered the buxom agent.

"That doesn't mean that the Drow don't have information we could use. Can you help me get to them?"

"My sources probably won't see you. Not even for me."

"Where is the closest group?" I demanded. "Modesto area?"

"No, those are Wood Elves. Sacramento," she said. "There is a Fey bar there, small and not very well known. Humans occasionally come with their preternatural friends. There are a Drow or two that I know frequent the place. Or rather, used to. They might still. I've been out of contact, like I said, for some time."

"Well, then. You and I are going to Sacramento," I declared.

CHAPTER TWENTY-FOUR

"It would have been faster to fly," I complained. Agent Gunnerson drove while Shelby rode shotgun. In the back next to me was Agent Mistry who had been pleasant company so far on the drive to Sacramento. "I can afford it."

"It's only three hours." Gunnerson's foot was heavy on the gas as we zipped along Interstate 99 North. I could see the grin on his face in the rear view mirror. "Two if traffic's not too bad."

"Don't kill Mr. Mosteller in the process," said Agent Shelby, his expression light.

"What about you, me and Shiandra?" Gunnerson feigned shock.

"We're always acceptable casualties in the game," said Shelby quietly and Gunnerson grew uncharacteristically quiet. I wondered what he was referring to but didn't ask.

"The car has magical shielding and there are a few special tools we couldn't bring on board a plane," continued Shelby responding to my complaint. "The chief said if you are going to ask the Drow some questions that we weren't to let you out of our sight."

"You know anything about this place?" I asked.

"We are aware of this particular establishment, *Iron's Bane*. The Drow occasionally frequent the place. We keep tabs on the preternaturals within the limits of the law."

"With the limited manpower the budget allows us." Gunnerson seemed far too happy driving through traffic at least twenty miles over the speed limit. I assumed the federal plates precluded police intervention, but it would be interesting to see the blonde agent pulled over.

"Then why send so many agents with us?" asked Mistry, motioning at the sedan behind us.

Gunnerson swerved around a ratty old van. "You might need protection. Devon is operating as a federal consultant and we don't want him going missing or with his face grafted into the trunk of a tree."

"You've seen that before?" I asked.

He practically glowed with nervous energy. "Oh man, yeah! It was freakin' awesome! The front half of this guy was fused with the tree. The M.E. declared he died of suffocation. They didn't kill him before they stuck him in the tree!"

"Wow," I muttered sarcastically and leaned back on the seat. Would I have been able to unravel the magic and get myself free? Somehow I doubted it. If I couldn't See it, how could I manipulate it?

"That wouldn't be Drow magic, Ivan." Mistry tapped the blonde on the shoulder in rebuke. "Wood Elves are known for that sort of merging of creatures. Not the Drow."

"It was natural magic, something only a non-Human could have done," added Shelby. "It's in cold case, but the Drow are still on the list. Wood Elves and High Elves, Hell, if it has 'Elf' after it, it's a suspect."

"Well, I don't know how comfortable you guys are gonna be there," muttered Mistry.

"I have no trouble with gay bars," said Gunnerson with a grin.

"A gay bar?" That put my dealing with any Drow in an entirely different perspective. "As long as you don't cramp my style," I teased the agents.

"Oh, I don't think *we're* gonna cramp your style," snickered Gunnerson. Even Shelby grinned at me.

"What's so funny?" I asked.

Neither of the federal agents would reply, but Agent Mistry finally turned and looked at me. Her eyes were playful as she answered.

"*Iron's Bane* is a lesbian bar."

CHAPTER TWENTY

I must have been fairly lost in thought, because when Agent Shelby's phone rang loudly in the car, I jumped. Mistry had actually fallen asleep or had pretended to. Her face was away from me against the car window and she didn't stir. Gunnerson was still speeding down 99, weaving around traffic.

Shelby listened for a few minutes. When he hung up, he turned to me. "Good news and bad news."

"Start with the good, I guess," I answered. Gunnerson looked in the rear view mirror at me and shook his head, as if I'd made the wrong choice.

"We found Kimric and Jake. They set up in the Squaw Valley area just above Orange Cove."

"I know the area. One of my best friends grew up in Orange Cove. Illegal aliens mostly and some first and second generation Mexicans. His grandparents still live there." Sonny Perez, one of my circle of five, now in San Diego. I didn't bother to mention that his grandparents were some of those illegal immigrants.

"The bad news is that Jake's supposed to undergo some ritual the next full moon."

"We knew that. Did they find out what?" I asked.

"Two agents went up to try and claim Jake as a federal witness. Kimric was waiting with two high-powered lawyers, which the agents thought was pretty strange."

"Why?"

"They were living like trailer trash in a few caravans and a single wide mobile home. Lots of junk on the five acre lot, but Kimric last reported twenty-three members. They must be sleeping three to a bed."

"So how could they hire powerful attorneys," I finished for him. He nodded. "And why try and keep Jake?"

"The thing is, the attorneys were prepared. They had case-law and a court order. That as a witness, not suspected of the actual crime, we couldn't hold Jake just for his own protection. The pack had the right to protect him. Furthermore, they found a judge who agreed that since Jake hadn't seen the murder, he wasn't actually a witness. How the fuck did they know he hadn't seen the murder. He can't talk in shifted form, right?"

"Lycanthropes are secretive second only to the Drow." I glanced at Mistry but she was still leaning against the glass, eyes closed. "We know a lot about their biology and stuff because that's not so private. Some Humans have had better luck studying some of their basic cultural rules. But all in all, Werewolves still don't like the moonless."

"The moonless?" asked Agent Gunnerson as he veered between two narrowly spaced vehicles. I gripped the arm of the door.

"It's a derogatory term that Lycanthropes use for non-Lycanthropes. We don't change at the cycle of the moon. They consider us inferior for that."

"Hey, if I could bench press a car, I'd consider ordinary men inferior too," retorted Gunnerson. "So we're moonless. Learn something new."

"You're saying you don't know?" Shelby gave Gunnerson a look.

"No, I mean," I looked at the sleeping Agent Mistry again. She had said Jake should have been able to speak in Werewolf form, but

Melanie had said that something had gone wrong. I gave him my answer. "My understanding is that they can speak in Werewolf form. But I'm also sure that Jake couldn't talk. Or he would have tried before they took him. Melanie, my friend the preternatural vet, said Mistry messed up the spell because he didn't look like a Werewolf should. Anatomically. But can the pack use Werewolf metaphysics to communicate with him? That I have no idea. I'd say it might be possible. But I don't know for sure."

"So we can't touch him?" asked Gunnerson.

"How many days till the next full moon?" I asked.

Shelby took a deep breath before replying. "Three if you include today."

"And today is almost over. Not much time to learn everything I can to get him back," I muttered. Agent Shelby started dialing his phone and I leaned back in my seat again. I rested my head against the thickly padded head rest and looked out the window.

My pulse raced and my palms grew sweaty. I'd had nightmares as a child about wandering into the center of an empty, fog surrounded place with a single large boulder jutting out of the ground. Then suddenly a pack of angry Werewolves appeared out of the mist and circled me. I knew they were going to kill me. When they attacked, I would wake in a panic. My old nightmare was about to become a reality.

CHAPTER TWENTY-ONE

"We're here." Agent Shelby's hand was on my shoulder. I must have dozed off after all.

"I'm up," I answered, shaking myself awake. Agent Mistry was sitting up staring out the window. I followed her gaze. We were parallel parked on a street in an older district of Sacramento. Weathered homes and newer shops adjoined to each other. "Where is it?"

Agent Gunnerson looked around confused. "This is the address." A window-boarded, former barbershop, too small to house a bar faced us. Agent Shelby tapped Gunnerson on the temple and Mistry grinned.

"Oh, yeah," Gunnerson touched the side of his sunglasses. I saw the flicker of a red light for just a moment. "There we go."

I turned to the empty barbershop and switched into magic mode. The world turned into shades of blue except for the barbershop. The mystic neon colors practically blinded me. "It's bespelled."

"Exactly," said Agent Shelby. "Invisible. In case of Anti-Preternaturalists."

"They keep well-meaning but annoying Humans out, too," said Mistry.

"Well, is it just hidden? Or shielded as well?" I asked.

"Shielded, but we've got it taken care of," said Shelby smugly. We got out of the car as another black sedan pulled up behind us. I glanced at Agent Mistry and she removed the heavy overcoat she'd been wearing the entire drive.

"Devon, can you hold this?" Underneath, she wore a very short, black evening gown which showed off her long, slim yet athletic legs. Her exposed brown skin showed she worked out just enough to be firm but feminine. The top of the sleeveless gown stopped just above the center of her breasts and ran under her arms to the back. The very top of her areolas showed above the dress-line, like dark chocolate on her brown skin. It was plain she wore nothing underneath the dress.

"Holy…!" I exclaimed, staring at her partially revealed breasts.

"Why, thank you, Devon," said Mistry. She had called me Devon twice. "Coming from a gay man, that reaction is very flattering."

"Devon?" I asked.

Agent Mistry really was the prettiest Indian woman I'd ever seen, and I had watched quite a few Bollywood films. "I'm your date for the evening. I can't call you 'Mr. Mosteller' in the bar. And please, call me 'Shiandra.'"

"My date?"

Agent Shelby folded his arms and smirked. "Yep."

"The bar is shielded against men entering solo," answered Gunnerson, unhappily.

"One man per woman." Shelby nodded at the other car. Agent Clark, dressed more conservatively, came up to us. Shelby extended his arm to Clark like a gentleman. She looked at it dubiously.

"Remember, it's 'Shiandra.'" The beautiful agent took my arm. "Shall we enter?"

I happily accepted Shiandra's lead and followed her through the magical façade into the dimly lighted bar. "You really do look amazing. Aren't you worried you'll be the most popular girl with the girls?" What I would have ordinarily asked in a low whisper, given the volume of the music, had to be considerably louder.

"You assume that I wouldn't want to be." Shiandra practically had to shout. I looked at her and returned her grin.

"*Et tu*, Shiandra?" I said. She was a gay like me.

We passed through a narrow space before reaching the entrance to the main bar. A short, pear-shaped woman with an 80's Mohawk and with more piercings on her face than I could quickly register sat behind a counter and stared at us. Her eyes flickered from me to rest fully upon Agent Mistry's peeking nipples.

"Wow," she said in a husky voice. Her ears could accommodate so many piercing because they were twice as large as the average Human's and naturally fluted on the outer edge. I had a chance to study her eyes briefly before she tore them away from Shiandra's lovely breasts. She raised them to the Indian woman's rich, brown eyes. "He with you?"

Shiandra appraised me frankly for a moment. "Yes, but only as a friend. He's family, too."

The large Fey woman actually made eye-contact with me. "The boys don't usually like to come here."

"I happen to prefer the company of lesbians to gay men," I said truthfully. Right answer, because she grinned and I saw two pair of pointy eye-teeth. Interesting but a bit intimidating in a lover. I was reminded of Jake as I had last seen him. They had made me nervous as well. At least, the thought of them sinking into my throat and tearing out the flesh.

"You're the first I've met," replied the door-woman. "But welcome then. As you can see," she pointed up at a handwritten sign above her head, "bare-breasts are free, men are twenty, sorry luv, and everyone else is ten."

"Not a problem," I answered amiably. The first gay bar I had ever hung out in had refused service to women for a couple of years.

Although illegal, they had gotten away with it. I had just come out and was young enough and cute enough that the owner had hoped to bed me, which gave me some latitude in getting my female friends served. That discrimination was still prevalent in the entire gay community, so I had no rancor at its reversal. "Gotta have standards."

I handed her thirty but she only took the twenty. "Her pips are showing enough to make the women happy. No charge," she chuckled then, repeating my joke, "Gotta have standards. You're welcome back anytime, as long as you don't start too many fights inside." She leaned forward conspiratorially at me, although her eyes were on Shiandra's bosom. "If you do want to start a fight, there's a tall, greenish chick with hair down to her butt!" She winked at me but both eyes stayed focused on Shiandra.

"Come along, you big flirt!" Shiandra grabbed me and pulled me into the main bar. She put a hand on the large woman as we passed. Despite the dim lighting, I swear the Fey woman turned a shade of aquamarine.

The main room of the bar was considerably larger than I had expected. It was packed, but we could maneuver. A couple of tables were actually free and we headed toward one. Most of the women were sprawled on lounge chairs or on the dance floor. It wasn't immediately apparent that they weren't Human.

"That was very early 80's, don't you think?" asked Shiandra as she looked around.

She looked back at the door woman and waved. Still no sign of Agent Clark and Agent Shelby. "Oh, her hair. Yeah. I understand it's coming back into fashion. Usually though it's the young 'uns."

"Baby butches with Mohawks?" She sighed. "I thought I'd survived ever having to see that again."

"You are actually quite charming for a fed, Shiandra," I said as Agent Mistry steered me over to one of the tall, round tables with four stools. Shiandra put her hand to the table to start to sit when a voice shouted out to us from the table.

"Sorry, Beautiful, but it's taken," said a very small female voice.

Shiandra pulled her hand back as if she had been stung. Sitting on what I had taken to be an ashtray were two doll-sized women. Female Sprites of some kind. They buzzed their wings the way a cricket vibrates its legs as they sat talking. I had thought that all sentient Fey were wingless, but I guessed I was wrong.

"My fault," Shiandra responded graciously and was rewarded by a flirtatious smile from both Sprites. The Indian agent took my hand and led me to the only other empty table. She carefully inspected it before sitting down. I preferred standing and took a position between her and a beam that supported the ceiling.

"What's keeping your fellow agents?" I asked Shiandra. She put a hand to my arm and I looked around.

A waitress came up to us and beamed a smile at us both. Nice to know I wasn't going to get the cold shoulder from every woman. The Fey were more territorial than Humans, although nothing on the scale of Lycanthropes.

"What can I get you two hotties?" I couldn't place her accent. She set her tray on the table and checked her cash box as she asked.

"I'll have Absolut and pineapple," I said. The waitress nodded but continued to arrange her bills so that they didn't stick out of the small plastic container.

"And you, doll?"

"Sex on the beach, please." Shiandra smiled at the waitress who picked up her tray and headed for the bar.

"Human enough." It was more a request for confirmation than a statement of certainty.

"Lycan I was thinking." Shiandra surveyed the bar as she spoke. "Did she smell Lycan on you?"

"What?"

"She seemed too friendly, even in a bar like this." She turned to look me in the eyes with frank curiosity. Too many people looked at me like I was something slightly out of focus. "If she smelled fellow Lycanthropes, it would account for her friendliness. She didn't flirt with either of us, so it wasn't sex."

"I—How would she smell Lycan on me?" I stuttered and she grinned.

"He was a little hottie. And I could feel the sexual tension between you guys. You were in the file. Him I guessed. My gaydar is pretty good, too."

"But I've showered since then," I retorted, feeling the blood rise to my cheeks. "Twice."

"Hm, gay men are usually fastidious about cleaning themselves. If you were straight, I'd have said twice wasn't enough to wash the smell of him off of you. Not completely."

"I've been accused of having heterosexual tendencies." I laughed at myself.

"I like you, Devon. That's good. I'm considering signing onto the Fresno division permanently. Right now I'm just on loan because of the Drow angle. What little is known about Drow magic *officially*, I know." She stopped speaking and gaped for a second. I followed the line of her vision.

Strolling toward us were Agents Clark and Gunnerson. The lean, white-haired Gunnerson was shirtless and his tie was wrapped around his neck like a collar. Clark walked in front of him, slightly embarrassed, searching frantically until she spotted us. She bee-lined for us as if trying to get away from Gunnerson. I looked down the line of his body and saw that he also wasn't wearing shoes.

"Aren't shoes mandatory in California bars?" I whispered to Mistry. She looked down and nodded.

"I hope you realize how mortifying this is!" Clark dropped onto the stool I had ignored. Gunnerson strolled up behind her and smacked her on the butt, grinning.

"What's up with the—er, lack of clothes?" I asked, admiring the definition of his sparsely haired chest. His shoulders were covered with freckles but otherwise his skin was flawless over very lean muscles.

"Clark made a comment about refusing to enter with anyone looking like a fed after she bothered to dress up," replied Gunnerson with wicked glee. "Since Shelby refused to remove his jacket and tie, I was volunteered. I'm not dressed like a fed and we're in."

Clark smacked the table. The waitress appeared as if on cue and set down our drinks. She looked at Gunnerson, down at his feet, and then at Clark. "What'll it be?"

"Nothing for me," snarled the embarrassed female agent.

"Just a coke," said Gunnerson, and the waitress went away.

"Why are you so angry?" Shiandra asked Clark. The burgundy-haired woman just sat there and sulked, looking away from us all.

Gunnerson leaned on the table. "She's mad because I told the butch at the door that I was into taller broads."

"That can't be all," prompted Mistry.

"No, it certainly wasn't!" sputtered Clark.

"Well, I did mention to the butch that Clark was so wild in bed that I had to tied her down to keep from getting my whole back and chest clawed to shreds," answered Gunnerson with innocent eyes. "Just keeping the money-collector entertained."

"Oh, my god!" I chortled, which earned me a nasty look from Clark.

"Oh, lighten up, Tina." Shiandra startled Agent Clark with her tone. "Be proud of a woman's sexual prowess. Experience should bring such things as greater skill in expressing passion, not the loss of passion."

"I am not that casual with my references to sex, especially in public," stammered the other woman. Speaking deflated her anger a bit. She looked at Gunnerson's silky naked chest and his tiny, pink nipples but then the blood rushed to her face again. "Though," she said slowly, "I wouldn't mind trying to wear out a fit, muscular man like that with a couple of days of non-stop love making."

The blonde agent blushed halfway down his chest, a look of panic on his face. Agent Clark let loose a nervous chuckle, which we all joined. "Better?"

We nodded at her.

"You deserved that Gunnerson." Shiandra resumed searching the room with her eyes. "You see any yet?"

"Yeah, far corner of the dance floor," said Gunnerson, suddenly serious.

"Any what?" asked Tina.

"Incoming." The blonde picked up Shiandra's drink and sniffed it, pretending not to notice the two women who approached.

The eyes of half the patrons of the bar were on them as well. I saw fear in those looks. All three agents tensed up, but no one spoke. The Drow, like all Elves, had extremely acute hearing.

The women were both about five-two and wore matching hair styles—long knotted pony-tails that curled at the end. The woman leading the strutting duo wore a bright red gown which flowed and hid her feet, held up by a strap which went behind her neck. Where the ends of the strap met the rest of her dress, the top was cut into a deep vee, revealing her small, pert cleavage. Black pearls adorned her neck with matching earrings. She wore a band on her forehead of copper, with inlayed intricate designs.

Her companion wore a green, tightly-fitted dress that shimmered in the dim bar light. It draped down her hips to mid-thigh, while the top encircled her throat. A Mandarin collar, with a flower-shaped opening, revealed her slightly more ample bust-line. Her feet were visible in dressy, low, black heels. Her earrings were white diamonds that seemed to be imbued with their own light source. The Drow were dark complexioned, like Shiandra, but unmistakably Fey. Their eyes were the blue of the water of an undisturbed lagoon and they wore lipstick the color of freshly spilt blood.

"Hello." The Drow in the red dress took Shiandra's hand and raised it to her lips. Her eyes ignored the rest of us, though her companion in green briefly studied our entire group haughtily. "You haven't been here before."

"How do you know?" asked Shiandra with flirtatious denial and careful disinterest.

"Because I never forget such beauty. I have never seen you before." She smiled as if she knew Shiandra would fall before her charms. "I am Lu'urna. This is my sister Ma'alma."

"I'm Shiandra. This is Devon, Ivan, and Tina." Shiandra motioned to each of us as she offered the women our names. Lu'urna acknowledged each of us with eye-contact, barely pausing when she came upon Agent Clark. "You like men."

"Might be fun to tempt," drawled Ma'alma. She glanced at her sister. "If she were plausibly attractive?"

"Come, sister. She is not worth that trouble." Apparently these Drow didn't bother with straight women. That was refreshing but inconvenient.

The two Elves turned to walk away when Shiandra stood up and put a hand on Lu'urna's bare shoulder. The Drow woman stopped and turned, placing her hand over Shiandra's where it touched her skin. "Wait, please."

"I do not normally wait for anyone. What do I gain if I wait?" The Drow woman's eyes gleamed with more than lust. She was dangerous. Their walking away had been a ploy of sorts.

"What would it take for you to sit with us," asked Shiandra cautiously.

Lu'urna looked at her sister with a cat-ate-the-canary smile and then turned back to Shiandra. "Get rid of the others, for a start."

Gunnerson spoke up, "Not a problem. Come along, sweetheart." He took Clark by the hand, helping her stand, and pulled the angry agent away from the table. They moved to the bar about fifteen feet away. Lu'urna and Ma'alma scowled as they passed by. Then the smile returned to the sisters' faces.

"Devon stays. I am not permitted to be out without a male companion." Shiandra stared at the Elves, but they did not challenge her.

"Very well, cultures are different among our species, not just across them. He may remain if he behaves." Lu'urna did not smile.

"Now, please sit down so we can talk," said Shiandra.

"Ah, I said for a start," replied Lu'urna, stroking Agent Mistry's arm.

"What else do you want, then?" I asked.

Lu'urna stopped, her fingertips resting on the Indian woman's flesh. She looked at me as if I was a dog that had begun speaking. "Why must you be here?" she asked me. "Go join your little friends at the bar."

"He has questions," answered Shiandra, truthfully. But there was nothing else to do. I had assumed that the federal agents could force the Drow to comply. Or that I would be able to persuade them on my own. Neither was the case.

"Why should I waste my time answering his questions?" purred Lu'urna. She leaned in and ran her lips along the line of Shiandra's ear without touching it. She caressed the woman with her breath. Agent Mistry shivered, despite herself.

"Because if you don't answer my questions, the federal government is going to accuse the Drow of using blood magic in a murder." I dropped any attempts at coyness. "And that would be an inexcusable violation of your agreement with the United States. I believe they threatened concentration camps if you should ever violate your end of the deal?"

Lu'urna stood up straight and removed her fingers from Shiandra. The two Drow looked at each other, uncertainty bleeding into their arrogant expressions. My fingers tingled in response to mystic energy. The Drow were communicating magically.

"You think because you use magic to keep us out of the conversation that it's private?" I asked. It was a bluff—one-hundred percent.

I saw the flicker of surprise before Lu'urna regained control of herself. She glared at Agent Mistry. "Are you even interested in women? Or are you like your friend?"

Shiandra smiled and put her own lips close to the Drow woman's ear. Putting heavy aspiration in her words, she whispered, "There's no part of a woman's body that I don't like to caress with my tongue, if that's what you mean by being 'interested.'"

I watched with amazement as Lu'urna's eyes rolled up in her head, her heavily lashed lids fluttered half closed and her mouth tightened with a swallow. She licked her lips. Shiandra had hit her mental g-spot.

"Is that an offer?" Ma'alma did not smile, but there was a look of anticipation. The sisters shared their women.

"The offer is this—answer my questions and I'll do my best to make sure the Drow are not blamed for something they didn't do," I said through gritted teeth.

"Is that the only offer?" Lu'urna gazed at Mistry with sour eyes, putting on the pretense of disinterest.

"Yes, that is the only offer." Shiandra looked down at her hands and then back up again, very somber. "My body is never a bartering chip. It's given out of desire or love or not at all."

Ma'alma put her hands on Lu'urna's shoulders, her expression very unfriendly. "My sister is not used to being denied. You may regret this. We will not answer your questions because you threaten us."

"I wonder how your leaders will feel when the Drow are accused of violating their treaty with the American government because two petty lipstick lesbians refused to answer some questions," I said.

"You government will not dare to take your word over the Drow Queen's denial. Not without proof," sneered Ma'alma.

Gunnerson was at the bar still talking to a trio of women, but Agent Clark had disappeared. Were the women with Gunnerson happy or angry at whatever he was saying? He seemed unaware that Clark had disappeared. I doubted the Elves would resort to magic, but we'd need his help if they did. Agent Shelby was trapped outside.

"If none of you remember why you're even here?" suggested Ma'alma. Lu'urna had remained silent since Mistry had refused her her body. I had thought that the silent sister was the dominant, but possibly I was wrong.

The Drow woman in green raised one hand as if to gesture when someone grabbed her wrist and jerked her around. The bartender looked furious and Ma'alma flinched.

"You know the rules! Magic is strictly forbidden here!" The Lycan snarled and motioned with her free hand. I looked over my shoulder and the door-person strode over. "Throw these two out of here, eighty-sixed for unauthorized magic use."

"My pleasure," said the chunky woman. She grabbed each Drow woman by one arm and pulled them toward the door. Ma'alma tried to use her free hand against the butch Fey, shaping arcane symbols in the air, but the pierced woman flared with gold and Ma'alma shrieked in pain. "Tsk, tsk. You never felt the feedback power of a Saggit Fairy?"

"We need to follow them," I whispered to Mistry. The federal agent stood but the waitress put her hand out to stop us.

"Sorry, can't let you," explained the Lycanthrope. "Bar rules. They broke the rules so they get thrown out, but you can't follow in case revenge is on your mind."

"We're federal agents," explained Mistry.

The cocktail waitress shook her head. "Doesn't matter. Bar rules supersede all other rules here," she smirked at Shiandra, "Without a court order, that is."

"There goes our chance to find out who's behind it," muttered Shiandra.

"Not necessarily," said a figure sitting on a nearby couch. Her cuddling partner stood and swaggered onto the dance floor alone. A muscular butch woman with a very feminine face wearing only daisy duke jeans. The figure on the couch was tiny by comparison, but Human-sized. "Most of us are grateful that you rid us of those two. And if it's the Drow you seek, there is one more."

The slim woman rose from the couch. Her startling violet eyes, set in deep, chocolate-colored skin, studied us in turn. Hair buzzed to a number two length did not hide delicately feminine features. One ear had a golden hoop at its base, though both of the pointed tips were capped in silver.

"I am Na'lima," said the petite Drow, barely four-foot-seven. Where the two sisters were shapely, she was thin. "You've made some serious enemies in those two."

"You will talk with us?" I asked Na'lima in surprise.

"This is one of the few places our kind can come to relax and express ourselves. Ma'alma and Lu'urna are, shall we say, more than mildly sadistic. Unfortunately, they cannot be banned for anything other than unauthorized magic."

"Why would they risk it?" asked Mistry. "I've heard of Ma'alma before, she wasn't supposed to be stupid."

Na'lima raised her hand to shyly hide a smirk. "Mental communication is not considered unauthorized use of magic here.

Perhaps Ma'alma was given bad advice because her sister was denied this lovely creature." She reached out, but stopped her hand inches from Shiandra's arm, remembering her manners.

"Or she *thought* it was her sister," suggested Shiandra with a smile.

Na'lima's own smile brightened but she tried to hide it under her dark hand. Agent Mistry reached out and gently held the thin woman's wrist, pulling Na'lima's hand away from her mouth. The Drow was only slightly darker than the agent.

"You should never hide such a beautiful smile."

Na'lima blushed, but an unpleasant look crossed her delicate features. "I told you I will answer your questions. You do not need to feed me false praise."

Shiandra did not let go of Na'lima's wrist as she leaned toward the petite Drow woman. "I never give false praise. Your smile is beautiful. I cannot have been the only one to have told you this."

Na'lima searched Agent Mistry's eyes for some sign of deception. After a moment, she let the gentle humor return to her eyes. Her lips were slow to follow, however. "My apologies. I am reminded constantly by Ma'alma and her sister how ugly I am by Drow standards. To be told that my smile is beautiful now makes me suspicious. You can see why we are glad to be rid of them here. Back home I must endure their torture."

"Should we talk here, or—?" I asked. Na'lima looked at me and her smile returned.

"There are no friends to those two here. That I speak with you will not get back to them unless either you or I reveal it. Come, the couch is free."

Na'lima motioned gracefully toward the empty cushions. Her extended arm had so little meat on the bones that I winced. I had never seen a Drow so undernourished. Not even Jake had looked so gaunt.

We moved to the couch as a group, except Gunnerson who was still talking animatedly with women at the bar. His audience now numbered five. I hoped he wasn't going to get us into a fight.

"What is it you wish to know?" asked Na'lima with a shy tilt of her head.

"There was a murder in Fresno," I began, but the petite woman interrupted.

"Forgive me, but who do you represent?"

"Shiandra and," I nodded over at the blonde man at the bar, "Ivan, are FBI. I'm an outside consultant."

"What is it that you do—?" she asked.

"Devon."

"What is it that you do, Devon, that the FBI cannot get from their own agents?" Her slow way of speaking matched her shy exterior.

"He is a *sovenjor*," interjected Shiandra. Na'lima's eyes widened and she looked at the beautiful agent as if she were jesting.

"You can affect magic?" whispered Na'lima. I nodded. "Then— then perhaps it is not I who should answer your questions."

"What, because I'm a *sovenjor* you won't talk to me?" I asked slightly offended.

"No, not that I will not, Devon. One of the elders of my people would be best suited to answer your questions. And in return, perhaps would ask a favor of you."

"Where do we find this elder?" asked Shiandra.

"Our enclave is actually not too far from here," replied the thin Drow.

"In the city?"

"It is not always convenient to find places in the country to build a life, away from the eyes of nosy Humans. Sometimes, one must improvise."

"How far is not too far?" I asked.

"Five minutes actually," said Na'lima raising her hand automatically to hide her grin. "If you don't mind walking that far."

CHAPTER TWENTY-TWO

On our way to the door, the Saggit Fairy stopped me. She stuffed something in my hand, "You picked a better fight than I could have hoped for." I glanced at it, afraid it might get her in trouble. It was a free pass to the bar.

"Thanks."

We returned to the street and found Agent Shelby looking bored, leaning against the front of his black sedan. I saw no evidence of the two sisters. I switched to the Sight and looked for spells.

"What are you doing?" asked Shelby.

"Looking for booby-traps the sisters might have left behind."

Na'lima stood next to me. "They fear the elders enough that whatever vengeance they might wish to exact on you, they would not do so in public."

"What sisters? What booby-traps?" asked Shelby as Na'lima started to walk down the street. Shiandra fell in line beside him and quietly recounted events to the black agent.

"My people are very mistrusting, Devon. In this case, there is that which is to our advantage. We have need of your help and it may be used as leverage to get the elders to cooperate," explained Na'lima.

"Why are you telling me all this," I asked, suspicious of her frank honesty.

"Because, like you, I do not fit in and am judged for it. I want to live in the Human world, where individual differences are better embraced."

"I'm glad you said 'better,'" I muttered.

She paused after a few blocks and we stood in front of a large, two-story Victorian set between two similar homes, each connected to the next by tall wooden fences. I saw nothing especially unique about the place.

"This it?" asked Agent Gunnerson from behind me.

Na'lima looked at me quizzically. Things didn't always appear as they really were and I could tell that this was a test. I switched into the Sight and the entire block blazed with an intricately woven pattern. Thick lines crisscrossed from the ground to the space above the tallest house. From where I stood, I could not tell if the mystic field spread any further beyond that point, because it seemed to go on forever.

I studied the lines. The nodes of the strands were woven into the arc of a secret door where this house's entrance stood. Finer strands of energy were spun into intricate designs overlapping the wood of the door. I stepped forward, climbing the stairs that led to the porch and approached it. I could feel Na'lima behind me and assumed the others followed.

I focused on the weaving of the door spell, looking for the places where the strands could come free. I suspected I would not be welcomed if I actually dismantled the spell, but I guessed from Na'lima's attitude that I was supposed to find my way in without damaging it. I'd never tried to dismantle a spell without destroying it. I didn't know if I could.

"What are you doing?" Gunnerson was still close behind me.

"Trying to unlock the door."

Aha! I saw a place where the strands were not actually woven together, but held together by a slender thread of another kind. I reached out my hand, a subconscious habit I'd never been able to break myself of and pulled the tiny thread of mystical energy free. The thread it had held in place slid away from its anchor and hung limp in the pattern.

"Whoa!" Gunnerson had his sunglasses on again and he must have seen something vaguely like what I saw. I'd have to borrow them sometime to compare biology and technology. The glasses, however, wouldn't let him manipulate whatever he saw.

"Nicely done." Na'lima walked through the opened portal as I went back to normal sight. She paused in what in fact a tunnel of dark rock and motioned for me to follow. I looked over my shoulder and Agent Shelby nodded. I entered the tunnel, my footsteps echoed by the federal agents behind me.

Na'lima waited until I caught up with her before she resumed walking. The tunnel was short and we stepped out of it into a forested night sky. Two shadows rose from the vegetation that framed the tunnel mouth and a silver blade was at my throat before I could react. Na'lima stepped forward and put a hand on the Drow warrior who held the weapon.

"He is my guest," she said meekly. "As are they." The federal agents stumbled out into the glade as other Drow warriors manifested around them.

"We do not bring outsiders here," seethed the warrior who held his halberd blade at my throat. "Never Humans!"

"I will suffer the elders' judgment, then, will I not?" Na'lima did not sound confident, but I watched her stand tall as she pushed the blade away from my throat. "Go or follow us to the enclave, but they will pass!"

"So, little Nama is growing up," laughed a rich, booming voice without a hint of merriment. The hair on the back of my neck stood up as a tall, broad-shouldered figure entered the glade. He was dressed in ornate black armor—black metal chest plate, helm and boots. Arms covered in dark leather gloves that left his fingers exposed. His eyes were the same blue as the two sisters from the bar.

"Do not speak, no matter what he says," she whispered to me. "But if you must speak, do not lie, at any cost!" She lifted her chin and glared defiantly at the armor-clad warrior. "I am full grown, Me'erik. And well within my rights to bring petitioners before the elders." I could hear the fear in her voice.

"You know they will be far harsher with you than I would," he said in that mocking voice. "You might enjoy some of what I would do to you."

"Hah!" She let loose a bark of derision but took a step back when he glowered. She bumped against me and squeaked as if she'd forgotten I was there. I heard her whisper and could not tell if it was to me or herself. "Hurry!"

Me'erik drew a cruelly barbed scimitar from the scabbard at his waist and raised it to point at her. He muttered something in Drow and Na'lima clutched her chest in pain, dropping to her knees. I switched my vision and Saw the spell he used against her. No time to study the pattern, I reached for the nearest knots and began tearing at it.

In the blue-grey shadows of my Sight, blinded by the numerous spells woven into every object in the Drow glade, I didn't see what happened, but I heard the scream of rage. I stopped and brought the real world back into focus.

Me'erik was now on his knees, his clothes smoldering, his blade twisted and half melted by whatever I had done to his spell. He raised his eyes and they were filled with loathing and perhaps a little fear.

"How did you do that?" he whispered like venom. Other of the warriors were putting out bits of cloth aflame or covering their eyes. Na'lima got to one knee weakly. Agent Mistry rushed to her side and helped her stand.

"Answer me, Nama! How did you break my spell?" he snarled.

"Na'lima did not do it!" I spat back at him.

His eyes flickered toward me and he waved his hand. The air was forced out of my lungs. Fire filled my throat and my nerves were pathways for a thousand volts of electricity. I couldn't See the spell even though I switched into the Sight. It was inside me, wrapped around me, binding me in pain.

"Stop, Me'erik!" screamed Na'lima. I felt a lessening of the pain and thought he had relented. But it was Na'lima's magic attacking Me'erik's spell, a barrier to the agony.

I was dizzy from the lack of air, but I Saw Na'lima's magic as it writhed weakly against Me'erik's. Recklessly, I took the threads of her spell and with my mind pictured them wrapped around the Drow warrior's throat. I pictured the threats growing thicker, the way stronger magics differed from weaker. Not a true spell, but what else could I do? I did what I always did—I attacked with rabid fury in defiance of my panic when I feared I was about to die.

The pain lessened again and I could breathe for a moment. Another spike of fire rushed through my lungs and throat, and this time, it burst into my brain and red-hued darkness followed. If it was death, at least the pain would end when my life did.

CHAPTER TWENTY-THREE

Unfortunately, I wasn't dead—because I was wishing I was dead. I think I was screaming except that I couldn't hear myself over the roaring in my ears. I opened my eyes, but all I saw was red, as if the flames in my throat and brain had burst out of my eye-balls.

'*Stop fighting me*,' said an unfamiliar voice in my head.

I knew it was in my head because I still couldn't hear anything.

'*Stop!*' commanded the voice a second time. Some mental switch was thrown because I heard myself screaming now. The roaring faded as the pain grew.

'*It will stop, now that you have stopped*,' said the voice, again in my head. The pain ebbed to a dull ache. The red that had filled my vision faded to the blue-grey shadows of mundane things as when I manipulated magic. How was I using my Sight unintentionally?

A deep blue shadow the shape of a wizened Elf stood over me, with faint green lines of power woven subtly about him. I tried to move my hand to touch him, to make sure he was real, but my hand refused to obey. Distracted by the effort, I stopped screaming.

'*You will recover*,' said the shadow. '*Let my magic work unmolested.*'

'*What do you mean?*' I asked in my head, because my throat was raw from screaming.

'*You kept dismantling my healing magic when we did not keep you bound,*' replied the voice with humor and annoyance. '*I would not have thought it possible.*'

Now that I was no longer focused on the pain, I could see other shadows behind the wizened Drow healer. I recognized some of those shadows as the federal agents. Their glasses were tightly corded with spells, as were the obvious shapes of their guns. Surrounding the feds were dozens of Drow warriors with equally magicked weapons, most of them pointed at my FBI friends.

"Na'lima?" I tried with my voice but it refused to obey me. The Elf responded to the sounds in my head.

'*Why should a Human worry about the fate of one of our kind?*' demanded the voice coldly in my mind. '*If you had cared, you would not have convinced her to bring you to us. It will go badly with you all.*'

'*She brought us. I didn't ask,*' I strung the words together in my head, though it was difficult. '*She said I could help.*'

'*And why can you help? We have sorcerers enough of our own,*' answered the mental voice with snide superiority.

'*Because I am a—*' What had the word been? "—*sovenjor,*" I managed to whisper the word and this time, I went to a painless unconsciousness.

When I woke, I saw the physical world in its natural brightness. Above me were green branches that swayed in a gentle breeze and early morning light. I stirred on satin sheets.

"'Bout time!" said a familiar voice, but definitely not in my head. Agent Shelby was sitting on a padded chair, designed to match the tree-woven ceiling.

"How long?" I raised myself slightly, but my head spun as I tried to sit up, so I settled back.

"All night. It's six-fifteen in the morning." Despite his gruffness, I could see the relief in his eyes. His sun glasses were in his jacket pocket. "Everyone else is alright. For now anyway."

"What's that supposed to mean?" I tried to force myself up again and this time I managed it. I was still in yesterday's clothes, which was a relief. I disliked being so out of it that someone could undress me without waking me. Control issues.

"What do you remember?" he asked me.

"That big Drow warrior tried to hurt Na'lima."

"Go on," said Shelby.

"I stopped his spell then he attacked me with another. Oh, I tried to stop him with Na'lima's magic."

"They think the girl did it." Agent Shelby's voice lacked any humor. "You wrapped her power around his throat long enough to distract him and the other guards. Gunnerson got a shot off before they took him out. That's what broke Me'erik's spell on you, but you collapsed at the same time. You were in bad shape. Na'lima argued with the *honchos* that showed up and they brought a healer for you. Except, even unconscious, you kept fighting their magic. We had to hold you down and he worked his voodoo on you."

"Where is everyone?"

I scanned the small room, taking in more of the details. The slate floor was partially covered by a Persian-style throw rug and the walls plastered except where bits of living trunk and root broke through to support the canopy of leaves over-head. An arch framed of smaller branches formed the door.

I replayed Shelby's comments in my head. "Is Gunnerson okay?"

"The others are in the next room. We can't get through to base and I don't think we'd survive a gunfight out of here."

"Didn't anyone know where we were going?" I asked surprised.

"I called in our approximate location before we entered this little fun-house. It's a large block to search. And I'm told that if they enter the house without dismantling the spell, they actually enter a house. But, of course, we aren't in the God-damned house!" roared Shelby. "They might see the magic, but they won't know how to get past it."

I stared at him and he grew sheepish. "Just venting a little." He rubbed his short cropped hair.

Shiandra came rushing in from the other room. "You okay, Devon?" Worry played in her huge dark eyes and I was grateful that she cared. I noticed, however, that she had shifted the dress up so that her nipples weren't visible.

"Pretty memorable first date," I said. "Now that Shelby's filled me in." She smiled and patted my hand.

"Hey, I'm getting jealous." Gunnerson appeared behind her, his face twisted into a mock pout.

"Okay, come here you big lug and I'll hold your hand, too," I said.

"Enough you clowns! This is serious," ordered Shelby.

I slid to the edge of the bed and Gunnerson helped stabilize me. The blonde lifted one of my eye-lids and I knocked his hand away. He didn't smile. "We're supposed to notify them when you wake up."

"I'm good. So let's do it!" I stood and found my legs would actually hold me up. "Hey, I really am good."

"The Drow healer said by morning you'd be completely healed," supplied Mistry. "It wasn't physical damage so much as magic poisoning, whatever *that* is. Still, a chance to see Drow magic first hand? My qualifications are growing exponentially."

"If you live to make use of it. Let's go," said Shelby with a nod of his head.

We all moved into the next room, a larger version of the room I'd awoken in. No bed, only couches and chairs, like the lobby of a hotel. And like the lobbies of some hotels, there was a large, wooden double-door that a rhinoceros could have walked through. We followed Shelby to the door and stood there looking at it expectantly.

"Do we just knock?" asked Gunnerson.

"Sure, why not?" replied Shiandra. She removed her gun from where it was hidden in her thigh holster and pounded on the wooden door with the handle.

"I'm surprised they let you keep those things," I noted.

"Human technology doesn't impress them much," said Shelby impatiently. "Nor Human magics."

The door swung open and an escort of Drow warriors stood there. Thirteen to our four. One of them was dressed slightly differently than the rest and she motioned for us to follow before walking off.

We fell in line behind her, trotting to keep up with our aloof escort. Gunnerson spoke to Mistry in a false whisper, "It's like at the academy, so serious!"

To my surprise, the woman we followed answered his blithe comment, "We take the death of one our own, very seriously."

After walking in silence through sections of forest-themed chambers, we entered through a final arched hallway into an expansive clearing. The glow of morning was visible in this open-air amphitheater. A tribunal chamber, six throne-like chairs set on a raised platform, each occupied by stern Drow elders. Given that Elves do not age very readily, that so many of these creatures looked wizened said something of their time on this earth—and their power.

Sitting on both the right and the left of the chamber were over a hundred Drow citizens, reclining on padded mats of exotic fabrics and designs, some tasseled, some trimmed in lace. Like of an outdoor concert in Los Angeles as they nibbled on basket meals and sipped wine. They turned to watch us with curiosity and more than a little hatred. A few, however, smiled with malevolent glee.

"They used to gather like this to watch public executions," I muttered.

"Come before us," exclaimed one of the elders.

I thought that was a bit over-played given that we were still walking behind our escort toward their thrones. I stopped in my tracks when I saw Na'lima dangling from the ceiling by a ropelike vine behind the council, almost hidden in the shadows. I so wanted to take back the public executions comment.

One of our escorts prodded me with a sharp edged weapon. I spun and grabbed the haft, yanking it out of his hands. The sitting audience murmured with interest but did nothing.

"Don't fucking prod me!" I snarled and threw the halberd onto the ground.

The Drow warrior hadn't expected resistance or I never would have had the strength to take his weapon. He looked embarrassed and furious with me. How to make friends and influence people—another one of my dubious gifts.

"What have you done to her?" I pointed up at the skinny Drow woman dangling half-conscious. There were bruises on her face, and I thought I could see the reddish black of dried blood at the corner of her lips.

"You will make no demands here!" roared the same wizened Elf who had commanded us to step forward.

My skin crawled with the presence of magic and I switched to the Sight. The tendrils of magic he cast were thick with power but moved slowly to wrap around my arms. I scanned the pattern, finding knots and overlaps and pulled the power apart. It resisted unraveling, which I had never experienced before. Not in the same fashion as the slippery death magic at the murder scene. No, it was because these strands were so thick with power.

I concentrated now that I expected the resistance and the spell broke apart. This time I left the magic on the ground in case I needed to use it again. I wasn't always a slow learner.

The crowd murmured again, louder this time and the council shifted on their chairs. They turned to each other in silent communication. I could feel the federal agents cluster behind me as the tension built. I imagined they had hands ready to draw weapons, even if we would all die here. Would the Drow simply cover up our deaths since no one could prove where we'd gone?

I could have just torn the bands of magic apart, instead of unraveling the knots and leaving the residue on the ground, but I didn't want to end up like Me'erik or that melted sword. Ripping spells apart made them explode with unintended effects. That was the reason I always had to be careful in the unraveling of magic on the job.

"I will make demands here under the law or the prized Drow autonomy will become imprisonment," I shouted back. Maybe I'd been reading too much on the obligatory rules of Lycanthrope culture. Who said that the Drow had to follow similar rules? If we survived, I'd have to ask Shiandra about that.

I should have been afraid that the Drow would kill us all on the spot, but it was true—I was only afraid of Werewolves, the great apes, psychotic Humans and apparently Trolls. Na'lima had brought us here because I needed questions answered. She also brought me here because the Drow needed my help. I would not allow her to be punished for that. Not without a fight.

"You threaten us?" asked another of the elders.

"No, councilwoman," I answered confidently, "you threaten yourselves. You violate the federal laws which grant you the limited protection of privacy and autonomy you enjoy. The government is just looking for an excuse to lock you in concentration—oh, excuse me—*internment* camps."

The councilwoman smiled and leaned back in her high-backed chair. "And you would have us believe you came here to keep us from such a fate?"

I remembered what Na'lima had said and knew that the sudden and intense conversations amongst the crowd had to do with the Drow ability to detect lies. I would have spoken the truth anyway, but I would be careful about what I said.

"I came here for two reasons. One, because I had questions to ask about a murder in which the Drow are implicated."

The murmuring of the audience included shouts of indignation or outrage, but I ignored the voyeurs. I spoke directly to the female elder. "It is my belief that while the Drow are somehow involved, they are being framed for the murder. I would like answers to my questions so that I may help solve this murder, and if possible, extricate the Drow as well."

I paused for a gulp of air, but the volume of my voice grew so that everyone would hear. Na'lima had brought us to help clear her people. They would know this no matter what they did to me afterwards. "The second reason that I am here, in your private enclave, is that Na'lima knew that you, her elders, have need of my help. She knew that it was better left to your superior understanding of the problem, whether you would ask for that help or not."

The audience rippled like the dull roar of the ocean as many different voices echoed together in the exposed chamber. The federal agents remained silent behind me and I resisted the desire to turn and look at them. The wizened Drow also remained silent.

"Na'lima did nothing wrong. Release her," I said again in the council's silence.

Agent Gunnerson whispered to me, "Don't push it, man."

"Don't whisper, Ivan. The Drow have excellent hearing," said Mistry unpleasantly. She had stressed 'hearing' to suggest that other senses were not excellent. I really liked this lesbian fed. I hoped she did become permanent to Fresno. And I'd like to go clubbing with her again. If she danced. First we had to leave here alive.

"Na'lima," replied another wizened female on the six thrones, "violated one of our most sacred rules. She brought outsiders into our enclave without permission. Worse, she brought unauthorized federal law enforcement. We are not so stupid as to act without checking your side of this matter. You have no warrant to enter this enclave."

"I—we were invited in. For that, we don't need a warrant," I answered.

"Ah, that is true. But that would have been Na'lima's only defense," replied another elder coldly, although I detected resignation in his voice. Perhaps Na'lima's punishment wasn't favored by the entire council.

"She had no reason to bring you here. We could never need the help of a Human," said another, who did not try to mask his hatred.

I looked from face to face, trying to find argument in her defense. I had exhibited my power, but they knew I could not thwart the entire combined forces of a Drow enclave.

Heads turned to look above the council. Even the elders craned their necks to look up at Na'lima. I looked, too. Na'lima repeated the same word over and over and I knew that word.

"So you have no need of a *sovenjor*? Then you are right, Na'lima is very stupid. Must be a Drow thing." I heard not only gasps from the audience but from Gunnerson and Mistry as well. I wasn't sure Shelby was still behind me because he was absolutely silent.

"So now you insult us?" shouted the woman who had tested my honesty.

She stood and I could see her fingers move in arcane deftness. She couldn't have been the only one, my entire skin itched with magic in the air. I was seriously considering just tearing it apart near the casters. Let them all explode in unpredictable magic, even if it took us with them. But a piercing voice broke through the chaos.

"He is right if you only hear insult in his words," said a previously silent elder. I looked closely at him and saw the threads of green magic which surrounded him. The healer who had saved me.

"What are you saying, Ti'mpal?" demanded the councilwoman.

"We spend our lives developing the skill of speaking the truth as unobviously as possible, so that deception may follow from inattention or false assumptions. Yet, because he is Human, you assume he has no skill in that style of communication."

Rather than argue, the woman turned back to me. She replayed my previously spoken words from memory. The faintest trace of smile played at her lips before she regained her somber composure.

"You are right. He implied that if we don't need a *sovenjor*, then Na'lima is stupid. And if Na'lima is stupid, then we do not teach our children very well. The second assumption is clearly true, if the premise is true. However, if we refute the premise, we must assume the falseness of the first statement. I applaud you Human. And I rebuke myself for my inattention."

"Do you need a *sovenjor*?" I asked directly. I had hoped that Na'lima wasn't stupid. Just as I was glad that Ma'alma had been.

The council returned to its silent communication and the murmuring of the crowd reduced to a low buzz. I could see the faintest smile on Na'lima's dried and cracked lips. Her eyes held mine for a second and I could have freed her. My magic Sight revealed that a spell held her there, not metal or rope. However, I had the elders' considering my words. I didn't want to antagonize them.

"Very well," said the councilwoman who had flickered a smile. "If we have need of a *sovenjor,* and if that need is met, then we would have no judgment against Na'lima."

"And if that need is met, not only would you have no judgment against Na'lima, but you would owe a debt to the *sovenjor*."

"What would that debt be, Human?" asked the healer suspiciously.

"Not only is Na'lima held judgment free, for all events associated with our presence here, but she should be recognized and rewarded for service to the community as is normal within Drow culture." It was worth a shot. I knew that there were at least three Drow who would want to hurt the woman for her interaction with us.

"That is easy enough," answered the woman but she hesitated. "That cannot be all."

"No. I admit I would like my questions answered without objection."

The council conferred and then the woman spoke firmly, "Five questions, no more."

The wish game. If the wish is even slightly vague, the genie will try and thwart your intentions by giving you less than you wanted or at least something different. By limiting the questions, it might take five to get a single answer, and little or no useful information.

"Only if the five questions are answered fully and as I intend the question to be answered. No evasion, misdirection or attempts to thwart the meaning of my question."

"What kind of game would it be with those limitations? No, if you cannot ask as you intend then we will not answer," replied the elder woman.

"Then five is not enough," I answered firmly.

"He is Human," sneered an elder. "Perhaps he needs more than we would."

He meant to bait me into accepting the offer. "Yes, perhaps I do. Make it twenty."

"No, twenty is too many," answered another of the elders, "even for a Human." They were playing a game. They had already decided on the maximum they would offer.

"Then, in truth, what is the maximum you will allow me?" I asked directly.

"Oh, he is much too direct. You are wrong," said one of the elders to Ti'mpal. "He does lack skill in this game."

"But I knew you had already decided upon a maximum, that says something," I retorted.

"Yes, it says something. But have you noticed that we have not answered your question? Would you have let it lie unanswered or counted it as answered?" asked the wizened woman on the end.

"The questions you grant me will be asked after I prove whether I can help you or not. These bargaining questions will not count," I added. Thank the gods I had been geek enough to play role-playing fantasy games as a teenager. Okay, major geek—Dungeon Master for two years straight.

"Very well, I bore of this trivial debate. You may have eleven questions and no more."

"Eleven will have to do. And we leave here, all of us, unharmed," I added as a final requirement.

"You stand before us as federal representatives. Of course we will let you leave here unharmed," answered a wizened male elder matter-of-factly.

"Then I accept," I declared. The elders seemed smug about something. It was too late. I had sealed the deal and was stuck with it. What had I missed? Whatever it was, it was bound to try and bite me— bad things always did.

CHAPTER TWENTY-FOUR

Shiandra and I, along with Na'lima, free of her bonds, were led to a chamber where the walls were black rock. Torches were lighted and set in grooves along the stone. Agent Mistry helped Na'lima stand while the wizened healer elder attended her. Agent Clark just kept an eye out for sudden attacks, although there was nothing she could have done. Shelby and Gunnerson had not been allowed to come, as they were men. Perhaps I was the exception because of my claim as *sovenjor*. I doubted it was because I was gay.

Another figure entered this small chamber—the councilwoman who had questioned me the most. She was not so wizened as she had looked upon the throne, although she was clearly not a young Drow.

"How is she?" The voice which had been so cold before was now worried.

"She'll survive undamaged," replied the healer.

"This way," said the councilwoman to me and she walked into a section of rock. My Sight revealed that the wall was an illusion.

"We're coming," insisted Na'lima. She staggered away from the healer and Shiandra hurried to support her. I wondered if the Drow woman might be Shiandra's type the way Ramirez had been mine. They walked slowly but steadily toward the spot on the wall where the councilwoman had vanished and were close behind me as I walked through the wall.

Inside was another dark chamber. Torches illuminated the space, revealing irregular passages that led in different directions. But what caught my eye was the shape of a naked woman carved in the stone. Her naked back and hair was so lifelike it had to have been the work of a master craftsman.

"Si'lith," whispered Na'lima with anguish.

I looked back at her. She stared with tears in her large, green eyes at the figure of stone. I turned back to the naked woman and switched my vision once more. The shape was infused with magic that was tied to the entire rocky surface. I remembered Gunnerson's comment about people being merged with trees by Wood Elves to kill them.

"My god! She's alive?"

"For now and ever," answered the councilwoman with sorrow. She forced her head up, lifting her chin proudly. "Unless you can do what you claim."

"How long as she been like this?" asked Shiandra.

"Three years."

"What did she do to deserve this?" asked the federal agent in a whisper.

"She did nothing! Nothing we know of. Someone did this to her. One of her enemies. One of my enemies. We do not know."

"Your enemies?" I asked, suspecting the answer.

"Si'lith is my daughter. One day Na'lima went to look for her and found this."

"Why can't you just undo what's been done?" I asked.

"It's not Drow magic, *sovenjor*!" seethed the councilwoman.

"My name is 'Devon.'"

The Drow elder put a slim hand to her eyes. The rest of her face reflected the pain she was trying to hide. Then she lowered her hand and I saw a mother's helplessness revealed.

"Forgive me, again. My name is Si'mara of the Tchel'in enclave. Well met, Devon, the *sovenjor.*" She bowed her head formally. "Can you save my daughter?" The pleading was plain her voice.

"I can but try." I walked closer to the wall. "You didn't want the male agents here because she is fully naked?"

"Men are not allowed to see our women naked once they are life-claimed," replied Na'lima. "It is not common among the other Fey, but we are sometimes more conservative. You are a necessity which I do not mind and I do not think Sith would."

"She is your partner?" asked Shiandra.

"Yes. We presented our claim to the elders only days before this!" whispered Na'lima.

"So," I spoke while I studied the pattern. I couldn't concentrate with so many people watching me otherwise, "do you contract names by taking the first syllable and combining it with the final syllable? Minus the initial onset of the final syllable?"

"I do not understand," replied Si'mara.

"Si'lith becomes Sith. Na'lima becomes Nama. Would you be Sira?" I clarified.

"It's not just the initial onset, Devon," pointed out Shiandra. "That would make it Si'ith."

"Ah right," I muttered. The pattern was vaguely familiar but I agreed with the woman—this spell was clearly not Drow. No matter how long I studied it, I couldn't place it.

"No one has called me 'Sira' in many, many centuries."

"My apologies." I switched to normal sight and glanced at the distraught Elf.

"No, my thanks. You brought back memories that I had thought lost in the expanse of time." She smiled and stepped beside me. "What do you see?"

I saw the worry in her eyes, the glow of love's fear and love's strength. A mother's love. My own mother had looked like that in her love for me once. I started to choke with emotion. "Put your hand on my arm."

When she touched me I switched my vision again. She gasped at the network of power in her daughter's body and the rock wall. She pulled her hand away and I knew that for her, the image returned to normal. Tentatively, she put her hand back and studied the shape of her daughter's imprisoned flesh.

"I want to see," said Na'lima. I felt another hand touch my arm. And then a third hand touched the back of my neck. Each woman gasped as they saw what I saw. I heard weeping and it was Na'lima.

"My beloved," she wept.

Si'mara released me and went to Na'lima, putting her slender arms around the tiny Drow lesbian. They wept and embraced. "Hope brings us back to our tears, does it not?" asked the older woman of her daughter's lover.

"As I thought nothing ever would," whispered Na'lima in reply.

I was going to try to unravel this spell as I had never tried before. The only thing stronger than my sense of justice was my respect for true love. If this wasn't it, there was no such thing. Whether between lovers or a mother and daughter, true love was worth any cost. Call me a hopeless romantic.

"If it's love, the lord won't mind," I quoted aloud from a book I'd once read when I'd been coming to terms with my own sexuality.

I reached a hand out for the first of the knots and tugged gently at it. It quivered more at one end than another and I followed the loose connection. I tugged at the weaving carefully because the spell was made the woman and the wall one thing. I could not simply just break it apart—it must be properly undone or I might kill her.

Every spell, no matter how complex, had a single node which held it all together. That one knot was the key to the puzzle. If the knot brought together multiple strands, it was possible to free them all with a single manipulation. If it anchored other knots together that held even more strands, it required a different approach. If the spell had just frozen her against the wall, it would have been simple to undo such a spell. But her flesh had become stone as well.

"Serious magic, alright," I muttered aloud. I figured the grieving women would want to know what I was doing at each moment. "If I can find the core node—there!"

One, two, three, I counted each of the attached nodes in my head. Four, five, six. "There are six key nodes that I have to undo simultaneously. It would be simpler to unravel from the outer edge of the spell, but that would take days if not weeks. And I'm not willing to stay here that long unless it's the only option."

"Will it hurt her?" asked Na'lima. Si'mara stroked the petite woman's head.

"Not if I'm careful. I've handled three nodes at a time without a problem. Six is a stretch. I just need to make sure I'm ready when I do it."

Si'mara nodded at me and pulled Na'lima's face against her bosom. Agent Mistry looked at me and smiled encouragement, although her hands went to stroke the back of the thin, butch-cut lesbian. It made me smile sweetly to see that affection.

I wrapped my mind around each of the six nodes, gathering the interim pattern in my mind, tracing lines of power from the core node to the outer nodes that bound all the rest together. My anthropology teacher Jackie Gillespie had taught me to use this technique instead of the tedious work of one knot at a time. I would have to thank her after this, regardless of my success.

After a few minutes, sweat had gathered on my brow, even though it wasn't warm in the cave-like room. Mental work was still work. I imagined gathering the nodes in my mind's eye and felt for them with my power. The web of power trembled as I drew the spell taut until each of the nodes in my mind pulled equally against it. Then I tugged with all my mental might. The spell fell apart more easily than I expected and I fell backwards onto my butt as if I'd been pulling with physical arms.

At the same time, Si'lith collapsed backwards from the rock onto the ground in front of me, her head landing on my thigh. Her mouth was open and her eyes were closed. She looked lifeless, although she was no longer stone.

Through the illusory door rushed the wizened healer, Ti'mpal. He picked up Si'lith as if she were a feather and shifted her to a pile of furs which I hadn't noticed earlier. My skin prickled with the feel of magic and I shifted my vision again. It was not the healer's magic that I felt. The spell which I had unraveled remained active in the mountain, waiting for a target. On the ground in front of me I saw the spell-key. A bit of rock glowed with power. Mistry saw the rock at the same time and reached down to pick it up.

"Stop!" I shouted and she froze, her fingers inches from triggering the spell again. The others turned to me. "That is what they used to activate the spell. It still holds the power. Give me a minute and I'll remove the magic."

"No," said Si'mara. "We may need it to track the guilty party or parties. If you remove the magic, our proof will be gone."

"But anyone who touches it will be turned to stone like your daughter."

"Then no one will touch it," said the elder councilwoman grimly.

CHAPTER TWENTY-FIVE

Ti'mpal led Shiandra and I down one of the side passages away from Si'lith. Si'mara and Na'lima had remained with the once more conscious woman. They had been torn between showering her with affection and demanding to know what had happened, but Ti'mpal stopped the interrogation as soon as she uttered her first words. Si'lith, although unharmed, had no recollection of who had attacked her.

I glanced at my two companions. Shiandra looked lost in thought while Ti'mpal simply looked straight ahead. He'd been helpful so far. Could I learn anything else useful before I was presented to the Drow elders?

"Who is going to answer my questions?" I asked the dark-skinned Elf.

He chuckled and flapped a hand in the air. "Don't worry, child, we didn't forget."

We turned right. A short while later, we entered a room filled with daylight and gentle rocking tree limbs for a ceiling. The walls were bright yellows and ochres while colorful fabrics were draped along the branches.

"Why the woodland settings?" I asked then panicked—"That is not one of my questions!"

"Calm down. While I will not answer more than you bartered for, until we begin anything formal, what you ask is merely conversation," replied the Drow bemused. "We were locked in the darkness for so many years. Some of our people still prefer the tunnels. But our enclave chose to live with reminders of our freedom, instead of our imprisonment."

He went to a large window, sat on the sill and looked out into the daylight. I walked up to him and looked out over his head. A panoramic vista of beautiful waterfalls and lush forests greeted my eyes. A flicker of my Sight revealed that while many of the underground plants were real and actual water ran along an Elf-made canal, mostly it was illusion. They used their glamour to fool even their own senses. Not much different from how many Humans lived.

"Now, ask your true questions," Ti'mpal prodded.

It was going to be just him for the Q&A. Was that because he knew more or less than the combined council would know? A moment earlier I had been excited to have him alone. Now I wondered.

I phrased my first question carefully. "There is a woman who was killed in Fresno about ten days ago. She was part-Drow and part-Human. Someone taught her some Drow spells, but she was not fluent in them. She shielded only the openings on her house, not the floor or walls." At this Ti'mpal's eyes flared with surprise and he nodded understanding.

Agent Mistry handed me a piece of paper from inside the holster strapped very high on her thigh. I hadn't noticed the concealed weapon in the bar, given the shortness of her skirt. That had been the point. I glanced at the paper—it was a picture of the nameless murder victim. I held it up to Ti'mpal for him to see. "Tell me everything you know or suspect about this woman."

"Nice, adding 'suspect.' I could have ignored anything that wasn't confirmed. Have you dealt with our people before, *sovenjor*?" asked the Drow coyly. "I can honestly say that I have never seen this female before in my life, and that is a long, long time. However—!?"

He took the photo and studied it carefully for a moment. "Yes, I suppose it could be. The jaw and eyes, certainly." He muttered to himself for a time. Then he looked at me and scratched his brow. "She looks like someone I once knew well, but who has been of a different enclave this last century. I would guess this is her granddaughter. If one of her offspring conceived a child with a Human, both the Drow parent and the child would have likely been discarded into the Human world. Give me a moment," he closed his eyes and I could feel the magic crawl along my skin.

A moment later his eyes flashed open. "Very well, her name, we believe, is 'Trina,' although she has also used 'Lenora' and 'Cheryl.' There was mention of a part-blood who came before the elders a few years back and asked for her blood-right. Her mother had been Human, her father unknown."

Ti'mpal stared out into the daylight as though he might not see it again. "She was refused in her request to join the enclave. But she was granted a single treasure—a small container of spells which were part of her Drow birth-right. If she could master them, then she could petition again. She would never have succeeded because they were blood spells mostly. She would have been captured by Human law and sentenced to death before she ever knocked on our doors again. We are not fond of our mixed offspring."

"She could have read the spells? Understood how to implement them?" I asked.

"On her own? Possibly, but highly unlikely. The few Human books that make reference to our magic do not depict such incantations in the common language. They were permitted to be written in an older version—to make it less accessible to your people. For that she would have needed one of us to help her translate. Even if she had mastered the words, it would have taken an enormous number of trials to implement any spell. Where would she get that much blood on a regular basis?"

"From a Werewolf," I said disgusted.

"A Werewolf? But how would she know to do that? Ah. Still, that explains it," said Ti'mpal. "She *did* master most of the spells. Although, 'master' isn't the right word. She crudely implemented them. Apparently, the enclave she first approached, the one her mother had told her of, changed locations after her visit." He chuckled, amused with himself.

"After she couldn't find it again, she came across our enclave. I was not here at the time. As a healer, I am often called to other places. I was told some part-blood had claimed that her father was a powerful Drow of the Pra'ten Enclave and that she had learned the spells as they had demanded. She cast a few for us, taking blood from a blonde child to work them. Naturally she and the child were sent away, although it puzzled us how she knew where we were located."

"But I thought by blood-right you had to accept her?" I asked.

"If she had mastered all the spells, then yes, she could challenge for a place in the enclave. We would have sent her to her father's tribe. But she failed one of the spells. It was enough to free us of our debt."

"You didn't keep tabs on her?" I asked.

"Of course we did, superficially. Me'erik volunteered." He studied me to see my reaction. "He in particular likes the discomfort of Humans. Well, Human women. A part-Drow does not have the same protections as a pure blood or even a claimed part-blood."

"Could he have killed her? No—the question is really, *did* he kill her and if not how can you be sure?"

"Hah, for free I will say, yes he could have killed her. But did he kill her? No, categorically not. Was she tortured?"

"Not from what we could tell. Though her soul was sent to a very specific hell for demonic torture. At least, that was the purpose of a spell used on her corpse." I looked at Shiandra with a flash of guilt, because I'd kept that much secret from the police. I realized then that I had also forgotten to share it with the feds. "And a second spell was also meant to deal with the afterlife."

"Our people do not have souls for any Human notion of heaven or hell. Our energy is recycled into the natural things of Earth." The healer sighed. "Me'erik would not have even thought of such a crime. If the body was not beaten and raped, then Me'erik had no part in her death. That is question number six, in case you hadn't been counting."

Six questions gone, but he had answered more fairly than I'd been expecting. "Do you know or suspect who killed her?"

"Not specifically who, no," he looked at me agitatedly. "Ask me what Me'erik discovered upon her death."

Was he trying to get me to waste a question after evading the last one? I looked at him long and hard and my instincts said he was trying to help. "What did Me'erik discover upon her death?"

He sighed again, as if he had been afraid I'd refuse. "Me'erik found her dead on his last visit to check on her. The spell you mentioned was meant to look like we had cast it and he wanted to obliterate the evidence. However, he was interrupted by someone entering the house. So instead, he tried later to recover our spell cache. It was missing. Whoever killed her took the cache of Drow spells. Or so we believe."

Shiandra paced the room and I looked at her, "Do you have a question?"

"Devon, you said the container was there when you found her. Which means someone came after that to steal it. But why didn't the police find it if anyone else could?"

"It was spelled against detection. I saw the magic surrounding it, not the thing itself," I replied.

"That's my point. Who besides the Drow could have seen it or detected it to take it?" she asked insightfully.

"Good question, thanks. Okay, Ti'mpal, who could have found or detected the hidden cache besides another Drow?"

He didn't answer right away, looking out into the sunlight. "I can never get enough of the sunlight. I never wish to be forced back into the darkness. It is important that my people prove they can be trusted in the daylight." He turned to me and shook his head. "Ordinarily I would have said any Fey creature. But the truth is only one of us could have seen it. Well, that's not true. One of us or one of you."

"A Human?"

"No, a *sovenjor*," he said softly. "Not even the strongest Light Elf could have penetrated the magics we place on the birth-right shells. They are meant to keep the part-bloods out of our enclaves, despite that our oldest laws guarantee them rights to it if they pass the tests. That is the rest of the answer to your previous question, in case you were wondering. Two remaining, Human."

Shit. Still, we knew a lot more than we had before. And I was left with the choices that it was another Human like me, or a Drow who had killed our murder victim. But if it had been a Dark Elf, why cast that spell to make it look like the Drow had done it. They could have easily borrowed other magics and placed the blame elsewhere. No one would have questioned Human anti-Drow terrorism.

I had spent all my time on this Drow business but done nothing to help Jake. I flashed back to that moment when Jake had followed the Kimric pack out the door. A question rose in my mind and I risked it. "What does *shabatka* mean?"

"*Shabatka*? How do you know that Drow term?" I had plainly caught him off-guard.

"When a federal witness was taken from my house, his pack-mate said it before they left."

"It is a rarely enacted Werewolf ritual where a male member of a pack is put to challenge. He must either survive attack by three of the strongest members of the pack or he must submit sexually to any and all members of the pack who claim him, even betas. Then, after they have used him, they can sell him outside the pack as a sexual slave. It is reserved for the worst Lycanthropic offenders and invented by the Drow when the Wolves were our slaves. What did he do to merit such a terrible fate?"

"I don't know, but they violated pack law to get him back," I muttered. "I will save my last question for later. I suspect when new evidence comes up I'll have something else to ask."

The Drow looked at me gravely and nodded, "You could ask later, but I think you will not have an opportunity. I was instructed not to let you leave till our debt to you for this was repaid. So your final question?"

Fine. What to ask? There was nothing that sprang to mind now that I could picture Jake being either killed or raped by half his people and sold. It made me desperate to save him.

"Tell me everything you know about Werewolf laws," I asked in desperation.

"While I would not mind spending weeks answering your question, I would prefer not to have to. I believe you said something along those lines about freeing Si'lith."

"Then tell me everything you know which might help me thwart Jake's pack from either killing him or raping him during *shabatka.*"

The wizened healer stood and sighed. The look on his face was sad and he put a slender dark hand on my forearm. "If the pack broke law to reclaim him, then they cannot hold him for *shabatka.* But the only way to hold them accountable is to provide a challenge that the pack itself cannot defeat. You are not strong enough. If the pack will not hold their Fenris responsible, then he must be challenged and killed. Otherwise, the pack will fall further into rogue behavior. Of course, if other packs were aware of this rogue pack's failure to obey pack law and they were willing to back you up and challenge on your behalf—

that could thwart *shabatka*. But they will not take your word for it. Of that I'm sure."

He removed his hand from me and looked briefly at Mistry. "As sure as I am that that was your last question. Now I have one before we let you leave. Na'lima is my niece. One of my only two surviving blood-kin after her parents were killed in the exterminations in Europe. If I could do something to help you, what would it be?"

"With the murder? I can't think of anything," I replied. "Now if you had some pull with other packs to challenge Kimric—?"

"I do not think they will do me any favors. I'm sorry." He shook his head and walked to a door that hadn't been there before. "Come, they know we are done."

Shiandra and I followed the healer. She took my arm as she had at the bar and I tried to return her hopeful smile, but couldn't. Jake was going to die and I could do nothing except die along with him while I did my best to keep my word to him.

We passed through the arch into a different style of room. It was completely enclosed by a real ceiling and there were no windows. Agents Shelby, Gunnerson and Clark were slumped in recliner type chairs. Drow warriors lined both sides of the door and two wiry Elves in loose tunics stood beside each of the federal agents.

"What's going on?" demanded Shiandra, warily.

"You promised we would be set free," I countered, feeling betrayed.

"Yes, you are being set free," the healer said without heat.

"What did you do to them?" Shiandra rushed over to our friends.

"We cannot let you leave with the memory of where we are and what you've seen." I saw a touch of regret in Ti'mpal's shining grey eyes. "You will only have the memories of what we have bargained for. Your eleven questions and anything before arriving here that you learned of us."

"You promised to leave us unharmed!" I shouted. "Or is the Drows' word worth nothing?"

"I'm sorry but by Drow definition, a little memory removal *is* unharmed."

I saw one of the Drow wizards point at Mistry's head. I flicked into my Sight and Saw the spell hit her between the eyes. I Saw the core knot and all the strands connected directly to it. But even as I did, the second Drow wizard hit me with his spell. I pulled at the knot in my mind, but blackness flooded all my senses before I could feel it give.

CHAPTER TWENTY-SIX

I sat up, feeling as if I'd drunk way too much. The fact that I couldn't remember how I'd gotten to the sidewalk meant I *had* drunk too much. Long Islands were my guess. That was the only liquor which left holes in my memory. Shelby and Gunnerson were standing in the gutter looking around. A black sedan pulled up and Shelby put his radio away. Beside me, Shiandra was sprawled on the ground. Clark knelt next to her anxiously.

"What happened?" I asked.

"Someone mugged us outside the bar," snarled Agent Shelby.

"Mugged?" I wondered if that was what was wrong with my head instead of booze. Mistry didn't stir and I was in no condition to pick her up. I motioned at the unconscious woman and Shelby nodded impatiently.

"Palmer help Clark get Mistry and put her in the back of the sedan," ordered Shelby. "Devon, hop in next to her. Gunnerson, ride shotgun. We're going to get you guys back to Fresno while I have the locals look into our assault."

Palmer got out of the driver's seat and helped Clark pick up their fellow agent. Gunnerson opened the back door and Palmer slid Mistry gently onto the leather seat, while Clark steered her legs into a folded position. I stumbled to the door and slipped in after her. Her skirt rode up and I pulled it down out of respect for her, but not before I noticed that she wasn't wearing any panties.

"Well, at least the Drow woman answered our questions before we were jumped," I offered, to mitigate the growing headache. "We know something about Lenora and her relationship to the Drow."

Shelby stuck his head in the open door. "Watch your sixes. We don't know that this attack isn't related to the murder." He slammed the door shut.

Palmer got back into the driver's seat and Gunnerson entered from the passenger side. We drove off, leaving Agent Shelby standing alone in front of a large Victorian house. I saw him head up the stairs to knock on the door. Turning back to face forward, dizziness combined with the lulling roar of the car's engine sent me back to sleep.

When I woke again, we were exiting the 99 onto Shaw Avenue. Shiandra watched me carefully. "Are you alright, Devon?"

"For being mugged, about as good as can be expected," I chortled. "Not that I'd ever been mugged before so I have nothing to compare it with."

"Even as a federal agent I haven't been hit on the back of the head too often," she said, but she seemed puzzled and stared out the window.

"We're going to drop you off at home, Mr. Mosteller," said Agent Palmer.

"Unless you need medical treatment?" asked Gunnerson.

"No, I'm okay." As my father had drilled into me, unless you're bleeding profusely, you don't need a doctor.

We turned off the main street onto Van Ness. "You'll let me know what else you find out about Kimric?" I asked. "Before the next full moon."

Mistry turned toward me. "Pardon?"

"Kimric? Information about the pack before the next full moon?"

"Oh, certainly," she said distractedly.

Palmer pulled the sedan into my drive and slowed down without stopping, "You recognize that vehicle?" he asked.

Agent Gunnerson leaned forward, "That's the Animal Control officer's truck."

"Yeah, Yuriko's. She has a key," I confirmed.

"Were you expecting her?" asked Palmer suspiciously.

"We headed out for Sacramento before I could tell anyone. She's probably worried about me. Damn it, I should have called her."

"We'll check it out first, just to be safe," said Agent Palmer.

All four doors opened when the engine stopped. Palmer and Gunnerson moved to the house before me, Shiandra covered my back and Clark remained by the car. Hands on their weapons but none drawn.

"We pulled the agents off your house when you left for Sacto. I got us here fifteen minutes faster than expected or they'd be here again," said Palmer.

The front door opened and Yuriko Morimoto stood there smiling, "Devon!"

"Hey Morimoto-*chan*!" I ran over and hugged her. I laughed out loud as she arched back so that only her chest pressed against me in her usual reticent manner.

"I was worried about you!" Yuriko pounded on my chest which aggravated my hangover. "The feds told me you went to Sacramento. What happened?"

Palmer rushed inside the house while Gunnerson stood at the entryway. Shiandra checked out the periphery of the house while Yuriko waited for me to reply. Clark, near the car, scanned all directions. I put my arm around Yuriko's neck and tried to press past Gunnerson. He put a hand up and shook his head. "Wait a minute."

"Clear!" called Palmer from inside, before heading back toward the car.

Shiandra rejoined us as well. "Nothing. You want us to wait till our replacements arrive?"

"No, I'll be safe with my own personal police officer here!" I laughed. "Besides, Palmer's the only one of us who wasn't whacked on the head! You need to rest, too."

"Okay, we'll be in touch." Gunnerson motioned for the other agents to get in the car. Yuriko and I stood under the eaves until they pulled out of the drive then I escorted her back inside.

"You here alone?" I pretended to look around for her boyfriend.

"Oh, stop it. Trust me, after last time, he won't come over here," she complained playfully. "I was just worried about you. Have the feds found out anything about Jake?"

I dropped my aching body onto the couch and closed my eyes. I felt Yuriko sit next to me. "I'm beat. We were in Sacramento following a lead when we were mugged."

"Mugged? By who? Are you hurt?"

"I don't think so. The weird thing is I don't remember everything. I remember leaving the bar, but that's about it." Until that memory loss, I hadn't considered the possibility of a concussion. Neither had my new federal friends, so I was probably fine.

"Well, thank goodness you are okay."

"The important thing is that I know what Kimric is planning on doing to Jake. And I've got to stop them." An idea popped into my head as I spoke. "The ideal thing would be to have another pack challenge them, but other Lycans won't take a non-Lycan's word for something this serious."

"You can't go on your own. It'll be dangerous. You don't have the strength of a Werewolf even in their Human form!" Yuriko tapped my beefy bicep lightly to emphasize her point.

"But he needs me," I said softly. "And he trusts me to save him."

"If you're going to get yourself killed, you're going to get me killed too," she said adamantly.

"You hungry?" I was suddenly famished. How many hours had it been since I'd eaten last?

"I had some chocolate a little while ago. I could eat something real."

"Fine, let's see what I have in the fridge." This time when I stood, the dizziness passed quickly. Another night's sleep and I'd be as good as new.

"How about pizza?" she asked.

"Ooh, sounds good. Pepperoni Lovers?"

Yuriko nodded with a frown. "You know pepperoni is fine. It's all we order."

If we survived the confrontation with Kimric, I could imagine the shit my friends would give me about taking on a furry lover. They knew how much I didn't care for body hair. Not that Jake had any as a Human. No doubt the bestiality jokes would proliferate. Great. But I'd be willing to deal with it because it would mean we were both still alive. The odds of that being true weren't so good.

I was reaching for the handset when it rang. I jumped and jerked my hand away. Yuriko chuckled as I answered it, ignoring her. "Hello?"

It was Shelby. "I just got word. Four agents are stationed outside your house. Two in front and two in back so don't freak out if you see someone in your yard." He sounded upset.

"What's wrong?"

The black FBI agent replied somberly, "Got word on the gossip mill that Kimric might take another run at you before the full moon. It's just a precaution."

"Great. Anything else on Jake?"

"We are in the process of getting a court order to extract Jake as a federal witness except those high-end Kimric attorneys are slowing down the process. That may be their plan. We hope to have the warrant in time for the full moon." Shelby didn't hide his disgust. "Otherwise we can't lawfully enter their territory."

"And I don't think they're gonna give us permission otherwise," I retorted bitterly. "Thanks, Agent Shelby."

"One more thing. I'll need you at the murder scene again tomorrow."

"Not a problem, I'll be there." Shelby hung up and I put the receiver down. Then I picked back up the phone and dialed my usual pizza parlor. Cheese in the crust and pepperoni—my body craved carbs and comfort food. Yuriko was right. It was all we ever ordered. But with all the chaos in my life, a guy had to have a little stability. Even if it was only pizza.

CHAPTER TWENTY-SEVEN

When I walked out of the house the next morning, Gunnerson and Shelby were once more standing next to their black sedan parked in the driveway. They wore identical black suits as they had the previous day and the same spelled sunglasses. A men-in-black moment and I smirked.

"Morning, boys." No other feds were in sight.

"You get a ride this morning, Mr. Mosteller." Gunnerson lacked his usual playful tone. "We're meeting the Chief downtown before we head to the murder scene."

Shelby opened the driver's side rear door and waited for me. Gunnerson slipped inside the car, his door open, while I approached the car. As I passed, Shelby whispered with minimal movement of his lips, "We're being watched."

I got in the car without responding and pulled out my cellphone and dialed Yuriko.

"Who you calling?" asked Gunnerson.

"Yuriko. She's meeting me at the crime scene in about thirty minutes. Except I won't be there."

"Good," he said.

Agent Shelby shut my door and got behind the wheel of the car. He adjusted the rear-view mirror. "I think it's the Lycans. Seems to just be surveillance. Nothing hostile."

He started the car and we headed onto Van Ness. I quickly explained to Yuriko and hung up before glancing out the rear window casually. The street appeared to be empty.

"They're gone." Gunnerson removed his dark glasses. It wasn't bright enough to need them just for the sun. "Two Humanoids concealed on the roof and a tree. Preternaturally quiet."

"Why do you think they're watching?"

"If it's Kimric, they want to see what you're up to," answered Shelby. "Probably expect you to try and sneak into their territory and steal Jake back. On the other hand, if it's about the murder investigation, it could be they want to see if you lead the trail to them." He watched me in the rearview mirror as he drove.

"Is that why the escort? Their surveillance?"

"We really are going to headquarters. But there is another matter within our jurisdiction."

"What?" I remembered to fasten my seat belt and leaned back.

"Jacobsen said to wait till you get there," replied Agent Shelby.

After that response, he drove and we all remained silent. Suddenly, I felt I was experiencing a case of pod people. Only, these were the real FBI and I was missing the friendly aliens. They didn't even talk to each other when we arrived at our destination.

The front of the Federal Building in downtown Fresno was fairly nondescript, except for the revolving glass door and a small squirrel house chained to a tree with a warning about the house's obnoxious occupant. It was seven stories tall, built out of blocky 1970s concrete and steel. Across from it were a parking lot and the historic Fresno Water Tower built in 1894, shaped like a round turret from some European village.

We parked in the side lot adjacent to the Federal Building and entered through the revolving glass door, just like ordinary citizens. Shelby and Gunnerson ignored the signs that said no cellphones allowed, and waved me through the metal detector. I followed them, even though the alarm went off, into the lobby. We paused as two other federal agents looked up from their station, one of them in mid football tossing motion, suddenly silent. They stared at my escort as if someone had left the front door open and a stray dog had appeared.

"Roswell team, huhn?" asked the man simulating a long pass. He wasn't anything like the agents I'd met so far, with grey in his hair and a beer belly, although he was wearing a snug fitting dark suit. "Like Fresno isn't enough of a joke."

I waited for Gunnerson or Shelby to respond, but they simply ignored the barb and so I felt compelled to say something on their behalf. "If you want the correct pejorative term, it's the 'Strange Squad.'" It wasn't a very good come back, but I was distracted by my fear for Jake and the strange behavior of my companions.

The greying agent scowled and turned back to his companion as if we weren't there before he resumed his comments of the current National League Football situation. Shelby stepped silently past them and pressed the elevator door which immediately opened. Gunnerson steered me forward by the elbow, rushing me as if afraid of what I would add to my initial comment. Shelby pressed the button inside and the doors closed.

"What is with you guys?" I asked, but they remained silent, staring ahead as if their personalities had been turned off. I folded my arms and decided to focus on the elevator's rocky movement upwards.

The second floor was the bankruptcy court and the third floor was the federal court offices, but I wasn't familiar with the fourth, fifth or sixth levels that we passed. We jerked to a stop on the seventh, topmost floor. On an earlier visit, I had been told it used to be a storage level, files and the like, since the basement was used for less dusty things. Now it was part storage and partly relegated to the newer federal units, such as the Preternatural Division of the FBI—dusty records and the Strange Squad.

The elevator opened and we entered a small foyer with two doors. One door led to the storage area and the other to our destination. A big Hispanic man sat on a stool behind a raised desk and looked at us briefly before looking down at his magazine. He was over three hundred pounds easily—more sumo wrestler than FBI. His name tag stated 'FBI,' nothing else. Gee, would never have guessed.

"One of the Strange Squad boys?" I tried to engage him in conversation since clearly Gunnerson and Shelby were having none of it.

"Naw." The Hispanic man chuckled without any real humor. He didn't even bother to look up from his magazine. "I'm not freaky enough for what goes on in there."

Shelby and Gunnerson remained silent as they led me through a wide, steel door. I wanted my pod people back! "What's up with you two?"

The steel door shut behind us and I was suddenly aware that we'd entered a busy office. Federal agents were scattered around the large room, some of the closest ones looked up from their various tasks at my outburst. I clamped my mouth shut in embarrassment, but most of them were too busy to pay attention. I didn't recognize most of them, but I did see Agent Mistry standing beside her desk. I knew it was hers because it had a Ganesh statue, the Hindu elephant God, next to a coffee mug adorned with Guajarati writing. Chief Jacobsen was standing close to her, speaking intensely.

I studied the other people, surprised at the diversity. A thin, older Chinese man shuffled papers at another desk, reminding me of an accountant rather than a field agent. Two female agents who could have passed for twin blonde strippers were bent over a long table, discussing a series of 8x10 photos. Their breasts bulged against their buttoned jackets but I seemed to be the only person to notice how uncomfortable they looked.

"So this is our manipulator." A handsome Hispanic man about my age stepped out of a back room. He had short-cropped hair and dark eyes, but his skin was pale compared to most of the local Mexicans. I studied his face and decided that his features were more Caucasian than Amerindian. He was either from some other South American country or had strong Spanish roots, but clearly he wasn't local to Fresno. "Agent Anzaldua."

I shook the proffered hand. "Devon Mosteller."

Shelby kept walking toward Jacobsen and Mistry, so I gave Anzaldua a quick shrug of apology and followed. Jacobsen seemed irritated and Shiandra looked at me furtively. This really was beginning to feel like a '*Twilight Zone*' episode.

"Agent Jacobsen."

"Mr. Mosteller, thank you for coming." The Chief extended a hand. "Please, this way."

Shelby stepped aside, so I followed Jacobsen through an unmarked door and saw a set of glass cubicles. The first cubicle was empty but I stopped at the second, confused. Melanie O'Keefe, the preternatural veterinarian and one of my five closest friends, was sitting there with bloodshot eyes, talking with another agent I'd never seen before. She was wearing a white doctor's smock, which meant they had called her in from her clinic.

"I didn't know Melanie worked with you guys. I guess I should have."

"She doesn't work with us. We have contacted her in the past about possible consultation but she's here as a suspect." Jacobsen watched for my reaction.

"For what?" I practically shouted. The rooms weren't sound proof because Melanie turned toward me. She stood up, relieved at the sight of me. I reached for the door and rushed inside as Shelby and Gunnerson tried to stop me.

"Melanie!"

"Devon, oh thank God!" She threw her arms around me and hugged me warmly. I felt her full breasts press hard against me in her urgency, but ignored the odd intimacy. I smelled apples and cinnamon on her skin and hair and it felt like home. Her hold on me stiffened and she pulled away. I saw Ulrich standing outside looking murderous.

She glided to the door as her husband tentatively came in. She threw her arms around him and he held her as if his own life were at stake.

"What are you accusing her of?" I asked Jacobsen through the open door as the couple hugged. Ulrich raised his brows and turned to the Chief.

"Troll trafficking." Jacobsen scowled. "We found a receipt for medical services in an eighteen-wheeler we stopped at the Nevada border—along with twelve Mountain Trolls chained inside a refrigeration unit meant for fruits destined for Florida. The receipt had her name on it."

You can't say 'fruits' and 'Trolls' in the same sentence and not expect to be taken seriously. However Jacobsen was nothing but serious.

"I had nothing to do with it," stammered Melanie, still embracing Ulrich. "I treat Trolls but I had nothing to do with their export."

"Who was the receipt made out to?" I asked.

"That's not for discussion in front of the suspect," answered the agent who had been speaking with Melanie. I immediately took a dislike to the bitter, arrogant expression on his face. It had nothing to do with the fact that he wasn't Human.

"You're a High Elf," I said surprised.

"We prefer to be called 'True Elves,'" replied the Elf in crisp, clear words. His beauty was marred by the expression on his face. "And I was not done with this suspect."

"You are now," said Ulrich in equally crisp German tones. "Without our attorney present, she will answer none of your questions."

"Jacobsen, I know that Melanie would never be involved with the illegal transport of an animal—anywhere! Unless it was to save it from harm. Melanie, did you have anything to do with it? Were you trying to protect them?"

She looked at me appalled then softened. "No, I had nothing to do with this Devon. The Trolls are safer in their mountains than in some other state. Especially a place like Florida where they shoot even Asian tourists."

"Her word is good enough for me," I stated unequivocally.

"Whoever you are, that is not how the FBI works," replied the Elf. "Your word means nothing to me."

"I'm just suggesting to Jacobsen that he not waste department resources investigating Melanie instead of enlisting her to find out who might be responsible," I said through gritted teeth.

Ever meet someone who, even though you were totally against violence, made you want to just belt them in the face? The Elf pushed that button in me as if he had used magic to do so.

"I'll consider that, Devon. Could we go into my office and discuss this?" It wasn't a request.

"Fine," I said, still miffed. Gunnerson and Shelby joined us. I sat opposite Jacobsen while the two other agents stood on either side of the door.

"I'm sorry, Devon, but I had to see your reaction to your friend being here," began Jacobsen. "If she were involved and you knew about it, you might be tempted to cover for her. It was obvious that this was not the case and I'm sorry to question your integrity. I would have done it with any of my operatives as well."

"I understand," I replied, glowering.

"Actually, we don't think she had anything to do with it. Her husband, however, is another matter. Not that we have evidence of his involvement. It's just, well, his immigration records don't exactly stand up under federal scrutiny. For example, he didn't legally exist until ten years ago. Oh, people remember him in the old country, when he was a boy, things like that. But there is no paper trail of Ulrich Gotterdam existing before then."

"So you thought if you shook up the wife, the husband might fess?" I asked still annoyed.

"Something like that," nodded Jacobsen. "To answer your earlier question, the receipt was made out to an alias. The address, however, is troubling."

"Why?" I leaned forward.

"Because it's 4501 Talon Drive." Jacobsen folded his hands on his lap.

"That's the murder scene!" I exclaimed.

"Exactly!"

I looked up at Shelby and Gunnerson. "Is there a problem with Agents Shelby and Gunnerson?"

Jacobsen sighed and tapped his pencil on the monthly calendar that served as a desk protector. He looked frustrated. "There is some evidence that they are hiding facts from us in the matter in Sacramento." He glared at his two subordinates. "While that is being investigated, they are under departmental observation as well."

"Observation? What does that mean?"

"There is a magical observation spell incorporated into their glasses, which they are now required to retain on their person at all times for the duration of the investigation. That spell has now been activated as a result of these discrepancies. Everything they say and or do is recorded and observed."

It relieved me to know that they were being forced to be typical humorless G-Men. But I didn't have to like it. "What facts? I can corroborate the events of our time there, if that will help."

"No, I'm afraid that will not help. You, apparently, were also unconscious during key points in the evening."

"We were mugged. I woke up with a splitting headache. Mistry was unconscious next to me when I woke," I argued.

"It is nothing with which to concern yourself, Devon" Chief Jacobsen waved his hand dismissively. Back to playing official federal agents again. The pod person, friendly Jacobsen, had left the building. "If your help is needed later we will ask for that help. Now, because she is your friend and I believe you when you say that she could have nothing to do with Troll smuggling, I would like *you* to question her about Trolls. We will monitor the interrogation from outside the room to put her at ease. Then I would like you to return to the murder scene with Mistry and Special Agent Thandryl. And this time, look for evidence of Trolls."

"I'm not sure how useful I'll be. I've already examined the place for magic. And I'm not a Troll expert." I tried to hide a shiver of revulsion.

"True, but if Lenora did not keep the Trolls on her property, she may have used a place nearby. Oh, and don't worry, Mistry reported the conversation in Sacramento with the Drow woman. I don't need it in an official report immediately. However, for corroboration, you should write up something like last time."

"Fine, not a problem," I said, reminded that I was only temporarily part of their team. "Why Thandryl?"

"He has a few particular talents that might be useful." Jacobsen's expression was carefully neutral.

"Why didn't you just have him examine the scene initially?" I persisted.

Jacobsen leaned back in his chair and looked through the glass window at the Elf still badgering Melanie. "Because, Devon, he was just shipped here this morning." The chief glanced at Shelby. "Get on with it. I've got work to do."

Agent Shelby walked to the back of my chair and tapped it twice. I stood without a word and followed Gunnerson outside. As we left, I heard Jacobsen whisper to Shelby. "Make sure than blasted Elf doesn't leave that crime scene until Mosteller's done!"

"How long should Devon be?" asked Shelby, with a hint of conspiracy. If I could hear this conversation, I had no doubt the Elf could.

"Tell him to stay until it gets so dark he can't see. Just keep him away and out of my hair the rest of the day," muttered Jacobsen while Shelby shut the door.

I saw Thandryl glance up at the door, his expression disgusted. Even Elves weren't perfect at hiding their real emotions. In his eyes, I saw the flicker of doubt.

CHAPTER TWENTY-EIGHT

True to their word, the feds left me alone with Melanie and Ulrich. I didn't see any conventional cameras, but I knew that the feds also used magic for surveillance.

"You understand that even though it's me asking the questions, the feds are listening in?"

Ulrich nodded without looking around but Melanie reflexively searched the room. "How?"

The German stared at me defiantly. "They use magic. Just like they use your relationship with him to interrogate you without our lawyer being present. We should wait, my Love."

"No, I trust Devon. If he feels we should answer the questions, I want this cleared up. I want the feds to know I have nothing to do with this!" Melanie held her husband's hand and rubbed his fingers with her own.

"Very well. It's not as if I have say in the matter," he muttered angrily, his accent stronger.

"Ulrich, I would never do anything to hurt Melanie. If I thought she were guilty I would tell you to wait for your lawyer." It occurred to me that by reassuring Ulrich, I might be defeating Agent Jacobsen's intention to catch him off-balanced.

"As long as they keep that bastard Elf away from me," seethed Melanie with real anger. That surprised me because she had adored Elves in college. She had, in fact, wanted desperately to date one. I guess if you can't become one, that's the next best thing. Some of us weren't happy with the weaknesses of our Humanity. I knew that from firsthand experience.

"What, he worse than me at making friends?" I asked playfully which brought a smile to her full lips. "Okay, first, are they talking about the Trolls I saw in your clinic?"

"No, those are still there. Though—." She concentrated on a memory. "Though someone tried to break in a couple of nights ago. A cop car happened to be passing by and scared them off. I thought they were going for the medicines. They warned us of that in vet school. But they could have been after the Trolls."

"How many other Trolls have you treated in the past couple of weeks?"

She looked at Ulrich and smiled. The look on her face may not have shown passion, but the love was undeniably real. "It'll be alright, Ulrich. The police aren't the same here as they are in Eastern Europe."

She looked at me, patting his hand. "You know I haven't been busy. Except, the number of Troll-sightings in the area have been higher than usual. Sometimes people call and want me to come get them. I don't go, because it's not my job to collect wild creatures. But there was one. A man called and said he found a wounded Troll on the side of the road. He offered to pay me to come treat it. I thought he was like me, just cared enough about things to make sure they didn't die."

"Melanie! You didn't tell me this. You cannot run off to meet strangers alone!" exclaimed Ulrich.

I could see both passion and love for my friend and I smiled. He loved her as she deserved to be loved. Even if it wasn't as she deserved to love.

"Oh, stop it Ulrich. I was fine."

"So you did go?" I asked.

"We needed the money. And sure enough there was a Troll trembling with fear on the side of the road, her leg badly cut up. She was pretty timid around Humans. I had to get the driver away from her so that she would calm down enough that I could treat her. Thankfully, it wasn't as serious as it looked. I told the driver that she would be fine, just let her amble back into the wild. He paid me and—"

"Paid, how?" I interrupted.

"Cash," sighed Melanie. "But I made out a receipt, like the law requires!" She raised her voice to speak to the hidden observers. Sheepishly she grinned in embarrassment at her childish outburst. "I'm sorry. I'm just saying I did everything that was reasonable. I didn't check his ID because it wasn't necessary for cash."

"Did he drive off?" I asked.

"Well, of course he drove off," she answered flippantly. I stared at her and she made a face of contrition. "Oh, did I see him drive off? No, I left first. I remember looking in the rear view mirror thinking it was nice that he worried enough to watch the Troll heading across an empty field. I just assumed—."

"It's okay, Melanie. It wasn't unreasonable, like you said," I reassured her. "Can you describe the car?"

"It wasn't a car. It was a king-cab truck, Silverado. Very nice too, brand new."

"How did you know it was new?" I asked puzzled.

"It didn't have its plates yet. The temporary sticker was still on the window-shield," she answered wistfully. "And the truck was cobalt blue."

"The very one you wanted?" asked Ulrich sadly. "I wish I could afford to buy it for you. There is so much in this world I want to give to you."

"Shh," replied the buxom woman. Her round blue eyes welled with tears, "You give me everything I could want. Stop doubting yourself."

"Did it have one of those dealer frames?" I asked.

"No, not that I noticed. I'm sorry. You know me and details like that. But the man, he was about his mid-twenties with strawberry blonde hair like mine. And tall. I'm sure he was taller than you, maybe taller than Ulrich."

"Thin? Chunky? A three hundred pound tanker?" I asked, thinking about the guard at the elevator door.

"Definitely muscley. Big arms and chest. But it was probably from the gym, because he had those chicken legs from not working everything out equally." Ulrich his brows raised. "Sweetheart, I notice these things because of Devon. Spend four years with a gay man who is also interested in biology and then tell me you don't notice the general oddities in both male and female morphology!" She looked at me and waggled her finger. "See what trouble you still get me into? It's the hardest habit to break."

"Trust me, I know," I bantered back. "Try having to explain to a boyfriend. 'No, I don't find him attractive, it's just that I'm amazed that his torso is too long for his legs or that he has no chin'. But then I get in trouble for checking out women. Really, they shouldn't be threatening to a boyfriend 'cause I'm gay."

"Fine, I am convinced!" Ulrich threw his hands up and tried to smile. "Is there anything else, Devon? I would like to get my wife back to her practice."

"Who's watching the Trolls?"

"Federal agents as they ransack the place," Ulrich replied bitterly.

"Then you better get the heck out of here," I joked and stood up. "Alright, Jacobsen, it's time to let the nice people get back to their lives."

A moment later, Jacobsen and Mistry appeared in the hallway and unlocked the door. Jacobsen stuck his head in and nodded to me,

"Thank you for the information, Dr. O'Keefe. I'm sorry we put you through so much anxiety."

"You need to have someone besides that Elf do the questioning then," she muttered belligerently.

"He is still a little rough around the edges," replied the Chief with a curt smile. "Devon, we'll follow up on the vehicle. I need you to head to the murder scene now."

"What about the driver of the semi?"

"He's not worth anything. Not his trailer, even though it's his cab. They actually swapped out his unit for the one we apprehended while he napped. If he was pulled over anywhere between here and Florida, he would have been clueless as to where his cargo came from."

"Alright, Melanie." I hugged her quickly and just as quickly reached out to hug Ulrich. "Ulrich."

He stiffened with shock. He loved her and I loved her. How could I not do my best to make him feel welcome? Eventually he would stop doubting us. I smiled and left the room in Jacobsen's shadow.

Shiandra Mistry fell in line beside me. "How are you?"

"Fine. Still a little fuzzy but I'm sure it will pass."

"So you don't remember anything more about—about our mugging?"

"No, although I haven't been trying. Is this related to the trouble Shelby and Gunnerson are in?" I whispered.

"Something like that," she murmured.

Thandryl stood near the elevator, a scowl on his face. Jacobsen put a hand on my shoulder. "I know that was hard on you. But you need to understand. If you are part of the federal team, even your own family is not off-limits." Jacobsen gave the Elf a stern look. "Now, find out the connection between our dead woman, the Trolls, and the man who paid O'Keefe for treating that Troll."

"Is that all?" sneered Thandryl.

He entered the elevator as it opened. Jacobsen and I shared a look then I followed the True Elf into the small box. I stood on the opposite side to give Thandryl his space. Mistry followed and pushed the button for the ground floor. My last sight of agent Jacobsen was of him rolling his eyes as the doors closed.

CHAPTER TWENTY-NINE

Shiandra led us to another black sedan. Thandryl tried to get behind the wheel but Agent Mistry slid in first. He stood there for a second as if he wouldn't accompany us. I got in behind her. A moment later, the front passenger door opened and the Elf sat noisily on the leather seat. He slammed the door, which given an Elf's strength, might not open again. Shiandra ignored his tantrum and drove us out of the parking lot until we reached the Ravenclaw complex.

News vans lurked on the street, although no reporters were visible. Two squad cars and another federal sedan were parked in front of 4501 Talon. We pulled into the parking spot behind the other unmarked government vehicle.

"Reporters," muttered Agent Mistry. The news van doors opened and reporters with portable vid-cams came running towards us.

"Allow me." Thandryl stepped out of the car with that perpetual arrogance and a mist rose between the house and the reporters.

"What did you do?" I asked.

"They are lost in the confusion of their own minds. The fog will hold them for a time," he chuckled low and bitterly.

"You are in so much trouble," said Shiandra. "We can't restrict lawful reporting of the news."

"It is merely a distraction, Mistry," said the Elf with angry eyes.

"Let's just get inside," I interrupted.

"Are you going to use fog every time we step outside to investigate?" continued the Indian FBI agent. Thandryl went toward the house. She grabbed his jacket sleeve and spun him around. "You may not like it but I out-rank you, Agent Thandryl."

"I am here as a Special Agent. I am not out-ranked by anyone," he said coldly.

"You still believe you'll return to Washington? They sent you to us to get rid of you. You are on indefinite loan to us!" she shouted with uncharacteristic heat.

Thandryl stormed inside the house. Mistry glared at his back and then looked at me embarrassed. "He just makes me so nuts!"

"It happens to the best of us," I said. Shiandra followed Special Agent Thandryl reluctantly inside, with me close on her heels.

At the threshold, the uniformed cop watching the door was Ramirez. I'd forgotten all about him with all my other concerns, but he had been the one to make it clear it was a no-go while Jake was in my life. I nodded and walked past him. Keeping it professional, I told myself.

Thandryl stood in the kitchen, his posture angry, his demeanor cocky. He used his Elf senses to look for evidence I might have missed. I could feel the magic on my skin.

"You sense something?"

"If there were anything here, I would know it," replied the Elf.

I flicked my vision so that I could see the spell he used. His entire body was covered in lines of power, which meant the magic was affecting him, not the house. In the patches of blue-grey of mundane counters and decorations, I also saw the magic woven into the walls, but the canister was still missing.

"Then there is nothing here?" I made it clear that I was challenging his abilities.

"If you mean the shielding of the windows and doors, of course there is something there. But that is all," said the Elf testily.

"Can you detect Trolls?" I walked further into the kitchen.

"We hunted Trolls for pleasure before Humans limited our rights."

"But can you detect them?" I repeated.

"Yes, of course I could. If I had a scent-beast," fudged the Elf.

"Well, we don't have one, do we?" Mistry came into the kitchen. "What we do have is a general description of a man linked with the Trolls. While you do your thing, I'm going to canvass the neighborhood. A tall ginger bloke should stand out."

"You don't have a strong British accent," I commented to Mistry. "Why now?"

"No thanks to Mum and Dad," she said with an exaggerated English accent. "I had to work extra hard to get rid of it as a child even though I was born in the States. Problem is, whenever the subject of ginger—red-headed lads comes up, I slip back. Complicated story."

"Didn't mean to pry."

"No problem," replied Mistry and she went outside.

Thandryl stood there scowling at me. I stared back. He didn't move, didn't say anything, just stood there looking at me.

"Fine, you win. What?" I finally asked.

"What do you mean, 'I win?'" He was puzzled and annoyed at the same time.

"You stare—don't say a word. I stare back, waiting. I got tired of waiting first and asked why you were staring," I explained. Despite their intellect and quick cultural assimilation, many of the Fey didn't have a native proficiency in English. I didn't speak High Elf, so I wasn't throwing stones.

"I win because you yielded first. Ah, a game we played as children," said Thandryl with something of a reminiscent smile. Then his scowl returned. "You know she favors females."

"Yeah," I answered.

"Then why do you flirt with her?" It was not a question I'd been expecting.

"I wasn't flirting with her," I said carefully. Oh what the hell. "I favor males. It was merely friendly banter."

His eyes flashed wide and then narrowed suspiciously. "Your kind are barbarically backwards about same-sex pairings. Why would you reveal such a secret to someone who obviously holds you as inferior?"

I laughed and his scowl turned into a snarl. "Special Agent Thandryl, first, it's not a secret. I make it plain to anyone who asks that I only fancy men. I don't like getting close to a guy and having him freak out later when he learns I'm gay. If he hasn't already figured it out. Second, if you consider me inferior, it is because I am Human. Elven culture understands the biological nature of homosexuality. If you *did* think me inferior for it, it would say something about you, not me."

I saw Thandryl looking over my shoulder and I turned. Ramirez was standing there listening to my explanation. His eyes held mine for a moment before he spoke. "That Animal Control officer, Morimoto, called about an hour ago. Said to remind you to call her when you got here." His voice was so male and sexy. My gaze was drawn to his fine featured hand as he brushed the bangs out of his face.

"Thanks," I called as Ramirez returned to his post. When I turned back to the kitchen, Thandryl was gone. "Happy happy—joy joy," I grumbled.

I searched the murder room, but it was empty. The body had finally been taken away. All the interior rooms of the house were empty, too. I retraced my steps and went to the garage. Thandryl stood in the semi-dark with the door open. My body cast a shadow using up half the light. The Elf stared at the countertop.

"Do you require something?" His tone was nearly civil. I realized then he had come here to be alone.

"Sorry. Didn't realize you wished to be alone." I paused. "I'll be in the first bedroom, the one the body was found in."

All I could see was the trickle of light reflecting off his eyes. "Did you know that True Elves and Black Elves are natural enemies? That I should rejoice in the death of one of them? Even a part-blood?"

"I knew there was bad blood. I didn't realize it was that strong," I replied slowly.

"Instead, I weep for another of the Fey lost to Humankind," he said, somberly. "Not just at the hand of a Human, but tainted by Human culture. We once knew right from wrong. Since we have been forced to live under Human laws as well as our own, we do not act naturally anymore."

"What do you mean?"

"I am a True Elf in the service of the very government that subjugates my people. The same government which limits them to reservations and restricts their powers. Can you imagine what that says about me, as you put it? How I am viewed by my own kind?"

"Then why did you—?" I asked but Thandryl turned back to the counter. I waited for him to look up or speak again. When he did not, I took a single, tentative step toward him. It was meant to be a moment of intended camaraderie. But I saw his head tilt away from me in response. That movement, so eloquent and definite, rejected me.

I turned and went back into the house, hoping that somehow we could trace the Trolls. That was, if they had ever shown up in this house. It was a long-shot, but it was our best hope at tying in Lenora, Kimric and whatever the hell was going on!

CHAPTER THIRTY

"Hi, Yuriko." I spoke on my cellphone as I walked into the bedroom. "Sorry, got sidetracked. We're back at 4501 Talon. Hey, do you know if the feds have hound dogs? No, no, I mean scent dogs?"

"Yeah, for bombs and drugs, just like the regular police," she answered. "Why?"

"I need something that will track Troll."

"Forget it then," she said definitely.

"Why?"

"Dogs hate the smell of Troll. Haven't been able to train a dog to hunt Trolls in the last thirty years." Her voice turned thoughtful. "You need a cat."

"A cat?" She had to be kidding me.

"Not a housecat, Devon!" She laughed at me. "You need a big cat trained specifically to hunt Trolls. Cheetahs mostly. That or possibly a Werewolf."

"Well, Werewolf is out for the next two days. Unless another one shows up in animal form between now and the full moon. Where would I get a trained cat?"

"Missouri. Maybe Wyoming," she replied seriously. "I can check."

"That won't work either. It'd take at least a couple of days to get an animal. I doubt the FBI will foot the bill for flying it out."

"And the trainer would have to come, too," she reminded me. "You can afford it. If it's that important, why not?"

"Because I'm not going to spend all of my money doing the federal government's job. You want me to spend money, let me spend it on you."

"I told you, you're my friend. You already spent too much money on me." Her Japanese accent grew strong with emotion.

"Then I guess we need a Werewolf. That might be the perfect excuse for confronting the pack."

"No! You are going to get killed. Visiting without ritual to offer you some protection is stupid. Stupider I mean!"

"Okay, okay, calm down," I repeated, trying to make her hear me. "Then we hope Thandryl or I can come up with something. Or that they track down the truck."

"What truck? Who's Thandryl? Is that even a Human name?" she asked.

"Sorry. The guy I told you about who has been trapping Trolls drove a cobalt blue Silverado king-cab. He may be linked to the murders. He gave 4501 Talon as the address when Melanie treated an injured Troll. And Thandryl is an Elf. A federal agent on loan to Fresno and here at the crime scene. Does that bring you current?"

"I have no idea what you are talking about, except that last bit," she laughed. "I'll be there in fifteen. I'm just down the street at Starbucks."

"Of course you are," I chortled back. "Bye."

I put the phone away and looked around the bedroom. I flicked into the Sight and saw that only the windows' defensive magic remained. The death pattern on the floor must have been thoroughly documented because it was wiped clean. What had happened to that last spell, the one which had felt like impossible necromancy?

Just because I could identify the classes of spells used by more traditional cultures didn't mean I knew for a fact that the spells worked that way. Yes, magic had been woven to do something, but I wasn't about to try it out first hand to confirm its effects—not necromancy.

I went to the closet and opened it. Inside the grey-blue shadows of her wardrobe was absolutely no evidence of spells. I separated items and looked at them carefully. I felt in pockets even though I knew the police or the feds had already done that.

I started to shut the closet when my fingers prickled with the proximity of magic. I stepped completely inside the closet and shut the door. In the darkness, peeking through a bit of paneling which had been glued over the inside of the sliding door was the tell-tale glow of magic. Like the canister, this panel had been protected from not only being seen, but being felt.

I peeled away the panel and there was an envelope taped underneath, masked by glamour. This was not a shoddy copycat spell nor was it the slightly flawed work of Lenora. Someone well-versed in Drow magic had woven this spell.

My fingers reached out as I learned the pattern, found the knots which bound it together. I released the first layer of the spells which masked the envelope. After three tries, the envelope was visible and touchable to normal sight. I peeled the tape from its edges and removed it from the door. I slid open the closet and then stepped back into the bedroom.

I cautiously checked for mystical booby-traps before opening the envelope. Whoever had spelled the outside had confidence in their magic, for the interior was free of charms. I pulled out a sheaf of documents and started reading. The first one was a birth certificate for one 'Trina Lenora Haim.' Under mother it listed 'Abigail Haim.' No father. I immediately looked at the date. Lenora had been born in 1927. As a part-bred, her life expectancy was considerably longer than a Human's.

I was glad for something to show Jacobsen. I wasn't proving to be a regular Sherlock Holmes. Not that Sir Arthur Conan Doyle would have written an overtly gay character like me, despite some literary gossip about his famed Holmes and Watson relationship.

The next document left me cold in the pit of my stomach. It was a bill of sale for a seven year old boy of the Kimric clan. Not Jake. This boy would have been around thirty-seven-years-old now. The name on the document was 'Brell.' No surname listed.

Two children sold into the hands of Trina Lenora Haim. What had happened to Brell? Was he back with Kimric or had he suffered a worse fate than Jake? And why would she have kept such incriminating documents? It was a serious crime, child slavery. Even the Elves had a mandatory death penalty. With or without torture, I didn't know.

The third document was the receipt for Jake, dated around eleven years ago. I couldn't read the signatures on the bottom. Each of the documents on the sale of the boys had express warranties as to their health and obligations as to their care.

Those warranties offered some protection to Kimric in case the documents were discovered—a two-edged sword, though. Lenora could use these documents to blackmail Kimric if they refused to provide her with children for bleeding. Kimric could claim that the children were meant to be fostered out and protected but that probably wouldn't hold up.

If the signatories could be confirmed, this would get that federal warrant—unless the judge was both conservative and ignorant and believed that Werewolves actually fostered out their offspring. It was the furthest thing from the truth about modern pack behavior.

I thumbed through the next few documents but they were irrelevant to the case. Among them was the deed to the house and related financial papers. I rushed into the kitchen but Thandryl wasn't there. Ramirez looked at me quizzically.

"Is Agent Thandryl still in the garage? Or have you seen Agent Mistry?" I asked anxiously.

"Haven't seen either one of them." Ramirez shook his head and I headed down the hallway.

I entered the garage and found the blonde Elf sitting on the counter, staring into space. I think I actually startled him because he jumped off the pressed wood and brushed his butt with his hands. "What now?"

"I've got something. Get Shelby on the radio."

"Jacobsen you mean," corrected Thandryl.

"Fine, Jacobsen. Habit, dealing with Shelby on this case more than Jacobsen. But get one of them on the radio. I need to talk to them."

"Do not give me orders," said the Elf.

I cursed and spun on my heels. Once I was back in the kitchen, I leaned against the marble countertop and pulled out my cellphone. Jacobsen was programmed in from the last case. I dialed him.

"Jacobsen."

"Devon here. I found some important documents hidden by a concealment spell. Jake wasn't the first boy sold to Lenora."

"Another Lycan?" asked the Chief.

"Bingo! Also Kimric."

"Why didn't Thandryl call this in?"

"Thandryl?" I repeated, before answering. "He's still investigating the house."

"Is he being a pain in the ass or is he helping out?"

"He's cooperating just fine, Chief." I hated making things harder for Thandryl, he had other problems. It didn't matter that I was pissed at him.

I looked over my shoulder. The Elf stood there looking at me suspiciously. "You need to talk to Jacobsen?" I asked.

Thandryl shook his head, frowning, and left the room.

Jacobsen's voice drew my attention. "Where's Mistry?"

"Agent Mistry is out interviewing the neighbors about the new information."

"Wait, if Thandryl is with you, who's with her?" I could hear the anger in the fed's voice.

"Er, she's alone."

"God damn it! What is wrong with you people? Palmer would never have left Mistry on her own. I knew sending Thandryl was a mistake!"

"Don't yell at me. I just follow orders."

"Sometimes," said Jacobsen sourly.

"Yeah, well for me, 'sometimes' is good," I joked. "And FYI, Agent Mistry made the call. She instructed Special Agent Thandryl and I to do our thing while she left."

"Just be thankful you are only a consultant. You can get away with breaking a few rules." There was a pause. "Why are you trying to protect the Elf?"

"What makes you think I'm trying to protect Thandryl?"

"What's going on Devon? Play straight with me. I mean—you know what I mean," he sputtered.

"Honest, Jacobsen, it happened like I said. Thandryl was in the garage checking out magic there while I was in the bedroom checking out stuff. Shiandra was the one who ordered us to do our investigation while she canvassed the neighborhood."

"Fine, have it your way," he said gruffly. But in his voice he let relief slip in. "If he works better with you, then maybe it's just as well. I'll send Palmer over for the documents. He just got back from Sacto."

"That's a lot of driving back and forth. Still working the mugging?" I asked.

"If it *was* a mugging, yeah," answered the fed. He sounded weary. "Be careful. We never found the sniper and I can't afford to keep that many agents in the neighborhood, so you're on your own. And give Palmer thirty, depending on traffic."

"Okay, talk to you later then." I heard Jacobsen hang up.

The envelope in my hands was critical evidence so I hated setting it down on the counter. But I didn't want to wander around with it either, in case I was obscuring fingerprints and other forensic evidence. I shouldn't have removed it from its hiding place but the crime-scene investigators had already gone through everything. In my head I had just been doing my job.

"Thandryl!" I called as I walked toward the garage. The Elf rushed out with his hands at the ready. A regular fed would have had his hands on his gun, instead I felt the prickle of magic on my skin. "Sorry. I need to give you this for safekeeping." I extended the envelope to him and he lowered his hands. The itching faded.

"I don't want it," he said surly.

"But it needs to be dusted and stuff," I countered.

"Do I look like I do menial chores like fingerprints?"

Behind me, I heard someone approach. It was Ramirez. "I have a fingerprint kit in the squad car," he said. "I'll bag it and dust it for you."

Thandryl turned and went back to the garage. I nodded at Ramirez who went outside for his kit. I stood there, torn between continuing to check out the house and my sense that Thandryl was a soul in distress.

Ramirez returned with a fingerprint kit and plastic bag. He was wearing gloves and carefully took the bag from me. "We'll need your prints, too."

"They're on file with the feds," I answered curtly and strode off to the garage.

It was still dark inside the garage except for what light came in under the metal door. I used to like to be alone and think in the semi-dark like that. Thandryl was walking in a circle, staring up at the rafters. His posture was vulnerable, his hands folded across his chest, gripping his biceps. He had heard me coming. An Elf only didn't hear you coming if he was lost in thought or a spell.

"There was fear here, considerable pain," said the Elf quietly.

"Jake was kept chained here."

"More than that. Blood magic, I can smell it. The blood is soaked into the cement. But the fear is strong and recent."

"Can you tell anything about the source?" I asked.

"You worried about your little Lycan?" he turned and made eye-contact.

"Yeah, I am."

He closed his eyes and breathed deeply. Some things were not in the realm of magic and what he sensed, my specific talent could not detect. "His fear is here. Along with his bowel movements and urine. Disgusting."

"Let's chain you up for a week and see if you can hold it that long," I criticized.

"Elves can withhold for a long time."

"For a week?"

"No," he answered grudgingly.

"What else can you say about what you feel?" I asked. It was a connection to Jake and I wanted to know everything about the twenty-year-old Werewolf, to help him when we got him back. I had to believe that would happen.

"It is none of your business what I feel, Human!" Thandryl snarled.

"I meant in the room."

His face crashed when he realized he had revealed something about his mental state. His perpetual scowl returned. "If you are asking can I sense the emotions of other creatures here. No. I do not remember what Trolls emote, but I do not smell them here."

"I forgot how preternaturally sharp Elven noses are."

"Not as good as a Lycan, I will even admit. But then," he sneered, "I am not an animal."

"What is your problem?" I complained without expecting a reply. "Fine, so we know there were no Trolls in the garage. Did the feds check for hidden underground rooms and stuff? This place is new and if she were going to smuggle Trolls, wouldn't she have prepared for it?"

"They ran a scan using sonographic equipment. There are no hidden cavities here," he answered plainly. "The Trolls were not kept in the house. The part-bred wouldn't be that stupid. They merely hope that she was forced to house a Troll here or that evidence of them on clothing would be present."

"So you came here in lieu of a scent-hound?" It was *totally* the wrong thing to say.

"I am not an animal! You may like to fornicate with beasts, but do not mistake me for one of them," Thandryl snarled and I took a step back.

My skin prickled all over and I my vision instinctively flickered to the other Sight. Power blazed from his entire body like white-fire. It was just pure energy, so there were no threads to unravel.

Thandryl seethed with his loathing for my kind. "Humans are one step above animals, but True Elves are the true children of this world!"

"I never said you were an animal," I replied. I wasn't interested in fornicating with him, either. "I meant that your abilities far out-rank Humans in that area," I wasn't sure he would calm down, no matter what I said. He didn't reply.

"I wish I could feel emotions or smell the faintest traces of something," I admitted, grudgingly acknowledging his abilities. "Animals happen to be better at that than Humans. And as I said, I'd forgotten Elves could as well."

"All the Fey," he repeated. "And of all the Fey, we once ruled. We were once feared and given the respect we deserved. Now I am forced to live among Humans, employed in their service."

"If you don't want to be here, then why are you?"

"Because it is my punishment!" he roared back at me. Then, like a switch had been thrown, he suddenly grew docile. "Not open to further discussion. Let us leave this dank room and search the rest of the house."

Sonny was the only bipolar friend I had, but I believed I had just witnessed the Fey equivalent—one minute raging, the next calm. When Sonny went off, I still took it personally at times, although I was getting better. That practice kept me from yelling back at Thandryl now.

"Sure, *Special* Agent Thandryl. Whatever you say," I watched the Elf walk into the house and shook my head at his back. And people wondered why I preferred the company of lesbians.

CHAPTER THIRTY-ONE

Agent Palmer took the envelope from Ramirez and glanced at the fingerprints taken by the uniformed Hispanic. "Good work, Officer."

Ramirez glowed in a shy manner under the praise. His coy innocence was incredibly attractive and I had to remind myself that he told me to stay clear until I was unambiguously single.

"Is Mistry back?" Thandryl came out of the garage but Palmer was looking at me.

"No, she's still out canvassing. Why?"

The conservative black agent seemed worried. "She's not answering her phone and it was sloppy of her to go out alone." He turned to Ramirez. "Did she take a uniform?"

"Are you expecting trouble?" I asked again.

Palmer looked at me and his eyes expressed worry. His words, however, didn't match that concern. "There's no problem. Jacobsen just wants all of us to focus on the new material. The vehicle search is taking longer than we expected. That particular model of truck is popular in cobalt blue. Sixty-five have been sold this last week alone in the U.S.. None of the registrations leads back to Fresno."

"Figured it'd be too easy," I muttered.

"Just because it may take longer doesn't mean it won't lead to our perp," encouraged Agent Palmer. He focused on the Elf. "Anyway, we need to go find Mistry."

"I'm coming too," I added.

"Why?" grumbled Thandryl in protest. His expression was odd—had been odd since my coming out to him. But I couldn't believe he was reacting just to me being gay.

I was missing something, but my reaction was sarcastic. "Because I'm curious about the neighborhood. I've only seen the inside of this house."

Palmer seemed to understand my real reason and he nodded. "Not a problem."

He lead us out the door into a bright Fresno morning. The three of us were immediately confronted by a small cluster of reporters and Palmer raised his hands to them. "Look, we're in the middle of a federal investigation. The official line is that we are following promising leads on the murder. To divulge anything more at this stage will compromise our investigation. Thank you for your cooperation."

He motioned and two uniforms held back the reporters as we moved east on Talon. Palmer had a swift, determined gait while Thandryl seemed impatient to get away from me. Trailing behind them, I studied the two very different men from my favorite vantage, the backside.

Palmer had sexy narrow hips and a bit of breadth on his chest, lean and athletic from sports. In contrast, Thandryl was Elf thin, with a nice vee-shaped frame consisting of broad shoulders over smooth hips, your basic quarterback frame without the muscling. In his case, the standard suit jacket drew the eyes up to the shoulders, which were his best features. Centered above those nice shoulders was his collar length blonde hair, which stood out against the dark suit. I didn't mind thin, but I wasn't as attracted to it as much as moderate muscling. Surprisingly, both men had square firm butts, even the Elf.

Normally, formal wear only flattered the thin and the thinner. For someone decently muscled, even as tightly as Palmer, jackets weren't worth the bother. But the slacks really hugged their thighs and rumps in a very distracting manner.

Of course, I had had several guys complain that my basic fashion sense of black jeans and plaid shirts with solid t-shirts underneath was too lesbianesque for them. Those now ex-boyfriends had wanted to enhance my wardrobe—using *my* money of course. My simple tastes were too masculine for their expectations. And maybe if I was too butch in plaid, they were too femme in Prada. There were reasons they were exes.

Agents Palmer ignored the completed houses, but rather strolled along the curving street until we were forced to turn left onto the next street—Pelt. There was no sign of Agent Mistry out in the open, which is where we expected to find her.

Out of curiosity, I switched into my other Sight. There were no traces of magic in the new construction and I was beginning to doubt that this was a specialty development for Lycanthropes. The street names drew too much attention for Preternaturals. More likely, they were geared toward Humans who admired the Fey—plain, innocent marketing.

I grew impatient with the silent walking. "She may have entered one of the houses."

"No, she wouldn't have been foolish enough to do that without back up," replied Palmer.

"She was foolish enough to canvass without back up." Thandryl's lips curved into a more pronounced sneer.

Palmer glanced at him but said nothing as he resumed walking. We turned left again and were soon in front of the house immediately behind 4501 Talon. Most of the lots on either side were empty, but then only about twenty percent of them had houses or were under construction.

"Where are the construction crews?" I asked.

"We're keeping them out. At least until the development owner gets a judge to force us to back off, which is usually how these things go."

"What makes the FBI think that anyone living nearby is involved in the murder?"

"We don't," answered the attractive black agent. "But there's a strong chance that someone here might have seen something or know something about her. Might have witnessed the driver of the blue truck. Speaking of which, the vic's car was nowhere to be seen. She bought the house under the name of Lenora Holmes. There were no cars with that registration."

"The documents Ramirez gave you show her as Trina Lenora Haim—H-a-i-m," I suggested.

"Wonder which one's the alias?" Palmer took out his radio and called it in. He gave me a slight smile, the first I'd seen, his pearly white teeth stand out against the handsome dark skin. "We should know something in a few. In the meanwhile, we need to start knocking on some doors. Find out which was the last house Agent Mistry visited before she disappeared."

"Why do you say disappeared?" asked Thandryl.

"Because she's not responded to her radio or phone for the last twenty minutes."

We headed to the nearest house and Palmer's radio buzzed. He answered it and nodded even though the person on the other end couldn't see him. He put the radio away and looked at us. "Well, that's that lead. A cobalt blue Silverado was purchased by a Trinity Haim two weeks ago in Denver, Colorado. Looks like our murder vic was definitely involved in Troll trafficking. But unless we find the truck, we may not find the accomplice."

Walking up to the front door, Palmer knocked while Thandryl stood stiffly on the opposite side of the black agent from me. The Elf scowled at me as if I'd done something objectionable. What had happened, now?

"Most of the owners are probably at work," I commented.

"Yeah, but there are always exceptions," countered Palmer. He knocked again, loudly. After a few moments without a response, we headed back the way we came, passing a partially constructed frame and two entirely empty lots. The next house had a Suzuki Samurai parked in the drive.

The door opened almost as soon as we knocked. A girl in her late teens opened the door, her sandy blonde hair in a ponytail and her expression pleasant. She wore a video store clerk's uniform. "Not Mormons. One too many," she said by way of greeting.

"FBI, Miss." Agent Palmer flashed his badge. The girl seemed impressed but not intimidated. "Has another federal agent been by within the last hour?"

"Nope. You guys are the first. Though, I've been listening to music and might have missed the door. You knocked just as I was getting ready to head out."

"Do you know much about your neighbors here?" I asked. She looked at me and flashed a flirtatious smile.

"I tend to be friendly, but in this development you learn to mind your own business pretty fast," she said with a knowing laugh. "Looking for anyone or anything in particular? I notice stuff on occasion."

"A blue pick-up truck?" I asked.

"A big, king-cab kind? Yeah, I've seen it. Pass it on the way home every day after school. Parked on the next street over in front of the, I don't know, is it a tan house? I don't notice houses. But shiny new cars that my dad won't buy me? Those I notice."

"What about the owner?" asked Palmer.

"The high-class chick with the sexy boy-toy?"

She beamed a playful smile at the black agent. Apparently she was an equal opportunity flirt. If he was affected by her obvious interest, he didn't show it. I was clearly immune, although I reacted to her mention of a 'boy-toy.' That had to be Jake.

"Yeah, I've seen her. Not recently. But her dog was howling something fierce last week. I'm just glad finals aren't for a few more days. Couldn't sleep hardly at all."

"You aren't aware that she's dead?" asked Agent Thandryl without any tact at all.

"Dead," sputtered the young woman. She stared at each of us for verification. "No. When? How? Pete's gonna be crushed."

"Pete? Who's Pete?" asked Agent Palmer quickly.

"He's the landscape guy. Does all the yards here at good old Ravenclaw." She puckered her lips into a unhappy smile. "Pete's cute, so I sometimes come out and flirt with him. Not as cute as a federal agent, apparently. He has—*had* a crush on—you know I never knew her name. We always called her H.C. Stands for 'High Class.' My name's Amanda, by the way. Amanda Walters"

"What does this Pete look like, Amanda?" I asked hopefully.

"Um, white with brown hair. About your height. Nice butt," she said without hesitation. I couldn't criticize her, they were usually the best feature on a man. "I don't think he ever had the nerve to ask her out, though. Not with a live-in boy-toy who was my age."

Palmer looked at me and shook his head. She'd given us as much as was likely to be useful. I nodded agreement and he turned to the girl. "Thank you for your help in this matter. If you see an East Indian woman who identifies herself as a federal agent, would you please tell her to call in?"

"Sure." The girl reluctantly closed the door when we started away, disappointed not to have gotten a phone number or some way to contact us again.

"She was telling the truth," blurted the Elf.

"Useful, very useful." It was my idea of an olive branch, but the Elf only glowered more.

We went from house to house until we reached the scene of the crime. One woman had admitted to seeing Agent Mistry, but no one in any of the two houses between the blond girl and the woman had answered Palmer's knocking.

"What do we do?" I asked.

Palmer got out his radio again. "We report an agent missing. This investigation just went up a notch."

CHAPTER THIRTY-TWO

Jacobsen arrived in his sedan followed by five other government vehicles. He ordered the twenty agents who piled out of the cars to search all the nearby houses. Warrants had been obtained on the grounds that a government agent had disappeared but Jacobsen was pissed!

"I can't believe she did something as novice as investigate alone! Palmer, get me profiles on all the owners of the houses. Now!" he shouted and Palmer rushed off.

"What about the empty lots?" I asked.

"What about them?" The Chief snarled back.

"Did you profile their owners?"

"They aren't occupied. What's the point?"

"Because the owners may not live here yet, but they would come to inspect their future home sites. Possibly frequently."

Jacobsen gave me a glower similar to Thandryl's and I was beginning to feel unloved. "You know, maybe we should make you an official departmental member, Mr. Mosteller." He roared for the black agent. "Palmer!"

Palmer popped out of one of the cars. Jacobsen pointed at him angrily. "Get me profiles on the owners of the empty lots as well."

"Yes, Chief." Palmer disappeared back into the vehicle.

"Any other suggestions?" Jacobsen let his worry for Mistry show.

"If you would allow me to use magic, I could find your missing agent." Thandryl's tone dripped with disgust.

"I told you, Elf, all agents are shielded against that sort of detection. It's standard issue!"

I suddenly felt sorry for Thandryl because Jacobsen was looking for a punching bag and the High Elf had given him a focus. "Would it hurt to let him try?"

Thandryl spun on me and pointed his finger in my face, an unintentional imitation of Jacobsen pointing at Palmer. "I can make my own arguments! I do not need you to support me. You will win no favors from me."

"Ease off, Special Agent," snarled Jacobsen. The stern federal agent turned his anger on me. "I thought you said he was cooperating with you?"

Before I could answer, Thandryl lowered his trembling arm and walked away. Jacobsen ran his hand through his hair while he tried to regain control of himself. "Wow, you managed to piss him off even more than we did."

"For a minute I thought he was actually warming up to me." What had I done to change that?

"Never mind. We'll find Mistry without his superior everything." Jacobsen responded to a call on his radio as Yuriko's truck pulled onto Talon. "You find her? Why the fuck not?!"

I left Jacobsen shouting at other officers to greet her.

"Sorry, I'm late." She stared at the number of federal agents and uniformed cops as she got out of her Apache. "What happened?"

"Agent Mistry is missing."

"The cute black one?"

"Shiandra. The East Indian woman. She was really nice."

"How did she go missing?" Yuriko rubbed my arm reassuringly.

"Abducted probably. In relation to the murder."

"Can I help?" Her offer was to help me, not the FBI. I hugged her and looked at the men rushing around.

"Tomorrow night is the full moon. You're already going to be helping me then. For now, it's in the hands of the feds."

"Devon!" I turned to see Palmer running toward us.

"Yes, Agent Palmer?"

"Jacobsen wants me to check out that landscape designer lead. I can't find Thandryl and wondered if you'd help me. I know Mistry made an impression on you and I need back-up." He looked over at Jacobsen who was micro-managing his agents at the moment. "The Chief needs all the people we have and I could use the help."

"Sure. Can Yuriko come?"

"If a civilian can come, why not police back-up," said Palmer.

"Where are we going?" I asked as we walked briskly toward his car.

"Peter Lyndigard has a design nursery about twenty minutes from here. He's been working a second project this week. That's why we haven't seen him here the last four days, according to his secretary. Today he's at the nursery."

"Should I take my truck?" asked Yuriko.

"Not unless you're going to buy a shit-load of trees." Palmer didn't smile as he unlocked his vehicle and we hopped in.

He had the car in gear and moving down the street before I'd finished latching my seat-belt. Although he drove quickly, unlike Gunnerson, there was nothing reckless about Agent Palmer.

"What are we hoping to find out?"

Palmer's grip on the wheel indicated how upset he was. "See if he knows the strawberry-blonde or the whereabouts of the truck. His crush on the victim makes him both a suspect and a likely witness. Keep an eye out for evidence that the Trolls might be hidden on the nursery grounds."

"If he had a crush on her, why kill her?" asked Yuriko from the back seat.

"Unrequited love or cheating are number one reasons for domestic murder, Officer Morimoto," replied Palmer. "Though, if he was involved with her in other areas, it might have been over the Troll trafficking. There is a lot of money to be made."

"How so?" I asked. "I mean, what do they use Trolls for?"

"Slaves," answered Yuriko. "The department sent out a flyer a few months ago. Trolls are being illegally used for domestic slaves and—," she didn't finish.

"And?" I prodded.

"What officer Morimoto is reluctant to mention is the fact that they are also used by a select few for sex slaves and pornography," answered Palmer.

"People pay to watch Trolls have sex?"

"Not with each other," said Yuriko.

"You mean a Human and a Troll?" I asked with a shiver.

The idea of a Troll and a Human having sex disturbed me. A whole lot more than having sex with a Werewolf in Wolfman form bothered me. Maybe I couldn't see past it being the rape of the Trolls. I may not like the dark-dwelling Troglodytes, but they were smarter than apes, smart enough to make functional domestic help, no matter how minimal their tasks. It would be like molesting children. I wanted to hit someone.

"And the video market for Fey-on-Human sex is booming," explained Palmer. "The legislature hasn't bothered to pass any laws about it yet. Not the way it's bolstering the economy. Slavers are getting about five-grand a Troll on the black market. More for females."

Palmer turned off of Herndon Avenue into the drive of a rustic looking nursery. The main building looked like a high-tech log cabin with huge window panes and beautifully landscaped.

"He's talented," I observed as Palmer parked close to the building. Yuriko got out of the car and nodded agreement. "It's beautiful."

"Look for signs of Trolls, not tulips," cautioned Agent Palmer as we walked to the front door.

Several Hispanic workers paused to glance at Palmer's suit and then Yuriko's tight blouse before returning to tending the trees and hauling stock around. We ignored them and entered the warehouse-sized building to find soft music playing against the sound of several waterfalls spilling into decorative, self-contained ponds. The interior was air conditioned, but not cold. The three of us walked slowly through the plants looking around.

"Don't see anyone," I said.

Agent Palmer went to a door which led to the nursery back-lot, opposite the one we entered. He pushed it open and looked around. A muscular man rushed out of the shrubs he had been working with and approached us, smiling warmly.

"Sorry about that. Trying to stem what I feared was a weevil problem. Turns out it was just a bad transplant job." The man was incredibly tan, around five-foot-nine with blue eyes and a pug-nose. His smile was a bit open-mouthed but his teeth were white and straight. His shirt, stretched over his broad chest, was embroidered with the nursery name and logo. Beneath it was his name—Peter. He had that masculine, earthy look about him that matched his name, but I didn't find him attractive. He felt like a salesman and I'd never been attracted to that type of personality.

"Pete Lyndigard, how can I help you?" He was slightly out of breath as he stepped behind the register and put his elbows on the counter. He leaned forward, his smile never faltered.

"I'm Agent Palmer of the FBI. Officer Morimoto. And Devon Mosteller, special consultant to the department."

"What can I do for the FBI, Mr. Palmer?"

"We understand you work at Ravenclaw as their landscape designer."

"Yep. Along with the Hartford Homes complex in West Fresno and Sullivan's in Reedley. It's a good time of year for my business." He puffed out a bit with pride.

"We also understand that you know a Lenora Haim at 4501 Talon." Palmer kept his voice dry and unemotional.

"I know Lenora, but her last name isn't Haim. It's Holmes. Why, is she in trouble?"

Before Palmer could follow up, I posed my own question, "We also understand that you have a romantic attachment to Lenora?"

Lyndigard stiffened, holding his breath. "Interest, yes. Attachment? No."

Yuriko picked up some products on the counter as if they were more interesting than the discussion and read the labels. Then I saw her gaze beyond the product, studying an area behind the register, looking for clues. If I'd been smart, I would have left the questioning to Palmer and done the same.

"Are you saying that you had no personal interaction with Miss H—Holmes?" asked the agent.

Peter Lyndigard attempted to look coy and I held his gaze so that he wouldn't notice Yuriko snooping. "Lenora and I talked a few times but that's as far as it got. Then I got so busy I decided to cool it down till the season passed." Peter grew upset. "I told her keeping a wolf chained up in the garage was illegal." He smiled, that salesman, gooey façade. "Can I do anything to help?"

No one had mentioned the wolf and my Spidey sense tingled. Palmer looked at me as if to say let him handle it. I held up my hands, palm out to him and kept my mouth shut. Palmer's demeanor was hard to read, but his tone was casual. "When did you last see, Lenora?"

"She had arranged for me to come over to discuss her back yard on my last day on the Ravenclaw job. Before I switched over to Hartford for a couple of weeks. That would make it the fifteenth. Yeah, the fifteenth." He didn't take very long to think about it.

Palmer and I exchanged glances. That was the day Lenora Haim had been killed according to the coroner. I studied Lyndigard and wondered to myself—what did Troll smugglers look like?

"See anything you might like to buy?" I asked Yuriko, but she shook her head. Nothing.

"Lena cancelled our meet the night before." Lyndigard seemed overly eager to keep us on his alibi. "Said she had to go out of town on business and that she'd call me when she got back. I work fourteen hour days on average and when I get home I usually watch a little TV and hit the sack. I'm a workaholic which is partly why I don't date. When she didn't call, I just assumed she was still out of town." He raised his brows and his eyes were too innocent. "Are you telling me she's back?"

"Yes, Mr. Lyndigard. She's back in town," said Agent Palmer dryly.

Peter Lyndigard looked upset again. His emotional shifts were like a rollercoaster of lies. Did people actual fall for it? "She isn't avoiding me is she? I wasn't stalking her or anything. She actually flirted with me first. I thought she seemed to genuinely like me. I know I really liked her."

"Mr. Lyndigard." Palmer stared out the large glass window that made up most of the back wall. "Are all your employees Hispanic?"

"Mexican? Yeah, every last one of them. Well except for Tobino, he's Filipino. Why?"

"Do you know a strawberry blonde or red-headed gentleman? Over six feet tall? Muscular?" asked the federal agent, still watching the activity outside.

"No, can't say that that rings any bell. I don't hire Whites. Hard to find anyone who works as hard as these people do for minimum wage."

"The Fey work hard. You ever hire any of them?" I asked.

"Why put out hard working migrants who have families to support just to be PC about a bunch of non-Humans who don't even need the work?" Lyndigard's anger was real.

"Many nurseries now exclusively employ part-Feys because they have special abilities with plants."

"Look, I have nothing against non-Humans, but these *people* count on me for jobs."

"Did you know that Lenora was a non-Human?" asked Palmer.

"What? What do you mean she was a non-Human?" The designer stiffened again, startled. "She was so beautiful and perfect."

"She was part Drow," I offered.

"I didn't know." Lyndigard acted nervous. "I've heard stories about the Drow but I've never met one. Or I didn't know I'd met one."

"Mr. Lyndigard, Lenora Haim AKA Lenora Holmes is dead," said Palmer finally.

"Lena is dead?" Peter whispered. Then rage filled him. "Who did it? I want them dead. This red-headed guy you're looking for?"

"We don't know for sure," said Palmer.

"You mind if I look around some outside?" asked Yuriko.

"No, but what are you looking for?" Lyndigard grew guarded.

"Don't worry, we're not after your workers. Even if some of them aren't documented," said Palmer.

Yuriko stepped forward and picked up one of Pete's cards. "While we're here, I want to get some tree ideas for my front yard."

She wandered outside and Palmer nodded permission, so I followed my friend. Lyndigard and Palmer stayed inside as Yuriko casually browsed potted plants. Apparently she was genuinely window shopping, so I trailed along thinking about everything that had happened in just a few short days. After almost an hour, she wound up buying three indoor shrubs and two flowering annuals for a planter, but neither of us had noticed anything suspicious.

Palmer waited until we were in the car with the doors closed, "You find anything?"

"Nothing except her plants," I answered. "What about Lyndigard?"

"I think he really cared about the victim, but I think he was lying about something. You remember how that girl said he had a crush but never talked to her? He admits to having a relationship with her. So why would he keep it a secret?"

"He have a wife or girlfriend already?" I asked. "Interested in— what was her name? Amanda, too?"

"No to the wife or girlfriend. We verified he's single. And I don't think Amanda was our Mr. Lyndigard's type."

"Maybe Lenora had a boyfriend. Asked Lyndigard to keep it on the sly," I tried again.

"That might be possible, but that would give Lyndigard more of an alibi, not less of one. I verified his contracts while you were shopping. He's as busy as he says. He may have nothing to do with her death or the Trolls. Either way, we don't have enough for a search warrant."

"He seemed pretty surprised at her death. Or he's a good actor," I said. "Not that his early extremes in emotions support that idea."

"His employment records and the other financials he shared with me show that he owns the place outright. He makes good money." Palmer started the car. "I don't see why he would get involved in Troll trafficking. Not worth it. And there's no evidence of anyone working or involved in the business except migrant Mexican laborers."

"It wasn't a total waste of time," said Yuriko, embracing her new plants with the affection people normally reserved for pets or people.

I grinned, but it didn't hide the fact that we drove back to Ravenclaw disappointed.

CHAPTER THIRTY-THREE

As soon as we returned to Ravenclaw, Jacobsen sent me home with Yuriko. All extraneous individuals had been ordered out of the area. I was frustrated and tired, so it was just as well. I needed rest before the upcoming full moon. I also needed to refresh my memory about the finer details of Werewolf law. In the past, everything I'd learned had been just personal curiosity about Lycans. Now I needed to know everything that I could.

Yuriko pulled onto Van Ness. "You want me to stay?"

"No, that's okay. To be honest, I've had too much company the last few days. I need some alone time."

"Well, call me if you change your mind."

"I will. Thank you. But I won't be all alone." In my driveway were two federal sedans.

"I thought they weren't watching your house while you aren't home?"

"Apparently that changed when Agent Mistry went missing."

She pulled into the drive and four federal agents surrounded the truck. Gunnerson peered through the tinted windows and motioned the rest of his team to back away.

"Sorry, Devon. All a bit jumpy," the blonde apologized as I stepped out of the idling vehicle. "Should have recognized this classic piece of metal." He patted Yuriko's 1957 Apache truck affectionately.

I shut the door with a parting comment. "See, completely safe."

Yuriko laughed and drove off with a wave as I stepped back. The feds returned to their positions and I went to the door. It took me a moment to find the right key and the phone started ringing before I made it inside. That happened often enough that I suspected a conspiracy. I got the door open and rushed to the phone.

"Hello?"

"Devon?" It was Melanie.

"Yeah." I walked back over to shut the door.

"Don't you check your machine? I've been calling all afternoon. What's going on with you?" She was angry but I hadn't a clue why this time. She was fighting tears. "When they had me in for interrogation, I heard one of the feds saying something about you going to a Werewolf ritual to rescue Jake. Tomorrow night at the full moon?"

"There's no choice."

Melanie started yelling. "Do you know how stupid that is? You of all people understand Lycanthrope mentality! Alone against a pack? Even one-on-one you're not strong enough—Sight or no Sight!"

"I'm counting on the rules." My argument sounded weak even to my own ears.

"The rules won't save you!" I could hear her breathing hard. "You saved me today by breaking the rules." Then the sobbing began and I heard Ulrich in the background trying to soothe her. I was glad he was witness to this, because I hadn't started it.

"Devon?" He was suddenly on the line. "I may not be a wealthy man, but I have honor and strengths. You will not go to this ritual—"

"Yes, I will!"

Ulrich repeated himself sternly, "You will not go to this ritual *alone*. I am coming with you."

I didn't know what to say. I had learned long ago never to rely on others. Certainly never to ask for help so that I wasn't disappointed when they refused. These friends, the ones I called my five best, were the exceptions. Although I made a point not to ask them for help, I had eventually learned not to feel guilty for accepting it.

I was touched by Ulrich's offer. It was something most people only offered a close friend. But he was offering to help a man he didn't even trust with his wife. Or hadn't. If I said 'no,' I would lose this step forward. But I didn't want him at risk. It was bad enough that I had agreed to let Yuriko come. I sighed. What was one more dead friend?

"I am honored." I had to at least make an effort. "But you are too important to Melanie."

"Didn't I mention?" he asked with a maudlin laugh. "She's coming, too."

CHAPTER THIRTY-FOUR

I spent the rest of the night on the internet at websites dedicated to Lycanthropes and their obsessive fans. Ulrich had offered up his password and log-in for the University so that I could search for full-text articles on Werewolf culture. He was currently enrolled in some outreach classes and I needed more than pop-cultural references to Lycans. Their lives, not just mine, could depend on it.

Some of the stuff on the internet was review, some plain wrong. I had to sift through it carefully. Before she let me off the phone, Melanie had asked me again why I was doing this. That question kept haunting me as I did my research.

Was it to rescue Jake or to prove that I could overcome my Werewolf phobia? It was important to know why I was risking my life—especially now that I was risking my friends' lives as well. It wasn't enough that I would have done it just to save Jake. Was that the *real* reason?

I looked at the clock and cursed. Three-twenty. If I didn't go to bed soon, I'd lose my last day of preparation. On the other hand, sleeping in late wasn't a bad idea because I'd have an even later night confronting Kimric on their home territory.

Melanie, Ulrich and Yuriko were all going to meet me at six in the evening. According to an online almanac, the sun was due to set at seven forty-three, which would get us there about thirty minutes before the start of the ritual, given an hour's driving time.

"I just hope that's enough."

I rubbed my eyes and shut down the computer, but I wasn't done. There was a good chance I'd die in this insane challenge. Should I leave a note? For who? No one in my family cared. I'd bought off my father with a hundred-grand. Mom was dead by gunshot. My favorite grandmother was also dead, but from a fall off of a mountainside hiking. There was no one left. No, that wasn't true. There was one person to call, but no way to reach him.

My grandfather, Colbert Tanner, my mother's father, was still alive, but I hadn't seen him in a long time. Not because he didn't love me. He just never stayed in one place long. Sometimes, he didn't want to be found.

Once in a while he appeared as if by magic. I was his reminder of the daughter he had lost. If I died, he would have been the only one to really miss me. I could have gone to my mother's grave and said goodbye to the lifeless ground that held her. But it wasn't her.

"Tomorrow I confront another of my fears, perhaps the greatest." I don't know why I felt compelled to say the words aloud. Maybe deep down I worried that the dead could hear the living. Regardless, I surveyed my large living room and its contents one last time before I went to bed.

Jake's scent on my sheets should have been reassuring, but my dreams were haunted anyway. In them, I left behind a field of mutilated bodies. I survived but my friends were the price I'd paid.

CHAPTER THIRTY-FIVE

The phone woke me. "Hello?" It was only nine-thirty and I was uncharacteristically groggy. So much for sleeping in.

"Mr. Mosteller?" The masculine voice was familiar but I didn't know why.

"Yes. This is Devon." I rolled over onto my belly and propped myself up on an elbow. I grabbed a notepad and pen, holding the phone with my cheek and shoulder.

"This is Officer Sorensen."

"Officer Sorensen. How can I help you?" I wrote his name down on the pad.

"It's how I can help you this time," he said gruffly. "But it has to be off the record. Completely confidential."

I was suddenly and completely awake. "Go ahead. My lines are federally secured." I crossed out his name.

"The police are not allowed to step foot into Werewolf registered territory. Not without a federal warrant. Even in hot pursuit." That much I already knew, so I listened impatiently. He hadn't called just to tell me that. "But outside it, those monsters have no rights ordinary folk don't have. You should know that as a personal favor, a few extra of my fellow officers will be patrolling in Squaw Valley tonight. Any indication of trouble and they will be able to offer assistance up to that boundary. *Only* to that boundary. Not the *inside* of it. You understand me?"

I got the hint. Lure them outside the boundary and the cops could arrest them for kidnapping or battery or whatever they could make stick. Or shoot them in my defense. Probably the latter, given his demand for confidentiality. Not to mention the not so subtle hints. I didn't approve of murder, not even Werewolves, but it was good to know.

"And how will these fine officers know what's registered territory?" I wrote 'registered territory' on the pad.

"The monsters have to file with the county and mark the key points with what they call them 'totems.'" His tone had relaxed—we were on the record again.

"I've heard about totems." I added the word to the cryptic notes, even if the information appeared useless at the moment. "To identify their pack for other Werewolves."

"Not exactly. Totems, by law, must be banded alternating red and white in addition to any other markings or designs. That isn't well known. Mandatory fences keep out wandering travelers and the totems warn the police not to cross the line. That's all we were told when Kimric moved into the county, but it was information the L.T.s drilled into our heads. Don't rely on fences or buildings or dead skulls on sticks for identifying the boundary. Only the red and white."

"Thank you, Sorensen. You're okay."

"Let's just say I repay my debts," he mumbled and the phone went dead.

There was no point trying for more sleep, I was too pumped up on fear. I also to get down to County Records and get a map of the filed territory. Leaving the notepad on my pillow, I slipped out of bed naked. I studied myself in the wall-length mirrors on the closet doors and played with my bangs. Longer than I liked. Funny that I should worry about my hair when I could be in a six-foot wooden-box after tonight.

I picked my briefs off the floor and slipped them on, then my gym shorts lying on the floor behind the bed. Fresh t-shirt from the closet. First, I was going to work out in the confidence course I had had installed in the back yard. My brain wasn't going to function well on six hours sleep unless I did. I'd already missed my Tae Kwan Do sessions twice that week.

I went down the hall, stopped in the kitchen and took a swig of Diet Pepsi before heading out back. Van Ness lots were atypically large. Some had larger front yards and others larger back yards. In my case, the front yard was small which meant I had room in the back for an oversized pool, workshop and a confidence course which included an obstacle run, monkey bars, gymnastic pommel horses and balance beams of differing widths and heights. It was the one thing I had done with my money that was just for me, so far.

When I walked around the workshop, I froze at what I saw. The two-inch thick rope nets had been torn into shreds and the monkey bars had been twisted into pretzel shapes. The balance beams, made of a thick metal alloy, were dented as if some giant fist had pummeled them. And the pommel horses were torn out of their cement anchors, the fabric shredded from their wooden cores.

"Fucking Lycanthropes," I snarled under my breath.

There was movement at the corner of my eye. I spun, fists balled defensively. How had I not noticed that a federal agent was sitting on one of the damaged balance beams?

"This piss you off? It would have pissed me off." Agent Shelby tapped the ruined metal under him. I was surprised that a high ranking agent would be doing basic surveillance.

"You been here long?" I asked.

"No."

"I guess I really pissed off those Lycans." I sat down next to him.

He turned to me with an odd expression. "Oh no, it wasn't the wolves."

I started to face him when I spotted a pair of black legs sticking out from under my Euonymus bushes. I jerked toward the body instead. It was then that something hit me on the back of the head. I knew then that Shelby wasn't Shelby, even as his laughter followed me into the blackness.

CHAPTER THIRTY-SIX

When I woke up, my vision was still blurry. I saw Christ hanging in front of me on a cross, his long, brown hair sprawled across his chest, his head hung down in shame. His skin was dark and I was pleased that my delusion was historically accurate. He wasn't some blonde Aryan born into a land of dark-haired, brown-skinned Middle Eastern people.

I shook the fantasy out of my head, which hurt where I'd been bludgeoned. The pain, on the other hand, cleared my sight. The figure still hung from a cross opposite me. It occurred to me that my arms were stretched out and tied in the same manner. That's when I began to feel other pains. My arms felt as if they were being pulled out of their sockets from supporting my weight.

The figure opposite me stirred. The dark hair rose, revealing firm, round breasts the color of caramel. Blood was caked under the left breast and trickled down the flat, tight belly. The face that looked back at me was Agent Shiandra Mistry.

"Shiandra!" I grew angry when I saw that both her eyes had been blackened and her lips cut up.

"Sorry," she said weakly.

A hand whipped out and struck the federal agent on her sleek, dark thigh. She winced and her chin dropped back down. The hand belonged to a Drow Elf I didn't recognize.

"Leave her alone, you bastard!" A handful of fingernails sank into my bare thigh, raking down hard, bringing with them bits of my flesh and of course blood trickled warmly down my leg. I cried out wordlessly. I was as nude as Mistry.

"You have no protection here, Human." I could not see my tormentor but she accommodated me by moving into my field of vision. Her I did recognize.

"Ma'alma?" I stumbled over her name. The memory was fuzzier than it should have been for events from only a couple of nights earlier.

"Ah, you remember that much, do you?" she crowed gleefully. "Good. I want you to remember why you are being punished. And who it is that is punishing you."

"Do you remember *me*, little Man?" asked the Drow male. His voice was deep and full of masculine spite.

"Er, nope. You know, I'm getting to the point where I can't remember everyone I've slept with, sorry," I joked. It wasn't in my best interest to piss off people who had me tied up, but when I got mad, even vulnerable, I grew a smart mouth. More than normal that is.

"Well, then I'll have to remind you. My idea of sex is rather painful. You won't ever forget it again." His laughter was so cold it actually made me shiver with fear.

Shit! I was hoping that by suggesting sex, it wouldn't happen. Usually it worked, because straight guys didn't want to be perceived as gay, even when torturing someone. This time the bad guy was gay and I was tied up like meat.

"If you survive it," laughed Ma'alma.

"Let—him—be." Each word cost Mistry pain.

"No Human shall ever tell me what to do!" The Drow struck her again. This time, his hand left a deep-blue bruise. "Especially not a female!"

"Why are you doing this?" I asked.

"He should be told." A new female voice spoke from the shadows. I twisted my head but the figure remained masked by darkness. I thought it was the sister, Lu'urna, but I couldn't be certain.

"His memories were taken away for a reason." The male spoke cautiously. "If he should survive our game, he shouldn't be allowed to know."

"Are you so weak that he will survive?" The hidden woman mocked him. Maybe it wasn't the other sister.

"I am not weak! You of all people know that!"

"Now, now, Mik," cooed Ma'alma to the male. "My brother is the strongest of the Drow and someday will lead the elders. For now, use that brute strength against these Humans who dared to humiliate us."

"Brother?" I asked. Ma'alma, Lu'urna and this Mik were sadistic siblings? That made sense, although referring to her brother in the third person when directly speaking to him was a bit mental. "If you three are such shits, what the fuck were your parents?"

I flinched when Ma'alma swung her hand around, expecting perhaps to wind up with a broken leg for that comment. Or worse, my genitals ripped from my exposed crotch. Instead, she tugged at her own hair where it dangled in front of her throat and laughed.

"They are dead, Human. They thought they could control what they had made." She studied me, as if unexpectedly pleased. "You are amusing. This one merely kept silent. You actually goad us to kill you."

"Hey, what's life without a little fun?"

Ma'alma slid her fingers along my bleeding thigh, painting on my skin with my own blood. Her other hand touched a part of me no woman had since I was an infant and I flinched. I knew I shouldn't have thought of her ripping things off and waited stiffly for my fear to become reality. But no pain followed. She laughed and stepped back so I could see her below me again. She stuck her fingers into her mouth and licked the blood clean.

"Do not worry. We are not Vampires. Blood for us is merely foreplay. Though, if a man were stupid enough to put certain things in my mouth, I do like fresh meat to chew on occasion." Ma'alma strode over to Shiandra and ran her pointed tongue from the back of the agent's knee, up her thigh until Ma'alma's face was hidden by her buttocks.

Shiandra arched forward, crying out as she jerked against the rope which held her in place. The Drow woman laughed wickedly and stepped from behind the federal agent grinning. She made a show of wiping her mouth with the back of her arm, but she stared at her brother, as if that was where the challenge lay.

Mik scowled at Ma'alma and glanced at the shadows. "We have them both here. Can we now begin to have our fun?" He ran his strong hand up Shiandra's inner thigh, not slowing down as he approached her vagina. His fingers brushed the lips of her labia and she flinched painfully. Were the two of them going to rape her first and then me?

"Not yet. Lu'urna was promised her revenge as well," ordered the shadow woman.

"Go and get her then!" snarled Mik to his sister. She glowered at him and folded her arms in a sexy pout. He rolled his eyes at her. "That works with other men, not me."

"That, brother, is because you've never had me." She sneered and slipped out of sight.

A sudden thought flashed into my head. How long had I been out? The Kimric ritual might have already started. A panic began to grow in my gut and I fought a desire to thrash against the rope holding me in place.

"All of this because you were thrown out of the bar?" That was my only memory of these people. But they had also mentioned 'missing' memories.

"You attempted to deny my sisters what they wanted," said Mik nastily. "Now they will have it. Only they have no reason to be gentle with the Human female. You might survive my tender affections, but she surely will not theirs."

"You actually mean to have sex with me?" I had still hoped he was just toying back with me.

"Rape is not sex," he purred. "It is just a form of power. Ask your Lycan friends about that. For you to know that I humiliated you, made you do things against your will—that serves my needs."

I didn't have a reply to that. The primitive part of my mind screamed and wanted to go into hiding before the pain. I flickered into that other Sight because of my fear.

In the shadows of our prison, the physical world grew even darker. I could See a glowing pattern of gold strands on Shiandra's body. It wasn't the work of the Drow. No, it was the mystic federal protection that Shelby had mentioned.

Something near my own body glowed faintly, drawing my attention and I looked down. Had it not been so dark, the tiny red spot on the ground beneath me wouldn't have been visible. It was the tiniest spell I'd ever seen, affixed to my shredded clothes. Where had that come from?

"Am I boring you Human?" Mik's strong fingers curled around my ankle. He jerked my feet like a whip and my entire naked body slammed against the cross. It hurt me as much as Shiandra had hurt herself at the Drow woman's touch. I cried out through gritted teeth.

With head still lowered against her chest, Mistry spoke to Mik, drawing his attention away from me. "You like sex with boys because you are afraid of women?"

I flinched at her words. No gay man wanted to hear that he was only gay because he was afraid of women. I was gay, so I *knew* that was a lie. But Mik wasn't really gay, just a sadist. He wouldn't know the lie in her words.

He roared and spun to face her. Maybe he *was* afraid of women. But she had bought me some time.

As he approached her, I focused on the magic on the ground. I could not cast spells, but if I could unravel it, perhaps I could use it as a weapon against him. But the red threads were so tiny and my arms were bound so that I couldn't use my hand to direct it closer. I turned to study the golden pattern embroidered onto Shiandra's skin, but some part of me warned that I shouldn't mess with her protections.

"I am not afraid of women. I enjoy raping them as well as men. I just promised my sisters that I would not touch you till they were done," warned Mik.

I returned my focus back on the magic beneath me, ignoring the conversation. I didn't care if the shadow woman watched. Even if they knew what I was, they wouldn't know what I was doing. Sweat gathered on my brow from the mental effort of using my ability as never before. Slowly, the threads seemed to grow clearer in the Sight and I felt a surge of hope.

It was a simple spell, as most were, with a single central node. I tried to unravel it with my mind, although without my fingers to direct my power, my first effort failed. Then I rushed a clumsy second attempt. Finally, the spell came free on the third try and I raised the unbound spell with the equivalent of metaphysical telekinesis. The magic floated in front of me, wobbling, but the power I was born with was growing with practice. It was the best I'd ever managed without being able to physically point at a spell.

But the truth was, I didn't really know how to use the unbound threads as a weapon. If I hurled it at the Drow, it might do nothing. The Drow were magical creatures and I couldn't tell what the spell did in the first place. If I tried to strangle him with it, like a physical force, it would only alert the other Drow.

I knew that if I tore the loose strands directly, that the spell could cause unintended consequences instead of simply exploding as I would have preferred. I was less afraid of the women than Mik. If I could take him out, it might buy us time. Though what the women might do to us—would their disemboweling be any more gentle than our rape? Choices, choices.

"Hey fuck face," I yelled.

Mik turned from whatever he was saying to Shiandra and opened his mouth to shout at me. I sent the magic hurtling into his opened mouth and willed a single strand apart. The magic exploded and a burst of red light shot out from his nose and from behind his eyes. He threw his hands to his throat and staggered.

"What's wrong, Mik?" I goaded. "You shouldn't suck if you can't swallow."

No sounds came from the shadows so I assumed that the mysterious watcher had left. That, or she didn't care what happened to Mik. Shiandra looked at the Elf as he fell to his knees with wide eyes.

"You said you can't cast spells."

"I can't," I replied. "But I can redirect existing magic."

"You didn't disable my body spell did you?" she asked horrified.

"No, not at all," I reassured her.

We heard female voices then, coming toward us in the darkness and they were bickering.

"Unconscious!" whispered Shiandra. She let her body relax. I did the same, the pain of my arms giving way to numbness.

"I want her to writhe in pain as I straddle her mouth," declared Ma'alma as they entered the room. There was the sound of clothes rustling and footsteps approaching. "Mik, what's wrong?"

I waited for her brother to reply, but instead there were just footsteps in the dark. I refused to open my eyes to see, for fear that the sisters would notice.

"They are unconscious," said Lu'urna. "All of them."

"She wouldn't have done this." They weren't talking about Shiandra.

"If Mik angered her sufficiently. A burst of power to make them all suffer," suggested Lu'urna.

"But why? She agreed to let us have our game. She asked us to take vengeance for their interference," complained Ma'alma.

"Perhaps she seeks to set us up. To raise her status in the enclave and make us prisoners," suggested Lu'urna. "She plays the game better than most."

"Listen!" whispered Ma'alma. Both Elves grew silent. After a time, I could not tell if they were still in the room. As much as I wanted to open my eyes, I resisted. The Fey could be preternaturally quiet.

I heard movement after what seemed like minutes and tried not to stiffen. "Shiandra! Devon!" The voice belonged to a certain blonde agent that I was growing very fond of.

"Gunnerson?" I opened my eyes and saw federal agents rushing into the room.

"Who did this? Kimric?" asked Gunnerson angrily.

"Drow," hissed Mistry as she was painfully cut free of the cross.

Light was let in through huge metal doors and I could finally see that we were in an insulated warehouse. When the agents cut me down, the pain returned in strength. I stumbled naked onto my knees. Someone put a blanket around me and I looked up gratefully.

"Never thought I'd see you naked," joked Yuriko. I could see the worry in her eyes and even apology.

"What time is it? Are we too late?"

She looked at me confused, then her eyes widened. "It's two hours before dark. You can't still go," she wailed softly.

Jacobsen and Shelby entered the illuminated warehouse. Their guns were drawn. "They okay?"

Gunnerson nodded and helped Shiandra stand. The men approached her, but refrained from doing more than touching her shoulders. "Who did this?"

"The Drow," said Shiandra. "Renegades."

"Not Kimric?" asked Shelby in disbelief.

"No, not related. How did you find us?" she asked.

"Officer Morimoto received an anonymous call." Jacobsen looked at Yuriko as if she were a suspect. "Told us exactly where to find you."

"Yuriko?" I asked as the paramedics arrived with a gurney and loaded Shiandra onto it. They carried her out despite her protests.

"I don't know," she whispered. "I don't think he was Human."

"There's a dead agent in your back yard, Mr. Mosteller." Jacobsen watched my reaction to his implied accusation. "Anything I should know?"

"Yeah. That I was about fifteen minutes away from being raped by a sadistic Drow bastard. Mistry was going to suffer the same. What do you think you should know?"

"How did someone know where to find you?" Jacobsen made no effort to be friendly. Suspicion ruined the best of friendships. We didn't even have that.

"I don't know. I have a personal stalker. He might have had a spell on me that somehow triggered the rescue call." It was only a guess, but Yuriko would have recognized Jiao's voice. "Otherwise, I don't know who could have left blood-magic on my clothes." I was in pain from supporting my own bodyweight, but I wasn't stupid. Jacobsen actually sneered at me contemptuously. He did everything but call me a liar.

I snarled at him, "If you think I'm not trustworthy, there's no point in us working together anymore."

I pulled the blanket more tightly around me, my muscles screaming in agony. I gritted my teeth and walked past the agents, with Yuriko close on my tail.

"Where are you going?" demanded Jacobsen.

"I've got a personal matter to attend, Agent. Go fuck yourself." I continued walking.

Outside, among all the official vehicles was Yuriko's truck. I walked directly up to it and waited as Yuriko rushed to open the door for me. I slid inside and she slammed it shut. I refused to look at the figure who had followed us to the car. I was so angry I was literally seeing red. Blood-red, like the magic that had let someone know my every movement.

Yuriko slid in the other side and started up the car. A piece of paper fell into my lap as we drove off. It was a map—a Werewolf territory map, stamped by the Fresno County clerk's office. I looked up, startled, but whoever had offered me this treasure was gone. I understood. The map was the only help I was going to get from anyone in the FBI.

CHAPTER THIRTY-SEVEN

"I can't believe you told a federal agent to go fuck himself!" declared Ulrich as we sat in my living room. I was still nursing my arm joints and chafed wrists but the pain was slowly fading.

"You haven't known Devon long enough." Melanie rubbed her husband's lean shoulders, smirking vindictively.

"I could really use that." I looked at Yuriko hopefully.

She didn't move from her stool. "If you are in pain, we shouldn't go."

"The painkillers Melanie gave me are doing the trick." I scowled at Yuriko before turning to Ulrich. "And Jacobsen deserved it. Just because someone happened to know where I was and called Yuriko was no reason for him to suspect me, or her, of being involved."

"His reaction was pretty strong," said Melanie, her smiled turning quizzical. "I wonder if it was something else?"

"Like what?" asked Ulrich.

"I don't know. Just from what Devon's told us, it was out of character."

After being conked on the head by the Shelby imposter, I seriously considered her suggestion. Could Jacobsen have been a Drow in disguise? Wouldn't the feds take precautions against that?

"So you're really not a federal consultant anymore?" asked Yuriko sadly.

"Would you work with people who suspected you of being one of the bad guys?"

"I was surprised you were able to work with the feds at all. You aren't good at dealing with authority." Melanie walked around the couch to sit next to her husband. He put an arm around her and looked at her dotingly.

"You sure you guys really want to do this?" I asked for the umpteenth time, ignoring the comment. I couldn't refute it but I didn't want to acknowledge it.

"No federal back up then?" asked Yuriko.

"Look, it's settled." Melanie glared at the other woman. "We've identified where the boundaries should be and it will be more impressive if you have back up. Clan to clan as it were."

I smiled despite myself. These friends were what got me through life in place of my disenfranchised and crappy family. I knew how lucky I was. "Okay, then we better get going. It's almost an hour drive."

"So no federal back up?" asked Yuriko again, this time with a grin.

"Who needs the feds," replied Melanie, also smiling at the insanity of what we were going to do. "Four humans against a pack of Werewolves. Sure, we stand a chance."

I stood and the joking died. Outside, the federal sedans were gone, but Yuriko's Apache, Melanie's 1986 GMC with its extended cab and my tiny S-10 were all there. "Gee, which pickup truck should we take?"

"Mine," said Melanie and to my surprise, Yuriko didn't protest. "Never know when we might need medical supplies."

We piled into her veterinary truck. Yuriko, Ulrich and Melanie sat on the front bench-seat while I climbed into the back of the cab and perched uncomfortably on a tool box. I might be sacrificing my life for a practical stranger, so I could certainly sacrifice my comfort for the friends who supported me in this mad venture.

The truck started up smoothly enough and we headed out. Melanie made snide comments in the front which had Yuriko laughing. Ulrich was quieter than normal, ignoring his wife's banter. And I sat behind them, alone with my thoughts.

I had the strangest wish that my mother could be with me, to stand at my side. Most sons would want their mother out of harm's way. But I saw my mother as a strong warrior type. I would have found strength in her strength. She was already dead, so I wasn't afraid of her dying again. Wanting her with me wasn't practical at the moment and, besides, I might be seeing her soon enough.

I focused instead on the possible options I would have when confronting the Kimric Fenris. If the pack was totally lawless, I had no chance at all. They would break the rules and kill us on the spot.

I had a rush of fear for my friends and almost backed out then. I could feel their love despite the innate conversation or awkward silences. But my promise to Jake weighed more heavily on me than forcing these brave and loyal people to let me face Kimric alone. It was mad, I knew. Kill three friends and myself to save one person?

'*The needs of the one outweigh the needs of the many,*' I quoted inanely to myself.

I felt the rustle of paper in my shirt pocket and took it out, smoothing out the wrinkles. Was it Shelby or Gunnerson who had slipped me the Kimric map? The chance that I could maneuver my confrontation with the Werewolves outside the pack domain was slight.

If I fell, my friends knew to run as fast as they could to that line. So obviously, the closer the better if I could manage it. And hopefully a squadron of cops would be there if they did run. God, would even a bastard like Sorensen set us up to die?

But there was the matter of Jacobsen which I couldn't let go. I was still bitter about the Chief's lack of faith in me, but our relationship wasn't personal. I didn't know how to have strictly professional relationships. People grew on me. I sometimes wished I could just keep someone at arm's length, like I pretended to do with Ramirez. But I knew the truth.

As far as Jacobsen accusing me of violating the law, I sometimes pushed things. I stayed within the intended limits of the law unless justice would be thwarted by some misguided legal requirement—like speeding on the way to save someone's life. But I never broke the law casually.

"Devon," repeated Melanie anxiously. From her expression, I'd probably not heard her the first couple of times. "You don't have the proof."

"What?"

"The documents!" She gripped the steering wheel so hard her pale knuckles were ghostly white. "You left them with the feds. Because you left pissed off, you didn't get the proof of the pack selling children."

"Shit! Too late now. We keep going. I just hope my powers of persuasion are better than I think."

"If they're gay boys, you'll be fine," said Yuriko smirking as if this were a night at the bar. "As long as they're mostly bottoms."

Bravado—my friends were as afraid as I was, but they wouldn't back down unless I did. It wasn't too late for me to save them. I could say let's just turn around, now! But that wasn't me. I'd made a promise and I couldn't let Jake down. And they came with me because they knew that I'd do exactly the same thing for any one of them. I wouldn't be the person they cared about if I wouldn't. I just hoped an answer to staying alive would present itself when we got there.

Melanie turned the truck onto the steep incline of Highway 180 heading into the foothills. Beyond Squaw Valley, 180 would take us all the way to the Sierra Nevada National Forest, although in this instance, we wouldn't go even as far as the tiny town itself.

"Remember, turn on Bramblepatch Road. It's the shortest distance from there to the ritual spot." I reminded Melanie.

"And we run like crazy if things go bad. I remember."

"You guys know I love you, right?" I said emotionally.

Everyone grew silent. Melanie wiped tears from her pale cheek. Yuriko stared out the window on the passenger side but I could see her trembling. Only Ulrich was unaffected by my words as he had been unaffected by their humor.

"Yeah, us, too," said Melanie sniffing. "Just don't make me cry again."

"Yeah!" wailed Yuriko playfully angry.

Ulrich spoke in the ensuing silence, his voice soft and serious. "I am stronger than I look. If it is a physical test, let me represent us."

I didn't reply, although I saw Melanie look at me in the rearview mirror as if to say 'please don't.' Yuriko stayed silent. About ten minutes later, Melanie slowed the truck and turned onto Bramblepatch. She leaned forward, shifting her grip on the wheel and looking for the territory markers.

According to the map, this was the only place that the totems actually abutted the road. The North and South borders were on property lines between five acre parcels. The Kimric clan owned three such parcels in a row, which meant that it might be hard for my friends, if they had to run for safety, to find this patch of road in the rocky foothills.

"I don't see anything," complained Melanie.

"There." Ulrich pointed to a short live-oak with bush-like branches. Behind it was one of the territory totems.

"Hidden from this side," muttered the veterinarian. "Those bastards."

She pulled onto the steep shoulder and jerked to a stop. I grabbed the wall to keep from sliding off the metal box. Melanie hopped out as if it were any ordinary medical call and opened the suicide door. I crawled out, rubbing the cheek of my ass where the metal had dug into it.

"Dark soon," I said, looking around. I smelled the familiar scents of mesquite and pungent kit-kit-dizze and other wild grasses I couldn't name. "Very soon."

"What's that smell?" Yuriko wrinkled her nose.

"Kit-kit-dizze—ain't it great? That's what we called it at camp—a Miwok Indian name if I remember right." I breathed deeply and smiled. "Also known as Bear Clover and Mountain Misery."

"You remember the dumbest stuff," replied Yuriko. "And it stinks."

"Says the woman whose native country eats fermented bean curds the consistency of semen."

"We all know how much you hate semen. You are seriously the worst gay man alive." Melanie went to the back of the truck and banged around in her kit. She came back with a small satchel. "Are you sure you won't carry any of the silver nitrate?"

I shook my head. "Not the worst gay man alive. There are some things I do very very well."

"Is this necessary?" demanded Ulrich and I realized he was the only one offended by our sex talk.

Melanie handed a duplicate satchel to Yuriko and I changed the subject. "As challenger I cannot carry silver. You are not challengers. You are witnesses which means by law, you can carry it purely for defense."

"Still don't have to like it." Melanie started off across the uneven slope onto Kimric property, kicking at the calf-high weeds. Ulrich rushed after her and Yuriko and I followed.

Yuriko's cellphone went off and we all jumped—all but the ever steadfast Ulrich. Melanie needed someone in her life who could anchor her. He was the opposite of what I was. Or rather, what I had been in our friendship. We paused while Yuriko answered the call, watching the shrub for wolf-like shapes.

"Hello, Agent Jacobsen." Yuriko's expression was sour as she strolled away from us to talk. It was habit, not personal. She looked pissed off when she came back. "Sorry, I'm ready."

I started to ask about the call—I'd never seen Yuriko look so pissed off, but Melanie interrupted me. "Why don't they have barbed wire around the property? It's required."

"Because," I moved toward her. "The pack can hunt anything that comes into their territory. Keeping animals out would be to their disadvantage." No fence meant that Kimric was even less lawful than I'd hoped.

"What about Humans?" asked Ulrich.

"A lack of fence should have given the feds grounds for a warrant. I don't know. Maybe no one physically came up here to inspect things." If we survived, I was going to have a long talk with the feds about their sloppy work. It would be a nice excuse to tell Jacobsen to fuck off again. Yeah, I was still pissed.

We didn't talk again once we started working our way through gullies and inclines, climbing around large boulders. Some of the wild grasses grew about a foot high and left fragrant bits of plant pollen on our pants and shoes. We stumbled occasional on the uneven terrain, but we waited, staying together.

We weren't far into the property when a shape dropped from one of the many boulders to land in our path. Melanie was in the lead and let out a startled scream. They knew we were here now for sure. As if there had been any doubt.

"You're trespassing," said a surly woman with shoulder length salt-n-pepper hair and wrinkled skin. Her bare arms were wiry but showed strong definition. Her clothes were soiled and she smelled of smoke and rotting meat. That troubled me. Werewolves were normally fastidious, like their wolf counterparts.

"We come under protection of challenge," I said formally. "I come to challenge the Fenris for violating pack law."

The woman gaped at me and then cackled. "He said you wouldn't come. No Human would protect one of us against our own. Not even for a bitch-boy who grew up as pretty as our Jakie."

"Who said?" I asked. "Jake?"

Jake couldn't speak the last I knew, but I believed that he might have thought that about me. I was glad I was going to prove him wrong.

"Not the boy. Though, for what you did to him, for that I should kill you." She spat on the ground. "Our Fenris made sure little Jakie knew hope was futile."

"You must let us pass by right of challenge," I repeated, surprisingly unafraid.

"I'm letting you pass because to deprive our Fenris of a chance to kill you himself would cause me a world of pain," said the older woman flatly. She scrambled back up the boulders with preternatural ease. This close to the full moon she probably could have leapt up twenty feet. Dusk started to make the real world into grays as if I were using my Sight.

"Come on. You can gape later," said Melanie back in the lead.

"If we still have eyes," added Yuriko. Sometimes her sense of humor was more disturbing than my own. Part of why were friends, I figured.

We kept walking, although Yuriko's twisted comment brought about a silence we didn't break. Above us, as the rocky outgrowths grew more numerous we detected shadowy shapes slipping along just out of sight, but they didn't stop us. Our progress slowed, however, as the dark settled into the foothills and a squirrel hole could mean a broken leg.

Finally, Melanie stumbled out into the center of a ring of irregularly shaped boulders, the shortest twice as tall as one of us. We knew we were in the right place as we walked into the center of an arena. Rock paintings marked nearly every inch of the stones. Haunting and menacing real-life figures sprawled throughout the clearing. Some were Human, some were full wolf forms. Only one was in a transitional stage—Jake and he was center stage.

Just like in a movie, every head turned to look at us. Surprise was written on most of their faces. Some were inquisitive and suspicious, others outright hostile. Jake sat huddled where he was, as if chained to the ground.

I searched the shapes that seemed most Human and made eye-contact with a familiar face. Carl. He seemed hopeful but my gaze was snatched away by a roar. I turned to a figure racing toward me. The sun wasn't completely down, but Lionel shifted as he ran. Only a few feet from me, a strange rippling finished his change from Human to Werebeast. It started at his head and worked its way down to his feet rather than everywhere at once.

I did the only thing I could think of. I pulled out the 10mm handgun hidden under my shirt. They weren't silver rounds—that would have been a violation of challenge. But even lead might slow him down. My delay in watching him transform meant that I never got the muzzle pointed above the ground. A gunshot sounded from beside me and I saw Yuriko standing in a braced position. Probably not the smartest thing for either of us to have considered. And we definitely should have told the other we were packing weapons.

Brains and one eye had splattered into the air behind the Lycan Yuriko shot. His face fell into the dirt as his front legs gave out on him. He quivered, but we watched in horror as the flesh and bone reknit itself into the bits the shot had removed. The eyes, even before the one was fully reformed, stared at us with violent hatred.

Growling filled the night as Humans throughout the arena became Werewolves. They snarled and chuffed as they closed in around us. In a moment or two, nothing we did or said would stop a group slaughter of us.

"Not silver!" I shouted. I looked at Yuriko for confirmation and she nodded. "The rounds were not silver!"

I took a step back, time to remind them why we were here again. "I came on challenge! Or does Kimric violate all pack laws?"

I kept repeating myself aloud. Physical force alone wasn't going to get us out alive, but perhaps a little shaming would help. If they would stop long enough to listen!

A silver-bellied wolf with champagne brown fur leapt toward me and I took a step back, bumping into Yuriko who had raised her gun once more. I held my gun reluctantly ready, but neither of us fired. The eyes of this Lycan bore into me with a strange warning. It felt like the promise of a threat if I failed him. I couldn't be sure I'd seen it right, because it turned and faced its fellow Lycanthropes. The wolf-head snarled at the closest pack members.

Unlike Jake, this beast spoke and I recognized his voice. It was the wolf-shape of Carl. "He is under protection of challenge! All are at the moment."

The Werewolves moved back, confused. I was a bit puzzled myself. They could speak, but Jake could not? Was that what they had meant by what I had done to him? Or rather what Agent Mistry had accidentally done to him? I couldn't exactly take credit and it was just as well. I assumed enough guilty responsibility without borrowing any.

"They shot Lionel!" snarled a white-furred individual with dark brown eyes.

Carl replied equally pissy, "He violated protection of challenge!"

This seemed to trouble the pack and confused them. They turned to look at a figure sitting calmly on his haunches atop a nearly flat boulder. The moon rose behind him, leaving him in silhouette. He was still in Human form, despite the moon growing visible in the dark.

I had read during those hours of preparation that it was considered a show of strength, staying Human longer than others, against the call of the moon. From what I'd understood, the strongest Fenris could resist the change the entire moon. Those types of alphas were rare. I hoped that this guy wasn't one of them.

"You protect the right of this Human to challenge us, Carl?" I knew he must be the Fenris of Kimric Pack.

"I protect the integrity of the clan," replied Carl. "He is in the holy circle. We are under the watchful eye of our Gods. Would you have them turn their back on us? We've already pushed away the other packs."

"Certainly not, though the Gods have not been with us in many years, Carl, my brother." The Fenris turned to me mockingly. "I am Lukas, Fenris of Kimric Clan. Who is it that enters our territory under claim of challenge? And what is that claim?" Ritual words which I vaguely remembered reading somewhere.

"I am Devon Mosteller, packless, challenging the Fenris of Kimric Clan for violating pack law."

The murmurs were a mix of Human and animal noises. Jake was alert now, looking at me and trembling. His mouth moved but the only noise that came from him was a long wailing howl. Some of the heads turned to look to him. When they gazed back at me, there were more looks of hate than before.

"You hold me in violation of clan law?" snarled Lukas. "I *am* clan law!"

"You ordered one of your pack to violate a challenge by rite of information in order to steal Jake from my care." I pointed at Jake, who was not the same as these Werewolves in the clearing. His proportions were different. I saw his skin rippling as if brushing off flies, but he remained as he was.

"Jake is subject to *shabatka*," sneered the Fenris. "He betrayed the clan. He sold our secrets to you for the pleasures of his body." Lukas paused, as though struggling against the pull of the moon. When he continued there was something less Human about his features, although it was hard to pinpoint anything specific. "His fate is sealed. Your challenge is ignored. If you wish to remain alive, leave now. You might actually survive your walk out."

"You cannot ignore the challenge!" shouted Carl frantically. There was grumbling among the wolves who looked from me to their Fenris, waiting for a battle of more than words. "Of all our laws, if you ignore a valid challenge on the night of a full moon, you are no longer Fenris."

"I told you, I am clan law! I have been Fenris of this clan for eighteen years, and shall remain Fenris. My word is law! Or must I have the clan fall upon you to remind you?"

A familiar voice snarled out of a wolfen mouth, "And she is Human law!" A reddish-brown Werewolf slunk into the circle, Connor Winters. He pointed at Yuriko with a long, muscular arm covered in sleek hair. "She is not allowed to be here. That is a violation of their laws and ours!"

Before I could do more than open my mouth, like when we'd drawn our weapons, Yuriko was faster. "I no longer work for the government. I already quit!"

Some of the nearest wolves sniffed the air, slinking in closer to her, without actually getting close enough to touch her.

"They can smell the truth," I said.

She looked at the wolves, gun in hand, not at me. "That's why I told the truth. I quit. Jacobsen said I couldn't come with you because I represented state and federal agencies at the moment. So I said what you said."

"You told him to fuck off?" I asked startled.

Melanie nudged my shoulder and I spun to aim the gun at her then lowered it. She chastised me, "Pay attention people. More important things than what she said to him, as long as she said it." She held a syringe of silver-nitrate in each hand. They looked small compared to the jaws of sharp teeth surrounding us.

The sniffing wolves slithered and slunk to their Fenris, the pack's ultimate alpha and growled and grumbled to him. He stared at Yuriko for a moment before turning to me once more. The look was the kind a wolf gives the rabbit pinned in its jaws before it clamps down and breaks the rabbit's neck.

"He has come here under challenge, a second time if you count your refusal to provide rite of information." Carl paced back and forth on all fours before me. "You may torture us all, but that does not change the facts. If the other clans learn that we have abandoned the most sacred rules that bind us—!"

"They will know nothing!" snapped Lukas. Carl went silent. "They live in the past, subject to rules and laws which have no place in the modern world. That is why we live as wolves because we obey rules as basic to life and truth as our animal counterparts do. We are men as well, and it is as men that we are strongest."

"You endanger us all by refusing his challenge," interjected another Lycan hesitantly. This one was nearly solid black with glossy fur. I could not tell if it was a male or female, given that their thick fur hid their genitalia. But I could see the fear in its eyes as it spoke, before it lowered its head submissively.

"You want me to honor the laws for this Human who did this to one of our own!?" Lukas pointed at Jake who took a step toward me and was jerked to a halt. It was then that I saw the metal collar and the chain which held him to the stone beneath him.

"I helped save Jake's life!" I yelled. "He was dying and only by forcing the Change would he live!"

"This is not the Change!" snarled one of the wolves, echoed by other Lycans. "It is an abomination."

"It saved his life!" shouted Melanie from beside me. "I am a preternatural vet and he barely survived despite the transformation. Would you really rather he died than live in this form for a short while?"

"He is still in this form, despite the moon!" snarled a mahogany-colored Werewolf with black paws. "And that Humans assign us veterinarians instead of doctors is reason enough to want to kill all the moonless."

"Devon, any idea why Jake is still in that form, given the moon is full?" asked Melanie softly. I shook my head and shrugged.

"Can you undo what you did?" suggested Ulrich quietly. I looked at the European and nodded thoughtfully. No point in reiterating that I hadn't done it.

"I can but try." I switched my Sight. The finely woven pattern which surrounded Jake looked very much like those of the Lycans surrounding us. I took a step forward, studied the white glow of mystical energy which was woven into Carl. Then I slowly compared it with Jake and saw how some of the threads were knotted up in the wrong places. It must have been a result of forcing the change and not being familiar with the spell. Shiandra had done her best, but it was wrong.

Something hit me in chest and I flew off my feet. I heard snarling and when my vision cleared, I saw a huge, grey wolf battling with the Lycan I knew to be Carl. The Fenris of Kimric Pack had transformed. The Human was no longer where he had been.

"You challenge me?" roared Lukas' from the jaws of the great, grey wolf. Carl backed off, head lowered slightly submissive.

"You did not answer challenge, Luk," whined Carl. Furtively he glanced from side to side at other pack members, moving as Lukas stalked him. "Saundra, Jorge, have we no longer any respect for our own clan?" He turned to two of the Lycanthropes pacing along the row of stones. "Chace, Mika, are you so afraid that soon none of our laws will bind us?"

"They will not help you, my brother," gloated Lukas. "You have only survived this long because we are blood. But tonight, Carl, you have proven you would usurp my power. Make Kimric chaotic and weak where we have built strength!"

"You call this strength?" asked Carl sorrowfully.

"We have avoided or won every challenge any clan has put to us. We have gained financial security where other clans live day to day hunting for prey. We are stepping into the modern world and leaving the restrictive past behind us!"

"If any other clan learns of what we have done, they will all come to tear us limb from limb. We are just now paying off our clan debts. I beg you, do not destroy us!" This triggered another bout of agitated snarling, Human voices mingling with the wolf noises.

"If anything, it is your weakness which will destroy us," snarled Lukas in disgust.

While they spoke, I leaned back and whispered to Melanie and Yuriko, "Get ready to run, weapons at the ready. They are more lawless than I had hoped."

Yelping drew my attention back to the confrontation between brothers. Two of the larger wolves, including one of those to whom he had pleaded, now held Carl down by fang and claw.

Jake wailed again and I flicked back into the Sight. Now that I knew what to look for, I quickly found the knots which were not supposed to be there. I tugged at them, directing my power with my hands, ignoring everything else going on around me.

Jake yelped in pain, but the first knot slipped. His body shimmered and his shape altered slightly. He was not fixed, but he was more like the others in the ritual circle.

Another large, furry shape hit me from behind and spun me to the ground. The air was knocked out of me and I couldn't shift my assailant's weight off of me for a frantic moment. Then I was suddenly free.

Rising to all fours, I saw a sight I had not expected. A Dark Elf, clearly one of the Drow, stood next to me, holding the unconscious form of Connor, the reddish-brown Werewolf, above me. The Elf took a moment to glance at me then inspected the wolves pacing the circle.

"Continue, Devon." He threw the Lycanthrope into the center of the arena with a heavy thud.

I turned back to Jake and found the other knot. This one was harder to break loose and Jake screamed in pain. I relented, but the look in his eyes pleaded with me. I crawled closer and saw that a third knot was next to the knot I had been tugging at. This node had to be freed first. Once I had done it, the last knot unraveled effortlessly. Jake's fur and skin rippled as his body changed from its unnatural shape to a full Werewolf.

"Who are you!?" screamed Lukas at the newcomer. The Fenris seemed afraid of the Drow standing beside me.

"We were once your keepers. Would you rather you went back to being our pets?" asked the Drow coldly.

"We have provided you with sources of blood!" complained the Fenris, showing his weakness. "It was not our fault Lenora died. We kept our pact."

Another Lycan, a female joined her Fenris. "You are in our sacred circle. Even when we were your slaves you had to obey the rules of the ritual circle. If only then."

"The power of this circle only holds if you obey the laws that give it that power," said the arrogant Drow. "And though you mistake me for another of my kind, I do not deny that you kept your pact with Lenora."

"Apparently you cannot keep your word for anything else, however," said a new voice, masculine and deep and entirely unfamiliar.

From the shadows behind me came the largest Werewolf I had ever seen. Bigger than a bear and blacker than the night. It stalked past Melanie and Ulrich and as it slid by me, my hair stood on the back of my arms and legs. My pulse raced and I felt the fear that made some people drop dead, stronger than seeing those Trolls in Melanie's office.

Other shapes dropped from the top of the rocks and slipped in through the opening we had found. More Werewolves and they surrounded us, facing Lukas. There was no way one Drow and four Humans could survive this many beasts.

"I am Lukas, Fenris of Kimric. Again I ask 'who are you?'" Lukas spoke this time to the huge Lycan intruder. What had we stumbled into here, I wondered?

Magic must have been triggered because my entire skin itched with it. I immediately guessed that the power two Fenris brought to a ritual circle must be strongly ruled by metaphysical laws. I doubted the glyphs on the walls, primitive though they seemed, were simply decorative.

"I am Tobaius, Fenris of Gaulteus Clan. I am here to witness the Human's challenge," said the bear-sized Werewolf.

"Why would Gaulteus Clan witness for a moonless?" asked Lukas suspiciously.

Tobaius looked askance at the Dark Elf. "It seems that I was persuaded by necessity in this instance."

"You come at the Black One's bidding?" shouted the Kimric Fenris in disbelief. "We were their slaves!" Spittle sprayed the air and dripped from his fanged jaws.

"That was another life, Fenris," shouted the Elf. "We were arrogant then. As you are becoming now."

Lukas paced back and forth before us, glaring at Tobaius. He then turned to the Drow and finally his gaze settled on me. His wolf lips pulled back into a Human grin that also served as a lupine threat.

"So he wants challenge, so he can have it," purred the Kimric Fenris. "Though how a moonless Human expects to survive a wolf's strength I do not know."

I swallowed hard then. If it was merely a matter of his strength over mine, I was dead. However, because he was in wolf form and I was not, there were rules. In Lycanthrope society, if a wolf form attacked a Human form, certain weapons were allowed in compensation. Knives, swords and even guns. I looked at my gun as I thought that.

"You are not allowed your weapon," said Tobaius in disdain. "You challenged him. Had he challenged you—"

Shit! He was right. The rules were meant to protect a Human form from attack by a lupine form, not to allow a Human form to threaten a wolf. But even a gun with plain ammunition wasn't much hope against a Werecreature, no matter the type. I had been counting on the rules, but really hoping for a miracle. If I prayed, it was to my own personal pantheon of gods, including the lupine God of Werewolves.

"Wasn't planning on using the gun," I said in false bravado. "However, as part of my challenge, I present evidence."

"Your challenge has been accepted, there is no need," said Lukas.

"It is the way of the ritual challenge. Or has the Fenris of Kimric forgotten?" I asked.

Tobaius nodded with grudging approval. "He has the way of it, Lukas."

"He will just tell lies!"

"Lukas ordered Connor of Kimric to reclaim Jake from my care, despite knowing that Connor refused my request for information. Pack law allowed me to decline the claim and released me from obeying pack restrictions since the request was not met."

"Is this true, Lukas?" Tobaius obviously relished this role as mediator. His resentment at being forced to attend had turned to interest.

"Jake is a member of Kimric. No one can keep him against his will. And look at what was done to our pack-mate!" Lukas turned and pointed at Jake. He was surprised to see a fully formed Lycanthrope chained to the stone by iron links instead of that inbetween form. The metal was either magically reinforced or Jake was an obedient participant because he hadn't burst free. His eyes were alert, watching me.

"He is healed, Lukas." Carl was no longer pinned by his pack-mates. Members of Gaulteus were standing aggressively behind him. I had read books suggesting that wolf size was the result of metaphysical strength and dominance, not just genetic make-up. Lukas was larger than most of the Kimric members but he was not nearly as big as the Gaulteus wolves.

"He hurt Jake!" roared Lukas. "He cannot be commended for healing what he has harmed."

"I don't know about that, Fenris," said the Drow smugly. "If the harming were intentional, perhaps not. But not all harm is done with such intention."

"Unlike you selling Jake into slavery as a child," I said clearly into the ensuing silence. Even Tobaius turned to me with outrage.

"We had been slaves many, many centuries," said Tobaius with a low, rumbling growl now directed at me. The hair on my arms and neck stood up again. Shit, I was going to be killed by one of the neutral guys. Not good. Not good at all! "You dare to accuse a Fenris, even *this* Fenris of such a crime?"

I saw Lukas grinning smugly at this change of events although he cautiously surveyed the surrounding wolves. He looked worried that most of them were not his.

"You heard him admit to providing us with blood, Tobaius. Where did you think this blood came from?" said the Drow. The black Fenris snarled and glared at Lukas.

I directed my words to the Kimric Fenris. "I challenge you for violating the most sacred of trusts. A Fenris is responsible for protecting the pack's children. And you sold not one, but two children!"

More of the wolves roared and snarled and I heard Melanie coaxing me from behind. "Pick your words more carefully. Say what needs to be said, but say it less Devon-like, for our sakes."

"How else would I know of Brell?" I ignored Melanie's instructions. If I played anything less than the alpha I was, the pack would sense it as weakness. "Formerly a member of Kimric, but like Jake, he was sold into slavery to a Drow for blood. At seven years old!"

"Is this true, Ti'mpal?" asked Tobaius of the wizened Dark Elf.

"Not for our use, Tobaius. But for the use of a part-blood, not raised with our kind." Ti'mpal selected his words carefully. "We would have stopped her had we but known. But it was Kimric who sold the children to her."

The muscular and massive Fenris of Gaulteus pack stalked around Lukas who no longer looked smug. His fear was palpable and the itching of magics in the air grew. Lukas kept turning so that his back was never to Tobaius' fanged jaws.

"If he does not speak the full truth, Lukas, then what blood were you offering? Your own?" growled Tobaius in those deep tones.

Lukas sputtered and backed away from the larger Fenris. "We offered," he started to lie. Lying to non-pack was permissible, but usually that was because it was to Humans who were incapable of smelling fear. During challenge, lying was another matter. Lukas dominated Kimric sufficiently that they did not question his lies. But Tobaius was clearly the stronger wolf.

"The Human's challenge precedes your claim, Tobaius," snarled Lukas frantically. "You may not harm me. And if he dies, then this claim is satisfied. Even you cannot challenge me again for enslaving two worthless runts to someone that could make better use of them."

Tobaius' eyes narrowed at Lukas' admission and his jaw dropped open, fangs showing like pearly white daggers. It was plain he wanted to rip out Lukas' throat, but unlike the Kimric Fenris, he obeyed pack law. It showed in his metaphysical power and the unquestioning cohesion of his pack.

"You are correct, Lukas. But if you kill the Human, as I've no doubt you will, we will be watching for any excuse to challenge you," replied Tobaius coldly.

Lukas and Tobaius stood there, glaring at each other—one with shrewd fear, the other with cold destruction. The two packs were silent, watching like frozen statues.

"If you know he's guilty, why don't one of you fight instead of Devon?" exclaimed Yuriko into the uncertain quiet.

She came up to stand next to me and I put my hand on the small of her back. I bit gently at her shoulder, more to reassure myself than her. Let's just say that biting to me was a form of affection. Yuriko slapped at me as gently as I nipped at her shirt. She seemed to understand I needed the contact of my face against her body.

"They cannot," said the Drow officiously.

"Only the wronged can stand in place of a challenger on their behalf." Carl had snuck up beside me. Damned quiet those Lycanthropes—reason enough to be afraid of them alone at night. "Jake is the only one who could. He would survive no better than you, Human."

As the two alpha wolves stared hatefully at each other, I looked at Jake. He looked lost and sad, even as a Werewolf. I went to him and took his large canine head into both my hands. I had come here to set him free. If I was going to die, it was silly that he didn't understand why.

"Jake," I whispered. I tried to remember the Human face and body underneath the thick wolf hair and skin. His eyes were the green that had amazed me during our love-making. They held that same trust now, as they had when he had wanted me inside him. "I'm sorry I let you down. Even though I came here to save you, I will probably die. But you don't need to ever be anyone's slave again. Set yourself free."

The voice I'd forgotten he had, spoke from that wolf mouth, deep and rumbling. "I don't want you to die. You're the first person to ever claim me for me. Not for my blood or money from the sale of my body. Don't fight him. Leave me here."

"The challenge cannot be withdrawn," declared Tobaius. I had whispered not because I'd forgotten that they could hear, but because it allowed me the illusion of privacy, of intimacy.

"You are worth dying for. Any person with any goodness at all in them is worth dying for," I whispered again. "I would die for any one of the friends who came with me. They came knowing they might die for me."

Jake began weeping, which was an uncomfortable thing to witness given he was a Wolfman. He pushed his muzzle against my chest, his right eye and cheek against my throat. "You have a true pack," he wept. "And I will never get to be part of it."

It broke my heart. Not because I hadn't realized just what I had. I knew that these people, who were not my family but cared for me like family, no, better than family, were as strongly tied together as any Werewolf pack. What I realized then was that Jake had never known this thing. He had been raised to expect it, to hope for it, but then had been made a slave and taken from it. A slave who was sliced and cut for his blood and his ability to heal.

I wrapped my arms around him and felt the chain linked to his collar against my skin. I switched my vision and Saw that indeed, the iron had magic reinforcement. I held him and unraveled the knots, letting the magic fall to the ground.

"You may have surprised Connor in his Human shape when he came to claim the boy, but you have no chance of defeating me. You would have been better off to accept Connor's refusal to acknowledge your attempt to enforce clan law," sneered Lukas, posturing.

"I'd rather kill you," I replied and stood up. Jake tried to follow, only to be reminded of the chain when it stopped him. "Let us get this over with, Lukas."

I walked toward the center of the ritual circle. The other wolves, including the Gaulteus pack, climbed or leapt up onto the circle of stones. The Drow Elf ushered my friends to a ground level opening between the rocks. They stood outside the circle, between the massive boulders. Tobaius did not leave the circle. Neither could Jake.

"Let him loose," I said, pointing at Jake.

"He is still subject to *shabatka*," snarled Lukas.

"On what grounds?" asked Tobaius, outraged. Lukas started to reply then stopped. From what I had been told, the basis for that ritual had been Lukas' own deception. He could not offer this same lie to Tobaius.

"Fine," Lukas growled and went to Jake. "*Manthrill!*" he said a single word, holding the chain in one furred hand. His fingers were longer than a Human's, his nails more like claws and the skin dark and hairy. He dropped the chain and faced me.

"I said free him," I repeated.

"The magic which makes the iron strong enough to hold one of us is gone. If he is not strong enough to break free on his own then he deserves to remain here," replied Lukas.

I didn't bother to tell him I'd already removed the magic. Tell the enemy as little as possible.

"I will be watching." Tobaius trotted to the edge of the circle and leapt up to a low rock. He pushed a couple of other wolves out of the way and took his prime vantage spot.

"Time to die," said Lukas chuckling. We heard a metallic thunk and both of us turned to see Jake struggling against his collar. He lunged and the chain struck futilely against the stone. "You are so pathetically weak, Jake. Even as a child, your preferences were obvious."

"Gay bashing as well?" I asked the Fenris with a hateful grimace. "I'd forgotten how homophobic Lycanthropes were."

Lukas ignored my goading and focused on the ritual, "As the challenged, I declare wolf-form. No weapons and to the death."

"Not so fast, Lukas," I said loudly. "Pack law gives me some discretion. Because my challenge to you is for fitness as Fenris, not for me to replace you should I win, I can select the nature of the challenge."

"Ridiculous," said Lukas. "When you challenge the Fenris of a pack it is always a physical contest and the challenged gets to choose degree of harm."

Tobaius spoke again, "There are some challenges with mandatory punishments, such as death or sexual submission. But there are no challenges, Human, which allow you to avoid fighting tooth and claw."

The wizened Elf spoke up, his voice clear and strong despite his age, "Perhaps it is because you have not known your freedom for the same length of time that you were our pets, but there are older laws of the pack. You once were more civilized. It was we who encouraged you to fight tooth and nail to keep you in line."

"And for your amusement." Tobaius was ungrateful for the reminder.

"Surely you have not forgotten the Laws of Sindak?" asked Ti'mpal, careful not to sound superior. Tobaius sat up and looked down at us.

Lukas glanced at the Elf uncertainly and bitter. "I know of no such laws."

"I recall something," said Tobaius. "They were rules which held when we were young as a species. When the clans used to get together once every few years. That was the last I heard of Sindak."

"Your laws are written down, not merely in the mind," suggested Ti'mpal.

The Elf looked down at me and I saw something like worry. I had never seen this stranger before and yet, he was here with Tobaius trying to keep me alive. Why?

"You have the Kimric Scrolls?" Tobaius raised his wolf-brows at Lukas.

I was interested, because they were like the holiest of relics for a pack. The history as well as the rules of pack behavior were detailed in them—sort of a Lycanthropic bible. No moonless had ever seen them.

Lukas refused to answer, but Carl once more risked the Fenris' wrath. "Ours was destroyed in a fire."

Tobaius looked at Lukas then to me and shrugged regretfully, "I'm sorry, but I will not take the word of one of the Black Ones that there are such laws specific to this challenge." He looked around the circle at the various shapes and colors of the two packs. "Are there any here of Kimric or Gaulteus, who, on threat of life, can swear they know of such rules and what they contain?"

I waited hopefully, looking from wolf face to wolf face. Most only glared back, although a handful looked away in shame or distress. Not every Werewolf was bloodthirsty by nature. You fought to survive. You fought to maintain social order. Some just liked to fight because killing was killing. The Drow had spent centuries bringing out the worst in them. No one spoke up.

"We could postpone challenge until this is confirmed," suggested a female voice from the shadows. Werewolves, unlike Humans, needed little light. But ritual braziers had been lighted so that some small amount of yellow glow enabled me to see only those close to the fires.

"No, the challenge was made this cycle, it must be met this cycle!" Lukas stared into the dark. He could see the speaker, even if I could not. I saw a shadow slink out of sight timidly. Kimric was not a cohesive pack.

"I must agree with the Fenris of Kimric," said Tobaius reluctantly. "This challenge will be of physical confrontation. I'm sorry Human, for your claim is just. If only one who was competent to do battle had offered the challenge."

Lukas grinned, relieved in his victory. He sat on his hind quarters, like some domestic beast and panted, waiting. I looked at my friends but they were being held back by the arms of the Elf. Yuriko actively struggled to get past him but I shook my head. With a sad look, she finally obeyed, standing there passively. Melanie's eyes were running with tears, and I wished I could make all the pain her loving me had caused disappear. My own tears were the only answer I could give her and she smiled at me. It took more strength than I'd given her credit for to wipe her face and offer me the thumbs up. Ulrich nodded at me, looking grim and proper as always. He'd get some peace out of my death, anyway.

I wished that my three other dearest friends could have been there if only to say good-bye. Sonny Perez was busy with the restaurant I had financed in San Diego, but I knew that he would be mad that I hadn't invited him to this madness. Evangelina Vera Cruz was in the Philippines, doing research for her doctorate on Ilocano, one of the many Filipino languages. Like Melanie, she was a friend from college whom I had grown very close to. Of all my straight girlfriends over the years, she alone hadn't fallen in love with me. But she had learned to love me as a friend, which was harder for her. She'd been gone ten months and I'd have no chance to remind her that I loved her, too. And then there was Nigel Evans in England. He was scheduled to come to San Francisco in a few weeks for his annual visit to the States, but I wouldn't be there. Nigel had offered me the other side of life to Sonny's. Sonny was carnal lust and Nigel was dignified temperance. I was that thing in the middle.

I thought about what Jake had said—that as a truly blessed man, I had formed my own pack. Not that I was their Fenris. No, if a pack had something like a representative child instead of leader, I was more that. I reminded them that loving someone, sometimes, wasn't a bad thing. I just was glad to have gotten to love them first. Now my world was safe knowing that I was loved back.

"Okay, Lukas," I said wiping away tears.

He laughed cruelly at me. "Already crying? Afraid of your death?"

"No, fuck-face! I'm sad because I'm leaving behind me some of the most amazingly good-hearted people on the planet."

I was pretty pissed. Why did the dummies always think that emotions and love were weaknesses? I'd had a couple of boyfriends like that, but they hadn't lasted long. I got rid of that type pretty fast, no matter how good the sex. Being the hard ass all the time was just too draining.

"So you acknowledge you are going to die?" asked Lukas, pleased.

"Well, since I'm Human and you've got like, super-strength, I think the outcome is pretty much assured," I said calmly. I looked once more at Jake who strained against the chain toward me. "Remember, Jake. You were made a prisoner—a slave as a child. You are a man now and if my death does anything, let it give you back your freedom."

It sounded cheesy in my own ears, but what other reason was good enough to die? I wasn't saving anyone's life anymore. No, that's not true. If I hadn't come, Jake would be eaten alive and his soul ripped out of his body as a sexual slave. My fairly quick death would keep him from a slow one. But if he didn't gain any strength, then I had failed. I may have been willing to die for him and my belief in protecting the weak if I had to, but I wanted it to mean something. I wasn't that selfless.

"Quit stalling. As challenger, you must tell the clan you are ready for battle." Lukas wanted me dead, to avoid some last minute reprieve. My death meant he was safe from other challenges. Me, I was trying to stall as long as possible.

"Fine. Hear me, Kimric Pack who has violated pack law more than once—and Gaulteus, who stand as honorable witnesses to this challenge," I struggled to remember the wording. If I wasn't about to die for real, I would have died of embarrassment. Being the center of attention was never my preference. "I, Devon Mosteller, unaffiliated with any clan, hereby declare my challenge against Lukas as Fenris of Kimric." I made fists—as if they would be any good in a fight with the thick furred Werebeast. "Open!"

On the last word, Lukas sprang with such speed that I flinched and dove flat on the ground and rolled. I surprised him because he was suddenly on the other side of me, spinning around to see where I had gone. I felt fire along my back and blood running down into the back of my pants. His claws had found their target, just not their mark. One lucky dodge before I was a rabbit in the wolf's jaws.

"You actually avoided my swipe?" he asked, amused. He could not see the blood or feel the pain which made my closed fists clench tighter. He raised his hand to his fingers and sniffed. Then licked. "Ah, you didn't. That's good. I was going to kill you fast, but now I see it might be more fun to do it slowly."

I couldn't pretend any longer and sank to my knees, reaching back to clutch at the shreds of the shirt. "Arrrrgh!" My hand came away smeared with blood. The lightheadedness was probably psychological from seeing the thick red liquid. As I dropped forward onto my unbloodied hand, I considered that my wooziness might be real.

"Dying already, Human?"

I tried to think of a snappy come-back. "Fuck you, Lukas."

Lukas' grinning wolf's jaws were suddenly inches from my face. He opened them in a yawn and his fangs dripped with spittle. I thought he was going to lick me before he bit off my face. I would have, just to be perverse.

"You need a breath mint." It wasn't true—his fangs were pearly white and all healthy Werewolves had sweet breath!

"Laugh, boy-lover," whispered Lukas. "I get to kill you and they can't touch me."

"At least Jake is free from *shabatka.*"

"Maybe, but he's back with us. We may not be able to sell him out, but he's beta to the core. We'll find equally fun ways to damage him." Lukas laughed.

"He can petition another pack to take him." I wasn't confident that that was true, but I hoped it was.

"Who will take such a pathetic weakling? Especially one so damaged as him?" Lukas snapped at me and I flinched back, wincing as my back-wounds flared.

"We will take him, if he petitions," said Tobaius clearly into the arena. Lukas looked over his shoulder and growled viciously.

"He can't petition if he doesn't survive tonight's challenges," growled Lukas evilly. I watched his face. His mouth opened as if something were forcing its way out. Lukas screamed. I thought his rage had finally driven him a bit mad. But the prickling which I had been feeling all along my skin suddenly was gone. Not the fire from the gashes on my back.

"Who interferes?" Tobaius turned to the Dark Elf.

"This is to be a fair fight, is it not?" The Elf shrugged calmly. "Lukas has been drawing power from the pack. Devon is unaffiliated. I could, if you'd rather, offer power to Devon instead?"

Tobaius scratched under his chin and looked down at us. "You only severed their links to the clan?" Ti'mpal nodded. "That is acceptable. Clan law forbids outside magic to assist a challenger. It has never been argued for clan energy. However, as witness, I approve. Any who disagrees may challenge me, immediately!"

Not a grumble or growl. Those who stood with Lukas believed he could kill me without their help. Nor did they want to challenge Tobaius. But the loss of pack metaphysics took a heavy toll on Lukas. He writhed on the ground as if it hurt. I wasn't stupid enough to launch an attack at him. He was still stronger than me and could heal himself if I gave him a non-fatal wound. The Fenris stood and shook himself. His confidence was shaken, but he was finished playing with me.

I tried to stand but bending hurt my back like crazy. I sat on my heels facing the Werewolf. Lukas hunched down, preparing to make his final, killing leap. I lifted my chin up high, fighting for courage.

I would not close my eyes. I would not!

Lukas roared and sprang at me. My mental discipline sucked. I couldn't remain sitting as the Fenris launched. My eyes clamped shut and I threw myself to the side. He hit me and I rolled hard against one of the stone walls. My back slapped the rocky surface and I screamed with agony.

Lukas didn't banter with me this time. He crouched again and leapt. I couldn't have moved if my life had depended on it. And of course it did. I watched everything as if in slow motion, his gaping jaws and extended claws reaching for me.

He fell forward onto the ground right in front of me, hard and sudden. Another furred form gripped Lukas from behind and there was a hush among the watching Werewolves. Jake had broken his chain and done the unthinkable. He had attacked the Kimric Fenris.

I looked up at Tobaius, afraid that a swarm of huge wolves were going to come into the circle and tear him apart. But Tobaius sat there nodding his approval.

Lukas reached over his shoulder and clutched at the weaker Jake. I couldn't see Jake's face, but I could hear his voice, crying over and over, "No. No. No."

The Fenris broke the smaller Werewolf's desperate grip on his body and threw Jake straight up over his head into the rock just above me. I heard him thunk painfully against the stone. An ordinary man would have been dead. Jake slid to the ground and collapsed next to me. He nuzzled me weakly before Lukas grabbed his leg and hurtled him against another rock. I used the boulder behind me to push myself completely up, hissing with pain but unwilling to give into it. Jake wouldn't survive Lukas' ferocity much longer than a Human would.

I looked around the circle. No weapons, they were forbidden. But my powers? They were a genetic part of me like the Lycan's fangs and fur. I shifted my Sight, looking at the world of shadows and darkness. I Saw the golden net that shielded the entire interior circle from the rest of the pack. Drow magic, clearly. I owed the wizened Elf gratitude, if I survived.

I turned my Sight on Lukas and Jake. I Saw the magic that made them Lycanthropes. I could hurt Lukas as I had hurt Jake tugging at those mystical nodes that tied the magic to them, but that would not stop the Fenris. I frantically scanned the rest of the arena. There was only one solitary glow in the small circle. The spell I had undone before Lukas had attempted to deactivate it. A bit of power that I might be able to use.

Until recently, I'd always limited myself to thinking that I could only unravel magic, not use it. Making that spell explode in Mik's jaws—I'd never needed to use magic for anything like that before and it had been a liberating moment. If it worked once, it might again. But unraveled as that nearby spell was, I had no way of knowing what effect it might have on a Werewolf. Now I didn't care.

I reached out for the threads of magic as I had done against my Drow captor. The magic faltered for a moment because I flinched when Jake was slammed against the blue-grey ground of the arena again. Lukas, aglow in the Sight with his Lycanthropic curse, began striking Jake so hard and with such rage that it would have frightened me even if Lukas had been an ordinary man.

The loose magic responded awkwardly to my power. I had to avoid being distracted by my worry for Jake and the violence he suffered. I pulled the threads toward me with greater focus, toward the Fenris. Lukas' fist paused in mid-blow and something made him look up.

"What are you doing?" he growled suspiciously. Jake's smaller blue-grey shape pulsed more dimly, his helix-shaped mystical threads fading as his life-force weakened. He was helpless beneath Lukas and Jake hadn't been healthy to begin with. Would even a Werewolf survive such trauma? His face was bloody and a couple of teeth had been knocked out of his upper jaw. They'd grow back if he survived but he looked battered to the point of death.

"There is one thing you forgot about," I said, looking at the bit of magic that rose into the air, still under my control.

Lukas turned to look behind him, to see what it was that I Saw. I tightened my mental control over the glowing magic. He didn't have my Sight and was unprepared for what happened.

"Die!" I forced the magic he couldn't see into the Werewolf's open jaws. For the first time, maybe because it was the first time I tried, even out of my actual Sight, I could still feel the magic as it slipped inside the wolf's throat. I tore those hidden threads with my mind and Lukas roared in pain as mystic energy blazed inside his head.

The world flickered back into ordinary shadows, not the blues of my Sight, and Lukas collapsed on top of Jake. I staggered toward the two Werewolves, gasping in agony. It was nothing compared to the pain of pulling the heavy Fenris off of Jake. I tried to turn my whimpers into a masculine growl but only to give myself strength. Jake was still breathing. But so was Lukas.

"Finish it," said Tobaius from the rock tops.

"I have to kill him?" I asked unhappily.

Tobaius looked at me as if I were mad. "He would have killed you. That was his intention."

"He didn't win!" yelled one of the Kimric wolves. It sounded like Connor. "There were two against one." Other beasts grumbled and snarled a chorus to his complaint.

Tobaius rose onto two legs and roared like a wild beast. Total silence followed his bellow, except for the rushing of blood in my ears and the ragged noise of my breath. "The participants did not object to Jake's presence in the circle. In fact, your Fenris refused to release him at the challenger's request. Jacob Winters and Devon Mosteller were within their rights."

I looked at the unconscious Werewolf next to Jake. I believed that I could kill to protect, although I'd never actually had to. But to kill when walking away was enough? I didn't have it in me.

My dad's voice echoed in my head—pussy. A couple of lesbian friends had argued that pussies were stronger than people gave them credit for. Maybe they were right. Regardless, I'd settle for being a pussy again if it meant I could live with myself.

"If I can be declared the victor without killing Lukas then I don't want to."

"It is your right." Tobaius glowered at me.

"What happens to Jake and Carl and the others if I don't kill him?"

"Jake is yours. That was the specific reason you made challenge. You could even take Lukas' place as Fenris if you had fought him alone."

"So he remains Fenris?" I reconsidered killing him. Other people counted on me to make the right choice.

"He is not!" declared Carl. "He lost the challenge. He violated clan honor."

"He remains Fenris," Tobaius snarled back at Carl, though his anger was for me. "You have won, whether you kill him or not. But he is still Fenris of Kimric."

Several of the Kimric wolves howled into the night. It was the saddest, most forlorn sound I'd ever heard. I looked at Lukas, his throat torn open, blood soaking into the ground. The spell had exploded. I didn't have anything left with which to kill him. I doubted the chain attached to Jake's collar would have sawed the beast's head off.

"Why couldn't he have made himself subject to Human laws instead of just Connor." I rested my forehead on Jake's body, listening to his heartbeat.

"What?" asked Tobaius. "Explain yourself." His sudden, animated interest gave me hope.

"When Connor refused my challenge for information, he said he would rather put himself under Human law than to answer my challenge," I explained. Had I overlooked something that could have saved me the blood loss and injuries we had suffered? "Connor said he made his claim for Jake under Human law."

"And it was after this that Lukas ordered Connor to ignore the challenge and claim Jake?" asked Tobaius significantly.

"Exactly," I replied but the world started spinning. I looked over at Yuriko and Melanie. They were no longer being held out of the circle but I could tell that they were afraid to enter for fear of costing me my victory. I smiled at them, happy we were all alive. And then I fell face down onto Jake and thought how comfortable his flat, furry belly was as I lost consciousness—again.

CHAPTER THIRTY-EIGHT

I woke on my stomach, lying on a blanket draped over the tail-gate of a cold vehicle. I felt a prickling at my back that wasn't magic but when I tried to stir, strong hands held me in place.

"I'm just sewing you up," said Melanie. Because I was held down, my cheek against the blanket, I couldn't see who was behind me. It wasn't a familiar position for me and I squirmed uncomfortably.

"We didn't think you'd want the police involved in this," said Ulrich.

"What happened? Where's Jake?"

"Relax, relax," coaxed Melanie. "You saved the day."

I heard Ulrich laugh for the first time since I'd met him. "You are the master at understatement, my Love."

"Are you going to tell me?" I asked, watching anxiously as she stuck the needle into me. I couldn't feel it and breathed relief. "Please tell me you didn't shoot me up with animal tranqs."

"If it's good enough for animals, it's good enough for you," chuckled Melanie. "Now hold still!"

"Who else is pinning me down with a vice-like grip?"

"I am here, Devon Mosteller. I pay my debts." The voice took me a second to place—Ti'mpal, the Drow Elf.

"What debts?" asked Ulrich.

"Let's just say that I was asked to intervene," said Ti'mpal with quiet humor.

"By whom?" My head hurt, but in a familiar way. I was suffering caffeine withdrawal. Great!

"Someone you know," said the Elf enigmatically. I left it alone.

"Well, thanks. To you and to whoever sent you," I added. "So, again—what happened!?"

"Done," said Melanie and the men released me. "Go ahead, Husband, explain so I can put my stuff away and we can go home."

I sat up, shirtless, but the evening was warm enough that I didn't shiver. Ulrich reached out to help me stand, but I put up a hand. "I think I need to sit a moment."

The lightheadedness from blood loss came back, just sitting on the tailgate. We were still parked on the side of the road at the edge of Kimric territory. No other vehicles in sight and the foothills were especially quiet.

"Well, where to begin?" said Ulrich to himself. His German accent had faded again. "You were declared the victor, so even though you passed out the issue had been formally settled. And although they couldn't help you, Gaulteus used some Lycanthropic metaphysics to feed energy into Jake. He's as good as new. The Elf offered to heal you, but?" Ulrich looked at Ti'mpal.

"My power cannot heal your body. Against foreign magic or perhaps certain other brain-related chemistries, my magic is effective on you. However, it seems your talent as *sovenjor* is not limited to conscious manipulation." Ti'mpal frowned but nodded as if I had agreed with him. "If you have no further need of me, I am finished here."

"*Sovenjor*?" I asked. The word sounded familiar but I couldn't recall where I'd heard it. The Elf simply ignored me so I let it go.

"Thanks for your help. Oh, wait! About those sisters, Lu'urna and Ma'alma?"

"I am aware of what transpired. Your friend Yuriko explained it to me before she left with the federal agents." Ti'mpal made eye-contact and I believed his promise. "It will be looked into."

"Yuriko went with the feds?" I glanced questioningly at Melanie as she came back from the cab.

"You saved the day," she began with a smirk. "Not just by helping defeat Lukas in the circle, but by mentioning Connor's reliance on Human law. If a Werewolf accepts Human law in a challenge and his Fenris supports him, the Fenris is subject to Human law."

"What does that mean?" I still wasn't following.

"He is now subject to criminal prosecution for slavery and child endangerment," said Ulrich. "Tobaius' people even escorted Lukas to the edge of the pack territory. Your friend Sorensen was here with a few Sheriff's cars and happily hauled him away. The feds showed up a short while later."

"Don't forget about conspiracy and manslaughter," added Melanie.

I turned back to look for Ti'mpal's reaction but the Elf was gone. No good-bye, nothing. "Is the Gaulteus Pack still around? I want to thank Tobaius."

A figure walked out of the shadows. "Tobaius took his clan home after they carried Lukas to where the cops were waiting outside our territory." It was Carl, still in Wolfman form. He looked at me oddly. "They invited Jake to go with them."

"Then he's gone." I couldn't keep the sorrow out of my voice. "Well, he's safe now. That's what's important. He'll learn how to be a member of a pack."

"But I want to learn how to be part of your pack." Jake emerged from the shadows to stand beside Carl. His Werewolf shape was larger than I remembered, probably the effects of Tobaius' healing him. "It was for you that I broke my chains."

I jumped off the tailgate without thinking and the blood rushed from my head immediately. Thankfully, Ulrich grabbed my arm and kept me from falling onto my face. He had to help me stand, so Jake came to me. He didn't touch me, keeping his furred arms dangling at his sides.

"Do I still repulse you? This is my moon-form. It is part of who I am." The boy was still part of the wolf, but there was also something older in him that hadn't been there before. Something had died in Jake. Not just his fear or passivity. Something good, too. He had helped me almost kill a man.

"I would like to try and learn to be comfortable with all of you." It was as much as I could promise him. "I admit I've grown very fond of you in just a few days."

Jake turned to Carl and the two wolf-beasts faced off. "Thank you for the offer, Carl. But if Devon will have me, I am more comfortable in his pack. I belong to him."

Carl nodded and looked at me. "Take care of him, Devon. Kimric owes you a very powerful debt. Do not hesitate to call us to task. We may take some time to grow back our heart and honor, but this you can be sure of." The Kimric Werewolf turned back to Jake. "Never be anyone's slave again. If you need us, we are also your family."

"Connor—!" I said unhappily but Carl interrupted.

"His uncle is very much regretting his part in this," chuckled the Lycan. "Tobaius let him know in no uncertain terms that any harm that came to Jake in the future would befall him. Ten fold. We do not take kindly to sellers of our kin. Even if to our shame we let it happen."

Jake put a hand on Carl's furry shoulder and squeezed. "I am safe now. I had a lot of years to wonder what was so horrible about me that I was given to my mistress. I never got angry at the clan but I grew to hate myself. Be content. I didn't die."

Carl slunk back into the shadows with one bitter parting comment. "Brell did."

I stared at the shadows. They were ordinary shadows that came with night and not my Sight. They covered the rolling hills and rocky outcroppings with a sense of eeriness. The bushy live-oaks made wicked looking silhouettes against the moon. Something told me that with Jake in my life, this wouldn't be the last time I stared at this same scene. Not that I had any trace of foreshadowing talent. Sometimes you just knew things.

"Come on, Devon. Just because I stitched you up doesn't mean you don't need better medical care. I just stopped the blood and cleaned the wound."

Melanie sighed and I reached out for Jake's head. I cupped the over-sized wolf ear and scratched behind it as if he were my favorite dog. "What's wrong?"

"I'm assuming that since it was a claw slash and not teeth that you didn't get any of his blood in your wounds," replied Melanie gravely. "But we won't know till next moon if you'll change."

It hadn't even occurred to me. I had been thinking rather poorly since the night of the mugging. Moments of fuzziness were more frequent. Maybe I did need to go in for a CAT-scan. Maybe I just needed to sleep a week. Although, with Jake around, sleeping wasn't likely to be my main activity in bed. There was the guest bedroom but I was pretty sure I wouldn't be able to banish him there, again. Nor would I honestly want to.

"I didn't get his blood on me. Even at the end, when I pulled Lukas off of Jake, I remember putting my head on Jake's belly, not his chest where the blood was," I argued. "It has to enter an open wound. I fell onto my face, and I don't have any cuts there."

"I know, I know," said Melanie frustrated. "You know I'm a pessimist sometimes. Just considering the possibilities. Like I worry about you and HIV sometimes."

"Such a beautiful woman with people who love her should never be pessimistic." Ulrich took his wife into his arms, squeezing her breasts against him as he leaned forward to kiss her chastely on the lips. She held him tightly back and I smiled. Jake shuffled up and took my hand in his clawed one. His skin was hotter than mine. I looked down and his green eyes shone in the moonlight. I'd fought to keep him and we'd actually won.

"You know what? I'm ready to get my ass home."

"Yeah, I'm sure it's your ass you want to get home." Melanie grinned as she pointedly looked at Jake's backside.

"Must it always come to sex with you two?" asked Ulrich, once again distressed.

For a change, Melanie didn't grow sad with his choice of words. She hugged him and grinned sensually up at him. "As if you'd complain about all that sex, Mister."

Embarrassed, Ulrich's gaze flickered at me as he nodded. "I think Devon is right. We need to get his ass home."

"You know, Ulrich, I think you're gonna fit in this pack just fine." I led Jake to the truck and this time he rode in the awkward back. But the whole drive home, his wolf-head rested on my shoulder and I'd never felt more loved.

CHAPTER THIRTY-NINE

Melanie and Ulrich dropped Jake and me off at my place. Inside, I shut the heavy cherrywood door and turned to face the room, pressing my back against the wood frame. Jake, in Werewolf form was curled up on the couch, his head resting on the back, staring at me. If a wolf could look contented, this one had mastered bliss. He sighed happily.

I was apprehensive. Jake as a Human was entirely my type but as a Werewolf he was about a hundred pounds heavier with nasty looking claws and fangs. Since the Gaulteus pack had fed him metaphysically he had increased muscle mass and there was something more feral about him. My flight response stirred. I knew he wouldn't tear my throat out. Or maybe I didn't know that. That was the problem. How much could I trust someone you'd only known a few days? Especially a Lycan?

"Well, Jake." I stopped myself. I had started to use my dog tonality with him. He wasn't even a person to me, already. I tried again, "Jake, look, I am not going to pretend I'm okay with this form."

"I know," he said. "I can smell your fear." This time he didn't seem sad. "But I know you are trying. You risked your life to save me. How better could you prove that you loved me?"

"Whoa, wait a second, Jake!" I exclaimed. "I care about you, sure. You put your faith in me, and that's an honor bound obligation for me to uphold. But I never said I loved you."

Jake raised his wolf-head and blinked at me. His expression was puzzled. "You care about me. Isn't that love?"

"Well, yes, on some level. I mean, if you're suggesting love is—," I tried to clarify what I'd meant but he interrupted.

"I'm saying that whatever you call what you did to me, what you did for me, that was love. And I know that what I feel for you is love," he said firmly. "For the first time in my life I'm not alone."

"But I need you to understand. You are welcome to live here, but, we are just dating."

As I listened to myself, I wondered who I was trying to convince. If I was both physically and emotionally attracted to someone— especially someone who liked me back, I normally considered them my boyfriend. Why was I trying to pretend this was different? I'd already slept with him, so I knew the sex was incredible. I could gaze at his face for hours without being turned off. I even knew that he'd found inner strength to protect me as I had tried to protect him. What the fuck more did I need?

"Dating? You mean just fucking?"

"No, not just fucking. I mean, yeah, I hope a lot of fucking," I confessed with an embarrassed grin. He smiled back at me still puzzled.

My body actually responded to the memory of being inside of him, of kissing his hairless flesh and biting the meaty bits of his shoulders, chest and back. Maybe I could get used to his turning furry during full moons. "I just don't want to make any promises. That's all. I always make promises before I even know someone. I'm tired of making promises I can't keep and feeling shitty about myself because of it."

Eventually the truth always found its way out of my mouth. I had made a promise that I'd never let anything happen to my mom. If I had been home maybe the burglars wouldn't have broken in. Maybe she wouldn't have gotten shot by my father. If only I had insisted she join me at the play!

"I don't want any promises. Well, except that you'll keep me and fuck me until you are sure you can never love me," he said with resignation.

The resignation in his voice made me sad. I wanted to hear excitement. But I couldn't bring him that excitement. And I realized that there was one more item to finish my full disclosure—the other guy actively in my life. Sort of.

"I have at least one other person I'm dating." The Santeria *hechecero* expected me to give him a chance and I'd given my word. Another promise. Shit!

"You mean fucking," Jake said sadly.

"Yeah, okay, this time I mean fucking," I replied truthfully. "Maybe more."

"But you'll keep me, too?"

"For now," I confirmed. "If I fall in love with someone, Jake, I can't be with someone else. Once, I thought I could be in love with two men at once. But I realized that that was because I wasn't in love with either of them."

"Then that's the only promise I want."

"What?" I asked uncertainly.

"That you don't send me away until you are in love with someone else. I've been alone my whole life. Every day with you is more than I've ever had. I will take that as long as you can give it." He rose off the couch and walked on two legs toward the bedroom. In beast form, he was almost seven feet and had to hunch over as he walked.

"Where are you going?" I asked nervously. I didn't think I could sleep with that shape he wore in my bed.

"To the spare room. In the morning I'll be Human again. I'll come to your bed then." He didn't sound disappointed. In fact, he sounded content. "Good-night, Devon."

"Good night." I watched him until he had disappeared down the hall.

I looked at the clock. Three a.m.. The pain in my back was increasing as the local wore off. I'd promised Melanie I'd see a doctor in the morning, but for tonight, I needed to sleep and let new blood be produced. Jake was going to be out of luck if he came to my bed in the morning, what, two hours or so from now? As it was, I was going to have to sleep on my stomach. So much for being comfortable.

CHAPTER FORTY

I reached out for the phone before I was even awake. Reaching for the phone strained the sutures Melanie had put in my back.

"Devon, are you alright?" shouted a voice from the receiver as it neared my ear. Agent Shelby.

"Yeah, just hurt my back. What's up?" I replied automatically. A hand touched the small of my back, below the injury and I winced in pain. "Still okay," I hissed through gritted teeth at the blonde in bed next to me, ignoring the phone for second. The local anesthetic had worn off.

Jake's face looked tragic with guilt and he pulled his hand away as if I'd slapped him. "Sorry." He shuffled off of the bed naked.

"Come back here," I said gently, glancing at his tightly muscled thighs and the flat line of his hairless belly with more than a little arousal. "I was just startled."

I turned back to the receiver still gritting my teeth while the pain rocked through me. "Agent Shelby, what can I do for you?" I reminded myself I was mad at Jacobsen, not Shelby.

"I hear you were hurt pretty badly last night," said the black federal agent. "Did you see a doctor?"

"My own personal veterinarian sewed me up but thanks for asking," I said sarcastically.

"I understand you not going to the hospital. Doctors have to ask too many questions. However, we have a medic on staff who offered to make sure you're okay."

"You have a doctor on staff in the preternatural division?" I asked surprised.

"Well, he's fully qualified, even if he was never officially certified," hedged Shelby. "You interested? Gashes like you took could leave serious scars without attention."

"What, my good looks will be ruined if I don't?" I joked. I didn't mind small scars. Melanie had said that the four gashes were six to eight inches long. "Sure, send him over." I paused. "You sure it's okay with Jacobsen since I told him to fuck himself?"

There was silence on the phone and then I realized Shelby was laughing. "He says it's good."

"He said 'it's good?' That's all?" I asked suspiciously. Jake's hand started caressing my naked ass and I turned to look at him. "Don't get any ideas. Only thing allowed there is a tongue. And—," I pushed his face away as he moved it toward my bare bottom, "with these injuries in my back, not even that! I'd squirm so much I'd rip out all the stitches."

"What's that?" asked Agent Shelby and I put the receiver back to my mouth.

"Nothing, Agent Shelby," I muttered slightly embarrassed. "So, you were saying?"

"Actually, Jacobsen's exact words were, 'I've decided to take 'fuck you' as an offer I'm declining, not a resignation. Take care of him.' End of quote," said Shelby.

"Well I'll be damned," I said. "Not that it makes me feel any better since he didn't trust me. But okay, then, send over the doctor."

"He's on his way. Oh, and just so you know, Jacobsen and Mistry are with him." Shelby hung up without waiting for a reply and I cursed.

"What's wrong?" asked Jake still rubbing my lower back and butt.

He looked very good naked and my libido reflected it. However, I couldn't move my back to do anything with him at all. The only way he could do all the work was if I laid on my back and that wasn't going to happen. Oh, I suppose there was oral sex, but since I didn't exactly like doing it, I wasn't comfortable asking someone else to.

"'No sex' is what's wrong," I grumbled. "But we're going to have company. We both need to put on some clothes.

"I don't have any," said the blond innocently gazing at my erection as I slid off the bed. I laughed and looked into his green eyes. God they were beautiful.

"I've got like three pairs of gym shorts in that top drawer. Go on. Get me a pair while you're at it, please."

"Where are the briefs?" I noticed he kept his ass facing me. It was a great view. My desire for him wracked my body. I decided to lie on the bed again, hiding my need for him from us both, though I could feel it crave release as I flattened it under my belly. I pulled the comforter over my lower half.

"Same drawer. Briefs on the right, gym shorts on the far left."

Jake dutifully went to the dresser and got us both underwear and the running shorts I liked to wear around the house. He put his on first and I continued to watch the sleek lines of his body as he bent over to pull them up. The pain helped me combat my desire for him, but barely.

Jake came to the bed and pulled the comforter off the lower half of my body. He slid the briefs on over my feet while I was still lying down. He carefully pulled them up onto my thighs, straddling the outside of my legs with his. He ran his hands along my skin as he pulled the underwear over my butt. I arched to let him slide them over my crotch but he licked playfully at my butt which made the process more difficult as I grew aroused again.

He took a minute to adjust the briefs. No matter what he did, a bit of soft flesh peeked through the top.

"Someone wants attention," he said playfully.

"Yeah, not gonna happen."

I slid off the bed and stood painfully to let Jake help with the gym shorts. When he knelt down in front of me, I throbbed inside the briefs again. He licked his soft lips and gazed up at me. There was flirtation and even lust in those green eyes. But he waited for me to give him permission. Later would be sooner after all.

"I can't promise how good I'll be. It'll be my first," said the blonde with clear infatuation in his eyes.

I sighed, giving in. His desire, my own gratification. "If you want."

At the first touch of his mouth on me, my back spasmed and I cried out through clenched teeth. He didn't want to stop and finally, I had to push him off of me. Climax would have been unbearably painful.

"What's wrong?" he asked, disappointed but still eager.

"The pain. I wouldn't have survived the spasms in my back."

He grinned and pulled my briefs back up, then the gym shorts. Standing, he licked my nipple and put his hands on the sides of my hips. "I'm glad you liked it. Like I said, it was my first time. I'll get better."

I blinked. "You'll get better? My body already thinks your every touch is heaven. My God, Jake!"

He chuckled and the little boy in the man was once more visible in his eyes. He touched my stomach, running his fingers along the slight indentations of where a six pack was forming. I trembled and had to grab his arm to keep from reacting with more pain.

"I can't wait till your back's healed," he whispered in my ear, his breath raising the hair on the back of my neck like the fear of Lukas had the night before. He brushed his lips against my ear as well, a soft touch that made me lurch inside my briefs. I had forgotten what it was like to be with a guy who could make my body tremble just with his lightest touches.

"Me either."

The door-bell rang and Jake stepped back. I was both grateful and sad that our intimacy had come to an end. Unfortunately, my body wasn't quite so obliging. "Can you answer that?" I tried to push my erection into a position which wasn't so noticeable.

"Why even bother trying? Like you can hide that thing," Jake said provocatively as he headed for the door.

"Dying car accident victims, wrinkled old woman's dugs." I struggled for a mantra of images that I'd hoped would kill my arousal.

I heard Jake greet someone and recognized Shiandra's voice. I glanced around the room, kicking my dirty underwear under the bed. I saw the blood on my sheets, small splatters from when I'd moved in my sleep—or maybe when I'd reached for the phone. That was enough to dull my sexual arousal. On occasion I might have liked to inflict a little pain with sex but not the kind that really hurt anyone. Especially myself.

"Where is he?" I heard Agent Jacobsen's voice and took that as my cue to exit the bedroom.

"He is here." I walked stiffly into the main house. To my surprise, Special Agent Thandryl and Yuriko were with them. Thandryl carried a white calfskin briefcase.

"I don't see any wounds." The High Elf scrutinized my exposed flesh uncomfortably.

I patted my stomach as if I had somehow gained weight under the combined stares of everyone in the room. I turned around and heard at least three of them gasp. I thought Jacobsen was the hold-out. Figures, since he was the heartless bastard among them.

"Where's this doctor?" I asked, still facing away.

Thandryl approached and stopped me from turning by clutching my arm. His other hand was cool against my back as he gently prodded the area around the gashes. "Slight inflammation. To be expected."

"Thandryl's the doctor?" I asked, still facing away. "But Ti'mpal, the Drow Elf last night, tried to use magic. It didn't work."

"That wizened Black Elf?" asked Thandryl irritated. "He may be old, but his power lacks finesse. Come. Lie on the couch here."

"I'm starting to get a complex being on my stomach all the time without someone underneath me," I joked.

"Don't worry, Devon, your reputation as a top isn't being tarnished," said Yuriko with gentle humor. "Let the Elf help you."

I walked stiffly to the couch, carefully putting myself onto my stomach but couldn't keep from gasping as the stitches strained and fire seared into my nerves.

Then the pain was gone.

"Is that better?" asked Thandryl, aloofly. If he could be diplomatic and dispassionate, I could too.

"Yes, thank you."

"Don't worry, Devon." Jake came to sit on the floor next to the end of the couch closest to my head. "If it would make you feel better, I could lie underneath you while the Elf works."

"No!" exclaimed Thandryl. "Not if you want my help!"

"It was a joke, Agent Thandryl," I said. He hadn't joined our laughter.

No one spoke for a few minutes. I watched Jake study Thandryl. There wasn't even the flicker of jealousy in me because Jake's expression was merely inquisitive. The only time I'd ever been jealous in the past was when there was an actual foundation for it. Jake wasn't interested in the High Elf.

Although I could see Jake watching Thandryl intently, I couldn't feel the Elf doing anything, magic or otherwise. "Er, what'cha doing back there, Thandryl?"

"Can't you feel anything?" Jake was surprised.

"No, he can't," replied the Elf. "I used a bit of mind magic to inhibit pain receptors. And as much as I regret saying it, while your mind accepted my magical influence readily enough, your body seems to be resistant to mystical healing. I hate to even agree slightly with one of the Dark Elves. Not impervious, however. I am removing the stitches one at a time as I seal up the wounds with magic."

"So it's working?" It wasn't vanity about the potential scars, honest.

"Dark Elf magic and True Elf magic are of two different sources." Thandryl was pleased to elaborate. "Ours comes from a connection with the Earth Spirit while theirs comes from blood magic. When they do not draw on another's blood, they draw upon their own."

"I didn't know that."

"It's not as if they would want it spread around. They agreed not to use blood from outsiders when they signed their federal treaty. The U.S. Government was afraid they'd kill Humans, make them look like natural deaths and then reap the benefits of their murdered victims' blood. They can take blood from donors, small animals or, unknown even to the federal government, from their own bodies."

"But that Elf didn't cut himself when he tried to heal Devon," commented Yuriko. "I watched closely."

"They don't have to. The blood is accessed from their body and simply passed through their system later. There are limits of course on how much magic they can use in this manner. Like Humans, Elves require time to replenish blood. Even when it runs cold and foul like theirs."

"So if the—True Elves know about this, why haven't they just spilled it to the feds so that the Drow will have fewer options if they break the treaty?" I asked. It seemed out of character that a race that hated another so much would keep its secrets.

"The Council's idea of honor, Human. The Black Elves wish to prove themselves changed. Our leaders wish to give them that chance. It does not mean we trust them or forgive them." Thandryl paused. "It is merely prudent."

I turned my head a bit more, trying to see what the Elf was doing, but I could only see the trunk of his body. Behind him I saw Jacobsen looking at me uncertainly.

"Look, Jacobsen," I started to apologize but the Chief of the Preternatural Division stopped me.

"No, Devon. You reacted like I'd hoped you would."

"What?" I asked, thrown off.

"You couldn't go into Kimric territory affiliated with our agency. I had to make sure there were plenty of witnesses that you had severed that affiliation." He studied my face for a reaction. My neck hurt from being at that angle so I laid my head back on the couch.

"Okay."

I relived the incident. Was that how it had happened? Did he do it on purpose or was he covering up for hurting me? Simply because now he needed me.

"And," he continued while I considered his words, "I just wanted you to know I never doubted you. But I know you aren't a very good liar, so I had to be the bad guy."

"He's right, Devon," said Yuriko, "You don't lie enough to be any good at it. I could teach you."

I laughed and Thandryl hissed at me to be still. I looked at Jake who sat there watching me adoringly. That sort of attachment was nice when you liked them back. And I liked him a lot. "So that's why you called Yuriko?" My question was a distraction while the Elf continued to work on me. "To get her to quit, too?"

"No, actually," answered Jacobsen wryly. "I've reviewed her file. She's damned good. Excellent marksman, mechanically inclined, bilingual. I didn't want her to jeopardize her position with the police because it would make it that much harder to recruit her."

"Recruit me? For what?" exclaimed Yuriko.

"Not just you," explained Agent Jacobsen. "You happened to be with law enforcement, so your record needs to be more pristine. But, Devon as well. Our department is looking for an outside team. Affiliated with us, but who can operate slightly outside of our guidelines. Like you did last night."

"That was personal," I said. "I wouldn't just risk my life for a complete stranger."

"I think you'd put yourself at risk for a complete stranger if it was the right thing. I don't mean jumping into a pack ritual-circle and challenging the head alpha. I still think that was stupid. Though how you got a Drow Elf and a second pack to show up as your back-up still intrigues me."

"I don't know why they were there. Ti'mpal said something about paying his debts. Tobaius was there because of him." I looked at Jake. "I think it was a debt due to Jake because Kimric sold him to Lenora for Drow magic rituals."

"Then you are one lucky son-of-a-bitch," said Jacobsen.

"I hardly think, Jacobsen, that Yuriko and I make a very serious team," I chuckled. "I had all my friends behind me or it might have turned out differently. We're no *Mission Impossible*."

"Exactly. We want to recruit the vet and her husband. And of course," he said and paused significantly. I craned my neck to look at him. Jacobsen was holding his breath apprehensively. "Thandryl."

"What?" exclaimed the Elf. He stood to challenge Jacobsen. "You cannot just palm me off on some Humans like I'm chattel."

"No one is palming you off," said Shiandra. She stepped between Jacobsen and the Elf. "The agency is offering you a permanent position here, as the official liaison and team member of the group. Sort of like G-men and junior G-men. Though, Devon's comment about *Mission Impossible* isn't too far from the truth either. Disavowed—officially unofficial. I'm staying on, too."

The Elf did not get the reference. He glanced down at me and scowled. Then he looked at Yuriko and Jake. "I suppose the pup is part of this also?"

Jacobsen smirked and looked at me, not Jake. "You think he's up to it? From what Yuriko said, he showed a lot of courage."

I smiled and nodded, "Yeah, he had that when it counted. If he wants to, he has potential."

"I told you'd I'd practice," he whispered to me playfully naughty. I laughed aloud and for once there was no responding agony. He gazed at me as he replied to Jacobsen. "If Devon says 'yes,' I say 'yes.'"

"Oh, what the fuck. If the Elf says 'yes,' I say 'yes,'" I teased.

Thandryl scowled again. "Do not mistake my aid as affection, Human."

"Oh, Thandryl, I do not mistake that you have any affection for me. That does not mean that I cannot maintain affection for you."

He had healed me, orders or not. That he was being punished for some crime I didn't understand and yet he tried to work with us Human types raised my sympathies. I grew attached very easily. He was a pain in the ass, but underneath it, he seemed almost Human. Not that I'd call him that to his face.

"Well, if Devon and Melanie say 'yes,' I guess I say 'yes,' too," added Yuriko.

"What, are we like the new *Mod Squad*?" I suggested. '*Mission impossible*' sounded too high tech for this bunch and I ignored the obvious 'odd squad' joke.

"Yuriko will operate in her usual Fresno County capacity. We managed to hide the fact that she was in Kimric territory during this event," said Jacobsen.

"Even though she shot one of the wolves right in the face?"

"That was you, Mr. Mosteller," corrected Agent Jacobsen and I looked at him. "Are you done, Thandryl? Can he get up so that he can look me in the eyes?"

"Oh, yes, he's done." Thandryl was staring into space, thinking hard.

I flipped over onto my back and there was no pain or rough edges of skin to catch on the cushions. "Good as new?"

Thandryl nodded and looked at Jacobsen carefully concealing his emotions, "Why am I being offered this? You've made it no secret I am a pain in your butts." He sounded uncomfortable using the Human metaphor.

Jacobsen looked at Shiandra who shrugged and smiled. Jacobsen nodded and the female agent answered, "Because you are only on special loan to us, so you are not already subject to federal restrictions on behavior. You are the only Fey our department presently has, as a result of xenophobia higher-up in the department. You have medical and magic training. You balance out the team and, simply put, we need you. Oh, and the fact that Devon said he didn't mind working with you didn't hurt any."

Thandryl looked at each of us again, his eyes lingering the longest on me. "You do not object to working with me, despite that I dislike you?"

I sighed and smiled sardonically. "I'm like a really twisted song, Thandryl. When you first hear it, you hate it. But after a while, the very twisted nature of the lyrics make you learn to like it. Then you start singing it. I'm like that. I have faith. Even you will eventually come around."

"I don't quite understand the analogy," said the Elf, "but I will accept that you have some false notion that I will come to like you."

"Perhaps not 'like,' Thandryl," said Shiandra kindly, "but perhaps respect?"

"Perhaps," said the Elf dubiously. "Very well, if you think you cannot function without me then I accept. But do not presume your affections upon me."

Thandryl stepped away from me and started putting away his medical toys. I looked at Jacobsen who still watched me expectantly. "Have you talked to Melanie?"

"Yes," said Jacobsen with a twinkle in his eyes. "How long have you been friends?"

"What, eleven years? Why?"

"Because she said that 'if Devon says 'yes,' then I say 'yes.'" He laughed. "I've known husbands and wives that start saying the exact things in similar contexts, even when away from each other. So I was just wondering. Oh, and that Ulrich character said if his wife was part of this, he would go wherever she went."

"Sounds like our European mystery man," I said. "So how does this team work?"

"We'll talk about the details in a few days," said Agent Jacobsen. "I'm still trying to get certain approvals. None of you will change your jobs or anything. You will just be covert operatives who can cross certain lines we can't. However, I still need your help, Devon, on the murder case. Yours and Jake's. You think you can make one more trip to the crime scene later? Jake's attorney is expecting a call to say when to meet her there. Jake is still a suspect, but only on paper."

"I don't know what else I might find, but, okay."

"Never know. I don't want my third case as head of this department to go cold." Jacobsen nodded to Mistry and Thandryl and started for the door.

I called to him as an afterthought, "Were you the one who dropped the map into the truck?"

"What, you thought it was Gunnerson?" He raised his brows at me in disapproval and then they walked out the door, Jacobsen, Mistry and Thandryl.

"You not with them?" I asked Yuriko, stretching my back and feeling the flexibility as good as new.

She shook her head. "No, I drove separately. Just in case."

"You wanna come, too?" I invited her to the crime scene. "Not that you need to. After what you did for me last night, that was real friendship."

"I'm kind of in trouble," she said sheepishly, glancing furtively at Jake. "Antonio didn't get sex last night."

"Ah, well, that would get you in trouble with me as well," I teased, although I didn't say what I really thought about her boyfriend besides 'closet case.' "I'm just glad my pig-headedness didn't get you hurt."

"I would never make you go without sex a whole day," added Jake, which embarrassed me as much as Yuriko.

"Go home then," I told her, blushing. "Jake and I will be fine."

"For the record," she said walking briskly to the door, "I never said he didn't get sex for a whole day, just not last night. You're not the only one fond of mornings and afternoon quickies."

She left grinning. When the door shut behind her, I sighed and sat back down onto the couch. Jake jumped up playfully and plopped kneeling onto my lap, his knees on either side of my waist, his butt firmly nestled onto my crotch.

"You're better now." He was grinning, too.

"Hm, where were we?" I asked him flirtatiously. He slid off the couch onto the carpet and tugged at my shorts much less carefully this time.

"Let me remind you," he said wickedly. There really was no pain and I was going to have a whole lot of reasons to thank Thandryl the next time I saw the snooty Elf.

CHAPTER FORTY-ONE

A few hours later, showered and freshly dressed, Jake and I pulled once more into the Ravenclaw complex. Jake was dressed in my gym shorts and a t-shirt but we had decided I would take him clothes shopping afterwards. I had money to burn and I couldn't have a live-in boyfriend naked all the time. I'd never get anything done!

And the moment I'd accidentally called him my boyfriend and he had glowed with joy like a thousand suns, I couldn't go back to calling him 'the guy I was dating.' Besides, Yuriko was right. If I was sleeping with a guy, I considered him my boyfriend. That was partly why things were so messy with Jiao. Technically, I guess I had two boyfriends now, although in truth, Jiao was something different. In my head I knew the distinction between the two relationships, even if I couldn't explain it to someone else.

There were no government vehicles or reporters on the street except for a single PD black and white. Mrs. Leung was scheduled to arrive shortly, even though no one planned on questioning Jake this go around. So when we parked my S-10 in front of 4501 Talon we sat there uninterrupted and I tried to really talk to Jake for the first time. It was the one place sex couldn't get in the way.

"Jake, when you were with Lenora," I wasn't sure how to ask the question, so I settled for my usual brashness. "Did you have sex with anyone? I know you said not her, but—?"

He glanced at his lap embarrassed. Then he gazed out the window, but didn't withdraw his hand from my thigh. I had my hand on his leg, too, just above his knee and squeezed it gently for reassurance.

When he finally turned back towards me, there was shame in his soulful green eyes. "When I was younger, twelve or thirteen. She needed money and there was a guy she knew."

Jake couldn't seem to find any words. He moved his lips silently, the panic in his eyes as he studied my reaction conveying more eloquently his feelings. I wanted to retract the question, to take away his shame, except, that I had to know. My need-to-know things about the people I was intimate with was a serious character flaw. "It won't change how I feel about you."

He leaned close and put his forehead on my bicep, his blonde bangs brushing my skin as he rubbed his cheek against my arm. When he raised his head, tears welled in his eyes. "I told you I'd never done that to someone. It was true. But this guy, he did that to me. He paid her to put his mouth there."

I wrapped my arms around Jake and held him tight against me. He gripped me around my waist, his breath hot against the crook of my neck. He didn't sob, but I could feel the wetness of his tears. After a moment, he continued.

"He wanted to do what you did to me, be inside me there. I knew I liked men. Lenora knew I liked men. She told him he could. She told me to let him. But he put his mouth on me like I was just this thing and he was hungry. Like he needed to eat and I was this thing he was going to consume. No feelings, no love, just hunger." Jake shuddered and I just held him tighter. I knew I couldn't hurt him with even my fiercest hug. He was a Lycanthrope.

"What happened?"

I didn't really want to know, but I had to. I was a guy and Jake was my new boyfriend. No one wanted to think of someone they cared about being raped. Men were funny about that. Rape victim as damaged goods. I'd dated at least five guys who had been raped as teenagers, although most of them had gotten over it. The two women I'd known who had been raped in their teen years were not nearly as well adjusted. I hadn't found the men as any less desirable or loveable. I'd just gotten angry and had wanted to castrate the ass-wipe that had hurt my boyfriend. That's what I was feeling now.

"Nothing." Jake laughed morosely. "He wanted to but I told him he'd catch it."

"What, you told him you had AIDS?" I was surprised. As lies went, didn't seem like it would be very convincing. Everyone knew that Lycanthropes couldn't contract Human STDs. "He wanted to do you without a condom?"

"Yeah. Oh that, yeah. He knew Lycans can't get HIV. But no, I told him he'd catch Lycanthropy from fucking me." Jake grinned like a kid who'd gotten away with something. Then his expression sobered up. "Mistress hurt me for a long time after that. Apparently he was willing to pay her a lot more for that than just putting his mouth on me. She tried to tell him that I'd lied, but he wouldn't believe her. When he knew he couldn't do that, he stopped coming around for the other. Afterwards she stopped trying to rent me out. Apparently she found another source of income."

"What?" I played with his hair and kissed his brow reassuringly.

"I don't know. Something about a different kind of sugar daddy. That's what she called the man who did that to me. He wanted to be my 'sugar daddy' she told me. She just said it was a man who wanted to spend money on me because I let him touch me. The other sugar daddy, I never saw him or met him."

A car pulled up beside us and the tinted window rolled down electronically. Mrs. Leung looked at us. "You boys okay?"

"Yeah, just talking. We're coming."

Jake sat up and wiped his face. He smiled at me but his eyes were duller than earlier. That trip down memory lane had cost him more of his innocence. I felt a tightening in my gut for hurting him, but I knew that in the long run, talking would restore more than it took from him.

"Ready?" I asked. He nodded and opened his door. I got out and he walked around to my side. "This time, we're looking for Trolls. We think it's that Fey smell you mentioned around Lenora's corpse."

"Okay." Jake held my forearm and wrist, his expression subdued. It was his automatic insecure posture, but I didn't mind. It felt very much like being possessed in a good way. The fact that his touching me in public didn't bother me said tons about my feelings for him.

"What's the plan?" Mrs. Leung joined us by my S-10, dressed in a suit and wearing sunglasses. She looked around the neighborhood but I got the impression it was to avoid looking at us. Her voice was husky with emotion. The feds must have told her about last night. "Glad you're okay. Both of you."

I started to reach out, to touch her reassuringly but that was too personal, too intimate for our relationship. I dropped my hand back to Jake's arm, rubbing his skin instead. "The connection seems to be Trolls, so we're looking for Trolls this time, Mrs. Leung."

"I take it that Jake is crucial in this matter?"

"His nose knows," I replied, trying to lighten the mood. My cellphone rang and it was Agent Jacobsen. "Hello, Agent Jacobsen. What's up?"

"We found Lenora's truck in an old barn out near Tollhouse. We think the Trolls are being trafficked out of there. Can you and Jake get down here right away? He's the closest thing we have to a scent hound for these things."

"Can we bring the lovely Mrs. Leung?" I winked at the Chinese attorney.

"Wouldn't want it any other way." In typical Jacobsen fashion, he hung up.

"What the? He didn't tell me where the fuck we're supposed to go?" I exclaimed.

"That's because we're taking you." Agent Gunnerson appeared on the walkway out of Lenora's house. Beside him was T. Ramirez, the gorgeous Mexican cop. I hoped Jake wouldn't smell my interest in him, because I couldn't help myself. "Short on vehicles today, so Officer Ramirez here volunteered to drive us. Mrs. Leung, would you care to ride with?"

"It would be a bit snug, Agent Gunnerson. While I'm sure you boys wouldn't mind being squeezed together, Mr. Leung isn't the understanding type." The woman smiled blithely. "I'll follow in my car."

"Who's watching the crime scene?" I motioned to the single cop car.

"Couple of uniforms inside, just in case. They parked one street over. Just in case the perps come back thinking we're done."

"Smart plan," I said.

"Who's riding shotgun?" asked Ramirez. From his unhappy glance at Jake, he expected it to be Gunnerson. I decided to surprise him.

"Me." I winked at Jake, hoping he was secure enough to understand. He looked at the handsome cop and frowned.

"Looks like one straight government employee in the front and one in the back," joked Gunnerson. "Come on Jake, I won't bite if you won't."

Jake looked confused but got into the back of the squad car. I would have hated being locked in the back like a prisoner, although it wasn't exactly a claustrophobic discomfort. I also wanted to establish some brief moments of separation from Jake so that he could grow more independent. Baby steps.

"Or blondes in the back and brunettes up front," replied to Gunnerson, hoping it would help Jake relax.

"Okay." Ramirez eyed me suspiciously as he opened his door. We got in and he pulled out of the driveway onto Talon and then stopped, idling. When Mrs. Leung caught up behind us, we caravanned North toward the Tollhouse foothill community.

"No sirens," warned Gunnerson. "We're surrounding the farm. Want to make it a surprise party."

"Understood," said Ramirez.

"How'd they find the truck?" I asked.

"Mistry followed up a hunch. With all the reportings of Troll sightings in the Tollhouse area, she figured they would be stupid to not keep them close to where they caught them. So she pulled some favors from the local sheriff," explained Gunnerson.

"Makes sense."

Ramirez sat stiffly in the driver's seat, not making any eye contact with me at all, although occasionally I saw him glance furtively at Jake in the rear view mirror. I couldn't see Jake's reaction, but I was sure it was equally uncomfortable.

"Take Herndon down to Tollhouse, and turn left at Adams Road," directed Gunnerson. He offered the directions without any of the imperiousness that I'd heard both Jacobsen and Thandryl use with the local officers.

"Does Adams go both West and East, or is that the one that only heads West from Tollhouse?" Ramirez peered at Gunnerson in the mirror for confirmation.

"I dunno," said Gunnerson. "I'm not local here. Just passing along the directions Chief Jacobsen gave to me."

"Speaking of Jacobsen," I said tentatively, "Are you still under official surveillance?"

"Finished actually," said Gunnerson without elaboration. For him, that was exceptionally cryptic and I left it alone. My character flaw, that need-to-know thing, would start gnawing away sooner or later, though.

"So, Jake, what do Trolls smell like?" asked Gunnerson.

I compared the two men in the back-seat, since both were obviously of Scandinavian ancestry. Gunnerson looked purely Nordic while Jake looked like an English blend of Scandinavian features. You'd never mistake the blondes as related.

"I don't know." Jake looked at me and I gave him a smile.

"Jake identified a smell on Lenora's body that he didn't recognize. We are assuming that it was Troll, but to be honest we don't know what it was. Other than Human, right Jake?"

"Not Human. Not cat or dog. I recognize zoo animals and farm animals too." He spoke like a young boy trying to impress his parents. "I think it was Fey, but it didn't smell the same. Like Elves smell Fey."

"What do Lycans smell like?" I asked him, curious.

"Human *and* wolf. They aren't natural, so they don't smell Fey," he replied thoughtfully.

"Not natural?" Ramirez was interested despite himself.

"You aren't born a Lycan unless you're conceived during the full moon," said Jake.

"What about you?" Ramirez stared at Jake in the rearview mirror.

I wanted to interfere and Gunnerson gave Ramirez a sour look, but neither of us said anything. Maybe we wanted to know more than we wanted to protect Jake's feelings. Or maybe I thought it was important that Jake stand up for himself.

"I was made as a kid," whispered Jake. He looked lost and lonely. "When Mom and Dad were killed. Uncle Connor said if I wanted to stay in the pack, I had to be one of the pack."

"That's awful!" exclaimed Gunnerson. "How old were you?"

Jake answered without hesitation, "Five. Uncle Connor took me to the ritual circle. I think Lukas told him to. He hadn't been our Fenris very long, maybe three years. I don't remember who our Fenris was before him because he died in the same attack that took my parents. That's why they said I couldn't stay Human. Humans hunted us and killed us. If I stayed moonless, I'd be killed too. Lukas bit me on the shoulder. It hurt so bad. They didn't even warn me."

"Just one more crime to blame Lukas for," I fumed.

"There isn't a legal age-limit on converting," warned Gunnerson, "if both parents were Lycans. From what you said, Jake, I gathered they were?"

"Yes. Mother was a natural. Father a converted, like me."

"Remember much about them?" Ramirez's tone was compassionate.

"Not really. I was two or three when they died. I just remember Dad telling me how I would get to choose when I was older if I wanted to be like him or stay fully Human. It was like he was trying to reassure me that I wouldn't always be like I was."

"Adams coming up," warned Ramirez and we directed our attention to the countryside. The foothills loomed high to the north and east, but we were heading toward the river, west.

"It's about a half a mile, past a vineyard, to the right," said Gunnerson.

"We stopping before we get there?" asked Ramirez.

"No, go past it. There's an access road for the fruit trees on the far side. We'll turn in there."

"You're the boss." Because we were close to our destination, Ramirez finally looked at me and offered a sympathetic smile. Then his attention was back on the road and I was left wondering what had changed his mind.

CHAPTER FORTY-TWO

As we passed the vineyard, I started looking for a house and evidence of federal agents. If they were there, they were hidden. The buildings were set far enough back that it was impossible to see more than rough shapes, although a crushed macadam drive indicated the property entrance. Fruit trees planted on the front acre to the East side of the macadam obscured the structures.

We continued driving past, looking for the access road between the rows of peaches. Fresno and Tulare Counties formed a big chunk of the San Joaquin Valley. We grew most of the fresh peaches, nectarines and raisin grapes, some olives, orange trees and increasing amounts of kiwi and persimmons. I'd lived here my whole life and I could identify most of the trees. It looked like a very ordinary farm.

"There it is." Gunnerson tapped at the mesh wire which separated the back seat from the front. He pointed to a dirt road about a hundred feet past the driveway. Ramirez grunted and slowed the car down.

Mrs. Leung's black car was right on our tail. "Jake's attorney managed to stay with us."

"She's a good lawyer." Gunnerson sounded impressed, something I hadn't heard in his voice before. "I did a background check on her. Lots of sealed files, but what I could see was serious shit. Why she's

THE DARK ELF'S PET | 347

in this rat-hole place instead of a high-end corporate office with a view of the bay, I don't know. I wouldn't give up a six figure income to come play house with my retired husband."

"You've never been in love." Jake looked at Gunnerson sadly.

"No." The agent grew uncharacteristically somber. "I guess I haven't."

"Blondes are all about the sex," I joked, hating to see his spark die any more than I liked seeing Jake suffer. "Gunnerson's too busy getting it on the run, never has a chance to fall in love."

"I wish. I'm more a voyeur. I can chat women up like—like I was a gay man. But when it comes to taking it home—" Gunnerson let his comment trail off and tapped the screen again. "Right there, behind that row of crates. And for the record, Jake's just as blonde as I am. He's definitely in love."

Ramirez stiffened in his seat at the remark. Gunnerson wasn't aware that Ramirez was gay or that he'd been interested in me. Still interested because he was definitely not happy hearing that Jake loved me. Another strike against any future with him.

The cop parked so that the large wooden crates were between the car and the obscured structures. He turned off the engine but none of us reached for the doors.

"I see only three federal vehicles." I peered around the stacked fruit crates. The wood was dusty from being stored outside. I would have thought they'd have been kept out of the elements until closer to picking season. Cheaper than buying new ones. The government sedans were parked so that they blended in with the dark boxes.

"This access road intersects a back road. Most of them are parked back there." Gunnerson tapped impatiently on the glass. The back doors could only be opened from the outside.

"Sorry." Ramirez glanced at me with frustration as he got out of the cruiser. I followed his example and opened the passenger-side back-door.

Agent Shelby appeared from between a stack of crates. He held his weapon and nodded to us silently. Mrs. Leung's car slowly approached us. She leaned forward, peering at us for instructions on where to park. I jogged over to her window which she rolled down. "Anywhere that keeps the car hidden. There's still a spot between those clusters of crates."

"Thanks, Devon. I'm not usually invited to this part of things." She rolled back up the window.

Shelby spoke softly to Gunnerson and Ramirez. The black agent caught my eye and waved me over. I took Jake's hand as I walked past him, tugging him along. There wasn't even a flicker of shame about being with him in public. I could never have done this with Jiao. I missed having a real boyfriend.

"We've only seen two people on the property. Neither one was the red-headed suspect. Both, in fact, were Hispanic types." Shelby held up his phone. "Either of these guys look familiar?"

"No, never seen them before." I shook my head. "Who are they?"

"We're running the photo as we speak."

"We waiting till then to move in?" Ramirez looked good in his uniform. Unlike the FBI suits, his pants hugged a very sexy butt.

I felt Jake's hand loosen from mine. He looked away but I could see the sadness in his eyes. He had seen me check out the cop. Attorney Leung approached us and Jake shifted toward her.

"No, we're moving in now. I wanted Devon here because," Shelby looked pained for a moment, "We discovered that the area is booby-trapped with spells. Fortunately our agents wear some mystical protection."

"But?" I asked.

"We have regular PD backing us up. Officer Sandoval was hurt pretty badly. You close?"

We all looked at Ramirez. The Hispanic cop looked grim and nodded. "She's a good officer. Has a husband and two teen-age boys. Where is she?"

"We got her quietly out of here and she's on her way to the hospital. Thandryl is riding with her, trying to heal what he can." Shelby gave a strange look. "He volunteered. Can you believe it?"

"Sometimes people just need to be given a chance to show their better sides."

"That kind of thinking gets cops killed." Shelby frowned and motioned toward the furrows. "We need you to scout the area with your Sight. Remove the traps and give us a clear path in."

"You got it."

"What do I do?" Jake watched the federal agents eagerly. He needed to prove to himself that he was good for more than blood and sex.

"If the Trolls are here, we'll need you to track them." Shelby scratched his temple. "Could you identify the person Lenora had sex with by smell?"

Mrs. Leung stepped forward and put a slim hand on Jake's back. The blonde man turned and she shook her head. "Check with me before answering questions. You're still officially a suspect."

Another agent appeared and hissed at Shelby. "Looks like they're getting ready to move out!" The unfamiliar man disappeared back into the orchard.

Shelby touched my elbow. "Follow me."

He rushed after the other fed and I followed. Gunnerson, Jake and Ramirez were behind us, while the Chinese attorney brought up the rear. As we cleared the stacks of pallets, I counted eight federal agents waiting at the edge of the orchard. One of them looked scorched, like he'd run through a fire. It must have been the agent caught in the same trap that hurt Sandoval.

"We need a single path from here to the barn cleared and then anything in plain sight around the barn which we might run into," instructed Shelby.

I nodded and walked to the edge of the orchard and shifted into the Sight. The trees looked dark and slightly creepy in shades of blue-greys and blacks, but along the ground, blood-red magic flared like scattered landmines. Although I couldn't see any detail of the spells from this far away, my gut instinct was that they were Lenora's work. An ugly question popped into my head and I glanced over my shoulder at Jake. Had the Werewolf's blood gone into forging them?

"Devon?" Shelby's tone conveyed urgency.

"Sorry."

I walked forward, pausing ten feet from the first magical trap. The lines of power came together to form three interrelated knots and I smiled, relieved. Three was the most strands I had ever freed at the same time so I was fairly confident that I could unravel them.

But the pattern grew fuzzy for a second and my head ached. I closed my eyes, confused by my reaction. The pain went away and I opened them again. I could See the magic clearly. Whatever it was had passed.

I reached out my hand to direct my Sight but the magic flared. I jerked my hand away and stepped back. Hands kept me from bumping into someone at my back. I turned and saw Jake. The rest of the team had remained a safe distance away.

"No, get back!" I pushed him and glanced down at the closest spell. The lines of power settled once more down into thin strands. Jake looked at me as if I betrayed him, but I didn't have time to coddle him. "Sorry, Jake, but the spells react to you. Your blood went into making them."

"Oh." He stood there looking lost and behind him, the feds were growing impatient. Only the enigmatic Mrs. Leung stood there calmly observing.

I turned back to the spell using my Sight. I gathered the three nodes with my mind and pulled simultaneously. The magic slipped apart and I willed it into the ether as ambient energy rather than leaving it as loose strands.

I hurried forward another thirty feet to the next trap. It was the same spell and just as easy to dismantle. After the agents finished this sting, I was going to have to walk the entire property to make sure I hadn't missed any.

I moved forward again, trying to stay within the cover of the trees. I could see the barn, a huge dark shape in my Sight but that was all I could make out form the orchard. I removed two more traps before I heard a noise from the barn. I pressed myself against the trunk of the nearest tree, shifting back into normal vision.

One of the two men came out of the barn and got into the cab of the cobalt blue Silverado truck. He started the engine. I looked at the last spell between me and the clearing. Shit, I had to move fast.

I motioned the agents forward and reached out from my position to take down the last spell. The agents raced past me, black shadows in the blue-grey world of my other Sight. I just managed to yank the threads of the final spell loose before they made contact with it.

The fuzziness in my head returned and I must have swayed because Jake was at my elbow, one arm around my waist supporting me. Mrs. Leung rushed up and studied me with motherly concern. "You okay?"

"I'm fine." I had used the other Sight much longer than this before without such ill effects. Maybe I was getting sick. Like any gift, physical health could impact it. "Thanks."

A gun went off and I jumped. The truck's engine was still running, but one of the tires was flat and four agents surrounded it while others flattened themselves on either side of the barn doors.

I moved out of Jake's grip and raced forward. I could hear Jake and Mrs. Leung behind me. Jake could use some time with his pack to learn that quiet stealth which other Lycans possessed.

Shelby motioned with his gun from against the barn wall. I scuttled toward him and he slammed me carefully against the wood. "I need you to check inside for more traps. It's probably not a problem. We've watched them come and go for about forty-five minutes now. But I don't want to lose an agent from carelessness."

"Isn't the other guy inside? He had to hear the gunshot."

"That's the problem. You have a weapon?" I shook my head and Shelby pulled a second gun from a back holster. It was a 9mm pistol, a weapon I was familiar with. "Just be careful."

"No problem, *jefe.*" I reached for the handle of the nearest door and pulled it slowly toward me. When the door was open enough for me to slide through, I was yanked backwards and a blonde blur raced inside past me. There was the sound of immediate gunfire—a much higher caliber weapon. Shotgun?

"Who?" I asked in a loud whisper.

Behind me Agent Shelby cursed. "Jake!"

I reached for the door handle again but the doors burst outward violently and my hand hit the wood hard enough that I was sure I'd broken something. Rather than Jake's dead body crashing out into the daylight, it was the other man. Two of the agents raced forward stood over him with weapons pointed at his head. He didn't move.

Jake strolled out of the barn, bleeding but holding a bent deer rifle in his hands. He looked smug and angry. "He was going to hurt you."

"And he did hurt you!"

Jake looked down at his chest as if he'd forgotten he'd been shot. He pulled at the ruined t-shirt, revealing the muscles underneath. Even as we watched, the skin pushed out the bullet and the wound closed. The blood remained but the damage had been healed.

"Never mind," I scowled.

"I hope you didn't kill him." Shelby couldn't hide a smirk at Jake's protectiveness of me.

"I don't think so." Jake saw me cupping my injured hand. "What happened?"

"The barn door." I tried to flex my knuckles, but it hurt too much. Once the pain faded I'd have a better idea of broken bones.

"I hurt you? I'm sorry!" Jake wrapped his arms around my waist and hugging me from the side, pressing himself hard against me. It had the innocence of a child's desperation.

"I'm okay. I may not be a Lycanthrope but I can survive a little rough and tumble."

Shelby peered into the open barn. "We still have Trolls to find. You see anything inside, Jake?"

"I didn't look." He reluctantly released me. "Want me to go back in?"

"Let's go together," I suggested. "I look for magic and you sniff for Trolls."

"Deal." Jake took my arm and kissed me on the mouth.

At least a few of the less familiar agents and police officers made snide remarks to each other, given the tone of their derisive laughter. They weren't out of Jake's hearing but he ignored them. He was too happy to be at my side.

I led him into the barn to avoid their further scrutiny. Mrs. Leung followed close behind. She didn't say a word but I could feel her smile.

Inside, the barn was well-lighted. I counted eight hanging lights and a few well-placed wall sconces. I didn't have to be a Werewolf to detect the smell of death, overlaid with something I couldn't place.

Jake apparently didn't like the smell either but he stayed inside the musty barn, sniffing the air cautiously. Mrs. Leung just stayed in the doorway, watching, but she covered her mouth.

"You don't have to do this," I told her but she shook her head.

Shrugging, I slipped into the Sight, hoping that the odd headache wouldn't come back. The pain in my wrist was already enough of a distraction. The barn grew dark under the blue-greys of the Sight.

Gentle shadows in the ordinary world became black shapes that bled into the dark blue-greys because there was nothing to illuminate the barn. There was no magic along the walls, nothing on the ceiling. Only Jake's soft, pulsing metaphysical DNA cast any light at all.

"It's clear," I called behind me.

Federal agents entered, including Shelby. They brushed past Mrs. Leung, their weapons drawn. They spread out in the large enclosure, cautious and organized. Jake moved between them like he was being pulled. He walked toward an office that had been built adjacent to one outer wall.

I trotted after him, once more relying on normal sight. "Wait. Before you open the door, let me check it out."

Jake stepped back and I ran my fingers over the wooden door looking for tell-tale bits of blood magic. There was no glow in that world of my Sight so I stepped back and let the Werewolf open the door. He was, after all, better equipped to survive another gun shot. These men clearly hadn't expected Lycanthropes. They had no silver bullets.

When Jake pulled open the door, the stench was the worst thing I'd ever smelled. It was like a dead animal had been left to ferment in its own feces. I doubled over and covered my mouth to keep from retching. I was embarrassed to be taken down by a mere odor. Jake wasn't overwhelmed by the smell, but he'd probably already detected it with his Werewolf hyper-senses.

Shelby walked past us and paused at the office door. He put his gun away and cursed. "Clear."

I held my breath and entered the makeshift office. At first, all I saw was Shelby's muscular back. But he moved and I saw the source of that smell. Hanging upside down from the ceiling was our missing strawberry-blonde suspect.

He looked strange dead, his features slack in a way they wouldn't have been alive. His mouth was open and flies were flitting in and out of it, landing about his teeth and swollen tongue, laying eggs inside him. Strangely, that didn't bother me.

It was the eyes gazing into nothing in a way only possible for the dead that disturbed me. My mother's eyes had been shut both times I had seen her before we put her in the ground. I would have had a lifetime of nightmares had I seen her like this.

I could tell that the dead man's spirit no longer clung to the hanging meat of his body. Just like the second time I'd seen my mother. So it hadn't been the embalming that had changed her. Time had been enough. That reassured me.

"I guess that ends that," said Agent Gunnerson from behind me. "Gunshot to the chest and one fewer shares of the loot."

Shelby and I exchanged frustrated looks. Jake on the other hand, squeezed my arm. "He's not the one."

"What?"

"She had sex with a man." Plainly Jake was referring to our first corpse, Lenora Haim. "He's not the one. He smells different." Jake looked at me, his green eyes wide with puzzlement. "This man had sex before he was killed, too. But not with a person. Sex with that strange smell."

"Sex with a Troll." Suddenly I didn't doubt that the red-head had gotten what he deserved.

CHAPTER FORTY-THREE

Finding the Trolls turned out to be more involved than we had expected. The *cholos* who had been getting ready to drive off and leave the barn behind had no idea where the creatures were being kept, or so they swore. Surprisingly, they admitted to killing Chuck Warkentin, the tall white man dangling from his ankles. Given that the body was right in front of us, I supposed that was reasonable. But there were no Trolls in their truck and the FBI agents seemed to believe them.

What they did have on their possession was about two-hundred-and-fifty grand, all in cash. That was why they had killed Chuck. It was the proceeds from previous sales of the Fey.

Apparently they had jumped the gun a bit, because he had moved all the remaining Trolls and had forgotten to tell them. Now they had no idea where the creatures were hidden. They really were sorry they had killed him, but their remorse was greed. They had been getting about seven thousand a head.

"The whole barn reeks of Troll and death," complained Jake as Shelby pressured him to give him an answer. "I don't know where they were taken."

"I don't believe that they've all been shipped out!" Shelby raised his voice, frustrated. "You said he had sex before he was killed. At least one God damned Troll must still be around here."

Jake looked like he was going to cry. Mrs. Leung stood between him and the black federal agent. "Leave him alone, Agent Shelby. He said he can't, he can't."

Shelby glowered for a second as if she were suddenly the enemy. Then he let out his breath and shook his head. "Sorry. So close and now our main suspect is dead. I've gone without sleep and suffered an internal investigation because of this case. I'm just on edge. It could be that these guys took out Lenora as well, but my gut says not."

"Not to mention that Jake says he's not the one she was screwing." Gunnerson waved his gun in the direction of the barn roof. "That means we're short one member of the gang. He probably has the Trolls."

"You sure?" Shelby directed his question to Jake. "There's no doubt that this man isn't the one who fucked her then killed her?"

"Definitely. This guy smells more acidic, an entirely different diet than the guy I smelled on the Mistress," said Jake. None of us corrected his slip into calling her that, although Mrs. Leung frowned disapprovingly.

"Shit!" The black agent paced back and forth and we watched quietly. Jake slipped a hand into my good one and I smiled at him. It reminded me—I flexed my injured hand. It wasn't broken.

"The area outside is secure. The farm house is empty." Another agent I didn't know stepped inside the barn. "What do you want us to do?"

"Search the barn," said Agent Shelby. "I want forensics on the body in there, but I want this place turned upside down for the Trolls. Ultra-sounds, the whole works!"

"Yes sir." The agent disappeared again outside.

"Hey, Shelby, I'm going to go dismantle the rest of those booby traps. Maybe I'll see something while I'm out there," I offered. The agent only grunted and I took that for assent. "Stay in here Jake, just in case you can help."

Jake didn't look happy but he obeyed. I was his new Fenris after all. I glanced at Gunnerson expectantly and he nodded, understanding. The blonde agent took a position near Jake and I knew he'd keep an eye on him for me.

I went outside as more feds entered. Looking at the assorted federal suits, I noticed that Shiandra wasn't among them. Someone had to staff the office, I guessed. I'd ask about her later.

I walked the perimeter of the barn and found scattered traps everywhere. I disabled each of them faster and faster as my mind recognized the nodes instead of needing to See the individual threads. Without the pressure of the feds waiting on me, I actually enjoyed exerting my mystic muscle. I even stopped walking. Instead, I pivoted slowly in place. I reached out for spells further and further away, testing my skill.

I really was getting better with practice. I chuckled, remembering Jake's comment along the same lines.

"It was all in your head." Special Agent Thandryl was there beside me. He looked somber but not particularly bitter for a change.

"What was?"

"The limitation you placed on your power," he replied. "Now that you know you can do it, you're able to stretch further."

"Thanks." I was surprised that he was talking to me without being forced to.

"If we are going to be a team, I decided, perhaps I had better stop acting like I was better than you," said the Elf uncertainly.

"Thanks."

"But that doesn't mean I have to tolerate any improper behavior. If you can agree to keeping your comments less personal."

"I'll try."

Sometimes I could be the bigger man. Although, from what I knew of Elven anatomy, that might not have been literally true. Promising not to be vulgar obviously wasn't going to be easy, but I kept that snide thought to myself. Even flattering the Elf about his kind's superior sexual size would probably go badly, joke or not. And some people didn't think I knew when to keep my mouth shut.

"Good," he said and walked away.

I averted my gaze, just in case he turned back towards me. Something told me I should leave well enough alone. It wasn't as if I intentionally noticed the butts on guys first and foremost. How can you not notice it when they walked and those muscles danced for attention?

If Thandryl had noticed me noticing, I'd probably lose what good will my restraint had gained. Instead, I finished the business of dismantling spells. Thirty or so minutes later I'd traversed the entire twenty acre parcel and returned to the barn. The farm was spell free. Most of the agents were gone and the suspects were in custody downtown. Gunnerson and Mrs. Leung were huddled together, talking, while Shelby stared at the barn as if that could force it to divulge its secrets. He sat on the hood of one of the federal sedans, his jacket and shirt folded neatly beside him. The wife-beater he wore underneath them seemed out of place.

I looked around for my new boyfriend and found Jake on the edge of a flat-bed trailer parked near the barn. He was lost in thought, which was a step up from watching my every movement for approval.

"What's the word?" I asked Shelby. He looked impressive sitting there, big arms folded across his broad chest.

He didn't take his gaze from the barn when he replied. "Nothing. Oh, we found a crude cellar hidden under the barn. Feces and bits of rotting fruit. The Trolls had been there for sure, though how long ago is anyone's guess. Your boy can't tell how old scents are. We checked the police records. Looks like the place was raided a few years back for smuggling illegal immigrants in from Mexico. That's why the cellar had been dug originally. The property is still in federal impound status while the owner's appeals are pending. No one is officially renting the place, either. It's supposed to be empty."

"So no paper trail."

Shelby grunted and stood up. "Okay, guess we can get out of here. This was a small time operation according to our *cholo* friends. You guys are done for now. Unless we find another lead, I don't have need of Jake's nose or your S&M gene."

The agent stuck out a strong black hand with such finality that I looked at it a moment before shaking it. Fortunately, it had been my left hand which the door had smashed. I reached out and took his hand in a firm grip. It was a moment of male appreciation, without any sexual aspect. I understood the difference, why didn't so many other gay men? Hell, why didn't so many straight men?

"It's been a pleasure, Mr. Mosteller." Agent Shelby spoke as if we'd never meet again. "I'm being transferred to DC, Presidential duty." He squeezed my hand once before letting it go.

"Will you be back?"

"You never know," he said with a wry grin. "It is a promotion. They want someone familiar with preternatural activities and I was selected. The wife's happy about getting out of Fresno."

"What about you?"

"Me? I'm not gonna miss Gunnerson, that's for sure," he joked as the platinum blonde agent walked up to us. "No discipline in that boy, not like Palmer."

"You told him?" asked Gunnerson without any frivolity. Losing a partner must be something like losing a boyfriend, except you didn't have to give up sex.

"Yeah, he told me," I answered. "If you have a party, I might be persuaded to attend."

"I don't know. Not big on goodbyes. Not formal ones." Shelby got into his car and Gunnerson raced around the front of the vehicle and slid into the passenger seat. I turned to wave once to the back of the government sedan, even though I couldn't see the occupants through the dark glass.

They sped off down the oiled dirt road and I walked over to Jake and Mrs. Leung. "You find Ramirez?" asked Jake.

"What?"

It hadn't occurred to me that the Mexican officer was missing. I hadn't seen him since I'd entered the orchard dismantling spells. None of the regular cops had actually participated in the raid.

"The feds made him stay at the periphery along with the rest of the police officers, in case you missed a trap or the suspects tried to flee." Mrs. Leung watched her young client unhappily. "Jake is under the impression that you had him stay inside so you could go find a certain attractive police officer."

"What?" I repeated annoyed. "Oh grief, Jake. I didn't know where Ramirez went and to be honest, I didn't think about it. I was too busy doing my job!"

"I saw you look at Gunnerson to keep me here," he said defensively.

"I looked at Gunnerson to make sure he looked after you, silly boy!" I didn't find the blonde's insecurity attractive. "I didn't know how much life experience you've had living with that bitch Lenora so I was asking someone I trusted to look out for you. Was that bad of me? It's my job as your alpha. You can smell the truth on me! Go on!"

"Actually, no I can't." Jake stared at me with helpless frustration. "For some reason, the strange smell—that Troll scent—numbed my nose. I can't smell anything except that." He rubbed his upper lip. "I've never had my nose fail before."

Interesting. That bit of information was something I would store away for future use in dealing with Werewolves. Not that I would have a handy bottle of Troll-scent available if I needed to numb a Lycan's sense of smell. Still, it might serve some purpose. For now it meant that Jake had to rely on trust instead of scent. I didn't think he had much of the former so I knew I was going to be sorely tested.

"Then you'll have to believe me for a change." I couldn't contain my annoyance. Being called a liar made me totally lose my cool.

"No one has told me the truth my whole life," said Jake and my stomach soured. "Except you." The sensation of being punched in the stomach faded.

"Does that mean you believe me?"

"You said you might date other guys. I said it was okay. I just didn't think you'd do it in front of me."

"I didn't."

"I know. I just found you. I can't stand the idea of losing you already!"

I chuckled and put my arms around him, although he pouted because I found humor in his pain. His waist was firm and sexy and I was distracted by the perfection of his body.

"Silly boy, you're not losing me." His emotion and our embrace stirred my libido. "By the way, just an FYI. A little insecurity is sexy, but too much is a turn off."

"Do you mind if we finish this conversation someplace more comfortable. And private," interjected Mrs. Leung rather awkwardly. She motioned with one arm toward the orchard where her car was parked.

"Yes, Ma'am," I said, properly rebuked and released him.

The attorney gave me a smart-aleck grin and walked toward the car. I started to follow when Jake grabbed my injured hand. I bit off a curse of pain and hissed at him.

Jake looked horrified and quickly withdrew his touch. I tried to reassure him but nothing I said relaxed him. Instead, he walked a few steps behind me, like he was afraid of me.

That was funny. He was afraid of me and I laughed. I wasn't the one who turned into a furry beast during the full moon.

CHAPTER FORTY-FOUR

Mrs. Leung drove us home in her car. Jake was in the back seat alone. He had insisted, still pouting.

"I talked with Agent Gunnerson," she said. "Jake's statement about there being a second man is confirmed. DNA came back. There were three types of hairs found at the house besides Lenora Haim's. The dead man, Chuck Warkentin is believed to be one set. They hadn't gotten the body in for analysis yet."

"So they think there were three killers?" asked Jake. I was glad he wasn't so emotionally fragile that he'd withdrawn completely.

"Of the three, one set confirms that Lenora Haim had some connection to the Troll smuggling. It was clearly from a Mountain Troll. Your hair samples, Jake, excluded you from the three found in the bedroom."

"I wasn't allowed in her bedroom. In the new house, I was only allowed in the garage and kitchen. And sometimes out in the yard."

"Well, that's good. The fact that she didn't touch you too much or let you interact with her socially worked in your favor this one time. You have been officially cleared in the murder," said Mrs. Leung with relief. "Only one of the three hair types is prevalent in the samples from the crime scene. They were clearly of a red-headed nature. What is problematic is that the DNA evidence points to Mr. Warkentin as the rapist and killer."

Jake made a strange noise from the back seat and we looked at him concerned. He shook his head, defiantly. "She wasn't raped! Whoever she fucked, it was because she had wanted to fuck him!"

"How can you be sure?" Mrs. Leung gripped the Lincoln's large steering wheel with both slender hands.

"She came through the house smelling ready. His scent was already on her body. She looked at me and sneered. Told me to be quiet, not to ruin this for her. Then she shut the door. I could hear her for a while, walking through the house shutting door after door so that eventually I couldn't hear what they said and did."

"Did she do that often?" asked the attorney again. It sounded like professional curiosity.

"Not at the old house. At the old house, there was magic on the door so I couldn't hear anything outside of my kennel," said Jake without rancor.

"Kennel?" I blurted angrily.

"That's what she called wherever she locked me in. In the last house, it was a bedroom because there was no garage."

"So you have no idea who this mystery man was?" asked Mrs. Leung.

"No. All I know is Mist—Lenora was excited about fucking him. I'd never seen her like that before," said Jake. "I think she liked this man. In the past, she only used men as tools."

"Well, if you hadn't raised the issue of this mystery man, the feds would have pinned it all on the dead Mr. Warkentin. There was blood under his nails. They are assuming it is Lenora's. However, there was no semen sample. They used a condom."

"So then Jake really is cleared?"

"Not completely. He may still be charged as an accessory. But because Jake helped in the investigation, Gunnerson doesn't think the bureau will put pressure on Jacobsen to hold him culpable. A lot will depend on whether they find this other man."

"Maybe now that we've identified two members of the gang, we'll get a clue!" I hesitated. There had been only one other man in Lenora Haim's life. And the way he had acted, something nagged at me. Something he had said. What was it? "Why does the image of the dead man seem like I should connect it with something?"

Mrs. Leung looked at me strangely. It was a bit of an idiosyncratic question, but I felt it was important. "Did he look familiar after all?"

"No, that's not it. Maybe he just reminded me of my dead mother. His eyes." Then it hit me. "His eyes!"

"What about his eyes?" asked Mrs. Leung.

"How would he have known about the eyes?" I exclaimed triumphantly. "Forget the house. Head to Alluvial and Fowler. There's a landscape design company there. And I think I know who our mystery man is."

Mrs. Leung didn't question me but she nodded. I leaned back in the plush leather seat and closed my eyes. We were fifteen minutes away. If I called in the feds and was wrong, I'd lose credibility. But there was back-up I could call. I'd been wrong in front of them more than once already. I pulled out the cellphone and put a plan into motion.

CHAPTER FORTY-FIVE

When we got to the landscape center, I had Mrs. Leung park far away from the main entrance. We sat with the engine off, watching the traffic come and go. It was a comfortably warm day and a lot of people had the same idea—to improve their yards with new plants. That was good. We were likely to blend in better.

"Here they come." I saw Melanie's vet truck pull into the parking lot.

She parked five or six stalls away from us. Ulrich got out, too well dressed for planting, but that was his style. Melanie on the other hand was wearing tattered jeans and a slightly too small, older t-shirt. Her breasts raised the shirt so that flashes of her smooth, creamy stomach were visible as she walked. Ulrich couldn't help but notice how sexy his wife was, because he kept staring at her as they walked into the nursery without even a glimpse in our direction.

"Nothing like a husband who still finds his wife a sex object," I said, approvingly. "That hour-glass shape will distract most of the men inside."

"Do we go in now?" asked Jake.

"Not yet. Mrs. Leung, your turn."

She removed her jacket and tie, and unbuttoned her pristine white blouse two buttons from the top. She looked like she was on her way someplace and needed some last minute plants. "Just walk around checking out flowers?"

"I'm going to push our suspect's buttons. I don't know what he'll do. The more eyes the better. The feds would have to get a warrant, but as customers we can be here no problem. Nice of you to help out, Li. We'll need someone to call Jacobsen if things get out of hand."

She pulled her sunglasses down over her eyes and looked at herself in the rearview mirror, touching the ends of her lips, making sure her lipstick was adequate. Then she got out of the car.

"She likes you," said Jake as we watched the petite woman disappear inside the nursery. I looked at him. "She wouldn't have done this for most people. I can tell."

"She's a pretty amazing woman, but I probably only stand out because her son-in-law is a real faggot. Anyway, we have to assume Peter knows what you look like." I brushed the hair out of Jake's eyes. "I want you to stay in the car. We've been through too much to rescue you to put you at risk. If he was the one who tried to shoot you that day—."

"I never saw him, how would he know what I look like?"

"Well, that girl commented about you being Lenora's boy-toy. If she knew about you in the complex, then this guy might have seen you as well."

"What girl?"

"When we were looking for Shiandra, a girl on the next street over commented about you and Lenora. If she knew about you, in all likelihood so does he." I explained. "So there's no point in us going in separately. If he sees you and me together, he's going to suspect we know something. And that means he might try something. I want to push his buttons but not by having our only witness just come strolling in."

"I'm not staying out here. I belong with you now. If you don't take me in, I'm going to come anyway!"

It was his turn to touch me, although he glanced at my injured hand. He brushed his fingers along the edge of my cheek. I shivered under his gentle touch. Amazing how the way a person felt about you translated into your reaction to their touch. He gave me goosebumps and a tightening in my pants.

"More of that would be nice," I murmured, my eyes half-closing. I reached out and stopped his hand, holding it a moment. "If you won't stay out here, then just stay with me and look confident. It would be nice to find a boyfriend who'll actually listen to me on the rare occasions I actually tell him to do something!" I sighed as Jake grinned defiantly at me. I wanted him to gain some independence. I couldn't criticize it now. "I'll do the talking once we get inside. Now let's go. God, I hope I'm right."

"My nose is working again, by the way," said Jake as we got out of the car. He started to take my hand, but as people walked out with their purchases passed us, he thought better of it. I smiled at him and it was his turn to sigh.

"Just walk beside me. We might be a couple, but I don't want that to throw a kink in the plan." I strode toward the doors of the hi-tech log cabin, pushing the door open for an older black woman with an armful of ground cover.

"Thank you," she said, slipping past me with a smile. I noticed through the open door that Yuriko had just pulled into the parking lot. My crew was complete. Jake noticed her too as we entered the air conditioned building.

He nudged my shoulder but I shook my head. "I saw."

There were only three other people milling about inside the building among the decorative pots and smelly fertilizers. Peter Lyndigard was helping an eight-year-old boy and his mother pick out seed packs, kneeling next to the young customer.

Jake and I strolled up near him on our way to the counter. He glanced up and started to greet us until he recognized me. Then he gave me a screwy smile and looked at Jake. I knew I was on the mark then, because he blanched. It took him only a second to recover. He quickly finished helping the boy pick zucchini over yellow squash. The mother and son went to look at plastic incubators and Peter walked over to the register.

"I see you're back." He stuck his hand out to Jake. "My name is Pete Lyndigard. You are?"

Jake looked at me and I gave him the smallest of nods. He shook Pete's hand and took a deep breath. His eyes widened with recognition. The designer saw the change in expression and released Jake's hand as if it were contagious.

"I'll be right back," said the designer. "I've got to help a customer out back. You're welcome to come with me. I assume you've more information on Lenora's death?" He didn't wait for my reply but walked out the back door. Jake and I rushed to follow. What the fuck was he up to?

Melanie and Ulrich were examining a blue spruce in an oversized planter just outside. Pete nodded at them as he strode past. They looked at me and I gave them the thumbs up. They went on the alert. I also saw Mrs. Leung at the far end of the flowering-plant tables and she saw us. Jake, Peter and I headed toward the back of the lot, where the storage sheds and a couple of small greenhouses sat.

"He's scared." Jake put his mouth close to my ear as we walked behind the designer.

"So, Mr. Lyndigard!" I said, trying to slow him down.

"It's Pete. Mr. Lyndigard was my grandfather," answered the designer amiably. He was a damned good actor. "I have a special order back here for that couple looking at the spruce."

Melanie and Ulrich hadn't placed a special order, which meant he was definitely leading us into a trap. I instinctively put my hands to my pockets, the way you check for keys or a wallet. The gun Agent Shelby had loaned me was gone and I hadn't brought my own. I had been counting on Jake's strength and my knowledge that this was a trap to keep us alive. Ideally, I wanted to keep us out of the trap entirely.

"Right in here." Pete held the door of the greenhouse open.

Jake and I paused to stare at each other. The blonde gave me a look that told me he was coming. Shit, might as well play it all the way out. I had started it after all.

I entered the thin door and Jake followed me inside. I turned fairly quickly to keep an eye on our host. Surprisingly, he just followed us and shut the door. "It's in the back. Would you mind leading the way?"

"Not a problem, Pete." I started to feel nervous. I really wanted Jake out of this place.

"I'm short a couple of workers. It's not like them to not show up," said the designer. "Not that I mind doing work. Just today's one of those busy days."

We reached the end of the greenhouse and I looked around. There were no tools that could be used as weapons nor did I see anything else threatening in the small, hot chamber. "Where is it?"

Pete smiled at us, much too benignly. Almost joyously, he motioned to some small ceramic pots on the end of the table. Jake picked up one of them and sniffed it, curious. "What are they?"

"A variety of belladonna. Wolfsbane." Lyndigard's voice was oddly distorted. The room began to spin and shift like reality was being altered. "Here, let me take that before you drop it." I heard his voice as if from far away. Jake collapsed to the ground and I tried to grab him. Instead, I only managed to stumble sideways, crashing into the table.

"Without him, there's no one to connect me to Lenora. Thanks for bringing my last loose end to me."

The table pushed me away and I fell backwards onto Jake. At least I thought it was Jake, as once more, I was sent into oblivion.

CHAPTER FORTY-SIX

This time when I came to, my head was preternaturally clear. I opened my eyes and could see I was in small, dark shed. I tried to move, but my arms were tied behind me to a heavy wooden chair. I tried shouting, but no noise came out of me.

"No need to bother." Peter Lyndigard stepped into my view. He wore work gloves and had shears in one fist. There was no blood on them yet. I tried not to think about how they might be used to prune parts of Jake or myself.

I couldn't see Jake in the small shed either. Pete smiled and continued to talk to me. "The belladonna is my own variety. You should feel wonderful right now, the epitome of physical health. Your voice will come back in a while. Of course, you won't be alive to use it by then."

I tried mouthing at him, which was somewhat successful because he answered my question. "The wolf-boy? That's the real point of belladonna, though, isn't it? It's very toxic to Lycanthropes." He shivered as he said the word. "I belong to a group very eager to rid our world of these non-Human abominations. This plant was bred specifically for that purpose. The ape-things I found another way to deal with. Couldn't blame Elves like I did with Lenora."

I didn't bother to reply, angry that I couldn't be heard. Melanie, Yuriko and Ulrich would be looking for us and hopefully Mrs. Leung had called the federal agents when we disappeared. Did Peter Lyndigard think we wouldn't be found?

"It doesn't matter who knows you're here," he said. "We aren't in the nursery any longer."

I definitely wanted to know what the fuck he was talking about. I heard customers milling about outside. I even thought I heard Melanie's voice calling to me in whispered urgency. Yeah, my hearing was especially acute.

"Where are we, you ask?" He seemed to take great pleasure in gloating over my capture. The villain played to an audience of one, a monologue explaining all the details of his dastardly plan. "Have you ever heard of pocket dimensions? It seems that I built my design center right at the edge of one. Perfect place to hide criminal activity. If I'd thought about it better, I would have trapped that mongrel, Lenora, here as well. Except I hadn't known what she was then."

I looked around the shed and saw nothing more than tools and extra pots. I sent air past my vocal chords but still there was no sound. Where had the bastard put Jake? And what did he mean by 'toxic?' Deadly toxic? Was Jake dead? Dead because I had been too embarrassed to have the feds know about my suspicions in the event I was wrong? God damn it! I cursed at myself.

"It takes a certain magic to enter pocket dimensions. Or the help of an accidentally found artifact."

He held up a strange key. It had a glowing gem in the handle. I switched my vision to the Sight and was blinded by the glow of the entire room. Quickly I went back to normal Human sight and blinked frantically. This magic even shined in the real world, I couldn't tell what it did metaphysically.

"I dug it up when I was breaking ground on the building. Seems like some race, older than the first Humans in the Americas, left a little something of their culture behind. Pure chance that I was the one to find it."

Peter Lyndigard looked at the key as if it were both boon and bane. A moment later he glanced up at me and there was cold hatred in his eyes. "I'm going to leave you here for a while. Can't have my customers wonder where I've gone. And if any of your FBI friends comes looking, I wasn't gone long enough to have run off with you anywhere. You will have just disappeared. It's what I should have done with that inhuman bitch as well."

The anger in his voice flared and he put loathing behind the word 'inhuman.' If he hated non-Humans so much, why had he taken up trafficking in Trolls with one? Why would he have used that key?

He stepped behind me. I heard the door of the shed open but wasn't able to make any noise. It shut again and I listened to be sure he was gone. Then I began to rock back and forth, roughly. The chair was damned heavy and all I did was chafe my skin where the ropes dug into me. I tried shouting again and heard my voice whisper weakly into the room. Good. The effects of the belladonna were wearing off.

I listened carefully for the sounds from the nursery. I could hear Yuriko and Melanie talking, agitatedly. Mrs. Leung was there, too.

"He claims that Devon and Jake left to look around," said Yuriko angrily.

"Bullshit!" swore Melanie. "I saw them go into that hot-house. We need to get inside and see if they are okay!"

"He's not watching us. Why not just go inside? There are no signs that say employees only," said Mrs. Leung.

"Yes there—!" replied Ulrich. I heard a ripping sound. "No, I guess now there aren't."

My heart leapt as I heard them approach the door. The handle rattled a second and then I didn't hear them anymore. I rocked frantically back and forth again, but couldn't free myself. My repeated shouts were merely unhearable whispers.

A few minutes later, I heard their voices again. "He wasn't in there."

Yes I am! I shouted mentally.

They hadn't even come inside! Or had they? I knew a little bit about pocket universes from reading comic books. Unless you walked in the right dimensional door, you could be standing in the very same spot as something else and never know it. Was the shed door like a train-track switch? If it was off you walked into the green house but if you needed to find this shed you had to turn it on?

My wrists and ankles were beginning to itch from the rope and my neck had rope burns from the rocking. I hated being helpless. On one of our visits to Oklahoma when I was a kid, my Uncle John had tied me up and thrown me on the front lawn to see how long before I freaked out. I'd freaked out right off the bat but he hadn't come and untied me for what seemed like hours. I was only five-years-old so it couldn't have been that long. But the discomfort and claustrophobia linked to that incident rose in me now. I couldn't even shout out my frustration!

I'd used up Jiao's hidden spell when the Drow siblings had captured Shiandra and me, so there was no way to let anyone know where I was. Maybe Thandryl would have been able detect the dimensional doorway, except they weren't looking for pocket universes.

Before now, as far as I knew, those had only existed in comic books. Like necromancy. But I had found a death spell the last time I'd seen Lenora's body. If one of them was real, why not both?

"Let me go!" I croaked, my voice coming back. I shouted through the door but there was no reaction. Apparently sounds could get in but they couldn't get out.

"Jake?" I said into the small room. I couldn't see behind me but it occurred to me that he might have been rendered mute as well. "Jake!"

There was no reply at first. If he had died because of me, I wanted to be dead, too. I rocked back and forth again, knowing that I deserved the pain the ropes inflicted. I cried then, not in frustration, but in mourning for that beautiful blonde Lycanthrope—a beauty that was in his soul not just his appearance. When the chair settled firmly into place again, I heard the faintest scratching. I looked up, but there was nothing but shed wall.

The scratching grew in volume and I saw one of the wallboards in front of me tremble. "Jake?" I said hopefully. "Jake, I'm here!"

The wood started to splinter and I saw a hairy paw tear at the wood. My first reaction was that Jake had once more managed to transform into a Werewolf. The hand withdrew and in the dollar-sized hole, a bloodshot pair of inhuman eyes glared into the room. The same inhuman eyes which Peter had mentioned in our first visit.

Those wicked looking eyes found me and stared at me with cold, unblinking malice. Mountain Troll. It began tearing at the wood in an effort to get to me. My heart lurched as if it had stopped and I reacted with sheer terror. It was the same kind of primeval horror that Tobaius had instilled in me when he had slunk past the previous night. I kicked back hard enough on the chair that I felt myself reach that point when I should rock forward again, but I kept going back—good old adrenaline.

I hit the ground hard and my head thunked against the chair's back. Pain exploded in my skull but I didn't lose consciousness. I could hear the scrabbling claws at work against the wood. The Troll was digging through the wall to get to me. It gibbered like a demented ape and I knew that if I didn't get free, I was going to be torn apart or eaten alive.

I screamed thinking that maybe someone would hear me. For a moment the clawing stopped and I thought perhaps I had frightened it off. But like the persistent gnawing of rats, the Troll started pounding against the wood harder.

Magic was the only thing left to save me. I flickered into the Sight but the glowing brilliance of the room forced me back into normal vision. No way I could endure the pain of that light long enough to forge some sort of tool.

Tools! I looked on the floor to both sides of where my head rested on the ground. There were no sharp edges anywhere to be seen.

I paused, listening over the pounding of my heart in my ears and my raspy breathing. Silence. The scrambling and shredding had stopped. I tried to still the booming beat of my heart that filled up my ears but it was as if the whole world had become that beating.

Shuffling noises, louder than my heart beat, drew close. The thing was in the room with me. I couldn't tell its breathing from my own short gasps. I was going to hyperventilate. At least then I wouldn't feel the pain as much as it sank those fangs into me. Something touched my ankle and I screamed out loud. The terror reflex left me mortified. I didn't care that it was a manly scream, it was a scream.

I waited for pain to follow the touch, but the Troll just waited. Was it toying with me? Or was it waiting for someone or something to join it? My imagination told me that all the missing Trolls were crawling silently through the torn wall to feast on my flesh. And here I thought I wasn't a drama queen!

Clawed fingers tugged at my ankle and I managed to bite back another cry. I gritted my teeth and waited for the fangs to sink into my leg. Instead, the creature kept tugging at my leg, like it was trying to drag me toward the hole from which it had come. Pain tore into my leg as the rope binding was forced hard against me. There was a snapping noise and I moaned aloud that the beast had broken my ankle. I couldn't feel the pressure from the rope any more. The whole leg had gone numb.

The Troll shuffled up along my field of vision. At first I could see the shadow of a bald, grey head move into sight, followed by those wicked, bloodshot eyes. It was worse than an ape's eyes. These were full of knowing hatred.

"Go away!" I yelled at the top of my lungs. I had the satisfaction of watching the Troll jump back a bit. But as I lay there gasping, it crept forward again.

I turned my face away, afraid it would take its first bite from my eye and cheek. I felt its hot, dry breath against my neck and shivered. My muscles twitched involuntarily—like anticipating a hard slap or the poke of a needle.

I screamed again when the thing touched my face. The scream turned into maniacal laughter when I recognized that what touched me was the Troll's tongue. It licked my neck slowly, tentatively. I was a fool. Melanie had said that they were gentle. But its eyes—!

"That a boy," I crooned. The licking stopped. I turned to look into those frightening eyes. They were pouting. I studied the features, looking at my fear up close and personal. Oh, I saw. "You're a good girl," I amended. How could I not have realized? She gibbered merrily, bouncing up and down.

Her hands went for my pants button and I yelled again. "Whoa, little lady!" She moved back to my face and looked at me from inches away. Her expression was getting easier to read. I thought I saw puzzlement. But those eyes were so cold, so deadly. No wonder people were afraid of them. Okay. No wonder *I* was afraid of them.

"If you want to undo something, try the ropes. Untie the ropes." I watched as she listened and looked at my situation. She went back to staring at my face. "Come on, do the ropes. Take off the ropes. On my legs and arms."

She seemed to understand and tugged uncertainly at the knots. It seemed so poignantly representative of my life. Untying the knots of magic with my ability to manipulate mystic energy. Unraveling the knots of my relationships. Now I needed someone, something else, to unravel these physical knots. I wasn't good at letting people help me.

I didn't think I was worth their help. My family had done a great job of undermining my self-esteem, despite my general confidence.

"Go on, girl. Keep going."

She gibbered and bobbed her head, something less apelike than crazed. I saw then that she had humanesque breasts, not apelike dugs, and her swollen vulva reminded me of a dog in heat. She had gone for my pants. Was this the Troll sex-slave of that strawberry blonde corpse, Chuck? She was like an innocent child! How could he have used her?

The ropes came loose from around my chest and arms. I burst out with a triumphant guffaw. "Thank you, you sweet little angel!" Then I shivered. God, I hoped that he hadn't talked to her like that.

I quickly freed myself from the rest of the ropes and stood up. The Troll bounced up and down at the hips, knuckles dragging along the ground like an ape, but her arms were much longer. Her breasts jiggled like a Human girls, only the flesh of them was grey and slightly scaled. I noticed a thin silver chain around her neck and a small rectangular bit of metal—a dog-tag that said 'Sally.'

Sally looked at me with anticipation and her eyes kept dropping to my crotch. I felt dirty. Dirty for the man who had conditioned this creature to expect sex from a Human. A man who had named her but who had to tag her to recognize which Troll she was.

I was finally able to look behind me. The door which led to the real world was there, but only that door. Jake was nowhere to be seen. I turned back to where the Troll had clawed her way through. I went and knelt to peer inside. I felt a clawed hand on my hair, stroking it like a lover. I tried not to react as I looked inside the opening.

It was another small room, with wooden walls on three of four sides, but the back was solid rock. Apparently, this pocket universe didn't match up exactly with the same geographically as our universe. There were no mountains next to the nursery. There was, however, another door in one of the two wooden walls. Perhaps it led to Jake's imprisonment. I crawled through the hole made by Sally.

It was big enough for me, because the Troll, though more petite, was large around the hips. By rolling my shoulders through the opening, I slid to the floor inside her former prison. It smelled foul and there was a rather full litter box in one corner. I don't think Chuck had expected to be gone so long—forever in this case.

"Where are your friends?" I asked her as she scrabbled back into her room after me. Sally gibbered in reply.

The small door was unlocked and I slowly turned the handle. I gagged. Troll was not a smell I'd forget. This must have been where they were kept. I stepped cautiously into the dark room, feeling for a switch by the door. Did pocket universes have electricity?

Sally stayed away from the door, like she was afraid. It made me hesitate. In the dark I heard something shuffle. No, make that somethings shuffling, because the sound came from different places in the dark. It could have been an echo, but my imagination was already primed and over-active. The Mountain Troll's nervousness didn't help me relax any.

I stepped back, trying to let light filter in from the first room. Something moved and I slammed the door shut. A powerful weight struck the door, popping it open eight inches against my body. I shoved back. I threw the latch as I slammed it into the frame. The heaving thudding repeated as that fleshy weight repeatedly hit the wood.

"Jake!?" I yelled through the closed door. Was he in there with whatever had attacked the door? Was something feeding on his helpless flesh? I grew cold with fright.

Sally gibbered at me from the corner, taking small steps forward and back, trying to draw me away from the door. I looked at the shuddering door and back at her. She seemed the smarter of us at that moment. I moved away and jumped when whatever it was thudded against the wood again. The wall with the door was seriously solid, while the wall Sally had clawed her way through was comprised of termite eaten wood and dry rot. The remaining wooden wall was a duplicate of the one opposite it, except without the door. Jake wasn't behind that wall and if he were, I wasn't going to get to him by scratching at the hard wood slats.

Sally crawled back through the hole she had made in the common wall to our respective prisons. I didn't feel capable of dealing with whatever lurked in the dark on the other side of that door, so I followed her through. My rope burns scraped against the irregular wood and I bit back a cry. When I hissed, however, Sally leapt across the room like she'd been bitten and turned snarling.

"Sorry, girl. It wasn't you." I used my best soothe-the-beast voice. She hesitated and slowly relaxed. "You afraid of snakes?"

My feet dropped into the room after the rest of me and I stood up once more. Might as well try the door and see if I could just walk out of this prison.

I put my hand on the knob, thinking I might feel otherworldly vibrations, but there was nothing. It was just a doorknob. I turned it and found it unlocked. I was free! Jerking open the door, ready to rush into the busy nursery, I motioned for Sally to stay where she was. Not that I had reason to suspect she understood what that meant.

When I turned to face the outside world, however, I saw just another small room. But not empty. Jake was lying on a dusty wooden table amid pots and miscellaneous gardening tools. I rushed to him, overjoyed until I stood over him, looking down at his motionless form.

"Jake!" I held his pale face in both of my hands, ignoring the pain. His lips were blue, and I saw all the signs that he was suffering from suffocation. I felt his pulse, but could only hear my own heartbeat. I put my lips on his and breathed air into his slack mouth. He was still warm, but just barely. Given that his body was normally hot, that was bad—very bad. "Come on Jake, hold on!"

Sally came in the room and knocked over some pots clambering onto the table next to Jake. She looked at him with interest, touching his crotch. I slapped her hand away and she held her arms tight against her body and gibbered sadly. "Sorry, Sally, but you mustn't touch him."

The door to the room shut and we were in near darkness. I let my Sight flicker on for a moment but the blinding glow was just as strong on this side of the door. Apparently my talent was worthless in a pocket dimension. Everything was as bright as gazing into the sun. But if the one door only led from this room to the other—oh, yeah, the key. I'd forgotten about that. It must change the door from a place in this dimension into a place in our dimension and versa visa.

"Jake, hold on, Baby." I breathed air into his lungs, again, ignoring the dark.

I didn't know if it helped or not, but I had to try something. Something. Could I risk the change again? Would transforming Jake into Werewolf fight off the poison or make it worse? Regular belladonna affected Werewolves but not like this. It didn't hurt the Human facet, only when they were in full beast mode. If I changed him, would it help him or kill him immediately?

"What should I do, Sally?"

She knocked another pot off the table and shuffled around. I reached out my hand and put it over his crotch. Sally's breath warmed the back of that hand. I had been right, she tried to touch him there again. "No, Sally! Bad, bad, Troll."

Light flared in the room and I turned to the door. It was ordinary light, not magic. I realized that the door between the two rooms and the two worlds was no longer fully 'there.' It became translucent as it was opened from the main universe, letting light flood in. I could see the knocked over chair and mess of ropes on the floor in my original prison.

"Your friends are gone. Gave up on you awfully—!" Lyndigard walked into the room and looked at the empty chair. He pulled a revolver out of his gardening vest and held it at waist level as he searched the room. It didn't take him more than a few seconds to find the hole that Sally had torn in the wall and took a step toward it.

"What the—?"

His surprise made me wonder if he had been the one to lock Sally in the pocket universe. My guess was he wasn't. I was betting Chuck had used this place for his perverse abuse of the Troll. It explained why she had been left alone in there with me. Lyndigard hadn't known she was hiding behind that wall.

He approached the opening with the same caution I had expressed, kneeling with the gun aimed in the opening. "Shit, a door!"

I watched him scramble into the opening, very much as I had done. He disappeared from sight then, because the door to the other universe closed and became tangible wood between rooms once more.

Jake hadn't moved, so I breathed one more puff of air into his mouth. I couldn't just wait for Lyndigard to find me, so I kissed Jake's soft lips before feeling my way to the door. I heard the designer scream before I could even touch the handle. It had been terror, not pain. His gun went off once and he screamed again. This time there was pain with his fear. I froze, my hand still on the door, listening.

Lyndigard began to plead incoherently and he cried out in anguish. The gun went off again, followed by silence.

My fierce grip on the handle began to hurt and I had to force myself to loosen my fingers. But I didn't release the knob. If anything came into the room through that hole, the door was all that stood between us and it.

I glanced behind me, where Jake lay unmoving, unbreathing. He needed my help! The longer I waited the less chance he had at pulling through.

"Sally, I'm going to have to leave you here with Jake. But stop touching him!"

In the dim light, I saw a pair of sheers on the floor near him. I went and grabbed them. Any weapon was better than none. Sally clambered off the table to follow me as I went to the door. Before she could reach me, I slipped through and shut it on her. If something happened to me, at least she and Jake would be safe a while longer.

I listened again, trying not to breath as I counted to ten. There was no sound from the hole so I risked a gasp of air. There was no movement, no further gun shots or noises from the designer. I heard footsteps and threw myself to the side of the hole, pressing myself flat against the wall. But the sounds came from the door I had just shut. The pounding on the door was followed by silence. It was the outside world. I focused on the hole again. Without that key, Jake would die. And Peter Lyndigard had the key.

I looked inside the hole in the wall, sheers ready to jab at anything which might try and grab me. It took a second for my eyes to adjust to the dim lighting. A body was face down near the interior door. The gun was still in Peter Lyndigard's hand. Blood pooled under his face and I knew that Peter had to be dead. Something taller than a Human shuffled out of the shadows from one corner. It teetered toward me and I scrambled away from the hole.

The monster that came forward resembled Sally, except that its head was three times as big. Its piggy eyes were still small and cold like Sally's. Its wide mouth was cluttered with jagged, over-sized teeth. Blood dripped from its mouth and hands and I knew I was looking my death in the eyes. This monster was not the work of my imagination.

I continued to scuttle backwards away from the hole. The thing's face appeared in the opening, like some mad doll. The piggy eyes moved in short arcs to focus on me. It stuck its head through the opening, but its body was too thick. It began to squeeze through, clawing at the wood as well. After a few minutes, only the head and neck had made it through. Shit, why not? I stood up and ran toward the thing which started to splinter the wood at my approach. I raised the shears and with both hands drove them down into the back of the thing's neck.

It was a horrible sound, those shears hitting the flesh. Horrible because they bounced right off without breaking the skin. I tried again, as the giant Troll broke further through the wall. Looking at its empty eyes, I felt my blood grow cold. One arm made it inside the room with me and it dragged itself forward. I hated those eyes. They made me unable to think.

Those eyes! Fear had made me foolish, but my brain latched onto that one useful thought. I used the shears and drove them into the closest of the piggy red orbs. The tip met with resistance, despite my muscles flexing their maximum. The adrenaline that flooded my system gave me just enough extra strength that I felt the eye-ball burst like caviar between molars. I leaned on the shears, shoving them further into the thing's face. The clawed hand stopped pulling the body into the room and slapped me off my feet into the opposite wall.

My head rang from the impact and I put a hand up to feel a serious lump. The wood splintered around the hole as the oddly shaped beast broke into the room. A sound from my right drew my attention away from it. The door handle turned and I was relieved. Jake was conscious and perhaps his Werewolf strength would help me get the key so we could escape.

"Jake!"

The door opened and a head appeared at waist height. Sally. She peered around the corner at me with that expressionlessness that made my skin crawl. The larger Troll-like beast saw her and roared. She let out a screech and dashed beside me, trying to hide behind me as I struggled to get back to my feet.

"Don't use me as a shield!" I yelled at her in panic as the thing lumbered toward us.

I leapt to the left and Sally screeched, running the opposite direction. The creature roared and went after her. I felt guilty that it hadn't chosen me to chase, but it gave me the chance I needed. I ran for the opening. My first reaction had been to grab the gun and go after the monster which was roaring as it chased the terrified Sally. But Lyndigard had tried the gun and he was dead.

I felt inside his work vest until my fingers identified a familiar shape. I pulled out the key and ran back toward the opening. Before I reached it, Sally bolted through and I jumped to the side again. Behind her the larger monster burst through the already enlargened hole, splintering wood into the room.

I darted past him, the key in my hand. Sally screamed in pain and I knew the beast had got her but I kept for the door. Maybe I'd feel bad later but Jake was more important than some sexualized Troll.

There was a small hole in the doorknob and I hoped that was it. I put the pointed tip of the key into the slot and the door pulsed with color. Pushing the door open, I saw the nursery through the frame.

"Sally!"

I propped the door open with the fallen chair and turned back to the tear in the wall. Sally clambered over the bits of shattered wood, one leg dragging uselessly behind her. The monster was right behind her, reaching for that dead limb.

"Hurry girl!"

I used the gun and shot at the beast's eyes. That slowed it down long enough for Sally to scurry on three legs through the door. The monster ambled quickly toward me, so I ran after Sally.

The light of day blinded me. I slammed into one of the display tables at hip level, knocking over ceramic pots with a loud crash. The pain of my bruised flesh was nothing against the cool breeze of freedom, and I kept trying to scurry away from the door.

Hands reached out for me and I fought them off, blinking against the daylight until I saw that they belonged to Gunnerson and Palmer. There were other federal agents in the nursery, but what reassured me most was Melanie and Ulrich rushing toward me.

"Devon, thank God!? Where were you?" asked Agent Gunnerson.

"Monster." I desperately tried to catch my breath.

"What?" Gunnerson clutched at my elbow.

I pointed at the thing which raced into the nursery in pursuit of Sally. At least three FBI guns were fired their weapons, but the bullets were deflected by its thick skin. Gunnerson was speechless for a change and I heard Melanie say, "Holy Shit!"

The creature lumbered past the other Humans, although it swiped at them with its long muscular arms. Palmer and another agent were knocked into some trees and it didn't slow down. It was a damned strong monster!

"Melanie! Jake's hurt. Belladonna. In there!"

I pointed at the gateway between universes as I fought to get back to my feet. She pulled away from her husband and helped me inside. Ulrich trailed us. The three of us got in each other's way as I looked for the door to Jake's room.

"In there—!" I realized that the door had to be disabled to get to Jake. "Hold on."

I pulled the chair out of the way so that the door would shut and removed the key. The color faded from the doorknob and I opened it again. Jake was still there, lying on the table. Ulrich brushed me aside and picked the Werewolf up like he was a child. The European may have been skinny, but he was as strong as he'd said.

He brought Jake out of that room and stood next to me, waiting for me to reactivate the door. For someone who wasn't very adventuresome, Ulrich seemed oddly comfortable with magic. Of course, he'd have to be, married to a preternatural vet.

I put the key in the knob and opened the doorway back into the nursery. I let Ulrich leave first with Jake, then urged Melanie through and finally I followed. I took the key this time and hobbled after my friends. The monster was destroying the nursery as Sally raced around on three limbs trying to avoid its deadly grip.

The FBI agents had stopped aiming for its torso. One of them managed to hit it in the eye and the monster rocked back for a moment. It stood there, hitting itself on the side of the head as if trying to get the bullet to come out. That was all the clue the rest of them needed, they began to fire at its face repeatedly.

"Is he still alive?" I asked Melanie as Ulrich put Jake gently on the ground.

She dropped to her knees roughly, cursing at the pain but ignoring it. She examined his eyes and lips and then turned her soft cheek to his mouth, feeling for breath. Ulrich ran off but he returned almost instantly with her kit. He set it down beside her without a word.

"Just barely. You said belladonna did this?" she asked amazed. "Belladonna doesn't do this. It's used to make atropine, an asthma drug and for other homeopathic treatments. It can be poisonous as well, but the symptoms aren't this, even for a Werewolf. How much did he ingest?"

"None. Lyndigard said it was a special variety he'd developed. To kill Lycans," I replied worriedly. "We just stood near it."

"Well it's fucking effective!" she snarled.

"Should I try and evoke the change?"

"No!" she snapped at me. "That would kill him for sure. No, we need—a tannic acid derivative." She looked at me with desperate apology. "I don't have any, Devon." Her clear blue eyes were wet with unshed tears and then she looked around the yard and slapped her arm. "Stupid Melanie! This is a nursery. White oak contains tannic acid. Red oak—hemlock does. Shit, even Manzanita leaves have about seven percent tannic acid content. Go! Pull the leaves off of whichever of them you can find, all of them, whatever! I have a portable torch in my truck. I can boil water and we can try and get it into him. But if this is a special strain of belladonna, I don't know, Devon." She had doubt in her eyes but that turned to impatience. "Get going! He has maybe minutes left, if that!"

I called to the blonde agent who had stepped away to shoot at the monster. "Gunnerson! We need to find oak, hemlock and Manzanita leaves. Can you get some agents to help us?"

Melanie yelled the plant descriptions over my shoulder again and we went from row to row of plants looking at all the trees and bushes. Other federal agents joined in the search, but because of the desert type ecology of the area, the nursery was stocked with drought resistant varieties. I thought we'd see lots of Manzanita, but perhaps the elevation was a problem.

"No!" I heard Melanie yell from the parking lot and I glanced over to see who had brought the wrong leaves.

She was alone with Jake, shaking him hard. I froze, emotion welling up. Melanie looked up from Jake to find me. There was no need for words to accompany the desolate expression on her face. The tears started down my face before my sobs quietly burst forth. I dropped to the ground onto my butt, my knees pulled up against my chest with my arms wrapped around them. I wept hidden against my legs.

It wasn't fair. He wasn't supposed to die. He was one of the good ones. One of the innocents! They weren't supposed to be the ones who died while the irresponsible ones like me and my father kept living. Mom shouldn't have died either while that bastard—!

I wiped my nose with the back of my arm, the way I'd seen Jake do before. It made me cry harder. I hadn't seen Mrs. Leung since I'd escaped from the pocket universe but I suddenly thought about her. I was glad she wasn't there. Her presence would have made the guilt unbearable.

That's why I didn't like to date blondes. I fucking hated blondes. They went up and died on you! I hated—hated—!

Have I mentioned that if I rambled enough, the truth eventually broke free? I fucking loved Jake and I hadn't told him. I'd said that I didn't love him so that I wouldn't have to make any promises. The promises I'd made to my mother hadn't kept her alive. My two special blonde angels, Jake and Mom. I hadn't been able to save either one of them. That was supposed to be my job. Since I was five my job had been to take care of her. Now I'd tried to take care of him and failed. What was the fucking point? It didn't matter whether it was familial love or romantic love, people died before their time because of me!

I could hear Melanie calling me, but I couldn't make myself approach his dead body. I would lose what little self-control I had. A wail like a wounded wolf wanted to escape my lips but I smashed my face against my knees.

I could sense people gathering around me, but none of them touched me, which was smart. Anger and sorrow warred within me until I thought I'd burst. I wept as quietly as I could, my face hidden in a selfish desire to be invisible in my pain. But despite that, I sobbed the way I had when I'd gotten the call about my mother's death. I squeezed my legs so hard I thought I'd break something. I wanted to break something. Something that would hurt more than my broken heart.

CHAPTER FORTY-SEVEN

Melanie drove me home alone in her veterinary truck. We'd been friends so long, only she knew not to say a word to me. Instead, she cried with me in silence. I cried more knowing that she wept, too. I'd never stopped loving her, even though it wasn't the way she had wanted or deserved. Her empathy was just one reason why she was worth loving.

Before we'd left the nursery, Gunnerson had taken the key from my hand. He'd had to pry it free while I sat in a state of denial. Inside the pocket universe, they found the missing Trolls. Bits of them anyway. The monster which had attacked Sally and me had been a Kree-Troll. Not really a Troll, but a distant relative that had a particular enmity toward Mountain Trolls. A carnivorous enmity.

Somehow it had been caught and locked up with the other Trolls. It had torn them limb from limb, literally. Bits of arms and toes and ears were scattered with unidentifiable parts that had been gnawed on or eaten from.

They were all dead. Dead like Jake. Dead like Peter Lyndigard who hated preternaturals because they weren't Human. Dead like my mother. Dead like anyone who loved me more than I deserved. They also found the rifle that Peter had used to shoot Jake in Ravenclaw. That evidence combined with my statement told them the entire story.

"No!" I spoke aloud, trying to banish thoughts of death. Melanie was still alive and Yuriko. Sonny, Evangelina and Nigel were happy and healthy and I knew they loved me. More than I deserved at times. I didn't want them to die because I'd thought that loving me was a death sentence. It was a superstitious fear, something to distract my intellect from my pain.

"You," started Melanie then she became silent again.

She knew that nothing would sound right now. When my mother had died, nothing anyone said was the right thing. All that had helped was having people who loved me around me.

My twin cousins Tommy and Carrie, both seventeen at the time, had come to my house and watched television with me until I fell asleep every night for the first week. We hadn't talked. We hadn't needed to talk. I hadn't even asked them to stay, but they had stayed anyway. It had been the right thing. I think they saved my life by being there for me back then.

Now they couldn't hide their disgust for what I was. But they had changed, not me. I didn't know what they hated more, that I was gay or that I could See magic.

We reached my house and my perspective had changed. I looked at the oversized Tudor and wondered what the hell one person needed with so much space. Where were the children and lover to share happy moments? When could I ever invite my mother over for homemade bread and cheesecake, her favorite luxuries?

I fought back the tears. I wouldn't cry again, not until I was alone. It didn't matter that I trusted Melanie and knew she loved me. Sometimes, sadness that deep needed to be shed in private. The soul got so emptied out that other people's emotions or spirits could sometimes creep into that empty space. It had happened to me when Mom died.

"I have to go back and take care of Sally." I heard the guilt in Melanie's voice. She knew I would have stayed with her if our situations had been reversed. But I didn't want her to stay.

"I'm glad. She saved my life."

"I can come by after?" she asked tentatively.

"No. No, tonight, I need to be alone."

She started to say something more, but the tears streamed down her rosy cheeks like waterworks and she blew her nose on a dirty handkerchief on the dash.

She idled the truck in the driveway and just gazed at me. I couldn't look at her directly. If I did, I was lost again. Instead, I opened the door and watched the ground. "Thanks."

I slammed the truck door shut and walked to the house. I stood at the door with my back to her, not moving until I heard her drive off. Then I leaned against the front door and started sobbing for real. It poured out of me, the loss of not just Jake, but the hope and memories he had represented. The reminder of my failure to be more than Human.

Getting my keys into the locks was harder than usual. When I finally made it inside the house, I felt the emptiness of the place. I was comfortable being alone, but this felt suddenly lonely. I could sense Jake in the rooms. I could remember his silky skin against mine. His boyish smile and the twinkle in his eyes when he laughed haunted my memory.

I wasn't going to be able to help the feds for a while. I would call Chief Jacobsen and tell him. Getting past this pain was going to take some time away from anything associated with Jake.

I had money, after all. When my mother had died, I was trapped with all the memories. Now I could fly away. Go someplace that had no associations with Werewolves or gay blonde men. I stared at the couch, picturing him curled there as a Werewolf and felt it like a blow to my gut.

I lifted my gaze to the counter where I—. The answering machine light was blinking and I prepared to be angry. I needed a distraction, but if they were sales calls, I was going to be angry dialing a few people. I went to the machine and pressed the play button. There were three messages.

"Devon, this Jiao!" The Brazilian did not sound his arrogant self. In fact, he sounded afraid. That was all that stopped me from pressing the erase button. "I'm in trouble. You must come to me! I know you said six months but it's life and death. *Mi padre*—!"

The message cut off and my heart raced. Definitely a distraction. I listened anxiously for the second recording, thinking he might have called back. What would make a filthy rich, powerful practitioner of magic afraid? And whose life was at stake? His or his father's?

The next message played. "Hi Devon, this is Evangelina!" My heart leapt in a smile at hearing her voice but made me cry all the same. It only helped ease the pain because it was one more person that I loved that was safe and sound. "I have a problem here in the Philippines. I won't be able to call again but you need to get here as soon as you can! Please, I'll explain it all when you get here. Dad will pay for your ticket, don't worry about the money."

Then the operator came on the recording, saying that she had run out of time. That message ended and I waited anxiously. I hoped the third call wasn't another problem.

"Devon Mosteller, this is Tobaius of Gaulteus Clan. We left Jake in your care. He was your responsibility and you let him die!" The deep, gravelly voice was heavy with accusation. "Last time we met, we supported you. Next time you cross our path, our interests no longer lie in helping you live. I would recommend you not choose to encounter us again."

My stomach filled with self-loathing. Jake was dead, as if that wasn't enough reason for guilt. Now Gaulteus pack intended to kill me if they got the chance. Not that I didn't deserve it.

If I hadn't gotten the other two calls, I might have just gone to face them and gotten it over with. But I wasn't going to just lay down and die just yet. Not until I made sure Evangelina was safe. And even that bastard Jiao.

It sucked that they were so far from each other, Brazil and the Philippines. Still, a no-brainer—Evangelina came first. I looked up the number for United Airlines, wiping tears from my cheeks. I'd worry about the Werewolves and any death-wish fulfillment when I got back. Tomorrow, I would fly to Manila. After that, well, Brazil would have to wait. And then maybe, just maybe, I could come back and tie up the loose ends I was leaving behind. My death could wait until then.

I dialed the airline and spoke into the phone, burying my sorrow as deep as it would go. "Next available flight to Manila, please."

The End

ABOUT THE AUTHOR

MICHAEL DON ANDERSON was born and raised in Fresno County, California. His first professional publication was in *Marion Zimmer Bradley's Fantasy Magazine* with a short story called '*The Lamp*,' although his writings have appeared in school-related newspapers, journals and competitions since his early teens.

His educational background includes two B.A.s (Anthropology and Linguistics) and an M.A. (Linguistics) from the California State University at Fresno, as well as an M.A. and Ph.D. (Linguistics) from the University of Arizona.

To contact Michael Don Anderson, please write him in care of the publisher CRIMSON WEREWOLF LIMITED, at 7260 W. Azure Dr., Ste 140-798, Las Vegas, NV 89130-7999.

For more information about our books, please visit our website at *www.crimsonwerewolf.com*

www.ingramcontent.com/pod-product-compliance
Lightning Source LLC
Chambersburg PA
CBHW070758180626
46818CB00001B/1